Bhajan

by Tim Garvin

Blue Bus Books
Durham, NC USA

Published in America.

Tiger image used for cover by Michael Strevens, www.mikstyx.com. Cover design ideas from Ashley Piediscalzi.

Acknowledgements: Grateful thanks to editor, Cynthia Drake, and beta readers Susan Garvin, John Migliorisi, Gary Lee, Chitra Alvarado, Randy Wasserstrom, and Marcia Lowe.

Quotations from *The Wayfarers* by William Donkin courtesy of Sheriar Foundation. Used with permission.

Quotations from *Discourses* by Meher Baba courtesy of Sheriar Foundation. Used with permission.

To be notified of upcoming books from Tim Garvin, email bluebusbooks@gmail.com.

ISBN-13: 978-1508753988
ISBN-10: 1508753989

Contents

1 1
2 23
3 29
4 41
5 51
6 65
7 91
8 111
9 117
10 131
11 155
12 173
13 195
14 197
15 225
16 245
17 263
18 267
19 285
20 305
21 325
22 347
23 361
24 369
25 373
26 381
27 393

For Cynthia,
whose light is reflected here,
and for
the One in all

1

When he was fifty-one, Bluey Macintosh, professor of mammals at Santa Rosa Exotic Animal College, foremost educator of America's zookeepers, had a heretical fundraising idea—a traveling zoo.

Need overcame stigma, and as the idea fulled, it pulled like a train—the air-conditioned trucks and RVs, a bamboo stockade, cleverly designed feed bins and freezers, cleverly designed stainless cages with squeeze walls, a fork lift, a website. Go out for a few weeks to state and county fairs, art fairs, town festivals, give kids a glimpse of nature, inspire the public with the glory of animals, make the local TV and newspapers, then return to the college and recuperate the beasts until the next stint. Hard on the beasts, but a good cause. Recruits, funding, longevity!—for the college and more importantly, longevity for the beasts' wild cousins whose extinction was accelerating.

He costed it, made diagrams and designs, jawed with the director of People for the Ethical Treatment of Animals (who said, bad idea, we'll organize protests, might sue, maybe not), jawed with lawyers, jawed with festival and fair directors and with the USDA and the Ventura County sheriff as a test case for law and licenses. It was a go everywhere—except PETA, but they hated all zoos.

That morning he submitted the proposal to Rudy Wheeler, the college president, and in the afternoon got a note in his mailbox—*I read it. Can you come at five?* Now he sat in Rudy's outer office. The receptionist-secretary, Maria, a large young woman with big glasses and spiked hair, smiled across to him from time to time. Perhaps she was churning with drama, and her smiles were pat-pats of empathy sent to ease disappointment. He returned the smiles, ignored the peck of worry. She had been one of his students, a former game warden. Santa Rosa's application process was arduous and usually weeded out the sentimental, but Maria had slipped through. She had not been good with animals, could not find a flow. Her only offer was from the petting zoo at an amusement park in Virginia. Rudy, the new president, had made a place for her.

Now a light flashed on her console. She smiled and said, "You can go in now, Dr. Macintosh."

Rudy, a slight, peppy man near forty, came around his massive desk and extended his hand. The desk perched on rhino horn legs—replicas—and on Rudy's arrival a year ago, Bluey had helped him disassemble and reassemble it to fit it into the office. Rudy wore jeans and a Santa Rosa's blue lion T-shirt, a casual Friday statement. He waved Bluey to a chair and sat across from him, spurning the presidential throne. Deference or pity? Wait.

Rudy bounced his head affirmatively and made an unhappy smile.

Pity then.

Rudy said, "I read it, Bluey. Amazing."

And Bluey heard, *something to read, not something to do.*

Rudy said, "It's sort of a nineteenth century idea, but you're being bold, right? And we need to be bold. A media war with PETA might even help us. I swear, it's like that Mickey Rooney movie, *Let's put on a show*!"

And Bluey heard, *you're a dreamer.*

"It must have taken a lot of time. It's so thorough."

Was that, *I suppose the college paid for the research?*

"And I know you worked hard on this."

Please don't get upset.

"But, Bluey, we got no dough, dude."

I'm a straight-shooter like you, man, but I'm not gambling what's left of my career.

Bluey had a spiritual moment. Pain, which had just flushed through him like hot water, drained away, and benevolence replaced it. He had a vivid impression of Wheeler's mind capsule, Wheeler in there suffocating, fogging the world with panic.

The legislature had cut the school's budget three years running. Developers eyed the campus and hired lobbyists. Legislators in Sacramento had caught the scent of money. Besides, they told themselves, why should the state subsidize crappy zoo-keeper jobs? Then the recession of 2009 arrived. Rudy had been hired as a savior and crucified by fortune.

Bluey put his thick hands on his thick knees, arched his back, and smiled.

Wheeler smiled routinely back. Then the benevolence penetrated. His smile faltered.

Bluey said, "Rudy, I guess I'll say two things." His mind was sharp, and the benevolence persisted. He had let go fast even after three weeks of nose down work. Good news for the inner man. He said, "First, yes, it's nineteenth century, but the public would love it. Second, it's your job to turn ideas down when they don't fit the big picture. I accept that."

Wheeler's face showed gratitude and regret. He said, "Well, it's not my job to—"

"Wait a minute, Rudy, here comes number three." Bluey had had a flashing thought—if a determined push might prevail, high-mindedness was an error. "Number three is, we're going down the tubes, which you certainly know. It's like a bad position in chess—" He spread his arms, producing between them an imaginary chessboard. "You can struggle, but the guy's closing in. You don't resign because you're afraid to quit hoping, so you cook until you're done. And we are cooking. Costs too high, tuition too low, the state government scared, and the public indifferent. We must act, or dry up and blow away."

Wheeler's smile had become grieved, the smile of a man contented with drying up, a man who wanted out. So number three was a mistake. It was hopeless and shouldered out benevolence. He was back to Bluey,

Australian cowboy academic, earthy whirlwind, smart, honest, self-possessed. But a self. With a stamped-on plan. And seated beside him the booted bureaucrat. Pain was back. He sighed. His head fell. He submitted.

This cued Wheeler to mention promised legislation, interested benefactors, increasing applications, federal grants. A bouquet of hope! He too had felt the benevolence depart. He ended with his mouth open, like a small bird, in need.

Bluey pushed his knees to hoist his bulk. "Hope you're right, Rudy. I have a class."

Wheeler stood, slightly rushing, and extended his hand. Bluey took it, and good will faintly returned. He found Wheeler's eyes and smiled into them. Wheeler's mouth closed as if enveloping this small morsel of forgiveness. He couldn't think of anything to say and watched the door swing shut. Two years later the school was bankrupt.

•

El Chastain recalled the day and the details of the day—in high school, sophomore year, in the hall with Betty Biggs, Betty talking to Jim Stokes—when she heard the expression, *What would Jesus do?* which Betty had asked Jim, something about lending his false ID to some little kid, Betty being ironic.

She remembered this vividly because from somewhere in the mist of childhood she had developed a habit of imagining what Pearl would do. Pearl was free and happy, quick to forget wounds, bright and interested, kind and courageous, patient and wise. Not a Goody Two Shoes, but not a rebel either. Instead, thoughtful. When she learned about imaginary friends, she thought, *Is Pearl that?* But she was not that. She was made of thought and certainly not real, but also not silly. She was a presence, without a face or body, like a serious fairy living inside. She floated up when El, for instance, lost the third grade spelling bee because of an *i before e* mess up in the word *neighborhood.* Or when she came home from school to find her puppy, Cinder, on the pavement in front of the house, squished. So then Pearl would come out and be there, inside her, for company. Or if she had to clean her room when she was lazy or bad-tempered. She helped her forget the spelling bee's lost glory, and was with her as she buried Cinder in the back yard under a cross of sticks and yarn, draped with her mother's pearl necklace, and helped her clean her room without pouting.

In high school, Pearl began to fade. Then in college she read in psychology and religion about higher selves and lower selves, and decided that Pearl had been a psychic formation of her own higher self trying to push through. She tried to revive her, but she was gone, a pale cast of thought, the way Hamlet put it. But could you get it back, if, say, you meditated or chanted or prayed or joined a sect or just a regular church, or were the atheists right, and higher and lower thought functioning merely part of evolution, the universe cruising mindlessly along? That was the whole thing summed up—was there a giant mind in back of the world? And if there was, what sort? And how could you find out? When she had time, she read up on religions and spiritual paths, and she also talked to people, ministers, sect people, professors. Everyone liked to be asked about truth by a bright young girl and offered their ideas. They said, come inside this nice cave I have, see how nice it is, how much better it is than other caves. But it *was* a cave, a thought cave. And inside that cave, no matter which cave, it was dark. And if you went in there, then you were supposed to go around after that with a dark heavy cave on. Even psychology and religion professors were cavemen, see how big our cave is!

Anyway, she had lots of other things to think about—organic chemistry, comparative anatomy, microbiology, on the way to vet school at first, and then on the way to the Santa Rosa Exotic Animal College. She had been there on a three day field trip and heard Bluey Macintosh speak, and then heard him speak again with some guys during the field trip farewell party, this time not about zoos and zoo politics, but about politics in general. The guys were second years, feeling safe and done, letting their conservative flavors out, crowding a couple of first years, a guy and a girl, into irritated meekness. Bluey had come up, paid the price of admission by listening for two minutes, and then in a pause said a few things and continued to mingle. Those few things convinced El to apply to the college. And now he had asked her to join him in an adventure.

•

Through the kitchen window, Bluey saw his neighbor, George Berreckman, exit his BMW and enter his house, back from surgery, still in scrubs. George's expression was intent and inward, sidewalk focused. Soon he would call, you busy? George had been divorced for less than a year from Vicki, his wife of over thirty years. Now Bluey, his neighbor and friend for twenty-two years, was leaving.

Bluey started the electric kettle. He found a knuckle of ginger and divided a thin slice for two cups of chai—tea, water, milk, cardamom. The house was empty of furniture, photographs, pictures, rugs. Even his bone collection, gathered over the years from his work as a zoo consultant, had been dispersed—the Australian mice skeletons to the Taronga zoo in Sydney, the skulls of seven African snakes to a colleague in Cape Town, the broken and rehealed *oosik*, a walrus penis bone, to the University of Alaska. All that remained was a twin bed, his suitcase of clothes, and in the living room a castle of cardboard boxes, which he had built that morning in several trips up and down the basement stairs—Rosa's shoes, dresses, coats, books, her grandmother's ceramic Christmas birds.

After her death and after grief had a little released him, he had returned to the questions that shape youth, what to do, where to live? The idea came in stages, first a gleam without breadth, then a few calls, discussions with colleagues, calls to land agents, calls to construction companies. When the land was found, more than three square miles of partly forested plateau just freed from a legal squabble, he flew to Tennessee.

He left the agent in a meadow and followed a creekside trail up a valley. Crows and blue jays talked in the tall trees, a mix of hardwood and pine, and the creek talked softly in mossy boulders. Eventually he found a waterfall and nearby the foundation of an old cabin, sprung with mature trees. The meadow was three hundred yards distant, so the ancient farmer, if he was that, had chosen beauty over convenience. He could choose beauty too. He build here and live surrounded by wilderness. He could forget the world. Or he could work.

He stood in the foundation of the cabin and closed his eyes and listened for the silence under the murmur of the forest. And felt the souls of beasts, like an audience of ghosts, awaiting his decision.

He would work. He would serve. He would build, gather, and organize. He was fifty-three and had twenty more years of vitality, maybe thirty. He would clear the foundation of the ancient cabin and build a new cabin and build an ecopark. He made a full price offer that day.

•

The phone rang.

"Shall I come?"

"Come."

Through the kitchen window, he saw George pick his way over flagstones, swing open the backyard gate. He was Bluey's age, tall, fair-skinned, freckled, large-boned, with a belly that came and went. When he and Vickie divorced, the belly had swelled but was again receding.

He came through the kitchen door, and Bluey handed him a mug. As they passed the castle of boxes, Bluey tapped a top box. He said, "These are the bird ornaments, and I'm disappointed you won't take them."

They settled in the two remaining patio chairs—these George would add to his own set, since they matched. George said, "Most of those birds have no beak. I was here when the tree fell, remember?"

They blew their tea. The scent of the spices contented them, and the memory of the tree catastrophe made them aware of their friendship, a sweet scent like the tea and comfortable with reminiscence. In his settlement with Vickie, George had given much to keep the house. Bluey and Rosa had been childless, but had been like second parents to George and Vickie's children.

Goose, Bluey's big blond Labrador, padded out of the shrubbery, made a quick hello circle, and settled between them on his rug.

Bluey said, "You're home early."

"My patient died."

"Oh, no."

"She died before I got to her, poor woman. Probably a blood clot."

"Did you know her well?"

"I met her yesterday. We chatted about her surgery. Now she is no more."

"You're upset."

George said, "I'm just tired of life not making enough sense. If you have some wisdom, I invite it."

Bluey could say, *sorrow is your consolation*. He could say, *your mood is medicine.* He said, "All I have is tea."

"Very delicious."

Bluey said, "You could come with me. Sew me up when I get mauled." He glanced and saw his fun had bounced. He reached, poked a thick finger against George's forearm, a dogged push at rue. He said, "There'll be a small fee for putting up with you."

"You mentioned camping. I might do that."

"Any time. We'll be out four months before we reach Tennessee."

"Charlie would come too, I bet. Grace would, but she can't." Charlie, George's son, had spent his high school summers working at the exotic animal college and was now a zoo vet in St. Louis. Grace was a dermatologist finishing her residency in Florida. "I'm going to the camping store."

"Tell Charlie I'll pay him, and he can check the beasts."

"He won't take your money, but I will. I'll give your crew some antibiotics, which they will likely need." George laid his large hand on his forehead, ran it slowly across his sandy hair. "Bluey, goddammit, someone will move in here, and I'll see them running around your house, and I'll say, you dirty bastards. I will feel friendless and alone, and it will be true."

"Charge out and date women. Expose your flank. Christ, a good-looking doctor, an experienced love machine."

"I weighed in at the Y this morning. Down twenty-one pounds."

"They say you live longer."

"I know it."

They held their tea two-handed before their faces like potions. After a moment, Goose lifted his head, looked at Bluey. Bluey laid his hand on the dog's snout, moved it across his eyes, closing them. Goose deposited his head on his paws again, huffed resignation and contentment.

"What about you?" said George.

"My weight or women?"

"Women."

Bluey said, "Women are now all my sisters. Except for twenty year old movie stars. I try to let them down gently."

George said, "Here's a thought. I think you and Rosa were a pressure on us. You were *in* love. Inside it, like in a bubble. Vickie and I were not in love. We were in infatuation once, but not love. First too young, then too bitter. You think that's ever happened to anyone else?"

"It might have."

"I believe we waited until Rosa was gone to let things come to a head. We couldn't bear to disappoint her. In short, you and Rosa modeled love and broke up my marriage."

The statement was a mixture of truth and whimsy. Neither felt like parsing it.

George said, "Maybe I'll buy your house. Then if it all falls to shit, I'll sell it back to you. At a considerable profit. How close are you?"

"The enclosures are almost ready. The trucks are finished. Then I have to get the beasts acclimated. Two or three weeks."

"Let me just say this—you're out of your fucking mind."

"I know it. Buy the house in case." Then, to fill the moment, to ease his friend from self-regard, he said, "I've never done anything like this. Zoo consulting is just, bring your mind and a pencil, a camera if you feel fancy. Now it's steel fabricators, mechanics, festival directors, website people. And all the permitting agencies, state, county, and municipal. And the USDA. I'm building a city."

"I'll quote you a line of poetry. Romeo says to Juliet, *Must I, like Atlas, uproot the repetitious earth and launch it deep into the giddy cave of stars toward fierce precipitous change?* I think you wrote that during your Milton phase."

Bluey smiled. "You didn't memorize that whole poem, did you?"

"Just that line. Anyway, that's you, trying to be Atlas at fifty-three. Also, here's something I may have said before—publish your fucking poetry."

"Here's the difference between Romeo and me. Romeo thought he had to change everything. I just want to get one shoulder—no, a fingertip—under a tiny flap of the world's indifference, and start shouting, *help.* If they don't come running, okay. New subject. I believe you remember my sister Annie?"

"Vaguely." George had known Annie for twenty years. He had steadfastly denied his infatuation to his wife, but not to Bluey.

"She called me from Bolinas. The money is gone. Which I already knew."

"Christ, how?"

"They bought a mansion just before the crash. And news is, Hardy is gone too. It turns out, he was a secret internet gambler. She's still in the house, but she can't even afford the utilities. She's coming to visit. I'm going to offer her a job."

"Damn, Bluey."

"Makes you think, doesn't it?"

George laughed. "My heart's beating. But then my heart—I look at a perfume ad, it starts up. But a free Annie—"

"I thought you'd perk up."

"I'm not prepared. Look at this." He patted the swell of his abdomen. "Here's my thought. I redouble my effort at the gym, become svelte, and charge like a buffalo."

"Like a lion."

"I think buffalo will have to do. What I feel might not be true love though. Annie might sense that."

"She does have antennae."

"So what will she do on the caravan?"

"Cook and gate-keeper. And she can drive the RV. She may say no."

"A good-looking woman at the gate has got to be worth something."

"Remember El? Last month at the yearend party? You spoke with her."

"I do. I was charmed."

"I've offered her a job too."

"Bright, as I recall."

"Very. In fact, I'm on my way to meet her."

"Damn. You should have said."

"I had time for a cup of tea. But I better move. I've got to walk Goose."

At the combination of the words *walk* and *Goose*, Goose got to his feet, watched Bluey's face.

They rose. Goose fast-footed into an alert radius ten feet away. As Bluey pinched up the emptied mugs, he looked at Goose, said, "Sit." Goose's haunches lowered, a spring compressing.

George said, "I'm on my way to the camping superstore. And I'll call Charlie. He'll be delighted to see his uncle Bluey. Don't tell Annie I'm coming. Or tell her, I don't know. I'll get one of those one man tents to disguise my intentions." He exited through the gate, closed it behind him. He said over his shoulder, "I must hit the gym with renewed devotion!" He climbed the steps of his back porch, waved, and went inside.

•

El opened the rear doors of building B and looked out again, listening. Nothing. If Bluey were out there, there would be plenty of vocalizations. His pockets were normally full of treats, and as he passed through the grounds, he woke a forward cone of yearning and left a trail of munchers. Yesterday afternoon in the parking lot he had given her a folder, instructed her to read it, then asked her to meet him at the admin office at one. She was the college's head keeper now, hired by Dr. Wheeler to remain until the last animals were placed and Bluey's caravan departed.

The school closing had been announced in January between semesters. Half of the first years did not return. The second years would be the college's last graduates. As the semester proceeded, Bluey Macintosh, everyone's favorite professor, announced to his second year classes—nutrition and behavior—that he had bought three miles of forest and farmland north of Memphis. He was building an ecopark. Bulldozers were clearing roadbeds. Carpenters and masons were at work on buildings. The plan included tour buses, clubs and day camps, summer camps, AARP and Elder Hostel volunteers, internet cameras, busloads of visitors. Students began to leave resumes and passionate letters in his mailbox. Then he revealed he was having transport enclosures built. They would lodge inside two tractor trailers and deliver the animals to Tennessee.

Then this—the cages would also be used for a traveling zoo.

The debate began, school-wide among the students and even professors. Bluey's argument was simple, if subversive—global warming, invasive species, habitat loss, the closing of migration corridors, bushmeat trade, exotic part trade, pollution and toxic spills, collapsing ocean and reef systems—these forces were dooming the majority of earth's animals to certain extinction. The world, stressed by terrorism, petty politics, and income inequality, had no time for the plight of beasts. The time for political correctness had passed. Without a revolution, the beasts were done.

But a traveling zoo? A circus? No, no, no—not a circus. A traveling zoo with rotating animals. The promotional flag of an ecopark. Out for a few weeks, then home to the park. A model for the future. A bold and resolute fight against the greed and indifference that were consuming the earth. In this fight, even animals would have to sacrifice. Eventually the automatic clamor—A traveling circus! Cages!—became more nuanced. Couldn't you advertise, make documentaries, maybe go around to schools with a single animal? What about a reality TV program? Train a cheetah! Zookeeper of the month! What about kids' TV? What about a youth program, something like AmeriCorps for animals, AnimalCorps? All good, said Bluey. Let's do everything. And everything included a traveling zoo.

Several students withdrew their resumes. His colleagues in major zoos around the world debated him in the forums. His presentation at last year's Association of Zoos and Aquariums convention divided the community.

Last night, El read the folder twice. He had told her in the parking lot that he knew she had been on both sides of the arguments. But she was his first choice. Read and think, he said. Well, she had thought. She had emailed Animal Kingdom that morning.

•

At the sound of George's porch door swinging shut, Goose's haunches lifted an inch, then resettled as Bluey glanced at him. Bluey gave the look a second more, then went to his back door, opened it, turned to Goose. He said, "Come." Goose bolted.

Blue rinsed the cups, set them upside down on the counter. Behind him, Goose made a brief clicking dance on the tile floor, then stilled, watching. As Bluey turned, the Labrador cocked his head. Bluey cocked his head in response. He opened a kitchen drawer, removed a poop bag, inspiring another tap dance. He said, "Sit. Stay." Goose again compressed his haunches, a fierce act of will. Bluey crossed to the front door, opened it, looked at Goose, who was faintly trembling now. He said, "Come."

Goose clattered across the wooden floors and into the world. A walk!

They were a familiar sight in the neighborhood, the thick, gray-haired, whisker-frosted man and his well-mannered lab, close at heel. It was Saturday, but except for two Mexican yard men the lawns were empty. As Bluey exchanged nods with the Mexicans, a bulldog appeared in a bay window, barked twice, disappeared, then reappeared to watch them out of sight. The bulldog, Rummy, sometimes got to walk with them. Today time was short.

They reached the undeveloped wood at the street's dead end and started down a worn path. At their destination, a downed tree across the creek, Bluey said, "Free."

Goose bounded into the creek, too shallow for a good swim, but with enough water for a splash and a slurp. Then he was up the other side and into the thicket of wirewood. Skunk! Squirrel! Coyote!

Bluey folded his arms and watched from his perch on the log. Goose had cocked his head in the kitchen. He cocked his own head again. That was what? That was moving the mind to a different space, trying to catch meaning, like a man angling his mouth under a faucet. Anything more? No. He was pressed against the force field where thinking ended. You could brightly notice, but always there was an edge, soft, black, and impenetrable. What mystics called the Ignorance. Science pushed there, but with the thick fingers of measurement, scribes measuring head cocks and guessing. Life and evolution had elbowed out space in it, had found enough food, shelter, and sexual partners to continue, had found ways to signal. These signals were his occupation. With animals, the higher mammals at least, he could flow, he could sense the edge of their ignorance, feel what they felt, feel what was close beyond them. He had a knack for knowing when they were with him, and importantly, especially with the big dangerous ones, when they weren't.

Goose was excavating a hole in a furious dog-paddle of digging. Bluey removed the throwing stick from its place on the roots of the tree, cracked it sharply against the trunk. Goose lifted his dirt-crumbed snout, and Bluey threw the stick into the creek, where Goose retrieved it with a hurricane of splash, brought it pantingly to Bluey's feet. He threw it several more times until Goose was clean.

"Did you poop?" he asked. If the lab had forgotten, this cue word would have inspired him to move his bowels, but Goose only stood, alert for another throw. Bluey replaced the stick in the roots. "Now, old Goose, will you sit? Sit."

Goose settled on his haunches, and Bluey swung a leg over him from behind, grasped his head with both hands, stilled him. Then he released and gently stroked the dog's face, eyes, snout, lightly and still more lightly. It was their communion, something transferring between them, a rain of heart love. He broke the spell by giving Goose a fierce ear scrub. Goose fell in at heel, and they went home.

•

He was late, which was unusual, and hadn't called, also unusual. The grounds were silent except for the faint flutter of a rake. El moved left a little on the concrete landing and saw Carlos raking the ostrich pen in Birdland a hundred yards away. Sara Livermore woke in memory. The ostrich had whacked her over the eyebrow, and the collar of her T-shirt was soaked with blood. Sara was a first year and deeply freaked. She had almost gone home after the whacking, but El was in the macaw enclosure and had seen it happen and sweet-talked her on the way to the infirmary, explained things, you crowded him, that's all, like magnets turned the wrong way, that's all, and besides he was nervy, I could see his rigid neck, I was just going to warn you. Sara got stitched up and stayed but was home now anyway, with no degree, in debt, partway to nowhere. Three weeks ago the students and staff had had their boozy party with hugs and promises of contact and then scattered. Probably El was the last student in town, except for her buddies, Ellen and Bretta, whom she was meeting later for coffee and a better goodbye.

With the students gone, most of the labor was gone, and Carlos had only JJ, the new guy, who unnerved her. JJ was mostly on the grounds in the afternoon, which is why El did not want to wander out there, at least until Bluey arrived. She couldn't see him, but it was after one o'clock, so he was there somewhere. Maybe he was preparing another ambush. Two days ago, he stepped out from behind a creosote bush with a poop shovel, said, hope I didn't scare you! Then he made a quick info dump—he was an Iraq army vet, didn't know squat about animals, except he worked for animal shelters sometimes. He was a videographer. He surfed and scuba dived.

She had been feeding the guanacos, Pumper and Nickel, when he popped up. She tried to look busy, tried to curve her way out of the conversation—better get back to work—but he was sticky. He had been in the battle of Fallujah. There were guys eating dogs over there, and there were dogs eating guys. He tagged along to the door of the chop shop and might have even come in, shovel and all, except El told him only she was permitted, sorry.

His eyes were slightly bugged, like a nocturnal's. His intensity was too innocent to be rude. She tried to feel him inwardly but couldn't. Then she thought, he's not getting the world in, which is why his eyes bug, trying to see. We're all like that though. Everyone's eyes bug a little, even animals, who were pushed from within and fixed on need, which was how you could train them. You flowed with what they saw, then flowed out ahead of them. That's what made a good animal person, which she was, which she had been since a girl. And what made some animals dangerous, because you could be wrong. People were fixed down deep on need too, like animals, but also fixed on top, between the eyes, sometimes mostly fixed on top, where JJ was fixed. Which bugged his eyes. Something like that. He had gotten under her emotional sheathe and creeped her out. After her JJ encounter, she tried to work where Carlos could see her.

She let the pneumatic door ease shut. Building B, the old, high-ceiling classroom building, was deserted. The squeaks from her rubber-soled clogs resonated on the stone walls. The building had been a monastery before the college converted it. She wandered into the micro lab, the beakers and titration stuff still scattered around. She drifted over to her old lab table, sat on her stool. From here, two years ago, she had participated in the infamous Dr. Feeney indole experiment, a sort of first year initiation. Indole was the molecule that made shit smell fecal and flowers smell sweet, and the experiment involved bringing a bit of your shit to class to determine why your shit smelled okay and the shit of others didn't. Same indole! It turned out to be a tricky question, so tricky that even Feeney didn't know the answer, but did the experiment every year anyway for the ice breaking and also the fame, no doubt. He was a tiny, fast-talking, long-faced guy, sweater and tie every day. Off in some biomedical lab now, probably missing the glory days of indole. He could tell his new colleagues, just bring some of your shit back in this vial, guys, and I'll blow your minds.

She checked the hallway and central office again—no Bluey—then wandered through amphibians, then reptiles, all the tanks empty now, all the denizens placed in zoos hopefully, easy to place in any case, though maybe a few euthanized by Dr. Peters, the college vet. Then wheeled to the incinerator by Carlos, who had that job now. Not so many as the Los Angeles animal shelter had to do and every day do, that's for sure. The death of a snake versus the death of a dog. The death of a dog versus the death of a person. People died every day on the news. What did you feel? Like snakes dying.

She was getting lonely thoughts in this lonely, empty place where there had been so much life, where she had zoomed around. It was like being in Sears after the A-bomb, a thought she had had as a kid sometimes, all the pretty dresses covered in dust, nobody left anywhere, just pigeons and broken windows. No zombies either, way before the current zombie craze. Right now, a zombie attack would pep her up. What if out of a cupboard bursts a zombie, completely unexpected! Thinking fast, she splashes acid in his eyes. She takes no joy in his death agonies and looks away, then catches the scent of indole and, just before his features melt, sees it is Dr. Feeney. Shoot, I've killed old Feeney, who would have thunk it?

She called Bluey's cell again, again got the message, *Bluey, here. Leave a number. Thanks.* She hit end. She had already left a message. He would be in traffic, couldn't hear the phone, or out of juice. Out of juice more like. He would have called. Since the semester ended a month ago, she had seen him several times on the zoo grounds, and each time he had been on the phone.

She stepped into the hallway and walked again to the double doors. She scanned the grounds. No JJ. Maybe he was off today. Anyway, she could always scrape him off at the chop shop. She pushed through the doors, sprung across the three steps onto the gravel pathway, and trotted out toward the carnivores. She wanted to tool around with the cougar, Clark, one of her second year animals, and thought of getting a couple of chicken necks, then decided no, leave the chop shop as a JJ refuge. Besides, Clark would work for love.

The cougar was lying on one of his elevated planks in the back of his long enclosure. He lifted his head as she approached, scanned her, let his head fall back onto the board for a moment, then smoothly up-gathered himself, like cloth drifting in water, and leapt onto the dirt floor. Then he moved fast, purposefully grazing along the rectangles of wire in front of her. After his head went by, she put her hand through and let her fingers ripple along his silky flank. He turned, and she withdrew her hand, letting the head by, then again let him stroke against her pressure.

In a field of dry grass, he would have been invisible, but here he was open, exposed, dependent. His long tail lashed from time to time, spilling energy. He had come to the zoo the previous year from a suburban backyard where the owner had gotten overwhelmed. El had been his first trainer. He had been irascible, a stereotypic pacer, a hisser and growler. She had used the entire basket of animal techniques—culinary and cosmetic scents, chicken necks hidden under wood chips and stuffed into boomer balls, and months of determined operant conditioning. The stereotypy vanished. Now he had a variety of behaviors, including some jokey behaviors for the amusement of her classmates.

"Carlos won't let me clean his cage, that's why you see that cougar shit. I'm not trained for carnivores." It was JJ, behind her, his voice timbrous in the silence and uselessly loud, the vocal equivalent of bugged eyes.

Clark was turning again, so she didn't move, waited for the head, let his flank roll along her fingers. She clapped twice, made a praying motion, then fast opened her hands. The cougar haunch sat in front of her, tossed his head, snapped open a fangy yawn, snapped it closed. Behind her she heard the gravel shift.

"I told him, Carlos, dude, I'm a carnivore myself."

She turned now, head only—busy here, got something going here—and said, "Hello."

JJ carried the shovel yoke style across his neck. He was in his mid-twenties, over six feet, in jeans and a white T-shirt, compactly muscled. He wore a large black baseball cap over hair shaved to a quarter inch stubble. He blinked rapidly. Both forearms bore the same tattoo, a black band with the word *REALITY* in skin-color.

He had stopped behind her. She felt the too close pressure of his body. She had met his eyes for an instant before turning back to Clark, felt his glance like stale light in a mirror prison. She felt herself flush and solidify with tension. She felt her breath shorten. For God sake, relax, she thought, he's not flashing a knife. His nearness was like a touch in a dark room. Where was Bluey? She had a wild thought. Free Clark! Flip up the lock cover and enter the combination!

Then fight rose. She turned, air-patted toward his chest. She said, "You're standing too close. And I'm working here, sorry."

He giant-stepped back, smirked brightly. "You're working? Doing what?"

She turned back to Clark, but kept JJ peripherally in view. But he had retreated. His smirk was submission. What did he want? Was he congested with lust? Did he need dominance? Like animals? She saw his neck flex against the shovel's shaft, saw him wring the wood, his knuckles paling. She felt a quick shimmer of compassion. It made her brave. She had an impulse—train him. Provide a reinforcer for his good behavior of giving space.

She said, "I'm providing enrichment for our friend, Clark, the fearsome puma. Aren't I, Clark?" With a push of will, she let JJ vanish from the edge of vision as she turned to Clark. She made a stirring motion with her left hand and Clark turned in a fast circle. She down-patted, and Clark sat. "Good Clark, good Clark." She turned back, glanced directly at JJ, offered him a mild, kind smile. She said, "Isn't he beautiful and super duper? I love him so much."

JJ's head made a series of jerking motions, his neck pressing spasmodically back against the handle, a sort of involuntary nod. He said, "I see these wild animals in cages, sometimes I want to jump out of my skin."

She thought of verbal play—oh, you'll need your skin!—but no, something respectful and plain. "I often think that too. In a sense, you may say that life has trapped us all."

Now his head fell slightly forward. Had he been enlisted? She offered a smile reward in case.

He said, "You're El right? Didn't get your name last time so I asked Carlos." His head moved methodically side to side. "You know my name?"

"JJ."

"That's right. Carlos should have introduced us, but he didn't. He don't *like* me." He pronounced the word *like* as *lack* in a put-on hick accent. "So the big dog's taking you on the wagon train, hunh?"

"Well, we're talking about it."

"Carlos says he got the cages built. Little bitty cages."

She offered a smile. "The proper term is transport enclosures. The animals are on the way to a Tennessee park where there's lots of space."

"And lots of fence."

"I see you are sympathetic to the plight of animals. We certainly have that in common. We both love animals."

He pulled his nose several times with one of the hands dangling from his shovel yoke. He made a series of snorting exhalations.

She said, "Well, I better get back to work."

"Get that panther to turn in a circle."

She made a small laugh and smiled. Her fear had melted. She said, "We call it enrichment. My work is to keep these animals happy as may be. It's sad to keep them penned, but what to do? Animal rights people and zookeepers are the ones that love animals the most." She had gone on thinking to disarm, but saw her words had somehow enclosed them, like entering a cage. Something sorrowful had moved her, some quick pity for his bug-eyed nature. Keepers got mauled that way, following pity into a cage. Her gaze moved past JJ, toward the entrance of the parking lot. Where was Bluey?

With his right hand he swung the shovel in a fast arc across his feet and up onto his left shoulder, either meaning to menace or oblivious of it. He said, "Gotta scoop some poop. Maybe you could train me to turn in a circle sometime." As he turned, he broke into song, his voice ringing and sonorous. "I'm sure I could do thaaaaaat, as good as any caaaaaat—" He cast a glad glance over his shoulder to collect her astonishment. He smirked and headed toward the ungulates.

She turned back to Clark, listening as JJ's steps faded behind her. She felt her heart beating. She flung hands at Clark, releasing him. The cougar yawned, dropped to his belly, then rolled onto his side. He held his head up for a moment, watching her—anything?—then let it fall onto the wood chips. He yawned with maximum width, shook briefly, blinked, watched her. Anything?

She felt her heart flood. Just this tiny signal—something more?—from a savage beast, and her heart flowed with gratitude and flowed over Clark and the zoo grounds and past fear and over JJ too, mad sullen soul, and over her being on earth, merely that. She was here on earth, and Bluey had prepared an adventure. She was going to travel and work with him, master consultant of world zoos, famous trainer and understander of animals, favorite of students, genial presence. Ups and downs, but a big up coming. Think of that, put that in front.

She heard a hoot from Monkeytown, one of the howlers, then heard murmured conversation. She moved to the gravel path, looked, and there at the other end of the zoo grounds saw Bluey speaking with Carlos.

2

On the freeway, he removed his phone from its holster to call El, then saw it had died. And yesterday he had crushed the car charger in the doorjamb. He was late, and El would wonder. Her number was on the dead phone.

He left the freeway, sped down feeder streets, past fast food joints, strip malls, buildings and businesses, then into brown chaparral hills toward the college. He was thinking of George, in thrall to Annie, up on the treadmill of hope. Then doubt. Then pain. Then despair. Or love could come.

He was suddenly deep. He ached. A line came—*the swindles of pleasure that jangle pretty nothingness in the face of discontent.* His phone was dead, and he could not email it to himself. He would write it later. He spoke it out loud. How lovely.

As he pulled into the lot, he saw the band of surveyors again, working along the upper hillside above the training zoo grounds. There were some suit and tie guys in among them today, each with a rolled up something, a map or plan. They were going to call it Monastery Mall, keep the nave and monks' cells, use a monastery theme. They had commissioned a giant bronze bell. He opened his briefcase, found a pen, and wrote the line of poetry of his notebook. It shimmered still.

There were three other cars in the lot. Carlos Rivera's pickup, El's grungy Fiat, Rudy Wheeler's BMW. He had expected to see JJ's SUV, but it was absent. Wheeler had hired him as a fill-in after the last two keepers married and went to the Lowry Zoo in Tampa. The zoo population was diminishing, but they still needed at least two assistant keepers until Bluey launched, and a month ago Wheeler arrived with JJ, whom he introduced as an army veteran. They shook hands, and Bluey asked him where he had served. JJ had said, Fallujah, heard of it? Bluey said he had and thought, here do not touch. It hadn't been Fallujah. It had been the antisepsis. It had been the boy's staring, white room mind. Here do not touch.

He entered the combination on the chain link gate, heard it click solidly behind him, then went down the gravel path and turned right into Birdland where Carlos was finishing with Sybil, the African gray parrot. Carlos was a squat leathery man with a long gray ponytail. His heavy eyebrows, protruding jaw, and flattened nose gave him a faintly Neanderthal appearance. He deposited a hand shovel of droppings into the wheelbarrow, latched the wire gate. Sybil watched with peripheral vision from her highest perch, rotated her head toward Bluey once as he approached, rotated it back.

"Morning, Dr. Bluey."

"Good morning, Carlos."

Carlos to Sybil—"That's all, folks. El be here pretty soon with a nice banana chip or whatever." Then to Bluey—"We gonna chat?" He hoisted the wheelbarrow, rolled it to the next enclosure where Spectra the peacock made several quick paces, then stopped, turned to the gate, head high, at attention. "I got to keep the pace or get home late, and Mariana ream me out. You looking for El? She was over with Clark. There she is."

Bluey looked across the grounds, saw El beside the puma enclosure. They exchanged waves.

Carlos opened the peacock's wire gate and entered with the hand poop shovel. He said to Spectra, "We friends, little man? I think so, but I'm watching you."

Bluey said, "The enclosures are looking great, Carlos. Many thanks. How's JJ working out?"

Carlos worked his way around the enclosure, scooping balls of peacock dung, using his shoe from time to time as pusher. "JJ, man. I give him a ride today. His SUV in the shop. He live out in Thousand Oaks with his mother. He met me at the guard station they got, probably didn't want me to see his mansion."

"How's he doing?"

"He keeping up. He scooping the poop." He looked at Bluey.

Bluey said, "And—"

Carlos scanned the surrounding enclosures. "He like to fuck with me. He thinks up some wild ass thing to say, see how I do. He told me he gonna rent a car, but I told him, man, I will pick you up. But it don't make no matter to JJ. On the ride in, he asked me if I wanted to get a sex change operation. A brave sombitch, since he don't know me. Maybe I could stab him."

"I'll talk to him."

"No, no. I'm not telling on him. Let him be. It's good practice for me with Mariana. He's a crazy vet, man, and you got to be sympathetic. He got the word *reality* tattooed on his arms, instead of like Sally or something. He laid his trip on me today, on the ride. He got some kind of theory of life. He's pretty smart. One thing, he don't like zoos. I say, man, what are you doing here? He says he's doing research. So I don't know. He could be animal rights, but then he's not very sneaky if he is. He's a little spooky. You always think, what kind of guy would starting shooting everybody? That's the guy, except he's a joker. Best thing, man, let's push him in with Demijohn." Demijohn was a full grown lion. Carlos kept a smile off his face.

"Okay."

"Hell, no. I'm not going down for no crime on an asshole."

"That's why there are so many assholes, Carlos. Nobody willing to step up."

Carlos cackled. "Naw, he's okay. Just a few weeks, right? When you bringing in the cages?"

"That's what I wanted to mention to you. Looks like next week we start. Should take a few days. I have a crew for that, but you guys will have to work around them. Big hassle. *Siento.*"

"No *problema*. Also, I'm seriously thinking about it. I said, Mariana, we moving to Tennessee. She said, hell no, it snows. I said look, green grass, pretty water. I looked at your spot on the internet. Looks nice."

"It is nice. You might come?"

"I would come. Mariana would too, pretty sure. She bitching on one side and thinking on the other. I say the word snow, her eyes twitch. She probably want to hit me with a snowball."

"It sometimes snows. Not that often."

"Just enough. Two, three snowballs a year, that's enough for Mariana. Anyway, right now, I'm starting with landscaping. Got my truck, my son put me up a little website, gonna put me up on Craigslist."

"We'll be ready in three or four months. I'll give you a call."

"Okay, man. Don't worry about the cages. We'll go around them."

As Bluey passed through the primates, he set off a chorus of complaint. Quanna the bonobo harrumphed, rolled onto her back. Taj, the De Brazza guenon, chuffed and banged his wire. Bluey rarely passed them without offering treats. Shindig the spider monkey threw himself from wall to wall in exasperation. Bluey resolutely ignored them. But he had a packet of dried apricot in his coat and would be back.

El was seated on a bench across from the cougar and stood as he approached. Bluey stopped in front of her, smiled, took her in. For Bluey, her face was a meadow, a pleasant place to rest the eyes. He gestured, and they sat. He said, "I apologize for being late. I would have called but my cell died."

"I figured."

"So what's the verdict?"

"You really truly have twelve million dollars?"

"I do."

He slid a paper from a pocket of the briefcase, handed it to her.

It was a bank statement. She read that his account contained $11,984,355. 34. She started to say not quite twelve, but kicked the thought as nerves. She handed back the paper.

She said, "Well, I'm coming. I emailed animal kingdom."

He found he had been holding his breath, and now let it escape, not hiding the sigh. She was turned toward him, her arm perched on the bench back, and, bowing slightly, he picked up her hand, gave it a slight shake, returned it.

El said, "Really, I'm excited. It wasn't that hard to decide. Well, it was, but not really."

"A traveling zoo."

"Yes, horrors. But also Disney. I had fantasies of being curator someday. But I get the argument. We're losing the battle. And you've got the bucks to do it. And the—the—"

"Are you hesitating on the Spanish slang for fortitude?"

"Yes. Anyway, I'm in. It is conflicting though. You have to concede that." She saw Bluey's broad face crease, a mix of sympathy and amused reproach. She laughed. She said, "Oh, concede. But I don't care. The main thing is, will it work? Will we be a raving success story in the zoo community and change the world? Or will my resume say, former member of the ill-fated Exotic Animal Caravan."

"You are brave."

"I guess. But I'm excited. I read the folder thoroughly. I love the land. It's got streams, ponds, perfect weather. So yes. Now what?"

Bluey outlined the schedule. The stainless cages would arrive next week and be cut into the enclosures so the animals could acclimate. They would launch in three weeks. Their route was first to a county fair in Oregon, then down to Nevada for a few weeks, then Colorado, then Kansas, finally arriving in Tennessee sometime in July.

El stood, approached the cougar enclosure, clapped her hands twice. Behind the rectangles of wire, Clark gathered his tawny length, quivered off a few clinging wood chips and haunch sat, alert. "We're taking Clark, right?"

"Definitely. The animals were in the folder. Did you skip that?"

"Yes, I did. I'm a coward. I'll say goodbye to every one of them and whichever ones are in the trucks will be Christmas. Is that okay?"

"Sure."

"We'll place the rest of them, don't you think?"

"I placed most of them already."

"I've already had my cry about Juniper." She clapped her hands twice again, raised them together as if in prayer. Clark froze with attention. She brought her hands to her left shoulder, and Clark rose, turned his left flank to the wire, leaned against it, a medical presentation. She clapped, and he haunch sat. She lowered her hands, palms down. Clark lay down. "You sweetie. You sweet cougar." She flung her fingers at him. He flipped his head, yawned, lay his chin on his paws. "You're sure you just don't want to go sit down somewhere, Dr. Macintosh? With your twelve million?"

"No, I don't. And now it's Bluey."

They started up the path toward the chop shop.

"Bluey," she said. "I will *like* to call you Bluey."

They passed the carnivore enclosures—Demijohn the lion, Bump the sun bear, Tooey the honey badger. She kept her eyes down. "Is Bump coming?"

"What's a traveling zoo without a bear? And Demijohn, and—"

"Don't tell me any more. Good though. Bump the lump!" Bump had been her other second year animal. She glanced back at him. His head was up, staring at her. She flung fingers at him, blew a kiss. She said, "You mention a cook-ticket taker and a big rig driver in the plan. Have you hired them?"

"I've got a collection of resumes for the driver. I think I may have the cook."

"Really? Who?"

"My sister, Annie. I haven't asked her, but it might just fit with where she is right now. Long story for later."

"Well, here's some shot in the dark news. I talked to my parents last night, told them all about everything. They're excited, by the way. So my mother tells me my cousin is now a big rig driver and got laid off. He's big as a house, which might be good. He's not fat. He's like you, like a column. He played college football. I haven't seen him in a while though. He might be fat by now, in case you don't hire the fat." She smiled at him. They were on their way, on an adventure. Joy had returned. She felt energy flowing, down her calves, into the earth.

"What did he major in?"

"Not sure. I knew him as a kid basically."

"What kind of kid?"

"A big one. A good pillow fighter. A big eater too, and you'll be feeding him, so there's that. Anyway, my mom, who as you know is madly in love with you, told me to mention him to you. His name is Roger."

"Do you have his contact information?"

"I'll email it."

3

The ad in the forum said, "Bengal tiger, pure-blood. With cage. Six years old." There was a photo too, a big tiger standing in a stainless cage, a small olive-skinned man nearby, both tiger and man impassive, staring at the camera. Bluey had called the number immediately, then forwarded the ad to El. Now they zoomed down the interstate in Bluey's pickup into rolling brown wine country.

They had talked logistics for a half hour, meat packers, meet-ups with Arnold's ZooFood trucks, the schedule of vet visits, the water systems, the refrigerators, disinfectants. He had received her cousin resume, and Roger was driving down from Oakland next week for an in-person interview.

They lapsed into silence. This was their first event together, and El felt herself unable to fully relax, her body unable to mold comfortably into the seat cushion. She kicked off her clogs, pressed her bare feet into the windshield, exchanged smiles with Bluey. He was inward somewhere. She began trying to wiggle her left little toe without moving the others. Her window was slightly open, and cool spring air whipped her short hair, a faint stinging near the eyebrows. A small sting to distract from the big sting.

Packer had been her first stint at living with someone, sharing a bathroom, dinner, breakfast, shopping, sex, TV, cars. He was a Canadian from Vancouver. They had been affable and considerate with each other. That was one thing, maybe everything, considerate, not attached. When the lavish Dubai hotel offered him lion trainee in its new menagerie, he showed her the email on his laptop that night, in bed. He said, I know, I know. Reality set in. She hadn't been that attached either. But enough. Anyway she thought *he* was. Was it pride then? No, something better. Heart pain. He was gone in a week.

Now it was back and forth between her toe and Packer. She flashed on cut-off heart tentacles bleeding into space, which she had read about somewhere. Did concentrating on the toe diminish the bleeding, or bracket it? That's what you had to do with every pain, all through livelong life. Bracket pain and concentrate elsewhere, your little toe, for instance, which represented new life and independence in the bracketing game, and the Packer pain old life and laughter at the breakfast table which she thought might lead somewhere, to kids and memories, all gone. If she and Bluey started talking again, she might open the subject, get some fatherly counsel. Except she might cry and alarm him. Anyway, he was inward. She concentrated on her left little toe. She could not move it, but could feel where the pathway lay.

They exited the interstate and started into the hills of greening vineyards. He glanced at her. He said, "I have to engage you in some family drama. I have a younger sister, and we both inherited from the sale of the family cattle station. Now she has lost her money and is broke. So I want to hire her. So on your behalf I feel apprehensive. Because she's family. So that's one thing."

"Not to worry. I get that."

"Thank you. She hasn't agreed, but she needs a place, so I think she will."

"How did she lose her money?"

"She and her boyfriend invested in real estate just before the recession. That took the biggest chunk. Then he played poker on the internet."

"Well, damn."

"I want to make her ticket taker and cook. She'll be your roommate in the RV."

"Fine. You said that was one thing."

"She has a nineteen year old son, my nephew, Dawson. He was in school at the University of Washington and had some trouble and lost his scholarship. Annie wants him to come with us. So I thought, well, I could use another vehicle anyway, a smaller RV for errands and shopping."

El waited, then said, "What trouble?"

"He wrote a hacking program which he didn't use, but someone else did. He has a history. He hacked the school board in high school and posted their minutes on the internet. The university declined to prosecute, but they took his scholarship. So that's the crew, you, me, Annie, and Dawson. And maybe Roger. They're untrained, so it's you and me in the lead. What do you think?"

"You train forty students a year. So I think we're off to see the wizard."

"That's what I think."

"What does Annie do? I mean what did she do? How old is she?"

"Forty-three. She worked in films, make-up artist, and a little acting. She quit when the station sold."

"I bet you'd like to find the boyfriend."

"Let him fade away. We've got something else to do."

This remark came like fatherly counsel. She honed in on her left little toe. A bit of twitch, definitely. She removed her feet from the windshield and worked them into her clogs. She said, "So who owns the tiger? Did you find out?"

"A corporation owns the vineyard, On the corporate prospectus there were pictures of middle Easterners. The animals are in the back, and they have a sign that says, Hafiz Menagerie. So I think Persians or Arabs."

"So what's this tiger's history? How old is he?"

"They're guessing six years. They got him from a village in India. He was part of their shrine or something."

Half an hour later the GPS led them through the ivied archway of Heaven's Gate Vineyards. They followed the twisting gravel drive to the summit of a hill where a cluster of white buildings stood, a sales store for the wine, offices, and behind, the vineyard sheds. As they parked in front of the office, a tall fiftyish man emerged. He walked toward them, hitching with every left foot. He was a tall thin man with a sun-lined face under a camouflage baseball cap.

He extended his hand to Bluey. "Tom Haley, Dr. Macintosh. Glad to know you. I read your books."

"Good to meet you, Tom. Call me Bluey. This is El Chastain. You're a trainer?"

"I'm a keeper, not a trainer." He shook hands with El.

"You got bit?" said El.

Tom looked at El. "Did you google me?"

Bluey said, "She didn't know your name. But a keeper with a limp might have been a trainer." He looked at El. "Is what she was thinking. Not that she should have mentioned it."

El frowned. "Well, that's true. Sorry."

Tom said, "Come on. I'll show you this tiger."

They fell in with him on the gravel road, Bluey in the middle, and walked past the vineyard sheds toward a stand of cottonwoods woven through with tall wire fencing. Haley bobbed along with energy. With each one of his hitching steps, El felt for something apologetic to say, but found nothing.

Haley said, "He's in good health, and the cage goes too. So that's a tiger and a stainless enclosure for twenty-five hundred. I expect you know a gift when you see it."

They passed under a steel archway with a crescent of Arabic script and beneath it, The Hafiz Menagerie. El tried to catch Bluey's eye, but he was looking forward, absorbing the layout and denizens of the park. There were camels, dromedaries, wild donkeys, lions, ostrich, flamingo, a variety of antelope, all in spacious zoo link squares, with shade canopies, ponds, feed and water troughs, dung free. Three Latino workers passed them, nodded to Haley.

"Well, you saw that sign, so you can guess it's Arabs. Not just any Arabs, but high up ones, right up there by the king. Saudis. The guy I work for is Fuad, and he is living the life. I been to Africa, China, Afghanistan. India is where we bought this tiger."

They approached a metal building with high wide doors for equipment. Two backhoe tractors and a bulldozer were parked neatly beside it. Haley opened a person-sized door beside the equipment entryway.

He said, "This is our quarantine shed. He's been here three weeks. Get ready for an interesting story."

They followed Haley through the door into the high-vaulted metal building. There was a concrete floor, high fluorescents, a miscellany of tool chests, a scattering of railroad ties, the smell of diesel fuel. In the center of the space on a platform of ties stood an eight by twenty foot stainless cage. At one end was a huge tiger, on his haunches, alerted, watching them. Zoo link fencing was wrapped around and over the cage and fastened with massive lag screws into the railroad ties.

Bluey laid a hand on the zoo link. He said, "It looks like you got him captured."

Haley laughed. "We do. His name is Bhajan. The Song of God. And when you hear him purr, you'll see why they named him that."

El said, "Tigers don't actually purr though."

"They don't except for this one. I've sat here for hours. It's like a waterfall, sort of."

"He purrs for hours?"

"He purrs at night, all night."

El followed Bluey in a slow circuit around the cage. Bhajan remained motionless, letting them fill their minds.

They returned to Haley, who was slouched on his right leg.

Bluey said, "A beautiful beast. What do you think, El?

"Beautiful. And pretty calm."

"I'd like to see his medical papers. But I want him."

They shook.

El said, "He's the king of the show. I can't wait to hear this purr. Why in the world have you got zoo fence all over here? He's not a dinosaur, for goodness sake."

Haley laughed. He said, "Let's sit, what say? Here's comes the story." They seated themselves on railroad ties. "We have a cage lift, by the way. We can put it right on a flatbed. The width is legal for the freeway. So Fuad wants a Bengal tiger. And it's got to be pure blood, not one of these mutts they got all over the states, half Siberian, quarter Bengal, whatever. They're gathering all the animals Arabs have come in contact with in their long history. We've got over a thousand acres here. These are just holding enclosures. We're building a major park. Anyway, he gets word there's this gorgeous tiger for sale in India. So we fly out in his corporate jet, which has got a conversion for animals. We land in Calcutta, then it's out in SUVs into the hinterland. I would say wilderness but in India there's always people just over the hill. Finally we get to a little village, and there's this tiger in a bamboo cage. Just bamboo now. It's on a pedestal, columns of painted concrete with Sanskrit. It's a shrine. And there's this naked guy, who is the handler and feeder and groomer. And he's dead buck naked. And he's got this wire brush, and he's combing this tiger, reaching his arm right through the bamboo, just combing away and the tiger's just lying there. The guy's got wild hair like he's wearing a bush on his head, and he's sort of dirt-caked. Doesn't give us the time of day. So we have a translator, and when the headman shows up—he's another old guy, but he's wearing a dhoti at least—that the keeper is a *mast*. It's spelled m-a-s-t, but pronounced *must*. Which is a god-intoxicated man."

Bluey said, "What was the name of the village?"

Haley smiled. "Why, you want another tiger?" When Bluey only waited, he said, "Hardeva. You ever heard of a god-intoxicated man?"

"Yes, I have."

"Really? Well, you're a world traveler. No one else I ever talked to has. Except Fuad. He knew what they were too. Another world traveler. Anyway, this is the guy who brought the tiger to the village. This was like six years ago. As a cub. So Fuad goes over and touches the guy's feet, which at the time I thought was, hey, show respect to the holy man, get a good price. But no, he meant it. Have you run across these masts?"

"I ran across a book."

"I didn't know there was a book. So when he touched the guy's feet, the guy swiped his back with the wire brush, then went right back to combing the tiger. Fuad had this white T-shirt on, and a minute later he had a red stripe on it. The guy got him a good one. The headman inspected the wound. Very propitious, supposedly. A couple of good scratches right down the spine. But it didn't affect the price, which started at five laks, which was five hundred thousand rupees, about ten grand."

"Why were they selling their tiger?" El said. She had folded her legs and half-pivoted to face the tiger, moving her hand from left to right,

right to left. Bhajan stared into her face, absorbing her, his eyes unmoving. Bluey watched, then dropped his hand gently across El's, lowering them. Bhajan looked at Bluey, absorbing him.

Haley said, "This tiger had got a mind of his own, doesn't he? Are you going for behaviors?"

Bluey said, "Not necessarily."

El looked at Bluey. "This is a very calm tiger. We could train this tiger." She swung back to Haley. "So why sell the holy tiger?"

"According to the headman, the mast told them to. So they bring tea, and we sit down in a circle with the elders of the village, and the rest of the village is standing all around us. Maybe two hundred people, perfectly silent. Very important moment. So the headman says, five hundred thousand. I'm doing the hard ass part, so I say, no, too much, best we can do is a hundred. So the headman says, okay, six hundred." Haley laughed. "So I say, come again? You went up a hundred? The headman wags his head apologetically. He says, very sorry, every time we object, the price must go up by one lak. So now Fuad says, no, too much. The head man wags his head, says, seven hundred. Too much. Eight hundred. Too much. Nine hundred. Too much. One million rupees. Fuad says, done!"

"That's a hard bargainer, that Fuad," said El.

"Well, you know, he's—"

"We get it. He's a philanthropist."

"He is. And devoted. Not a fundamentalist or anything. So we get a cage made in Delhi, fly it by military helicopter into Hardeva. Big ceremony. They lose their beloved tiger, only now they get electricity, nice school, computers. Fuad is funding the school. Over and above. His people are taking care of that."

El said, "But why—"

Haley raised a finger. "Why are *we* selling the tiger?"

"Right."

"Because Fuad says this is not his tiger. He said, put an announcement in a forum, whoever responds first, sell the tiger and cage for twenty-five hundred dollars. That's the owner. I told him Bluey Macintosh responded. He was very happy. He also knows your books."

Bluey said, "Did he have a dream or something?" He could feel his pulse going, felt a hot charge push up.

Haley stared at Bluey. "Well, you got there ahead of me. He did have a dream. The same dream three times. He came up to the tiger, and the tiger turned his back. A little bitty dream, but he had it three nights running. The tiger would not face him. So he said, sell the tiger, and the dream stopped. Fuad told me to tell you this tiger is destined for you. He wanted to meet you, but he's in Bahrain. And that's the complete fairy tale around this tiger."

"That is the coolest story." said El. "What happened to the holy man?"

"We never saw him again. I looked around for him during the bargaining, thinking, yeah, he's the guy that put them up to that raise-it-a-hundred deal, but he was gone. When we came back with the cage, the headman said he was gone for good."

The charge in Bluey widened, slowed. He said, "Tell Prince Fuad I would love to meet him someday. And thank him kindly for this gift."

"I will. I will miss this fellow's purring. I want to make a recording. I guess we can go sign papers."

El said, "You were going to tell us about the extra fence."

Haley laughed. "That's because the first night I freaked out. That tiger got under my skin. I freaked out, and next morning I had the guys wrap the cage in zoo link. You asked about my limp? I got my knee into the jaws of a Kodiak bear. Trying to make a Hollywood bear. I have a case of PTSD. Sometimes I can't close my eyes without a bear jumping on me. I can't even get in with the camels anymore. Anyway, I wanted to hear that purr, but I was too jumpy to stay in here. Now you know my secrets. I'll miss that purr, guaranteed. I'll get the fencing off there today. I believe I could stand it now anyway. That purr has fairly calmed me down."

They entered the small office at the side of the vineyard retail shop. On the desk lay a book opened to a page with a photograph, and Bluey recognized it as one from his book, *How to Run a Zoo*. Bluey and El sat in guest chairs. Haley sat behind the desk, closed the book, held it forth. "Do you sign your books? I thought Fuad might appreciate it."

"Happy to," said Bluey. While Haley rummaged in a filing cabinet, he held the book on his lap, thumbed to the title page. He had the impulse to say something foundational. There had been India, and a mast, and a dream. Nothing came. Then simplicity flowed. He wrote, "Thank you, Fuad. Bluey Macintosh."

Arrangements were made to collect the tiger in two weeks. Papers were signed. Haley walked them to the truck, then said, "Damn, just a sec."

He returned from the office with a small cardboard box, handed it to Bluey through the window. "Fuad said you might want this. Drive safe." He waved them down the driveway.

El said, "Can I open it?"

Bluey turned onto the road toward the freeway. He said, "Open it." He thought he knew what it was.

El tore away the paper and tape. Inside the box was a dirty wire brush. She said, "So cool." She perched it in her palm, held it forth. "The wire brush of the holy man." She glanced at Bluey, felt his gravity like correction. But her heart flowed. She kissed the brush. "God, Bluey, I'm just so excited. If we install a squeeze wall in the cage we can use this on Bhajan. You don't want to rename him, do you?"

He said, "No. Bhajan is good."

"So what book had masts in it? That's pretty interesting."

"It's called *The Wayfarers*. It's about group of people in India searching for the god-intoxicated."

"Really? Do you have it? I'd like to read it."

"I have it."

"Great. So what are the god-intoxicated?"

"I haven't read the book."

"Oh. Where'd you get it?"

"It was given to me."

"Well, definitely bring it along, okay? Hey, how about some coffee?"

They were nearing the freeway, and a MacDonald's had appeared. They got coffee and headed south.

El had become faintly nervous. Bluey seemed to have fallen into inwardness again. He had been a teacher, a mentor, now an employer, but here was a private Bluey, who had a past and a life. She let few moments of silence pass. They entered the freeway. She rolled her window up, and the new quiet invited. She said, "Do you believe in God? Since the subject came up. I mean with the masts." The question hung, made the truck cab seem suddenly intimate. "I always hate to ask anyone that. It's like challenge or something." She added formally, "Whatever you tell me will be held in strictest confidence."

He smiled. He said, "I'll tell you this. I think it's a bad question."

"Okay—"

"I mean, if you feel God, who cares what you believe? And if you don't, who cares what you believe."

"Ah." She thought, that's perfectly right and true. She said, "Do you feel God?"

"From time to time."

She could ask, what does he feel like? But didn't. His simplicity had struck some seam in her.

She said, "You know why I came to Santa Rosa? I was all set to be a vet, then came to the college on a field trip."

"I remember."

"Now I'm going to tell you something I've always wanted to tell you. So you guys threw a little goodbye party for the field trippers, and we were over at your house. And there was this argument going on in the back yard about the election. This was 2012. So these two second years were sort of trouncing these other people. They were both hard ass conservatives."

"Ah."

"Do you remember that?"

"No, but I bet I know the two guys. Both guys, right? Ray and Jesse, mid-thirties, one bald, one black hair."

"Right. So I was listening, and I wanted to jump in, but I'm an outsider, and I don't know these people, who were big deal second years anyway. Also it was down to facts and figures, so much percentage this or that, which I hate. But here comes Bluey with a margarita. And you said this most soothing and smart thing. Do you remember that?"

"Not yet."

"You said if you had a liberal and a conservative both make a list of all the human virtues that they believed were the most important, you'd have stuff on both those lists like courage, love, patience, wisdom, all those great things. And then if you compared the lists, you'd say, hey, these are the same lists, maybe in a little different order, but exactly the same. So the difference between conservative and liberals really comes down to the ordering of virtue. Do you recall any of that?"

"I recall that thought. I like that thought."

"Well, anyway, that particular moment is why I'm here! I mean all this tribal fireworks and then suddenly this sweet clear thought. It was the higher self stepping out, and all those facts and figures had to scatter like spiders. So that's why I'm here. It sounds naive, which it probably is."

"I'm very happy to hear that story."

"You could start thinking about fate and all that."

Bluey smiled.

She said, "I'm probably an atheist, by the way."

"You're an atheist that wants to read about masts?"

"Well, who knows what that is? I mean I believe in ESP too. I've been reading the new atheists. Have you read any of those guys?"

"I know their views."

"So what did you think?"

Bluey let a moment pass. He said, "I think you don't have to be much of a shot to hit bullshit, since it's what we're mostly made of. But it takes marksmanship to hit the truth."

El smiled. "That's good. That's a quotable quote." She felt a rush of joy, rolled the window open an inch, conversation done, and let the exuberant wind roughhouse in her hair.

4

JJ skipped lunch to give willpower a workout. He sat across from Carlos, watching him chew up three tamales, tried to think up comments. The break room had great light from a big window out to the zoo grounds, and if he slumped, the hat cam caught Carlos straight on.

He was silent until the last tamale, giving Carlos a pressure gaze. Then he said, "This just in. Mexico has become the fattest nation in the world. That's probably what finished off the Aztecs. Too fat to fight."

Carlos smirked and shook his head. Not much. JJ let it go. Carlos had armored up, and you had to poke hard to get something going. JJ wasn't much into it today. He had already taped more than an hour of indignant Carlos anyway, so plenty. Except if Carlos took a swing, which could be a capper, something for the last clip. The end of the zoo gig though, and no more El.

He finished at three. He was finishing earlier every day as the animal population whittled down, and he became an accomplished poop-scooper. He drove toward Thousand Oaks, then decided to hit Famous Raymond's before home. Famous Raymond had opened a new tattoo joint on Graciano Street and had been running ads in the weekly about his new Q-Switched laser, latest greatest for tattoo removal.

JJ followed his phone's map and found it, about fifteen feet of glass squeezed between a Chinese restaurant and a coffee shop. He found a spot five cars down and tucked the SUV in, then headed back up the sidewalk, passed a few strollers, then passed a short wide woman in a tug-of-war with her wiry little something dog, the dog looking windblown against the leash. El wouldn't put up with that. El would have that dog tucked in at ankle, ready to stop or start, yes, sir, ma'am. How would it be, quick as a flash, he picks the dog up, too bad, lady, and punts it into the street? Quick as a flash, big surprise for the lady, big surprise for the dog. That put a smile on his face. Just funning, lady, but train your dog.

A couple of guys entered the Chinese restaurant as he went by. They had a buffet up front wafting, and he caught the scent. He didn't care for buffet's that much, but he might give it a look after the tat shop, maybe they had something fresh. Unlikely since those guys cooked everything as far as he could tell, probably cooked lettuce.

There it was, famous Raymond's famous tattoo joint sign of a tattooed butt, and on the window in big lowclass-looking red and yellow paint, "Just arrived! Q-Switched laser for tattoo removal." He pushed through the glass door. On the left a counter and clerk, on the right a wall of tattoo art and a guy browsing. The clerk was a high school girl or just out, maybe Famous Raymond's daughter, but probably not, since he had three parlors. There was a door to the back where the gear and chairs would be and maybe Raymond too, but unlikely since he rotated. He was high dollar, and if you wanted Raymond you had to wait. Last year JJ waited two weeks, and when he showed Raymond his tat plan, an ink bracelet with the word *reality* in the font Verdana, Raymond had been off put. He went professional after that and took the money, but he didn't make much effort with his disdain. JJ stayed meek, since he wanted Raymond's excellence. But when Raymond got bent over and head down into it, he thought of whipping out his Gerber knife and stabbing him, just in the temple, say, a punish stab. *Christ! You stabbed me!* Yes, I did, Famous Raymond, because how about live and let live? He kept the knife strapped over his right kidney on an elastic belt. It had been his battle knife. He also kept a five shot thirty-two Smith in his front pocket, slim and invisible. He had gotten it at a gun show after Afghanistan, and it had somewhat calmed him down. Two weeks ago, he fired it a couple of times in the back yard to prove it, saw a security cruiser browsing a half hour later, but no door knock. Sir, did you fire a gun and frighten my millionaires? Of course not, officer. Okay, then.

The girl clerk said, "Hi. Can I help you?" She had scraggly brown hair and a thin tweaker's face but likely wasn't since her shoulders and arms were swollen with food. She wore a tank top, standard tattoo joint costume, and her arms and shoulders swirled with jungle birds.

"I want to get some removal, then some re-tattoo. But first I have some questions. Your sign says Q-Switched, but do you have the ND Yag?"

"Yep. That's the one."

"You use the Kirby-Desai scale?"

"I think they do. I've heard them mention that."

"Raymond?"

"No, Gina. She went to school."

"She went to school for tattoo removal?"

"Well, to conventions they have. They have seminars."

"Okay. Sign me up." Then JJ wanted fun. He said, "See this right here, where it says *reality*, which is what we're all looking for. Only sometimes we miss it because we're too lazy to be alert. So to represent that on my right arm I want two minus signs, here and here, each side of reality. And sometimes we're preoccupied and full of shit, and for that I want two plus signs on my left arm, here and here. They have to be skin color because reality is natural so the black has to be removed and then tatted back leaving the pluses and minuses. That way I can be reminded to stay centered in reality. How's that?"

The girl gave off a friendly smile. "Sounds like a plan," she said. JJ saw she was blocking strange and saw her life strategy on her face, plain as a tattoo, smile nice, block strange, eat food. She addressed her computer terminal, done with making friends. Not too scared either. Getting through bumpy old life. He felt a presence drifting in on his left and looked. It was the guy from across the room, a smallish, longhaired guy, dark as a hajji, but copper not olive, so a surfer, best guess. JJ had his forearms on the counter, and the guy was inspecting them and nodding. I'm a fellow appreciator of reality, is what I am, dude. JJ ignored him. He said to the girl, "I'm open after two weeks. Give me whatever you got, first one."

"You know removal takes a few months to take effect, right?"

"I do know that."

She made him an appointment, wrote it on a card, handed it over. She said, "You want to know some prices?"

He said, "It is my fortune to be rich and indifferent to price." He caught their looks as he turned, headed out. Was money really right down here among us?

He gave the Chinese joint a pass, clenching off hunger, what the tattoo girl couldn't do, obviously, missing an important sphincter. He got into the SUV, snugged the belt, then sat, letting a plan come. He started the engine and pulled into traffic. He would head out to Edmond's Point, smoke a joint, hit the surf. Then he could get an avocado at a roadside stand. His mother would be into her programs when he got home. How was work? Work was good. He would make a salad, unclench hunger and feast under the patio lights with the insects. He could cut the lights and sleep out there in a lounger, wear a sweatshirt, take some sheets, cover his head until he was asleep, then let the mosquitoes land, who cares, since he was immune to their chemicals. If he could get to sleep. Sometimes the couch worked, sometimes the carpet.

He hit sixty on La Brea. He would be in the water in under an hour. He had a good complicated stereo and opened his appetite. But music or talk? Before he could think, El appeared in his head, floating up beside him in the other lounger, her little self tucked under sheets, listening to the loud bugs. *Isn't this fun? Is that your lettuce? Do we have bugspray?* That produced a fine crisp pain, chest-centered, which he clenched off. Then she floated up again, behind, past his guard. She asked again, *Do we have bugspray?* And the *we* cut like a knife.

He hard craved a joint. He had some Queen's Delicious from the excellent Yuba City guys. Two tokes of Queen's, drift on, hit the surf, see if a shark would bite him, which he expected any day might happen, probably would, so what. They warned you, don't surf in the evening. But he looked on the web. Most bites were in the daylight hours. What the fuck, guys! Anyway, if a shark's got your name on it—like a bullet. The good guys coming down the street, the bad guys busy on the rooftops carving names in bullets. They carved Mississippi Marty on three of them.

After the first ambush they all said, Jesus, it was like a video game, tracers zipping, everything booming and bouncing, until Mississippi Marty broke from behind an engine block in the middle of the street, trying to get to the concrete Texas barrier and got the front of his face shot off. Then, for JJ, it was still like a video game, fiercely real and unreal together, Marty crawling blind with his face hanging, everybody scrunched in rubble, the sergeants shouting, cover fire, and everybody thinking, *Do we get him? Do we get Marty?* The bad guys spraying their shitty-aimed death blossoms, everybody shooting at tracers trying to scare the bad guys down, but some badass bad guy wanted Marty enough he stayed up to aim and finally got Marty again, this time twice through the neck, and he made a blood fountain ten feet from the squad on the other side of some bricks, going dizzy, his head up and waving, then his eyes flickering out, his head dumping down hard. Which was some relief, because then you didn't have to rescue him, and because, Marty, dude, your face, man, Jesus.

El was back in the lounger, her head poking out of the sheet, smiling like it was Halloween fun. He was snagged on her, like a nail, and when he tried to live on, she pulled him back, or he pulled her. Like a ghost, whoosh, back in front, in the lounger. If he had said to her, El, I like the way you move, and the way you look over somewhere and see something and get interested in it, I like that, and the way you smile, I have to say, is attractive and is a soft simple smile, all connected to your heart. But he went menace, his customary deployment. He swung that shovel to give her a jolt. Something draws you, get it by the shirtfront. She was kind in the lounger though. She said, *our bugspray.* One way, someday, fire a bullet through your head. Other way, you toke some Queen's, swim with sharks, work was good, try for sleep.

What if he got out his phone map right now and found a Wal-Mart to get some bugspray? That would definitely be a sign. He would probably get a giant can of the best kind. Read bug spray blurbs and spend ten minutes deciding between the last two best kinds. *Do I have bugspray, El? Sure thing, got this big can of the best kind.* He would leave the Wal-Mart, return to the SUV, take the bugspray out of the sack, set it on the seat so they would find it beside him like a farewell note. *See this bug-spray? I was losing grip and had to get off.* Then the little Smith. Up through the palette.

He could say, El, man, I was having a bad day. I confess it to you. El, man, I'm having a bad life, is the thing. I had this uncle, and grade school, and high school, and Fallujah. Never look at a dead kid you shot, El, because their ghost blows through you. It's all trends and forces, El, not just in history, but also in psychology, trends and forces issuing from the hidden land, of which I am a seeker and a victim.

JJ was born in fourth grade, is how he thought about it. Before then, blank. That's when his uncle had killed himself in the basement, and he was pretty sure, had to be, that his uncle had abused him down there, maybe since an infant. His brother, Trey, who was six years older, could have definitely been in on it. Maybe Uncle Jimmy got him first, said, now, sweet Trey, go get your brother. Both dead now and not talking, Uncle Jimmy with a razor in the basement and Trey in Seattle with the needle still in his hand. Trey had been a singer in a grunge band. He remembered Trey, who was thin and pissed and kept his room sloppy. He knew Uncle Jimmy only from pictures, not memories, smiling in his ice cream parlor, the parlor funded by his mother, his mother funded by his father, his father Mr. Hedge Fund. On the phone his father said, *you joined the fucking army?* Using his hip voice, unable to say anything without his hip voice, like it was installed in his throat. *Why not the fucking Marines, man? I mean if you're proving something, prove the shit out of it.* Because, father, they are proud, which is a form of dishonesty, which I do not condone. *Can you dig me, father, with your hip ways and beautiful wife?*

Or maybe something else happened in the basement, which he had to go down into all those years doing the laundry, his chore for allowance before the trust fund kicked in, part of his mother's raise-her-remaining-son better plan. A murder down there, or they tortured him, except no scars, or kept him chained up, or someone else chained up and tortured. But no. It was plain old everyday sexual abuse, had to be. Something with his little fourth grade weenie, and he had blocked it tight. It made him an odd kid and a violent fighter. In sixth grade he beat down Tashon, who was plaguing him and every other kid too, with his huge, held-back size. When Tashon went down he kicked him cold-aimed in the face and crotch until the teachers got there. Everybody was scared and JJ too. But he thought, so that's how it's done. They sent him to crazy kid's school where he played sullen with the counselor and hid the pills under his tongue. He gave it a while, then he moved to sorry, and the guy sent him back. He took martial arts then, two kinds, and won tournaments. In junior high and high school, the wrestling coaches called his mother. Maybe you could talk to him. He could be state champ, ma'am. Until he fucked up their heavyweight champ, who was beleaguering him about his lack of school spirit, and when they got into it, left his scrotum exposed. That was another bad situation, with a hospital and district attorney involved before it was dropped. So the rule was, in grade school and junior high and high school, don't mess with JJ, or talk to him much either because he's a hot burning fire.

So join the army. And turn down all those extra schools they offer when they find out how intelligent you are. Head for combat with your band of brothers, a scraped up mix from crazytown, off to battle the nation's enemies. Who were from crazytown across the sea. Combat was just right though, just what you thought it would be, with bullets pinging and blood and shit and corpse-eating dogs and plenty of pissed off hajjis to shoot at. He was in the armored cavalry, and his second day in Ramadi, he killed two college kids, looked like, out for a nice day of shooting at Americans. He was on point down an alley, then into a side alley, and it was him and two guys twenty feet apart. It was shoot or get shot, and he shot first and saw their blood fly. They both had big horn-rimmed glasses and were head to toe in insurgent black. One guy had black tennis shoes. The other guy had white tennis shoes he had magic markered black. After a few months, it was evident to all he was one cool dude under fire, and they made him sergeant and squad leader. He shot many hajjis. Then Second Fallujah opened, and he was clearing a house and heard metal scrap inside a cupboard and emptied the clip of his M4. Out of the cupboard fell a little kid and his father, and he felt the kid's ghost blow through him. A fourth grade kid about. The scrape had been a frying pan, the dad's weapon or else the dad was holding it in front of his son like a shield, and when that memory pushed up which it used to daily do and still did now and then, that's what he thought about, weapon or shield? For a long time he hated that father with black bitter hatred, but the father was fading now, back farther in his mind, on a little bench back there with his son, calmed down a little, not scraping that frying pan every chance he got. He told the army he was all right, but they didn't think so and detached him to Germany for a month. He went to Amsterdam for ten days, where he stayed stoned with prostitutes. Then he was deployed to Afghanistan where the fighting had died out for a while. Then he came home.

In community college he took psychology, then history, then video production. When he was twenty-one he got his money, and Trey's too, which put him over twenty million. He bought a big house at the end of a canyon and lived in it for a year. Three months ago a brush fire burned it to ash. So it was a hotel for a month, then his mother's invitation and a return to the big beautiful basement house.

The basement drew him. It was like a force field and blanked him, but he videoed it and studied the video in his room. He waited for something, a pipe, a nail, and mark on the ping pong table, to trigger something. His uncle had walled off a basement corner for a bedroom where he had his bed and a desk and an end table and rock band posters. He videoed it all with his high end kit, with slow sweeps, some well-lit, some not, and made disks which he let run on a computer all day every day. He installed surveillance cameras around the property so he could tell his mother he was monitoring feeds. Good for you, JJ, for being productive and helpful, though, really, this is a gated community with bunches of security, but good for you. Not really good for him, though, since he stayed on top, in his used-to mind, where he was weightless and spacewalking and blank.

He got good at video. He put up a website, got work, weddings, birthday parties, conventions, adopt-a-pet videos for animal shelters, which he did gratis, school events where he became a go-to guy because of his quality and dependability. He had a YouTube channel with time lapse and slow motion projects. He got certified in scuba, got an underwater kit, went out with dive boats. He worked surfing competitions. Then, through his mother's old buddy, he got the zoo job, thinking, time for some undercover, film some truth, animals in prison for your pleasure, you people of the earth, except there was El.

At Edmond's Point, the surfers were clearing out, obedient to the dusk theory, so it was just a black kid still out there on the water. JJ rolled into the back seat and got his suit on, then broke out the Queen's from a baggie under the floor mat, had his two tokes. Excellent Queen's. He got the separation from him and himself then, and started sliding, on vacation from reality now, and if El came up or if he got one of those bullet zips or RPG explosions which still came back here and there, or if frying pan daddy showed up, it wouldn't flinch him but would slide smooth by, unconnected and no harm.

He put his board under his left arm, trotted down the beach a couple of hundred yards, switched it to his right, trotted back, breathing hard now and ready to cool. He stroked out, fifty feet from the black kid. They flicked nods. The sun was flaring the clouds red and gold, and at the horizon burning a hot red hole. He sat his board straight-backed, kicking now and then to stay right against the chop, feeling the rollers lift and drop. He would take two, maybe three. The black kid turned his board, liking the dark one coming, glanced at JJ. JJ didn't show he noticed, let the kid go off to the beach. Then he was alone. This is what he liked, solidly alone, the ocean pulsing and brining, his feet waving at the dangerous dark. The ocean was like the living skin of a big beast, and he was so little the beast couldn't notice him. The ocean was like the mind, bumpy and foamy up here where you floated, and way down deep, fast dark sharks.

5

"Well, you've reeled me in, and here I am flopping on your shore. Another change, so what?"

They were in Bluey's kitchen, Bluey leaning on the counter facing Annie, his big, furred forearms like crossed logs. Annie perched on a stool, one leg over the other, foot dancing, puffing from time to time on an electronic cigarette.

She said, "And we can be together, at long last. Who could have seen that coming? You're being kind, I know. Some part of me says, well, he has to be kind, that's his nature, you don't owe him anything. Can you believe thoughts like that get into my little brain? Your call was a vine in the quicksand, as you can imagine. Oh god. I'm still trembling, even if I'm not physically. You're calming me down with your aura. You are never far from my thoughts. Do you think of me much? Tell the truth."

"I do. And warmly."

"Ah." She flicked an imaginary ash into the sink. She was forty-three, her faced faintly lined, but nicely boned, strong straight nose, agile mouth, still sharply pretty. "That's what wrong with these electronic cigarettes, you can never flick the ash. That's an invention waiting to happen, make a note. Fake ashes for e-cigs. Well, I'm saved then. In case you're wondering, will your altruism be rewarded, it will be. It wouldn't be altruism then, by the way. Anyway, main thing to know and believe is that I'm done with men. There's a blankness here." She moved her palm across her chest, testing the force field of her heart. "There's no invitation. I love animals too, by the way. I was raised on an Australian cattle station, too. When I smell horse shit, I perk up. And you can teach me. I will attend you, sir. I will cook and be a good cook. I can be organized, never fear. I am willing one hundred percent. I will cook with love and gratitude, and therefore my food will be tasty. There's probably a website, the RV gourmet."

"We can make a menu. We'll get it all organized."

"We will march together and swing our arms. That's a small jibe. I'm going to be your little sister forever. I must learn love, so that everywhere I go I shine, on king and pauper. See? I remember our talks. Rosa had that. I loved her too, Bluey. And she loved me. She got me all those auditions. There is a little shrine inside me for Rosa. Bluey, let me ask you this. Tell the whole truth. Do you love me?"

"I do, Annie."

"Well, goddammit, that's great." A sob erupted and her head fell forward. "That feels super. It does, I'm not kidding." She came quickly around the counter. Bluey unbent, and she hugged his thick body with one arm, the other holding the e-cig at her side. She laid her head against his chest, and he laid one hand on her thick dark hair, the other on her back. Then she bucked away. She puffed her cigarette, went back to her stool.

"I'm going to quit these e-cigs. Let my veins dilate. That could be half the problem right there. A bloodless brain. So I'll cook, I'll drive, I'll man the gate. And don't think I can't help with the animals. I don't mind cleaning cages. Just show me the procedure. You know, PETA's gonna be after you. Little cages, packed in trucks. They'll be on you, Bluey. They could organize protests."

"They might."

She frowned. "Well, they'd be right, wouldn't they? I mean, it doesn't sound too humane to me either."

"It's not, but it's only for three or four months. Then we install them in the ecopark. And we just go out from time to time, make our noise, and back home. And yes, I want you to work with the animals. They'll need all the attention we can give."

"Oh Bluey, you're putting my little butt in the palm of your hand, aren't you? You're lifting me up. And I'm loathsome, loathsome, as Dostoyevsky puts it." She adopted a Brooklyn accent. "Nobody would loan me money, then you loan me money because you're the only dumb shit sucker that would loan me money." She cocked her head. "Mean Streets. So now we come to this difficult subject. Bluey—oh Bluey—" Her voice broke, and she buried her face in the V of her palms. "I've done something so awful. I can hardly bear to open my eyes in the morning." Tears broke free and ran into the heels of her hands. "The money was gone. Hardy confessed and then what to do? We were broke. So I took the college money, two hundred thousand, and used it to live. Then Hardy took that too and disappeared. And so here I am and so is Dawson, washed up on your shore. He can't pay for anything, and the scholarship is gone, never to return. I want him to go with us, but he might not. You don't have to pay him, just feed him. He's got your brains. He's a whiz kid, actually. He's an artist, too. The scholarship thing was not his fault, by the way. His roommates got hold of his laptop, and used some of his hacking programs, which was forbidden for him to have, and the shit hit the fan. Then right out in the provost's office he admitted the thing in high school, which was sealed, and he didn't have to. After I spent all that money out-lawyering them. So they took his scholarship. He could maybe get a loan, but he won't try. I told him I'd ask you for the money, by the way, and I would have, but he said no. He's got my pride, that's for sure. He's a sweet kid. He's a special special boy. That's a mother talking, but it's true. Hey, do you have a website? Because he can do that big time. He can YouTube and Twitter, whatever. Would you have given him the money?"

"Probably."

"You would have. You need a website, right?"

"I do. Put your mind at ease. I'll talk to him. We'll see about a paycheck too. There's plenty to do."

Annie put her head down on the counter for a long moment, then lifted her head, peered at Bluey. "Sometimes I need to cry so much and can't. This is the best thing that could have happened, you calling me out of the blue. The absolute best thing, and it's still crappy. Can I admit that, or do I have to be a good girl? I don't know if Dawson will even come. He might just go be homeless or something. Or crash with a chum. He's pretty much disgusted with me."

"Does he have a cell phone?"

"Yes. You may not know this, but you were his father, in a way. He always had you in the background. We're going to Uncle Bluey's? That little awake face. So call him, with the phone and with your heart. That would be great."

"I will."

"Oh my." She covered her face. "Loathsome, loathsome!" She sobbed, then quickly scrubbed her palms across her face. She shook her head fiercely, let her hair fluff. She tore a paper towel, found a pencil in a cup near the phone, wrote a number. "He has a phone for now. The lava of my inequity will soon leave all a charred and barren waste. I could have been a writer, you know."

"You may yet."

"Really, Dawson is a find for you. Definitely computers, and also he can really draw. He uses computer programs. In high school he had this whole business going. He's my little whiz kid." She drew deeply on her cigarette, luxuriantly sighed forth fumes. "You know why I don't get depressed?"

Bluey smiled. "Because you keep moving."

"Bluey, you sharp cookie! Like a shark, that's right. Like a shark in cement. If I stop, the cement will set. One minute, I condemn myself, next minute, the most important minute, I forgive myself. You know why?"

Bluey smiled. "Because pretty soon you're gonna find a Starbucks and have a good cup of coffee, and you want to be able to enjoy it."

"Ha! You pass my tests, sharp cookie. I'm like a queen that just lost a battle. Twenty thousand dead! Execute those generals. What's this? Ah, delicious curry! They all want to kill her, but she keeps moving. And here I come again, you big massive brother, who has always let me off with a warning. You are a forgiving soul. You don't condemn and then forgive, like religion, which is psychologically impossible. Ha! I'm laughing because that's from you, and now it seems like my thought. You were my father more than Father, you know. Our parents were glancers. As opposed to long intent lookers. I have a whole interesting theory which I will relate later. Something for the road. Why certain generations of parents are glancers. Please remind me, or it will be lost to humanity."

"I will. I look forward to that."

She took a last drag on her e-cig, capped it, slid it into her shirt pocket. "I better get going. Bluey, thank you. There's a shrine in my heart for you too, you know. Right besides Rosa's. I always had this big strong brother to catch me. Well, thanks to all. I need a good long cry."

"How about a cup of tea?"

"No, I have to go. I have to fight traffic."

"Why not stay over, leave in the morning?"

"You have one goddamn bed. Anyway, I have to get up to Seattle and deal with Dawson. He's there in his dorm room, probably hacking away, nothing to lose. I have to get him to a park or something and speak with him. What can I tell him?"

"Tell him his uncle needs his help."

"Great. I'll tell him that and hold him in my arms, which he will permit for a microsecond. I am not a glancer when it comes to Dawson. I'm a long intent looker. I hope he comes. Don't call him yet. Wait til I talk to him. I'll call you."

"Remember my neighbor, George?"

"Sure, good old George, the somber surgeon."

"He says he's coming for a visit when we get going. He's getting a tent to camp."

"Okay." She delivered a look, waiting for the rest.

"Well, he and Sarah are no more. She left last year."

"Aha."

"He was coming to camp before he knew you were involved."

"And when he heard I was involved?"

"He's still a bit taken with you."

"Good god."

"He says he'll get a one man tent so there will be no mistaking his intentions."

"So his intention is to ignore the person he's taken with? Remember I said I was blank for men? Perhaps you'll give him some kind guidance."

He and Goose walked her to the curb. She found Goose's ears, gave them a brisk scrub, seized his muzzle, wagged it. Bluey recognized the maneuver, which he used himself. From his father? Or his mother. Glancers, yes, but kind, the main thing. Their childhood was like a friendly motel. Had a good rest? Off you go, safe travels.

They hugged. Annie got into her black Mercedes, waved goodbye, and was off. As he waved, another car, a small dingy Honda, pulled to the curb, and a young man got out. He was huge and thick-necked with close cropped hair. His nose and jaw were large, his forehead slightly puffed, like a boxer's after a fight.

They met on the sidewalk, shook hands.

"You must be Cousin Roger," said Bluey.

"Nice to meet you, Dr. Macintosh."

As Bluey released the hand, he felt foreboding. The hand was flaccid. The smile was affable, not stupid. But something limp somewhere. Or pride working its way out through scorn of custom.

"Likewise, Roger." He would wait before asking to be called Bluey, if he ever did. "Let's have a seat on the porch, what say?" They walked up the sidewalk to the concrete porch and sat facing the street, Roger on the backs of his hands. Goose trotted up, took scent, then plopped under the nandinas where he had a nest in the bark mulch.

Bluey looked into the street, looked at Roger, back at the street. Some fold in his mood would not smooth. But he bade kindness come, and it did. He smiled at Roger, whose forehead had creased as he waited.

Bluey said, "Well, we talked, and I read your resume. You studied horticulture?"

"Yes, I did."

"And then you started driving a truck."

"Yes, I did."

Bluey let a silence instruct that more was wanted.

Roger said, "I wanted more money. To start a business. Not much money working in a greenhouse."

"A horticulture business?"

"Right. That's my ideal."

This innocent phrasing was touching but faintly troubling. Bluey pushed forward. "I want you to have a clear understanding of what we're about here. I know you've made road trips and lived in your truck, but here there's no going home. I need six months' commitment. Hopefully, it'll be only four months. It could be three."

"Listen, Dr. Macintosh, I'm all in on this. I've thought a lot about it. I'm your guy."

"Also, when you're not driving, you'll be on duty. You might get an afternoon off now and then, but there's not many of us, so that'll be irregular."

"I know. Lots to do. I talked to El. Cleaning cages, putting up the stockade. I drove a fork lift in high school. And I know it can be dangerous. Not fork lifts, I mean the animals."

"I'll never ask you to do anything with the animals I haven't trained you to do, so then it's not dangerous. But it's mindful work."

"Right."

"When you're on that fork lift, the animals will be the ones in danger."

"Sure."

"That's why we're always mindful, not just for our sakes, but for theirs too."

"Right."

"I see I have led you to the land of safe answers." Roger opened his mouth, chuffed benignly, colored. Bluey said, "You played football for Oregon?"

"Yes, I did. I played offensive guard." He frowned, apparently efforting to make his answer more ample. He said, "Did you play football?"

"I played rugby."

"Oh, sure, right. You're from Australia. El said that. I can hear the accent. And they call you Bluey because that's what they call red-haired guys in Australia. They should call you Frosty now."

Roger's face showed alarm at his boldness, but Bluey said helpfully, "You may call me Frosty."

"Ha!"

"Call me Bluey." He was going to hire this guy. Who had said he was all in, which had sold him. "Six months, all right?"

"More if you need me."

Bluey offered his hand. "Big handshake!" he said vigorously. But the hand he clasped was only slightly more firm. He followed an impulse. "Is your father alive?"

"Oh, yeah. Both of them. I mean my mother too. My dad's remarried."

"Well, didn't your father, or coach, or anybody ever teach you how to shake hands? Particularly with somebody that wants to hire you for a job?"

"Well—"

"Because, son, you don't shake hands for shit."

Roger chuffed. "That's right. I'm a bad handshaker, I guess."

His chagrin was open, without grudge, and Bluey felt him more fully, a large man, but hunched within, seeking the periphery. He clapped his shoulder. "So first lesson from your friend, Bluey. Because we'll be meeting the public. Handshakes must be firm. C'mon."

They shook, and Roger squeezed.

Bluey said, "Now that's a terrific handshake. Still want the job even if I bug you about handshaking?"

"Absolutely." Then with sudden gratitude—"I know I'm a crappy handshaker. I got a block or something. But see, you just jump right in anytime I need to learn something. I'm dead certain about this job. You won't be sorry, Dr. Macintosh. Shake on it."

They shook again, firmly. They smiled at each other.

Bluey outlined the plan. Their first setup was a county fair in Oregon. Roger would drive the tandem with the herbivore and omnivore cages in the long rear section, and in the short front section the stockade, the feed bins, the refrigerators and freezers. Bluey would drive the flatbed with the carnivore cages and the fork lift. El and Annie would drive the RV. Also, there would possibly be a van for his nephew. They would eat together in the big RV, breakfast, lunch, and dinner, each with rotating kitchen duties. He and Roger would sleep in their truck cubbies, El and Annie in the big RV, his nephew, if he came, in the van. They would gather in two weeks, Thursday morning, at the college. Read this folder thoroughly. Questions?

Roger shook his head. "Probably, but I can't think of them. But as we go, I'll think of them. You'll probably get sick of me asking."

Bluey walked him to his car, followed by Goose. They shook hands again, firmly.

Roger said, "See, I already learned something."

Bluey watched him drive away. He had flowed to this young man, and the young man had felt it. He felt grave and happy. He headed for the house, tagged by Goose. Lots to do. Very good though. Roger would do.

•

El had packed her apartment. There were five boxes. In her suitcase she kept only three jeans, plus the ones she wore, five tops, two sweatshirts, six T-shirts, socks, underwear, and two pairs of shoes, tennis for running and clogs for everything else. She took the boxes to the post office and sent them home, called Sacramento from the parking lot.

"They're on the way. Only five. Just put them in my room, okay?"

"Well, your dad's threatening to clear your room, you know. He wants to cover the floor in plastic and have a pottery studio."

"I'm on the phone," said her dad. "Hi, El, little darling."

"Hi, Dad. Really, a pottery studio in my bedroom? Go for it. When I come home, I can sleep on the couch."

Her father said, "I was thinking the shed. I'll just push some tools around, make you a pallet."

"She can sleep in the guest room," said her mother, who they counted on to ground them. "Well, you were my last hope, El. Now I'll have clay all over the house."

"But pots too," said El.

"I already have pots."

"But money!" said her father. At a local community center, he had learned to make vases and bowls. He consigned them at a craft gallery, and they sold quickly for hundreds of dollars. They were all black and white, with careful Paleolithic etching. When the first one sold, he listed his dentistry lab with a broker. At the family meeting, El had sided with him, and they wore her mother down. But the lab sold quickly. Now she was happy to have a happier husband, but was not above pulling a face to remind them of their debt. She was an attorney, still earning well, and was herself in a life transition—from family law to criminal. She had had two jury trials, drug possession cases, and won them both. Calypso cases, she told her colleagues, because DA overreach was DAO, day-o. Now the assistant DAs heard the phrase around the courthouse cafes. She was free and fearless in a courtroom and could pay close attention.

"On a happier note," her mother said. "I listed my name with the public defender. I might get second chair in a murder one day."

"Oh lord," said El. "Let's hope you get somebody who didn't do it. If I had to defend a murdering rapist, I would work hard to appear to be working hard, and then secretly make sure the guy got convicted."

"Well, dear," said her mother. "They don't tell you they did it. If it goes to trial, it's because they say they didn't. So that means there's a mystery, and twelve people get to think it over."

"Well, that's horrible, when you think about it. If it's a mystery, then they're just guessing."

"It is horrible, in a way."

"And thrilling," said her father.

"I'm a thrill-seeker, it's true," her mother said.

"Well, about time," said El. "You both are. I'm proud of you both, for what it's worth."

"It's worth a lot," they said together. Then her mother said, "El, we talked it over and decided we want to tell you something."

"What?"

"El, I did a—well, I took it on myself to search the criminal records, and I found out that Roger has a felony marijuana charge in Oregon. He's on probation. I called Aunt Jane, and she admitted it. He was busted with some friends of his. They were actually growing the plants. One of them went to prison for selling to high school kids, and three got probation. I was quite pissed at Jane, the little weasel, but there it is. She asked me to beg you not to tell Bluey, but you use your own judgment. She says he's clean and has turned the leaf. I'm so sorry, El. I really should have done this before I told you he needed a job. I just searched on a whim."

"When was this?"

"Two years ago. That's why he's been driving trucks. He lost his job."

"Well, boo," said El. "Now it's on me. Bluey hired him. He said they had a nice talk. Well boo boo boo."

"Like your mother said, El, you use your judgment."

"Well, should I tell Bluey, is the thing. If you talk to him, don't tell him, just in case I don't tell him."

"It might be just fine. Jane says he's not drugging," said her mother.

"I'll talk to Roger and go from there. What did Aunt Jane say, by the way? Is he depressed?"

Her mother said, "I think he'd be a little sad, don't you? But I don't know. Has Packer left for Dubai?"

"Oh, Mother, Packer and I are kaput."

"Well, I'm just saying, doors that don't close all the way are still open, however little."

"Mother, that door closed."

"Oh, poor baby."

They said their goodbyes, said their loves, and she ended the call.

•

She met Elaine and Bretta at a Cup of Joes. They were both graduates, and each had landed a good job, Elaine in North Carolina and Bretta in San Diego. They sat at the window bar, facing the street, El in the center where they could get at her from both sides. After a compulsory session of Packer dissing, they moved to her new job. She saw it was a conspiracy. They had been strategizing. She was touched.

She smiled from side to side. "Those are great points. A lesser person than myself would succumb." The points had been—a career dead end, participation in the stressing of animals for selfish ends, Bluey was using her. Did Bluey have a nasty eye on her?

"Maybe you think we're jealous because he didn't ask us," said Bretta. She was tall, chunky girl, a lover of primates, and a lesbian. In her heart, the skillful, intelligent, natural El was on a pedestal, a prize never to be possessed, but always to be protected. But like all the students, she prized Bluey too. Now both united and gone together! A pain to be resisted before acceptance.

"Of course, we're jealous," said Elaine, who was off to the reptiles of the North Carolina Zoo. She was a short, compact mother of two, who before being accepted at the Exotic Animal College, had been a pharmacist. They could all imagine her thriving with a safari hat and radio mike, broadcasting pep to the public. "Not that I could have said yes even if he had asked me. But really, doesn't it seem a bit selfish? He knew you'd say yes. And really, El, you're going to be a deck hand. There's no research. And you say education? People see the animals in these little cooped up cages like fifty years ago."

"It's only for four months. Then it's the ecopark. And there *is* education. He's got lots of signs and brochures. And we're going to do a show. They'll be a super duper website. Then at the ecopark, it will grow, is the plan. We are designing the zoo of the future, girls. And get money money money and save the animals. You guys will be working for me one day, count on it." El put her arms around their shoulders, pulled them in. They laid their heads on her shoulders. "You guys are sweet."

They straightened, took up their coffees. Elaine lifted her mug. "Well, fuck it. Here's to your every success."

El lifted her mug, and she and Elaine watched as Bretta, with inching, frowning slowness, moved her cup across to make a triplet of clinks.

"Fuck it," said Bretta.

"Fuck it," said El.

A surge of fellowship. They sipped their coffees.

"What's he paying you?" said Bretta.

"Fifty thousand a year, plus free room and board."

Elaine said, "Holy shit."

"Damn!" said Bretta. "You know what I'm making?"

"Yes, I do," said El. "You're making crappy zoo money."

Elaine said, "We need a union."

Bretta said, "Then there wouldn't be any zoos, and all the animals would die. By the way, are you taking Thane?" Thane was a mandrill baboon, one of Bretta's second year animals.

"I don't know."

"He hasn't been placed, I know that," said Bretta. "Ask Bluey, will you, and text me."

"I will. And guess what? We found a fantastic tiger. And he purrs."

6

From the east, he could see a pulse of light. The darkness of the zoo grounds became a murky cityscape of wire and pipe. Bluey sat on the bench under the wisteria trellis, waiting to be revealed. A sprinkle of birdsong had started. When the chittering, hooting, and chuffing began, he would go to the chop shop to fill the treat bucket and make the morning rounds.

He came once or twice a week like this, waiting silently to be uncovered by dawn, inspired by a story Rosa had told him, how Mani, Meher Baba's sister, could not emerge from grief after he had dropped his body, as they put it. Then Eruch, one of Baba's men, brought her one dark morning to the pasture to listen to the sheep bleat, *ba ba.* They watched the dawn uncover the shepherd and heard the sheep quiet as they became aware of him. Eruch said, *Just see, how their shepherd was always present,* and Mani's grief, it was said, began to lift. The story was true, said Rosa, told to her by Ellen Auster, her Baba contact, an important person in someone's Baba life, the one who told you about him.

Perhaps the story itself was too perfect, shaped in retelling for the clutch of sentiment, but the idea had struck him, and for six years he had come once or twice a week to wait for dawn on the central bench near the ungulates.

Now came a whoop from Nubia, the spotted hyena, followed instantly by a shrill from Spectra the peacock. The morning discussion had begun, the last discussion at the Exotic Animal College. Bluey would depart today with twenty-four of the animals. Most of the others had been placed and shipped, leaving three for Dr. Peters, who would arrive that afternoon.

Bluey rose now, made a silent circuit of the pens and cages, declaring himself. He continued to the chop shop, with its banks of refrigerators and bins, its tables of cutting boards and scales, and spent fifteen minutes slicing, mostly apple and pear today, until he had a gallon plastic bag filled and arranged in the bucket. On top, he added a smaller bag with ten grapes and two carrots, another small bag with two frozen cricket bars, and a gallon bag of chicken wings and legs, thawed yesterday and waiting in the meat fridge. He filled the pockets of his treat jacket with seeds, nuts, raisins, and a few paper cones, then turned off the lights and toted the bucket down the chop shop steps and onto the gravel paths.

A week earlier, Bluey's bright new cages had arrived. The doors had been opened and fixed against the old cages, then passageways cut so the animals could pass freely back and forth, old house, new house, new house, old house. He had made several morning rounds already, proffering treats always in the new house, and strangeness had departed. Even Demijohn the lion would now enter his new space to receive his morning chicken legs.

He began with Monkeytown, as always, at the south end where the grounds narrowed between the parking lot and the Building B. That way he could make a neat circuit without doubling back, monkeys, ungulates, birds, carnivores. As he passed through the carnivores, Bump the sun bear, lying on his back in his new steel cage, waved a paw in the air, a mild salute.

Monkeytown had been reduced to five denizens, four for Bluey, one for Dr. Peters. The rest, two chimpanzees and nine old and new world monkeys, had been placed. He began reciting immediately, a new poem, still fresh, still settling. His voice boomed above the gravel growl of his boots.

"As I sit this morning to think of God,

A spider crawls into my hat,
And somewhere a dog is barking.
No matter—soon love begins to circle, looking for need."

Thane, the mandrill, who had watched him approach, now stepped down from his log perch and crossed into his new cage, moving methodically and with full concentration, as if not to miss a word. Bluey pushed a triangle of pear through the stainless zoo mesh, watched Thane take it with nimble fingers, pop it in with the apple slice, make a puff-cheeked grimace, showing a perfect pair of canines. Bluey pivoted, military style, his signal, done with you, little daddy, and Thane haunch-sat on his rainbow butt. He lipped the pear into a black fist and began to chew the apple.

Bluey moved to Quanna the bonobo, keeping his voice loud, but conversational, friend to friend, rapt, as if to the rapt.

"Sighs pour out like sweetness from a sewer.
I know if I approach, love's cold and quick away.
I've relearned that a thousand times.
So I set my hunger free and watch it roam."

He pushed a pear, then an apple slice through the wire, feeling Quanna's light caress as she received her treat, a quick stroke along his index finger. He held his hand at the wire in case she wanted more contact. But the fruit had her now, and she turned even before his pivot to settle in a corner of her new home, a black crumple-faced beast, first a thoughtful suck, then a thoughtful nibble.

A pivot to Shindig the spider monkey, who made a fast raking climb along the zoo link as he approached, then descended headfirst.

"I've heard that somewhere in this mist there is a doorway.
That makes such perfect sense that doubt is out of place here."

Shindig snatched the fruit slices, apple for the teeth, pear for the hand, and bounded to his new upper platform to settle and chew, his chocolate eyes holding Bluey and blinking blankly as Bluey made his pivot.

"Still hunger hasn't found it yet.
I don't mind."

He had come now to old Juniper, the big brown hamadryas baboon, *Papio hamadryas.* He had felt his voice grow slightly louder, recognized the reflex of sorrow. Juniper had an three month old abscess on his pink leather bottom and was not coming with them. The abscess, Peters said, would only grow deeper. Juniper no longer rump-sat, but instead slung his good leg awkwardly under him as padding. He came to the wire, rowing like a cripple on a skate, and took the fruit pieces directly into his mouth. Bluey considered a bonus, another pear, another apple, but that would have been for him, not Juniper. As he made his pivot, he felt some inner substance sheer, and stood without moving.

"I'm like a man who's lost his wallet,
Then recalls he left it home,
Then lets it be.
That it's somewhere by has eased the long neck of worry.
In time I will be home again."

That last for Juniper, a goodbye.

He crossed to Taj, the De Brazza guenon.

"For now I'll keep our bargain of silence,
Though if that doorway doesn't appear in a thousand years,
I might speak up."

Taj, a white-bearded, agate-eyed old world monkey, pushed both fruit pieces into cheek pouches, then cocked his bulging face and extended a wrist through the wire. His delicate black hand hung disconsolately as Bluey pivoted and left Monkeytown for the omnivores.

"I suppose I'm bluffing.
When complaint meets the soul, it forgets even its shame,
And in this radiant universe,
I'm happy to be anywhere, or anyone."

He pushed fruit through the wire to Chortle, the American raccoon, who made a fast examination, deciding on the pear, letting the apple tumble on the floor, where it freckled with wood chips. He nibbled absentmindedly. From time to time he received an oyster treat. All other food was not oysters, and so devoured temperately and with mild reluctance.

Bluey made his pivot. Ballyhoo the binturong watched him languidly, draped on her worn log perch, which had been repositioned in her new home. He held the cricket bars at the wire, finished the recitation.

"The morning goes as usual.
Hunger returns unsatisfied.
Love kindly withdraws.
He knows I have business with that spider,
And that mutt is starting to drive me crazy."

Ballyhoo rose, undoing her comfort with apparent reluctance, and, gripping with hands and long, leather-bottomed tail, half swung, half clambered to the wire wall. As she plucked the cricket bars from his hand, he caught her faint buttered popcorn scent. She swung away, repositioned herself on the log, and considered her bounty. She nibbled.

As he entered Birdland, he began another poem—"Sometimes I think I should go on out to Africa," then stopped, listening. He had heard a car in the parking lot, then car doors, then voices, Carlos and JJ, Carlos making some point, disdainful and querulous. Except for a few friends, Bluey kept his poems private, so he stopped. Henry's Agincourt speech came to mind and would fuel his mood, a band of brothers setting forth, and would get him through the birds and maybe the carnivores. But Carlos was through the gate and heading his way, stepping fast, ten feet in front of JJ, his face knotted with indignation.

"Siento, Dr. Bluey. Am I breaking up the poetry? Yo, this dude's telling me keepers are killers." Then to JJ—"Dr. Bluey's a killer too, right? Tell him he's a killer. It don't matter now. Show your colors."

JJ smiled. "We were having a discussion which Carlos didn't like."

Bluey spoke with friendly command. "I trust you gentlemen will work out your disputes. For now—" He lifted his hand to forestall Carlos, who had opened his mouth and shifted his weight with a peppery bounce. "—let's remove all dung from the new cages and freshen the cedar chips. Don't worry about the old enclosures for now. You can clean those after we load. When I finish the morning treats, we'll close the doors and start loading. The fork lift driver is on the way."

Carlos said, "I can drive that fork lift, Dr. Bluey."

"I know you can, Carlos. But I need to see my new man in action. If he impales some poor beast, you'll have to come running." He had inadvertently strayed into the arena of their dispute, harm to animals, saw Carlos exerting for words and forestalled him—"So off you go, my main men. Squeaky clean, fresh chips, then back to me."

Carlos said, "You got it, Dr. Bluey. What do we got today, little Shakespeare?"

"What else?" said Bluey. Carlos and JJ walked north toward the tractor shed, JJ falling in behind again, and Bluey entered Birdland, announced by a carved wooden sign of a trumpet spilling notes, work of a long ago student. Birdland was empty now except for Sybil, the African gray, Spectra the peacock, and Bart the ostrich.

"He which hath no stomach to this fight,
Let him depart. His passport shall be made,
And crowns for convoy put into his purse.
We would not die in that man's company
That fears his fellowship to die with us."

He was charmed by aptness, and his volume grew as he recited. Bart stepped into his new enclosure with his careful paddling gait and stood at attention. Bluey scooped two paper cones of pumpkin seeds and raisins from his safari jacket and poured them into the waist high treat pan.

He heard a diesel belch as the compact tractor started, then its throbbing rumble, faintly tinny in the metal shed. They would be hitching the divided tumbril, one side for cedar chips, one for dung. For Bluey, this was the last day of such expansive ease. In the caravan, the implements and storage compartments for cleaning and feeding, the chief tasks of any zoo, were scaled for travel and tucked neatly into a mere two trucks. It was the central challenge and had been eventually solved with months of design and the patience of Lew Charring, the supervisor at the fabrication shop. Did the bear enclosure need a deeper chip pan? No problem. You redesigned the hold-downs again? Okay. We're gonna stack the lynx on the puma instead of the dhole? No problem. Several times he and El had brought lunch for the crew, who promised to follow his travels when the website was launched. Lew broke a champagne bottle on the bumper of the tandem the day Bluey drove it away.

"This day is called the feast of Crispian.
He that outlives this day, and comes safe home,
Will stand a tiptoe when this day is named—"

Sybil hopped and beaked her way into her new space. She gripped her oak branch and stoically received her portion of Henry's speech and a cone of raisins and nuts. She was a large sleek silvery bird, an African gray parrot, famous talker of the animal world. Sybil, however, had spoken only once, when Bluey introduced Eve Carson, a second year. "Eve Carson, this is Sybil. Sybil meet Eve Carson." And Sybil had immediately pronounced *Carson,* exciting all. She had never spoken again, but had at least proved her anatomy. After Eve, though Sybil was no longer assigned by the staff, she was always chosen by some valiant, and eventually defeated, student.

He passed the empty enclosures of the toucans and macaws and reached, *Old men forget, yet all shall be forgot,* as he stopped before the peacock pen. As Spectra paced into his new enclosure, Bluey spread his arms wide. The peacock turned to face him, fanned his exultant tail, and Bluey could not resist skipping forward in the speech. "We few, we happy few, we band of brothers."

As Bluey recited, Rudy Wheeler, college president, approached silently along the gravel and stood five feet behind him, boyishly gratified by his exploit of stalking. He had come for work, wearing a red baseball cap, sweatshirt, jeans, and tennis shoes. He said, "How much Shakespeare do you actually know?"

Bluey, without turning, folded his arms across his chest. Spectra, gradually, then swiftly, collapsed his tail, which fell behind him on the cedar chips like an extravagant broom. He approached his treat pan and began to peck.

Bluey turned now, said, "All of it. Give me a test. Act and line."

"MacBeth. Act five, line twenty-seven."

"Canst thou not minister to a mind diseased? Raze out the written troubles and so on."

Wheeler frowned. "Bullshit."

"Correct. That is from MacBeth though. Might even be fifth act. Many thanks for coming, Rudy."

They shook. Bluey noted Wheeler's effort to smile away chagrin. Produced by what—his stealthy approach going unremarked? Or humiliation from halfway believing the Shakespeare boast? He was a delicately balanced man, in any case, and must be fed personality in small doses. But the combination of Spectra's fan and Henry's finale had made Bluey ardent and inattentive, and playful braggadocio had escaped. Without releasing his grip, he swung to Wheeler's side, dropped his arm across Wheeler's slight shoulders, a sideways hug, a brisk amend. He looked out and forward, toward the fresh sun. See Rudy, where the suns rises?

Wheeler had arrived five years earlier from the St. Louis zoo with a degree in zoology and a Stanford MBA, charged and ready to matter. But the ground beneath him had given way. He had not yet found a job.

Bluey felt him shift, done with hugging. He stepped away, bent to pick up his bucket. "Follow me, young sir. I will show you how we feed the beasts."

Wheeler cocked him a smile and fell in at Bluey's side. The animals were made faintly restless by his unaccustomed silence. But he could not recite. Wheeler would want to talk.

On the way to the carnivores, Bluey fed pellets to the Somali wild ass, the blue sheep, the two wild llamas. He showed Cloe, the okapi, the pellet in his right hand, palmed it, put his fists together, transferring the pellet into his left, offered both fists. Cloe knew the game, chose left, nuzzling Bluey's closed fingers until they slowly opened. She plucked up the pellet with rubbery lips, gave her head a shake, flipped the pellet to her molars with her prehensile tongue. Bluey seized her head, thumb stroked her closed eyes, then pushed her orange white forehead lightly away with his palm, made his pivot. He felt Wheeler watching him, noted peripherally his pleasure and admiration. Wheeler had not found a job, he said. He had not been looking that hard. He had made a few calls. He had sent a few letters. He was tooling around the forums. He said, "I may knock at your door one day. If you get this thing off the ground."

Bluey clapped him on the shoulder. "If I have a spot, I'd hire you in a heartbeat."

Wheeler said, "Really?"

Bluey turned to face him. "Would I really hire a dumb ass like you? I would." He had used profanity as medicine, something to jolt. "You're a fine administrator, Rudy. We just got caught in a drought." They started toward the carnivores.

Wheeler smiled. He said, "That sort of hurts."

"Why?"

"That I need to be reminded I'm a good administrator. I am, I think. In St. Louis, I was. I start thinking, maybe I was too slick with the corporate guys. Why give him money? He's doing fine."

"Probably that's overthink. It's just rascal people. We pass hungry kids on the way to feed monkeys, and then get bored, and the monkeys starve. To enter the public arena, we must gird our loins."

"Christ, I'm going to miss you, Bluey. I need someone to remind me of that every day."

"So do I. I'm about to get out amongst them."

"Yes, you are."

They heard the tractor's diesel thrum increase and change tone as it left the metal shed, pulling the tumbril. Carlos drove. JJ followed with a square shovel held behind his head.

Wheeler touched Bluey's arm, stopping him. "That's my cue. Wait a second." They watched the tractor, which turned away from them toward Monkeytown. "I have a confession to make. See if you think I'm a fine administer. I told you why I hired JJ. His mother is Sherry's old friend, childhood friend? So full disclosure. Marge comes for dinner, a long sad dinner with tears and wine. She's divorced and has lots of money but a sad life. Her brother killed himself, her oldest boy ODed on heroin, and JJ is an army vet and had some harrowing experiences. He just moved home after his house burned down. He was in Ramadi and Fallujah, the worst places. And she says, give him a job. He asked her to ask me. So I said, all right, two months. The plug had been pulled, and we were down a couple of keepers already, so I said, okay, do a favor. I got lobbied on the home front. Besides I have a soft spot for vets. So yesterday Marge calls Sherry to report that JJ has been making videos. She found them on his computer. He's a videographer, which Marge helpfully forgot to mention. He's got a camera in his baseball cap, for god's sake. He says he's not affiliated with PETA or any of the other weirder ones, and it's not animal rights. He loves animals and wanted to try working with them. She promised JJ she wouldn't tell, but she did, her old buddy, Sherry. So JJ doesn't know we know. So I may have committed a serious blunder. My abject apologies, Bluey."

"He was riling up Carlos this morning."

"He was? How?"

"Probably the euthanasia."

"Oh, Christ."

"No harm. There's no drama here. We are a grand and noble enterprise. After they finish cleaning, I'll send them both home. Let us not confront this fellow, whoever he may be."

"Marge says he has a bunch of medals. I asked him about Fallujah, and he just stared at me. Anyway, my bad. Tears and wine."

"You were doing a kindness."

"Well, sort of. I also wanted to hear about Fallujah. Anyway, I'm here to help. What's the plan?"

"I'm going to entice the beasts into cages with delicious food, and we are going to drop the doors and load. El has gone to get her cousin at the bus station, who is my fork lift man. And this is my sister arriving with my nephew."

They looked across to the lot. A taxi had pulled in.

"It's a family affair," said Wheeler.

"It is."

They started again, now headed toward the rear gate.

"Bluey, it's been a pleasure to know you." He touched Bluey's arm and stopped, and Bluey, after a step further, stopped too and turned. From the lot he heard voices and a car door open and shut. But when he gazed at Wheeler, he felt the man's uncomfort. He gave himself to patience.

Wheeler said, "You are a generous man, and you are a kind man. I have not really been your friend, I know that. Hell, I haven't been anybody's friend. I told Sherry that this morning, and we both burst into tears right there in the hallway. I hardly know what I'm talking about. But you do, don't you? You know exactly what I'm talking about, don't you?"

Bluey laid a palm against Wheeler's chest, then swung in at his side, clasping his shoulders. He said quietly, "Now then, we start from here. My sister is arriving and is a clamorous woman, and my nephew is distressed, and we have lots of work. But we will also be here, having spoken dearly to each other."

Wheeler said, “Christ almighty.” Bluey made a slight pressure on his shoulder, and they started down the gravel to the rear gate.

The taxi had pulled beside the RV and Annie was out, hailing Bluey from across the lot. Dawson sat in the rear seat, head lowered, busy with something in his lap. Annie bent and rapped the window. Dawson, in slow motion, raised his head without looking at his mother, then slowly clambered out.

Annie paid the taxi, and they crossed the lot, leaving a cluster of luggage on the asphalt. Dawson trailed twenty feet behind. He was tall and thin with two fangs of black hair bracketing his face, the rest swept into short pony tail. His nose was large and straight, the cheekbones sharp, the brow high, Annie's features, but only partly her beauty. His gaze flashed around the parking lot, the trucks and two RVs, through the fencing into the zoo, the new cages cut into the enclosures, the dark shapes of monkeys. His gaze seemed to say, *I get this, I see this, so what?*

Bluey and Wheeler met them on the gravel path beside the mandrill, who crossed his cage toward them, changed his mind, and returned to perch on a log. Annie wore jeans and a crisp white shirt, a hint of tan and lipstick, looking good. “Well, let's get this show on the road. I'm assuming that big one is my new digs.” She turned directly into Wheeler's front, offered her hand. “Annie Macintosh.”

Wheeler shook with her. “Rudy Wheeler.”

She glanced at Bluey, “Back to my maiden name. They'll think we're married.”

Bluey nodded. His sister, he saw, could not resist shaking out a few plumes, a sweet thing, and fun. He said, “Annie's the cook and all purpose roustabout. And here is my long lost nephew, Dawson.”

“Hey, Uncle Bluey.” Dawson offered a hesitant hand, but Bluey quickly enfolded him, then held his slight shoulders at arm's length. “Good you have come. When I heard you had accepted, my mind began to work.” He released him, gestured to Wheeler. “Dr. Wheeler, this is my nephew, Dawson, rumored to understand computers.”

Wheeler and Dawson shook.

“Good to meet you,” said Wheeler.

Dawson's eyes flicked up to Wheeler's face, then down. He said, “Hey.”

Annie said, "Dawson's not cheery today. We must improve him."

Dawson said slowly, "How can anyone be cheery with so many starving?"

This remark fell hatefully among them, breaking the spell of tact among strangers. A moment's silence before Dawson, with reluctant irony, pronounced, "Just kidding."

Annie said, "Oh, for god's sake."

Bluey laughed. "You had a good night's sleep?"

Annie said, "Oh, yes. You paid for two rooms, for god's sake. We could have bunked together."

"A last luxury before your new duties. Which start now. Dawson, see that red van? That's your new home. Annie, how about you and Dawson get unpacked and settled. Rudy and I have to capture the beasts."

"Nice to meet you," said Wheeler.

"Likewise," said Annie. She was discomposed and did not bother to flash a parting plume. "C'mon, buddy," she said to Dawson, who trailed her across the lot.

Bluey watched them for a moment. Dawson would not submit to handling, so patience there. The beasts might draw him, if he could notice them. There was courage in anger though. So that at least. He turned to Wheeler, found himself intently regarded.

He said, "Young man, let us begin."

•

El had sold her car and used Bluey's pickup to collect Roger at the bus station at dawn. It had been five Christmases since she had seen him. He had been a star at Oregon then, scouted by the NFL. Now he was a tricky felon. He rose from a bench as she pulled to the curb, shouldered his army duffel. He tossed it into the truck bed, and they embraced, her head below his shoulder, like hugging a building. His smile was affable and ironic, and seemed to say, I like things, including you. She smiled and liked him back.

As they drove, the talk was first about whether he had been able to sleep on the bus—he had, could sleep anywhere—then about his mother and his remarried, conservative father, who was running for state representative, then her parents and their life changes, then Bluey.

"He's a wizard with animals. He's like that psychologist, I forget his name, who could talk to crazy people."

"Erickson."

"That's right, Erickson." she said. She delivered an appraising glance.

"And you thought I was a dumb football player."

"I hate to tell you, but you're still a dumb football player."

"Ha!"

"I have some sad news for you, Roger. You got a felony drug conviction that I happen to know about." She surprised herself with this easy entrance.

"Damn," said Roger.

"You didn't tell Bluey, is the problem. He's my chum, so either you kill me before we get to the college, or convince me I don't need to tell him."

A moment passed. He said, "Pull over and let me kill you." Then he said, "You can tell him if you want to."

"I'm not asking you to beg. Tell me what happened."

"I didn't make the pros, is what happened. And then there were these guys I played with in high school. Who didn't even make college ball, so we had something in common again, back in my little hometown. You want to hear this sad tale?"

"So you were selling drugs to kids."

"Oh, for Christ's sake, no. I had a garden with a few plants, and Leon Delaney was selling at the school, which got us all busted, which we didn't even know. Not that I got a big issue about it. They were high school kids, not little kids. They got to have their weed, right? Not that I was on Leon's side, but mostly because he's a chief asshole, and lied to us. So that's the story. I was not selling dope, but I was busted on felony cultivation. Because of Leon."

"Do you still smoke dope?"

"No, because if I did I would go to deep ass prison for five years." He smiled. "So you're gonna have to hold our stash."

El smirked, feeling, a dumb ass football player with wit, and a straight shooter. "Okay, here's my deal. We'll go along for a while and then tell him. Let him get to like you and depend on you. Then we'll spring the big surprise, ha ha, you hired a criminal." She looked at him, and he looked back, both wondering whether that was too much. He made her a mock frown. She punched him on the shoulder, big solid shoulder.

•

It took Bluey and Wheeler only an hour and a half to recage all twenty-four animals. After luring them with treats into their new enclosures, from opposite sides they slid four red bamboo poles through the stainless mesh creating a temporary barrier. Bluey cut away the old wire with snips, freeing the door, then slid the door shut and heard the lock engage. He kept up a continuous drone of Shakespeare, not play excerpts, but sonnets, so that Wheeler could enjoy them without context. When El and Roger drove into the rear lot, the cages were ready to load.

Wheeler said, "Well, that was just efficient as hell. You should write up a presentation for the AZA by the way, about using Shakespeare. I see the rest of your crew has arrived."

"They have, and I've got to tend to them. They don't know each other."

"I'll say goodbye then."

Bluey slid the snips into his back pocket, squared to Wheeler, drew him into a firm embrace. "Rudy, I will stay in contact with you. If things fall out as hoped, we may work together again. Thank you for coming today."

"My pleasure, Bluey. I'll follow your progress on the web."

"And email or call from time to time, let me know how you and Sherry are doing. You will be in my thoughts."

"I will." Wheeler turned and walked away, chin down, heavy-seeming, like a man pushing through fog. Bluey had the impulse to speak again. He let it pass. But he would stay in touch with this man. Wheeler's unexpected vulnerability had connected them.

He met El and Roger at the rear gate, shook hands with Roger, both men acknowledging its firmness with a smile. Bluey led them to the large RV, knocked against the silver blue frame. Annie appeared and descended the steps. She gazed at the young people, then at Bluey, awaiting his introduction.

"El Chastain, Roger Shaw, this is my sister Annie Macintosh. She is our cook, so be kind to her."

"Definitely," said Roger.

"Ha. Nice to meet you," said El.

"Have we lost Dawson?" said Bluey.

Annie said, "He's in the van unpacking. Probably planning his escape."

"He wants to escape?" said El.

Annie said, "Oh, sort of."

Dawson, in the driver's seat, got out as they approached. After exchanging names with El and Roger, his gaze darted, unready to settle, held downward, then drifted again to El's face. Annie watched. She said, "How do you like the van?"

"It's new," said Dawson.

Bluey said, "Now then, excellent crew of the Exotic Animal Caravan, kindly follow me. We will have a tour, and then we will load and go."

They trailed him across the parking lot, Dawson last. They passed through the gate, through Monkeytown, and stopped finally before Nubia, the spotted hyena, who was lying on a raked-together pad of wood chips. Nubia lifted his head to appraise them, then dropped it back onto the chips. They caught the sharp scent of urine.

"These shiny steel boxes you see poking out everywhere are the transport enclosures. They will be home to our companions until we reach the ecopark in Tennessee. Each of you has a particular and essential duty. *My* first duty is to make a little speech, and yours is to listen. Dawson, you and I will have a private discussion later about your pay."

Annie opened her mouth, and Bluey said, "He will be paid, Mother, like all of you, and he must work." Bluey noted Dawson's new alertness beneath his indifference. He went on. "My speech is about our obligation to these beasts. They will be in a new prison, and this new prison will bring them pain. The enclosures here at the college were not much larger than these, but there at least they had regularity. Now they are being disturbed. Some will be aggressive. Some will be depressed, or nervous, or behave oddly. Whatever your daily duty, your main and chief duty is to these beasts. You can ease their pain by being properly with them. El and I are trained, and we will train you. When we reach Tennessee, they will find better lives. Their enclosures there will be spacious, and if we do our work well, they will complete their lives there. In days to come I believe that will be the fate of all wild animals on our little planet. Our ecopark is intended to be a model for future ecoparks, and our traveling caravan is meant to spread the word of tolerance and generosity to beasts. And get us money to continue. Forgive my lapse into teacherly prose but it saves time. So that's the plan. My chief misgiving is that by necessity we have gathered in haste, and so we are untrained and untested. That will make it interesting but also challenging. There is no eloquence that will lift your hearts to this task. Interest in animals, and love for them, cannot be compelled, but if you have it, or can develop it, you will find a channel for that here."

"Everyone likes animals," said Dawson. "Or else they hate themselves."

They all looked at him.

"Well, that's seems true," said Annie, raising her eyebrows.

"Definitely," said El.

"Absolutely," said Roger.

And Bluey felt, a gift, the alone-most one unifying them. "Now let's meet the cast of this show. This is Nubia, a spotted hyena. He's noisy, which is great, so the public will be interested and give money. That's the second mention of money, and if I don't mention it again, know that it's a central thought, because money is food, shelter, and longevity for these beasts."

They moved along the pathway to Bump, the sun bear, who lay back against the zoo link fence like a hobo, arms to the side, palms up. Bluey said, "This is Bump, the sun bear of India. He's El's good buddy. Each second year student in the college had the primary care for two animals each year, and Bump was one of El's. El has the gift of flow." He stopped and faced them. He said, "Now I will describe the gift of flow. It's like poetry. There is a poetry of beasts. When you read a poem, you read it best most simply, without putting in hammed up feeling to help the poem along. If poetry is in the poem, it will emerge and spread itself like perfume. In the same way, when you commune with a beast, you don't project your feelings, but instead you forget yourself and attend. Dawson is right, if you like yourself then you will like animals, because you came from them. They are in you. I don't mean genetically, but in your psyche. You came from them. So here's the secret—be simple and mean no harm. They will see that. Beasts are simple, but they are also true. If you mean them well, they will like you, and their prisons will enlarge to include you, and that's a generosity to them, and it's what we want." He had been glancing through their four faces as he spoke, noting their reactions—Annie, admiring, swept away by her big brother in his element, but also shaded with chagrin, some unease in herself; Dawson, way off but listening, tasting through a long straw, but with a so-far-so-good frown on his face; Roger, brow creased, intent, smiling a faint protective smile; and El, glowing with appreciation. He had been teaching, but also campaigning for leadership and was satisfied he had won election.

El crossed to Bump, put her hand on the zoo link near his snout. His head rolled, and he sniffed her palm. She said, "Ho, Bumpy."

He took them one by one through the cages, introducing the animals, noting their histories and temperaments. That morning, he said, he had emailed them a five hundred word description of each animal which they must commit to memory. Dawson put his smart phone in his breast pocket and began taping. Give him an email address, he announced to the gravel pathway, and he would email the tape to everyone.

Next, Bluey showed them the trucks—the big new air-conditioned tandem, with its rear section for the herbivore and omnivore cages and front for feed and water, and a roomy luxurious sleeping compartment for Roger; the flatbed for the carnivore cages and fork lift and with a compartment for Bluey, not new and not luxurious; the big new RV for El and Annie and for meals; the smaller RV van for Dawson and for running errands.

The introductory talk was done. The women and Dawson went to their quarters. Bluey led Roger to the flatbed. On the truck's rear, a forklift was hung in a steel cradle. Bluey reached for the descend lever, then stopped and swung fully about to face Roger, who stood a pace away, still covered with his half-smile.

Bluey said, "I don't know you, and I have the least connection with you of any of these people. But I have a high regard for fate, and here you are, and you are most welcome."

Roger colored. His mouth opened. He said, "Well—"

Bluey offered his hand, and Roger shook it hard and well. Roger said, "Thank you, Dr. Macintosh." Bluey started to speak, and Roger said, "It's Bluey. I know."

Bluey turned to the instrument panel and began to instruct. This lever, that lock, this release. The forklift descended to the asphalt. Roger climbed aboard, a giant in a bright yellow clown car.

Bluey explained the loading procedure. There were numbered metal plates at the bottom of each cage, and corresponding numbers on the floor of the flatbed and the tandem. They would load the rear section of the tandem first, big cages on the bottom, smaller cages nested and locked on top, a specific and thought through order. Roger drove the fork lift with youth's deft ostentation, but when he closed on the cages he focused, slowed, and became cautious. Bluey was content.

They loaded Charlie, the Somali wild ass first, Roger guiding the fork neatly into the receiver slots on the cage bottom, Bluey alongside gesturing palm up, five inches, enough, palms down, Bluey speaking something loudly, but cadenced and calm while Charlie stepped noisily, nervously for balance in his suddenly shifting world. Roger backed for clearance, then went slowly forward across the lot and up the long ramp into the rear cavern of the bright-lighted tandem, Bluey alongside, and it was Shakespeare he spoke, *tomorrow and tomorrow, I will the multitudinous seas incarnadine,* walking alongside, one hand on the stainless mesh of the cage wall, up the ramp, down the length, directing the gentle settling onto the floor space outlined in white paint, identified with an engraved metal plate. The floor was heavy wooden planks and when Roger nudged the cage into position, Bluey removed a pair of pressure clamps from the wall opposite, dropped the pegs of the clamps into half inch holes in the planking, then engaged the holder's lever with his foot so the cage's grooved rim was fastened firmly to the floor. Behind a narrow door in the back wall, a generator droned. Three cooling fans poured breeze over their heads.

They returned and brought Phoenix, the Himalayan blue sheep, Bluey alongside reciting, Roger deft and careful. *What a cool holding system,* Roger said. *Did Bluey design it?* He had. *Was that Shakespeare?* It was. *Did he design the cages?* He did. *Those rounded corners, that was to make them easy to clean.* That's right. *The screen on the floors, that was to let urine through?* Correct. *And what, there's a catch basin under each one?* Yes. *And you're gonna answer all these questions later, and right now I should shut up and let you concentrate on the animals?* Thank you.

When the rear tandem was packed, Bluey went to the front tandem which held the freezers, refrigerators, and feed bins, then returned with a five gallon plastic bucket of treats—pellets, frozen fruit, and nuts. He strolled the length twice, speaking loudly, *When in disgrace with fortune and men's eyes,* back and forth until the sonnet ended and the treats had been dispersed. Roger lifted the ramp, slid it into the undercarriage on its bearings, locked it in place. Bluey felt the cool air of the fans, descended the rear ladder, dimmed the lights with the wall switch. The trailer fell into shadow. He gently swung the doors closed and latched them. He felt the heartache of a jailer, too familiar for notice.

•

The RV had a center compartment that converted into a bedroom when the fold-down mattress was lowered. El and Annie stood in the central living area and regarded their luggage, two fat brown leather rectangles for Annie, one lavender duffel for El. The who-would-sleep-where decision had arrived.

El, in an attempt to preempt discussion, said, "See, it makes into a little bedroom, and it's got little steps, and you can get right down at night to go to the bathroom. It's me all over. It that okay?"

"That's not fair, is it? I get the bedroom all to myself? We should at least switch out."

"I don't mind where I sleep, really. One time I slept on a friend's floor for a month. You take the bedroom, and if later I just have to get away from everyone or something—oh, I won't. I'm kidding. I'm perfectly happy and am not sacrificing."

"You're a sweetie then. Okay. I don't snore by the way."

"I do, just kidding."

They inspected the kitchen, lots of pots and pans, coffee pot, crock pot, electric frying pan, microwave, gas oven, a four burner grill. The cupboards were empty.

Annie said, "Well, okay then, starting from pure scratch. Before we hit the grocery store, we better hit a bookstore and pick up *Joy of Cooking*. That's what my mother had."

"So does mine, actually. Are you a—" El hesitated. Then—"An enthusiastic cook?"

"Ha! Well, I told Bluey I would cook with love, and I mean to. Don't worry. I can cook. I understand food must be mixed and heated. By the way, did you dream a lot when you slept on the floor?"

"You mean at my friends'? I don't think so. Maybe. Why?"

"They say astral energy pools on the floor and makes you dream."

"Really? I think I remember that."

"You do? Are you a student of the occult?"

"Well, no. But I read a lot. Are you?"

"Sort of." Annie was looking out of the kitchen window. "What's Bluey doing, talking to the animals?"

"He recites Shakespeare. So they don't spook."

"Really. He has always loved Shakespeare. You know, I've never read Bluey's books. I better now though. You have them?"

"I brought *How to Run a Zoo*. That's the one he keeps up-to-date. It's in its third edition now."

"God, he's an ant. I'm the grasshopper of the family."

El watched Bluey and Roger through the window beside the settee. Roger seemed expert with the fork lift, a relief. She waited to hear what Annie would say next. Her impression so far was—a vigorous spirit, comfortable with honesty.

She heard Annie say, "Really, we need to hit the bookstore." Then saw Annie's head fall and a sob erupt. Then a snort, dismissive and abrupt, then a laugh. She turned and saw Annie's face lift, her green eyes wet.

Annie said, "You're rooming with a wacky woman. I won't keep you in the dark. I'm having a midlife crisis. Can women have those? I just left a chief asshole, plus I lost all my money. Which maybe Bluey told you. A huge amount of money. And my son hates me. Oh well. Honey, you are such a sweetheart, looking at me so sweetly. I'm starved for that so you better stop. Anyway, I'm older than you. You should come to *me* for comfort. So you've landed in a drama. Don't worry, you have a minor part, no part at all really. But you have a heart, and if you have a heart everywhere you go, you're in the play. Too bad."

El said, "I just got a broken heart myself."

"Really? Well, shoot. There's no pain like man pain. It gets right down into your creases like bacteria. You're a good-looking gal. You could probably give me advice about men. I could have used it when I was your age, since my dear mother was an innocent. I was not granted a daughter. They were probably all sitting around the table, what do you think, a daughter for Annie Macintosh? Eyebrows were raised, and the subject was dropped." She noted El's thinking frown. "The gods. Around the table." El smiled, nodded. "Instead I had Dawson, who has Bluey's brains, by the way. He's got X-ray vision and can see you coming a mile away. I can't wait until he's fifty, and we can be friends. I'm pouring a nice dose of Annie down your throat. Well, we'll be living together. I think that's my instinct, get it out there. Sit down, will you?"

They sat across from each other at the settee booth. Through the window, they watched Roger ascend the ramp with Thane, the mandrill baboon, Bluey alongside reciting.

Annie said, "Give me your hands. There." She held El's hands for a moment, then returned them firmly, folded her own hands in front of her, hung her head, lifted it. "Bluey said this twenty-two year old wunderkind was coming along, and I thought, well, maybe she's unattractive, and here you are, and you're attractive, and Dawson will fall for you, and there'll be trouble in the land."

El touched Annie's hands, pressed them briefly, made a frowning smile.

Annie smirked her gratitude, then sighed energetically. "I wrote a paper about all this, two papers actually, in college. About how we trade energy with men. Some people can see that actually, little currents of energy zipping back and forth. I can almost see it myself, but that's just my wild imagination. Anyway, Dawson will trip and fall, boo hoo. He's a lovely brilliant nerd, but he's a bud. I'm not standing guard. If you're going to hurt him, oh well. I haven't given you a hug yet, but when we get up from this table I will. You're just listening away."

El thought, get up now and give her a hug, but didn't. Annie might say something else, this bouncy, bounding woman.

Annie said, "Did you hear my Bluey talk to us? All my life I thought, one day I will sit by that fire. Now I'm free, and there's perfume in the air, and I don't believe it. From here on, I will be a tidy and well-mannered cook." Annie got up. "We don't have to hug. Can we though?"

El rose. She said, "Yes, let's hug. A nice hug, best we can do."

They embraced. Annie lay her head against El's shoulder. She said, "Really nice to meet you."

•

Dawson had unpacked his small suitcase, jeans, shorts, a hooded sweatshirt, t-shirts, white socks, white boxers. His RV had an upper double bed close to the roof, a small settee booth, a two-burner range, a toilet-shower combo he had to stoop to enter. Like a tiny dorm room, only new and smelling new. Sheets, blankets, two towels, and a pillow were stacked on the mattress. And soap in the bathroom, and dish soap and a sponge under the sink. His cave. Through the side door window, he saw the blocky form of his uncle walking toward him. He slid open the door to let him in.

"Hey, man."

"Hey," said Bluey.

"Time for our private confab?"

"Right. You get all squared away?"

Bluey hoisted himself aboard, sat at the settee, patted the table for Dawson to sit. Dawson slid in across from him, his eyes flicking, resting on Bluey's face for an instant before scanning away. He hadn't bothered to answer about getting squared away, and Bluey let the silence run. He gazed at Dawson's face, saw the young man alert for condescension.

"Dawson, you are an unexpected addition to our little enterprise but welcome as hell, because as soon as I put you in the scheme, I saw how much I needed you. Your mother tells me about your skill in computers and graphics, and I've been thinking about that. First we talk money, then—"

"Shouldn't we talk about what I can offer before we talk money?"

"I thought you might prefer money first."

"I would prefer to wait."

"So we'll talk duties. There's driving, and your mother says you've never had a ticket. Good. We never drive for more than a day without taking the animals out and getting them some air. Even if we don't set up the compound, we air the beasts. We have a route and a schedule to keep, and we have to be organized. So driving, and then set-up, and that's genuine work. We have a stockade to assemble, and the cages to place, beasts to water and feed, and manure to gather and discard, cages to disinfect, straw and wood chips to replace. During the show, someone has to take tickets, which will be your mother, and we may eventually have a souvenir booth, which can be you. Roger will be background labor, and El and I will talk about the ecopark and be with the beasts, and put on a show if we can."

"I don't know much about the ecopark."

"We have two thousand acres in Tennessee about fifty miles from Memphis. It's being put together now and should be ready for us in four or five months. That's where we're heading, and where these beasts will live their lives, except from time to time we'll tour to gin up support and money. Which means we need publicity. Which brings me to your—"

"So this is all about an ecopark."

"Yes. A home for wild beasts."

"So they don't go extinct?"

"That's right. In a hundred years if we don't develop a culture of ecoparks, there will only be pigeons left."

"What 's wrong with pigeons?"

"Do you mean what's wrong with no wild beasts?"

Dawson's gaze stopped shifting and stopped on Bluey. "Is there an answer for that?"

"Why not let wild animals pass into memory? What is their value to mankind? That's the question, isn't it? It's not a question of rights either, is it? Animals are in our power and have no rights unless we bestow them. And why should we?"

Dawson said, smiling faintly, "Yes, why should we?"

"For the same reason we preserve old forts and temples, and lavish money on museums and on art from ages past. We came from that. It's our heritage."

"But do we need our heritage?"

Bluey felt Dawson's courage, pushing him to the edges where thought didn't come in packages, saw also Dawson's faint bemusement—am I smarter than you? Bluey nodded. He spread his thought, a carpet between them. "Yes, that's the point, and I was begging the question. So I say this—I conceive of consciousness as a great pyramid that is built from all history and all life that precedes us. We're way on top, so mental and disconnected. And in order to be balanced and grounded and integrated, we need museums and ecoparks. In the future, mankind will visit those parks and feel the root of himself and be grateful."

A moment passed in silence. Bluey watched his nephew's face, felt his point work its way into him. Dawson lifted his eyes briefly to Bluey's face, said, "Okay, what about the money?"

"I'll pay you fifty thousand dollars for six months commitment, room and board thrown in."

"Fuck! Really?"

"Fucking right."

They smiled together.

Dawson said, "It's a deal."

Bluey offered his hand, and they shook. Dawson's hand was firm.

"So now we come to your rumored talent."

"So you need someone to put up a website, make videos, get the word out on the internet?"

"Actually, I already have a company doing—"

"Well, fire them, save some dough. It's all about dough, right? I can do the whole thing, top and bottom. We can use Joomla and PHP, completely free. We can haunt the forums, post everywhere, Facebook and Twitter and YouTube. We can set up a livecam. Cheap. It's the programing that costs, and you have me. I'm a hundred percent trained and available. I'm a graphic artist too. I did that for money in high school. We'll need lots of material though. You know that little talk you gave us, the poetry of animals? We'll video that. Talk about the park and the pyramid. You should be the star. El, too, because she's pretty. And mother, she would love it. Watch out, coming to your town soon, the Exotic Animal Caravan, to make you feel balanced and integrated."

He glanced at Bluey from under intent brows and saw Bluey's benign smile.

•

They gathered again in the large RV, four seated at the settee, Bluey swiveled toward them from the front passenger seat. From the big pockets of his cargo coat he produced four hand held radios and passed them out. They were to wear the radio during the day and sleep beside it. To work together effectively they had to be connected. Besides, part of their cargo was large carnivorous beasts and communication was essential. On the highway, they would drive in a column, five miles an hour under the limit, always in the right lane, Bluey leading in the flatbed, then Roger in the tandem, then the RVs. They would reach the Mississippi in three or four months, depending on the bookings, which were still being arranged. After that, the caravan would launch from time to time, and the ecopark would grow. If they were successful, permanent jobs would be available. So far they had four state fairs booked, Oregon, Nevada, Colorado, and Kansas, as well as several festivals and a few malls. More bookings would be coming. Sometimes they would leave the highway to visit farms where they would replenish their feedstock and bedding. Today, their destination was Heavenly Vineyards, where they would add a tiger to the caravan and practice their set up. He described his conversation with Dawson about internet promotion. Questions?

Roger, who was fiddling with his radio, said into the mic, "Ten four, good buddy." Feedback screeched from the other radios. Everyone smiled, and Roger blushed.

7

Roger had never driven a new truck, or even a new car, and felt princely wellbeing. After a few turns, he had gotten the hang of the tandem, swing wide, watch it come around in the wing mirrors. Bluey took a six lane route out to the highway, though, so easy anyway. They were heading up the west side freeway and should be north of San Luis Obispo in a couple of hours. Then they would swing west toward Paso Robles and should reach the Heavenly Vineyard before noon. He could see the flatbed ahead of him locked in at sixty-five and in the mirror the big RV behind. Bluey had sent the skinny Dawson kid on an excursion into LA, trusting him not to get lost, which Roger thought was maybe weak. The kid seemed half here, up in his head.

The truck was a slick new Peterbuilt, had new car smell in the cab and in the deluxe sleeping compartment, which had a TV, a stereo, even a little sink and coffee alcove, and underneath fifty gallons of water. There was an outside hand hose too. He could take a shower out there, get some PVC and rig a shower curtain or just in his underwear. Or inside just take a PTA bath, as his mom called them, and he flashed on the day his eleven year old buddy, Dougy, said, what's that, and she splayed back a little at the dinette, gave off her flirty slant smile, said, pussy, tits, and armpits.

A laptop was open on the console showing a four inch *72 degrees,* the temperature in the rear tandem. Every half hour he had to radio

Bluey the temp and also if it ever went over seventy-five, which meant they had to hit a truck stop and set up the inside fans, wait til night, travel at night. So far, holding at seventy-two sunny California spring degrees. Bluey had built it all, or thought it up at least. And paid for it. All those specialized cages, the racks of feed bins, the freezers, the propane system, that stockade, which was going to be a bitch setting up, and no doubt why he was along, all two hundred ninety pounds of him. Actually, be honest, more like three hundred ten currently. Three hundred fifteen probably if he actually got on a scale.

At the end of six months he would have an amazing fifty grand in the bank, but less taxes, so maybe forty. Get his accountant mother to handle the forms, find some strong tax strategies. Then maybe a masters in horticulture, or else Canada for football. Graduate school was a gamble because there was the felony, and you'd always have that *ever been convicted of a felony* question in an interview. His dad, who sold farm equipment and was running for state office, was pissed by the conviction since he was starting in politics. The evening before in Redding they had had a tense discussion.

He could make the Canadian league, since he almost made the pros, last one cut. Or try the NFL again, get his head on straight, learn to shake hands firmly. Learn to try hard, which was what he had left out for some deep reason deep down in him where he couldn't get at it. In the spring camp something depressed him. He could feel the guy they lined him up against, Bosco James, find his handle and get a better grip each time they set up. Something inside him wasn't all in, even in college, but his size hid it. Also, he didn't like to get personally pissed to get revved, which was the strategy most guys used. Disagreeable and also fake, screaming at each other on the sidelines, banging pads. But he was a quarter step slow, and they cut him, didn't even offer the practice squad. Sorry kid, we wanted your ass to play for us. If you're around next year give us a call. Which maybe he would do. With his forty thousand.

Now he was driving a herd of wild animals around the country, monitoring temperature, and meant for hard labor. Bluey was good, so that was good. A kind man. And smart. With his Shakespeare.

Roger checked his phone and saw he had three more responses from the dating site. The night before at his dad's house, after their politics tussle, he spent over two hours on his profile, took his picture with the phone, straight up in crappy lamplight, even mentioned he was getting a TINY spare tire, capitalizing *tiny* for the joke of it, and had to get back to the gym, or run, which he could do with the zoo's feed bags. Didn't mention the felony but stayed honest otherwise and no flash. Revealed that he liked action movies, but also chick flicks if they were funny or *literate,* boldly using that word.

And man, did the world of women respond. Sad, sort of. So he was down the road with so far seven women waving him over. He wouldn't have posted his profile if he weren't leaving, he could admit that. Sorry girls, have to drive animals. But seven responses actually got him in the mood. Who knows, maybe set up dates as they went along in case some of those girls were on their route. Coming soon to your town, Roger Dodger, big and fun. Really, he would like to get to know a girl, get to know her family, meet her brothers and sisters, show her little brother how to tackle.

He had not known one girl well yet, except for Sue Chen, Taiwanese cheerleader at Oregon State, who said when they broke up she was just dabbling in him. She was a porcelain beauty, a phrase he had read somewhere, but it fit Sue for sure, with her crust of beauty and springy cheerleaderness. Her parents lived across the seas. Sue was proud to date a guy on the first string. He was dabbling too though. He got up to the edge where if you stepped off you would fall in love, he guessed, or at least in commitment, but saw Sue was not stepping off, so he didn't either. Six months of dabbling, that was his experience with women, not counting Linda, two houses down, who he had a two week copulation with at fourteen, just before his parents split up, and he moved away with his mother, a sort of goodbye gift from Linda, who was sixteen and probably thought she'd never see this huge fourteen year old kid again. And she hadn't. He might see her on the dating site, never know. She was probably married. She watched soap operas as soon as she got home from school. She had a rope swing her father put up, and she used to straddle it in a dress and swing without underpants. Those were exciting horny days, but now he wouldn't mind meeting someone, get to know her parents and her little brother. Instead, he was driving animals, living in a truck and getting out of shape. And a felon. With no future except forty thousand dollars, a quarter step slow.

Ahead of him, the flatbed's blinker went on. He checked the GPS. The turn was coming. He hit the turn signal, eased on the brakes. The monitor still said seventy-two. They were all back there, feeling the deceleration, nobody to talk Shakespeare to them. Gentle as he could, he eased on the brakes.

•

El was driving. Patti, a thick-bodied shovel-faced black and gray dog, lay between them on the floor. Annie had gotten her from the pound after her divorce. She was currently a stowaway and would be revealed to her brother the caravan master when they reached Heavenly Vineyard. Annie had been afraid she would growl at the zoo animals or Bluey's lab, and when Bluey was out of sight in the tandem had led him discreetly into the RV. She had formed an attachment. It was her divorce dog and yes, the dog was a bit of a growler, a bit sullen, but wasn't Bluey the famous maestro of animals? Patti seemed to like El, too, and lifted her head with pleasure when El streamed fingers across her back.

El had gotten Annie talking about life on the Australian plains, asking questions, was she a cowgirl, how'd they go to school?—giving Annie a chance to chat away her tearful turmoil.

After describing the ranch—thirty square miles of woods and grassland, cattle and kangaroos, a herd of feral camels—Annie said, "We had nice parents and rode horses and went to school in school of the air, which was over short wave radio. There were a few cowboy families on the ranch so I had friends, but I was crazy to grow up and get to college and start living. Which I did. By the way, I know I hit you with a load this morning. Don't worry, I'm done, and I'm a good roommate, very clean and not messy. You were sweet this morning. That's what us girls do for each other, we talk. We put up wallpaper with talk, make a pleasant place. Us nice girls anyway. Do you sense my conversation tends towards the philosophical?"

El laughed. "It does, doesn't it?"

"Yes. I'm sort of a recovering—whatever that is. They should have AA for the suddenly poor."

"Maybe they do."

"We bought a twenty-three million dollar mansion on the beautiful Pacific Ocean which is now worth about ten, if that. The idea was to sell the mansion for thirty in a few years, do that forever and live like kings. We took one of those real estate seminars with the amazing Dr. Greed, who had made his money and now wanted only to give back from his incredible store of real estate wisdom."

"Damn."

"That's what I said, only really loud. But you know what, I was laying around the pool in a bikini, if that, drinking too much, all my old friends still working, wishing I had a prenup because my husband had gotten inattentive. Bored out of my head. Then it was gone."

"That much change must have been hard."

"From a bikini on the sea to homeless and divorced." It was on the tip of her tongue to mention Dawson's money, that it was gambled away, but no, too too black. She felt a flash of unease, dishonesty with her new friend. She said, "I fell in love with an asshole. But assholes marry assholes, so there's a sad truth."

"That's too harsh."

"Yeah. It's too harsh. I'm a sine wave, up and down. Hardy's not an asshole, just a lost child. He's an actor, back into auditions. I met him on set—did you know I was a make-up artist? Also a player of bit parts. Rosa got me my first job. Actually she's the one who encouraged me to go to cosmetic school. After my first divorce. I showed up at their house like a wet cat. She was a sweet woman. She was a selfless woman, is the right thing to say. They wanted her on set. She was a producer, you know. She had a calming vibe. If someone got pissy, she could tell them to grow up. Off-set, in a nice way, and they would go back to work. She was a Baba lover when she died. Ever heard of that?"

"I think—I'm not sure."

"Well google Meher Baba. She was a stately gal, and a good friend to me."

"She died of cancer—"

"Yes. Right in the middle of everything good, like someone turned off the movie. Hey, I'm watching that!" Annie's voice had gotten husky. "See that? There's still a sore place in my heart."

They were silent for a moment. El said, "It must have been hard for Bluey."

"Yes, but he doesn't show his feelings. He doesn't lean. I always hated that in him. And loved it too." After another silence, Annie said, "Well goddamn, girl, we need some flowers on this wallpaper. So on to El. El is short for what, Ellen?"

"My name is actually just El."

"Well, there's a tale."

"From my father, who found it in a history book. It's Egyptian."

They spent a moment on El's dentist-turned-potter dad, and her lawyer mother turned defense attorney.

Annie said, "I named Dawson Dawson because I thought it sounded great. I wouldn't do it again though. I would probably go with John. Or Smith. Smith Macintosh."

"Make it simple."

"Yes, stop painting so much. Let it be."

"Is his name Macintosh?"

"He took my name. Eventually. Actually, I think he took Bluey's name. So this guy broke your heart, the bastard."

"Well, cracked it. He took a job far away and said goodbye for good."

"Not just, let's have a break?"

El raised her eyebrows, shook her head, thought of her mother's comment, doors that don't close all the way are still open. And then wondered, is she checking my availability for Dawson?

But she eased when Annie said, with high-voiced primness, "Well, sometimes these things just don't work out, dear."

El smiled, wagged her head.

Annie said, "Before I started marrying, I had some fellows push away from my table. Well, not that many, actually two. The rest I had to throw a fork at. But those two, the soccer player and the writer, were heart-breakers."

"Heart tentacles out of alignment."

"Just that. The suction cups didn't quite line up. What the human race needs is a giant suction cup data base, and you just enter your data, and it spits out—Carl Akuba of Ghana!"

"But would Carl's spit out Annie Macintosh?"

They laughed. Annie said, "It wouldn't matter anyway because of karma. You don't get what you want, you get what you need. So that finally the universe is rubbed shiny. That's from Bluey. He's a mystic, in case you didn't know."

"Really?"

"When we were kids, he was. He was sort of my father. Ten years older. What he thinks now, god knows. He didn't go for Meher Baba, that I know."

They were silent for a moment. Then El said, "So what happened with the two heart-breakers?"

Annie said, "I scared the soccer player off, and the writer really, painful to recall, just didn't like me that much. He did love my body."

"You can't love a body though."

"Well, isn't that the truth."

"There's only one suction cup on a body anyway."

"I can think of three."

"Jesus. I'll grant you two."

They laughed.

"You know what my writer said when he met me? Your beauty is frightening. You must fart to put me at my ease."

"Ha! And did you?"

"God no. I wanted him frightened. Later, I did, but it was too late. Farts could not win his heart."

They laughed.

"We're a jolly crew," said Annie. "Good for us, goddammit."

Ahead of them, El saw the turn signal of the tandem go on. She said, "You're about to meet a really pretty tiger all the way from India."

•

Dawson found *The Joy of Cooking* and tucked it under his arm while he browsed the computer and digital photography section, looking for a book on how to work green screens. There wasn't one, but there was a section about it in one of the big fat photography bibles. He scanned it, got the idea and thought, don't need the book, but got it anyway in case, and also because the book had sources in the back. Then he went to the graphic art section and browsed for logo ideas, but not for long, because one had already flowered in his mind, a cornucopia of animals tumbling around the ornate Ringling-style script of the words, *Exotic Animal Caravan.* A logo for the web and also for the trucks and a graphic for the stockade with a crowd of people with their backs turned, peering onto this wondrous zoo, lots of kids and mothers. Get it all printed on vinyl, magnetic for the trucks, a couple of thousand bucks and done. He could get animal photos from the web, sketch it with Illustrator—he had his pen tablet with him—and sit Bluey down for a big deal presentation. Or just tell him. No, show him, since you could never tell what someone could imagine. Also they would need a good color laser printer for the green screen idea. And also a decent digital video camera. Say another thousand, maybe two, maybe three, so say five tops for everything. Good investment though.

He was charged, flashing now and then that he wanted to impress Bluey, flashing that Bluey trusted him enough to right away send him on this book and grocery errand, which bespoke trust that he could find a bookstore, get groceries, and show up at the vineyard squared away. When he got behind the wheel and started thinking about the Exotic Animal Caravan, all the ideas cascaded down, and he had to pull into a parking lot to email them to himself. He even took out a piece of notebook paper and drew the *E* of exotic with lots of corny serifs, raised and shaded, and with some kind of monkey hanging from its tail on the upper horizontal. Bluey would think, I'm already getting my money's worth out of you, kid. He was reaching for the apple of approbation, but he was getting fifty grand, so why not? Reach high. Then with the fifty finish school and into high tech. Or else have this impressive portfolio of zoo work and start his own web biz, graphics biz, maybe don't need school, maybe take the fifty and the portfolio and hang a shingle on the web.

He paid for the photography bible with his own money, using the credit card for the cookbook. Out in the van he checked the time, almost three. What he really wanted to do was hit a Panera or Starbucks for some coffee, use their internet, and get some animal images into his laptop so he could start thinking. But he was supposed to show up to help unload the trucks, and he still had to hit the special grocery store for the chow-chow his mother wanted. If he was late, it would be for a good cause though. But he would get a patient frown from Bluey and a pissed mother, rat kid already fucking up. He could wait. If he got going tonight, he could be done in a week with the graphics, unless he was busy shoveling shit or whatever else he had to do.

As he pulled out of the bookstore parking lot, he got the idea for the kids' club and the collectible figurines and almost pulled back in to email himself.

•

Bluey drove the Mac flatbed he had picked up at auction. It had a sleeping cubby, but the truck was almost twenty years old, and the compartment was scuffed and covered with mystery stains. Still, the truck had a rebuilt motor and transmission, less than ten thousand on them, so good to go mechanically, with a sweet loud diesel drone.

The voyage had begun well, the crew halfway happenstance and so far untroubled, though there was always Annie, who might become a privileged complainer when her gratitude wore off. Or get bored and reach out to an old boyfriend, meet me in New Orleans. But so far all well and on schedule. They could only carry enough provisions for a couple of weeks at a time, but Arnold's ZooFood would make runs with a box truck to refill them. Expensive, but this was the training run, partly for the crew, if they stayed with him, but mostly for him so he could see how a traveling zoo worked, what the public thought, what the logistical issues were, how the beasts behaved, what layout was best, what advertisement.

Dawson was a find. Young and up in his head, but up there a bright-eyed hawk. He had needed a reason to get involved, wouldn't come down from the heights until his got his ideals lined up, so Bluey gave him the humanity-in-balance riff, animals vanishing fast, and we must preserve them to appreciate our roots. It was a pitch well worn from the classroom, and true enough, except that it was morality, and so, for Bluey, it was bogus, part of his teacher persona and frontal man, unconnected to his heart, where need lived, and recognition, and love.

On his eighteenth birthday Bluey had an experience which shaped his life. He had come to Lake Matilda, as his father called their five acre cattle pond, and was seated in his familiar spot under the stringybark eucalyptus. He had come to draw the cattle as he had done many times before, becoming blank and harmless, letting harmlessness spread from him in waves, penetrating the beasts and drawing them like a candle in their dark. And they came until they were spokes around his hub, their wet pebbly noses wavering before his face, a few moving closer to taste his cheek or brow with rough tongues. Then he heard the station horn's distant blare, his mother calling him to his birthday lunch and cake and ice cream with the hands.

He had gotten into a state, and the will to respond to his mother's summons was outside the state, waiting, like the wheel of cows. Then some invisible barrier gave way, and the world became energy and radiant, and the cows emerged radiant from their hairy shells as beings suspended in being, dimly conscious and drawn by yearning to his greater consciousness, and when he stood finally, numb with wonder, and saw the brown water of Lake Matilda spread before him, he felt it flattened and held in its muddy bowl by some present and working energy, and felt the universe alive, and always working, and always alive. Then it all fell away, like a dream gone, and he was a stick figure among stick figures again. The cows milled and wandered. The horn blared once more, and he began the walk home.

A month later, in Melbourne with his father to buy horses at auction, he found an afternoon to visit the big library on Flinders Lane and browsed the religion section, Christianity, Islam, Buddhism, then Vedanta, then mysticism finally and read names like Yogananda, Ramakrishna, Krishnamurti, Gurjieff, Schiller. He could take ten books only and deliberated long over his selection, taking finally a commentary on the Buddha's sutras, the Bhagavad Gita, seven books by various mystics, and finally, as he was leaving, swapped Swedenborg for Aurobindo

Ghose's Letters to his Disciples, Volume II, which had headings entitled *Planes and Parts of Being* and *Reason, Science, and Yoga.*

He kept a book always in his saddle bag that summer, the ringers and his father getting used to his disappearance into the bush for an hour or two during the day, and him getting used to their ribbing—"Jackaroo, that Shiller is a lying sack of shit." His mildly religious mother, an Anglican, and his irreligious father were curious but did not pry, thinking mostly, he is using his mind, good. He had at first immersed himself in all the writers, a paragraph here, a chapter there, then more and more read only Aurobindo, whose thought seemed clearly to emerge from inner experience and seemed to map his own state with assured accuracy. From the chapter, *The Planes and Parts of Being,* he was able to assemble a rough geography of the psyche. Eventually he confided to his sister Annie his experience under the eucalyptus, how the cows had become more apparent, beings in a matrix of being, how he had felt the water held flat. At first she mocked him—*They call it gravity, you wanker.* But through that summer's muster and into the fall until Bluey left the station for Melbourne and college, she listened to passages about love and aspiration and ever-present divinity, and gradually something in her submitted, partly to what she heard, partly to his authority. When he left for college that year and through the following years, they talked frequently, satellites checking in.

In college he returned to the Melbourne library and read the other two volumes of Aurobindo's letters and also *The Synthesis of Yoga* and *The Future Poetry.* He discovered on one of them a typed square of paper pasted on the title page, "donated by Evelyn Welker." He found her in the phone book, called her, and was invited to visit. She was an old woman, a widow, and recounted that in her sixties she and her husband had lived in the French enclave of Pondicherry near Madras, India for a year, and had studied at the Aurobindo ashram. This was in the mid-seventies and Aurobindo was long dead. Mirra Alfassa, called the Mother, had taken charge but had also died. It was a period of disturbance and tension in the ashram, and Evelyn recounted a web of intrigue and complaint. He heard of whispered scandal, of the failed attempt to manifest the supermind at the cellular level, even of a struggle over land

and power. Bluey listened, bewildered and disheartened. He had come, a youth seeking fellowship, and heard a report of division.

On the long bus ride back to the university he sat among the jostling city people who rose and sat and stared and read and talked, and more than ever they seemed denizens of the *out there,* and a conviction rose that the *in here*, which he sensed was forming in him, was the sole harbor. The intellect itself, hungry to map the world, was part of the out there and unreliable. It took positions, defended guesses, and so made a fortress for pride and disappointment. No one was immune, not aspirants, and not their leaders.

He was seated at the window and watched the neighborhoods stream by. A small man smelling of aftershave and wearing a blue baseball cap sat beside him. In front of him two young girls chatted, both blonds, their long hair breaking over the metal bar behind their seat top. A sadness too deep for bitterness invaded him. His eyes wet, and he lowered his head so that tears, if they formed, would fall unnoticed. The sadness built, massive and relentless, and though at first he held it away like a weight, at last something in him gave way, and he let it take him. Then it fell away and calm came. Assurance blossomed in the center of his chest, and beneath it, tremulous as a reflection in moving water, love emerged. He thought, it has come forward, what Aurobindo called the psychic being, the soul force, it has come forward. It expanded to move out from his heart center into his limbs, then into space, and the baseball cap man and the blond girls were suspended in love. The being of all beings and had come, what Jesus said, only knock. After a time, like the experience under the eucalyptus, it faded.

Life became simpler. The boundary between the out there and the in here, though never fixed and clear, was useful. In here was where love could come. Out there was emptiness. All thought, even introspective thought, and all science, to which he devoted his working life, though useful and even essential for life, was not truth. Thought was mind merely and about something, a map of something, and the something itself was truth and approachable only through a part of the being inaccessible to intellect. At best, thought was subtractive and could clear the way for the part beneath that needed and yearned and could open and surrender. He read many more thinkers, discovered the existence of the perennial philosophy throughout history, but in the end came to consider most writers mapmakers, not explorers, and the real explorers, like Frances of Assisi or Hafiz or Rumi, only pointed, said truth is that way, go, and you'll recognize it.

He was young and sometimes neglected the in here for weeks and months at a time, swept away by a love affair, or competing on the varsity rugby team, or working on a paper. Sometimes, when his yearning built, and he wanted contact, he found his soul stubbornly silence. In time he accepted the secret, which was inner nakedness and patience. Love could not be summoned by will or duty, but came only in response to need, and even then only when some dark shifting within had occurred to prepare the ground. Hence patience, and also watchfulness, so that the lower vital, as Aurobindo called it, with its pride, anger, greed, and lust, did not gain too strong a hold. His experience under the eucalyptus was never repeated, and he came to think of it as merely a trigger and otherwise unimportant. Only love, which encompassed all valuable states and attributes and was the elusive fragrance of the soul, was important.

He finished undergraduate school, then earned a doctorate in animal husbandry. His first job was at the Taronga Zoo in Sidney, and he spent his nights enlarging his doctoral thesis into *How to Run a Zoo*, the book which brought him worldwide attention and led to work as a consultant.

He met Rosa in Schezwan, China, where she had come to do a film on the almost extinct south China tiger, and where he had been invited as adviser. He became part of her film, and they spent two months together. They lighted when they came near each other. They were glad in each other's company. When the film wrapped, she returned to California, and he to the Taronga Zoo, where he had become the curator of mammals. He rattled in his life like a bean in a bottle. They talked on the phone. She said, "If you're ever in sunny California, why don't you marry me?" Two days later he was on an airplane. They returned to Australia to marry, and a year later, he accepted a professorship at the Exotic Animal College, and California became his home.

Twenty-two years together. Then she was gone. Chemo first, then radiation, then a wait for death. Through a friend, she learned about

Meher Baba. Annie arrived and spent hours reading his discourses to her. Bluey listened from time to time, and though the content seemed coincident with Aurobindo and his own experience, Meher Baba's assertion of divinity rang wrong, seemed part of the out there with its warfare of claims and counterclaims. For Rosa though Bluey was glad. Meher Baba's words and photograph were a comfort.

Finally, she began drifting. She told him she had flown around their neighborhood in her room, steering it like a car. She said she could sometimes look down on her body from the ceiling. She said, we did not fall in love, we rose in love. One day she asked him for wrapping paper, scotch tape, and ribbon and made him leave, then called him back. She pushed a clumsily wrapped package across the sheet. He opened the gift, and it was a book, *The Wayfarers.* She smiled her lovely smile, said, read it when you feel like it.

Just past noon the turn for Heavenly Vineyard came up. Bluey lifted the turn signal, glanced into the rear view mirror, saw the tandem's signal come on a second later, Roger on the ball. The evening of Rosa's gift, after she slept, he had opened the book, standing at the counter in their bright yellow kitchen. He glanced at the mad eyes of ragged men, read a few paragraphs, felt simultaneous interest and aversion, then closed it and had not opened it again.

He removed his foot from the accelerator, letting the truck slow gradually. He eased on the brake. Goose lifted his head from sleep on the passenger seat, then stood, looked interestedly about, checked Bluey, anything up? Bluey leaned to grip his snout and smooth a hand across his brow.

Goose shook himself vigorously awake, then seated himself to watch for developments.

Bluey said, "We're going to get a tiger."

When Haley told his story about the mast-raised tiger, Bluey's heart had quickened. He had steadied it. You can think, this is more than coincidence and even be right. But still it's presumption to assume, like putting words in god's mouth. When he got home, he searched for and found the book. It had been buried in one of his packing boxes, and he had known which box exactly, the green-lettered liquor store box, marked in memory by a pulse of grief as the book's white cover left his hand. When he retrieved it, he checked the title page and saw it had been first published in 1948, sixty-six years ago. Likely none of the masts in the book had raised his tiger then. Still, his glance landed on a paragraph describing a man villagers believed to be over 130 years old. He browsed the book again, read a passage here and there, studied again the mad luminous faces of the god-intoxicated, felt again the suspicion and attraction. Now the book lay between the seats on the console. If Haley mentioned it, he would let him browse. He wouldn't lend it to him.

•

Haley waved them forward, and they drove behind his golfcart up the hill, then around the camel and Arabian horse enclosures to a flat acre of grassy ground. In the center stood the big stainless cage, a group of four Hispanic workers lounging in the grassy shade beneath it. Bhajan was sitting and alert, looking across the circle of men to the approaching cart and trucks.

Haley walked briskly to the cab as Bluey descended and pumped his hand. Bluey thought, did he limp?

Roger descended his truck and met Bluey at the control panel behind the flatbed.

Bluey said, "How's the temperature?"

"Seventy-two."

While Roger brought the fork lift down, Bluey rolled the motorized canopy back. He smelled a whiff of vomit, spotted it on the cedar chips of the sun bear's cage. He walked down one side of the truck, then the other, emitting a series of grunts, making his presence known. The lion stood, opened his cavernous mouth in a yawn. The hyena lifted his head, made a few inquiring yips. The rest of the carnivores lay in place, unconcerned.

He found El already in the rear tandem, heard her soft chatter, *hello, babies, little darlings.* He again smelled vomit and found it in the baboon and honey badger cages. Toohey, the badger, lay in a corner, peering up with still miserable eyes, but the baboon was alert. El stood at Toohey's cage. "How about dramamine?" she said. "Just a speck, see how it works?

The rest of these guys are great though. They're saying, hey, let's get moving!"

Haley led Bluey across the grassy field toward the tiger cage. He said, "You got more than two hundred feet here. What do you think? We're getting it ready for wolves."

"It looks perfect," said Bluey. "We won't leave a trace and many thanks." Haley's gait was definitely smoother. Where the hitch had been there was now a rolling motion.

Haley said, "Sorry to see this tiger go, goddammit. See these guys?" He indicated the Latinos beside the tiger cage. "They're here to say goodbye to their tiger. I let them go on break when we spotted your trucks. They can help you set up if you want. Happy to lend them. Did I tell you I started sleeping in the warehouse so I could listen to the purr? Anyway, I got company the last week or so. All these sad hombres who are sad to see their tiger go. I told Fuad, let's keep this tiger. I told him, let's send him the money back with a penalty. But he had a dream, and there you go. You're getting a special tiger, my friend. A purring tiger. Which I have halfway concluded is the long lost fountain of youth. You ever hear of the lost chord? These Mexicans told me about it. They believe in everything. Look it up on the internet." Haley laughed. "I sound crazy, but trust me, Dr. Macintosh, you will pay attention."

They had reached the cage. Bhajan haunch-sat gazing at them. His tongue emerged and made a swift circuit around his whiskers, nose, opposite whiskers, gleaming them, briefly revealing his immense canines. The Hispanic men had risen and gathered behind them. Bluey glanced, caught a few eyes, felt their restiveness.

Haley said, "These hombres showed up this morning with four thousand dollars. They checked the internet, thought that was a good price. One of them has a rabbit farm in Acapulco and said he would feed him rabbits. I brought them down to the office and showed them your book. I said, this man has got dibs. They said okay. Hey, Santino, okay?"

A short burly man nodded. "Okay."

They stood five feet from the cage, Bhajan three feet from the bars. His eyes held Bluey's, softly blinking from time to time.

Haley said, "I believe he knows you're his next stop. You could fire a pistol, I don't think that tiger would flinch."

•

They set up the zoo that afternoon, the carnivores and herbivores on opposite sides in a hundred foot diameter wheel of cages with the tiger as the hub. El walked alongside the fork lift as Roger worked, muttering, *oh, little baby, howdy doody, sweetie pie.* Goose followed them for a while, then plopped at the end of Bump the sun bear's cage, who observed him carefully, then came to sit companionably close. When the animals were in place, Roger wrestled the bamboo stockade pieces from the front tandem, stacked them five at a time on the fork lift, and dropped them at intervals around the perimeter. Bluey, El, and Annie, wearing leather gloves, Annie with a purple burnoose swept around her head, lifted the stockade into position, and slid the steel pins into their hinges. In the rear of the stockade directly across from the entrance gate, they left a pedestrian gap, with a concealing parenthesis of bamboo, and parked the vehicles just beyond it. When Dawson pulled up in the grass with groceries and *The Joy of Cooking*, Annie gave him her gloves, and he joined the stockade assembly with Bluey and El while his mother made lunch. In less than two hours, all the animals were in place, a seven foot bamboo stockade surrounded the zoo, and the crew was hungry.

Annie spread a blanket in the shade of the tiger cage. Using the RV's dish drainer as a picnic basket, she brought smoked turkey, tomato, and chow-chow sandwiches with chips and orange juice. They settled in a circle. Bluey informed them that they would not put up the interior crowd fencing, the ticket gate, or the signs. They needed the time to learn cage cleaning and feeding. A feeling of unity and purpose connected them. They had worked together and built a city.

Goose resettled under the lip of the tiger cage. He had been to the college zoo many times and understood enclosures, so a huge tiger a few feet away did not concern him. He had come to watch them eat. Bluey did not dispense handouts from the table, but perhaps the others?

The sandwiches were delicious, said everyone. Annie shrugged and smiled. The chow-chow had sealed the deal. Bhajan, lying hugely on his side, watched them, from time to time lashing his tail through the cedar chips to send a light brown rain onto Goose's head. From the perimeter, they heard an occasional hoot, chitter, or yip.

When he had finished, Bluey wiped his hands and broad face with a paper towel. He said, "So here's Roger, who Annie and Dawson don't know. And here's Dawson, who Roger and El don't know, and here's Annie, who El knows a little by now, but who Roger doesn't, and I know everybody. So here's your introductions. Dawson is a junior at University of Washington in computer engineering, and he's nineteen so he must be working hard. Or took courses in high school. You did, right?"

Dawson said, "Yes." He had not mentioned his ideas to Bluey as they erected the stockade. That would have been zealous. Besides, he wanted Bluey across a table and intent. Now the searchlight of attention compressed him, and he was relieved when the attention shifted to El.

Bluey said, "El is from Sacramento and has a degree from Berkeley in zoology and one from the Exotic Animal College in curatorship. She's twenty-two and has empathy for beasts. If she asks you to do something, please do it."

Roger said, "So she's my boss?"

El said, "Yes, Roger, I am your boss. Deal with it. Now I would like two chips, chop chop."

Roger choose two potato chips and handed them over. He said, "Damn."

Bluey said, "Roger is El's cousin, son of her mother's sister, and is twenty-four. And Annie, that's the last age I'll mention. He played football for Oregon, offensive lineman, and majored in horticulture. He is a skilled driver of big rigs, which is why he's driving the tandem. And he is a skilled driver of fork lifts, as we all observed. Annie is my sister, has a degree in humanities and promises to be a wonderful cook. If she asks you to do something, you are free to ignore her. Except for you, Dawson." As he was delivering this remark, there came a fortuitous hoot from Taj, the guenon monkey, and they laughed.

Bluey said, "Finally, I'm an Australian cowboy who hopes like hell this little enterprise works out. The work is partly setting up and taking down, and you saw how that goes. And the work is feeding and cleaning, and you'll see that in a minute. But the work is also representing to the public, and that's dawn to dusk. When you're inside the perimeter of the zoo, you're on duty. You'll wear a brown safari shirt with your name on it, which I hope will be delivered in time for our first set up, which is six hundred miles north in Oregon in the Willamette Valley. It's a county fair. We may not make much money, but we can practice. We have lots to learn. That's enough for now. Any questions?"

Dawson said, "We will leave a trail of psychologically balanced people." This was meant as inside humor between him and Bluey but ended shy, odd, and flat. They looked at him curiously, Annie throwing off a mild corrective scowl. Bluey laughed, said they definitely would. Dawson bit his sandwich with a lowered head.

When they finished eating, Bluey retrieved four notebooks and pens from his truck and passed them out. He said, "We're going to go beast by beast and learn how to feed and remove dung. Each animal is different, so make complete notes. El and I will guide you. The rules are, one, be careful, two, be considerate. We've got two carts, one for feed, the other for dung. We load the feed cart each morning, by weight for each animal. There's a master chart in the front tandem where the food is stored. That's the morning feeding. Then in the afternoon, we prepare treats, which means cutting up whatever vegetables and fruit we can get. And Dawson, from time to time, that'll be something for you, to hit the local farmer's markets or roadside stands and pick up veggies. We use the squeeze walls when we're clearing dung and that requires patience and consideration. We'll roll the dung cart into the tandem until we find a dumpster or a farmer with a manure pile. It's got fork lift slots, so it's easy to dump. I've got the feed cart loaded for today. Let's start with the okapi and move right around."

Annie said, "Well, let me clear up first. And Bluey, give me a hand, will you." She caught his eye meaningly, and he helped her gather the plates and empty bottles into the dish drainer, followed her to the RV, tagged by Goose.

Bluey shifted his load and reached for the door, but she moved in front. "Now Bluey, I hate to tell you this last thing, but the thing is, I did not tell you an important thing. I have a dog. She's right in there, just waiting to see what the hell I've got her into."

"Oh, for god's sake. What sort of dog?"

"Well, you'll know better than me. It's a shelter dog, I don't even know how old, but they said a few years."

"How long have you had her?"

"Three weeks. She's a nice dog, but she does growl a little bit. I'm thinking you could—oh, shit, I know I should have told you, but Bluey I just couldn't take her back, and she growls a bit and who knows what she's been through? Anyway, I'm going to open the door, and Goose is right here so what do you think?"

"I'll open the door." He led Goose to the front of the RV, gave the stay command. He tumbled the dishes onto the grass, and with the dish drainer held in front of him, opened the door. Patti watched him from the head of the steps, emitted a low growl. He stepped onto the first step, grunting, leading with the drainer, backing Patti off, then was in the RV, backing the dog down the length of the vehicle into the bedroom and up against the rear wall beside the bed, still murmuring, now emphatically. Patti tossed her head uncertainly, crowded, unable even to jump onto the bed. She stopped growling. She submitted. He lay his thick hand on her flat head, ruffed it, then stroked it gently three times. "C'mon, chum," he said. Patti followed him. When she descended the steps, she saw Goose, began a growl. Bluey grunted, and the growl ceased. He said, "Free," and Goose approached. The dogs completed a ritual sniff, circled, seemed all right together. Bluey said, "You got any snakes in there?"

"What sort of dog is she?"

"Bull terrier, maybe, maybe some pit. God knows."

"Well, will she be okay?"

They watched the two dogs move away together to investigate the zoo.

Bluey said, "Probably."

8

JJ had collected almost thirty Carlos vignettes. JJ would say, "I saw your wife picking you up yesterday. Decent hot. You guys ever swing? Swap around? Just asking." And Carlos would get that whiny look and break out with, "What the fuck's wrong with you, man! You say some shit like that!" Or JJ would say, "Carlos, did you defecate in the wild dog pen? There's a human turd in there. You shit in there, didn't you?" Or he would say, "Carlos, can I pat you on the ass a little bit?" Just any wild thing that popped into his head, and Carlos was like a jukebox, nickel in, music out. He had put them in the editor, strung them like beads with corny-cool wipes, just over two minutes, this frisky little Latino dude jumping with upset. "What the fuck, man! Shut that fuck up, man! Get the fuck away from me, man!" Bouncing up and down, swinging that ponytail, quick wipe to a different setting every time, high def right on the face with the hat cam. Gutbusting hilarious. He could show some casting agent—I have an actor who has caught the quintessence of outrage. He couldn't watch the video, even for the twentieth time, without heh-heh's bubbling up.

Which sometimes brought his mother to the door. "JJ, what is so funny?" Opening the door and blowing in a gust of fear and false with her perfume. And he would flick the dead eye glance and say, "Just my work." Which got him an eye roll and hurt feelings begging before the door slowly closed.

For two months now he had lived in his mother's house, the basement house of childhood, where the hidden land began, his Eden, what he woke with and lived with and slept with. He let the basement videos run all day, burning at the edge of vision like prison bars, which they were, crowding him into solitary confinement, which was right and true. Isolation whispered courage, and courage made the world clear, and people clear, who were ghosts, stuck in bodies and lives, submerged and drowned in lives and content with that and no hope and no desire and no desperation to swim up and get a breath of reality. Reality mattered and was all that mattered and started in the basement. One day he might get bored and tired of pushing crazy, if reality was impossible. Then one day pull the five shot on some sidewalk, bang and black.

Work was good. Projects like the hilarious Carlos video were good. Something to grip while he waited. Patience was courage too. But weary if it had no end. Useless if it had no end. You finish all the magazines in the waiting room, and you're still out there, dum de dum. If no one was home, he wasn't going to cry about it. If the hidden land was locked, and always locked, if it was always only dirtball earth and nothing behind the screen, and if he felt his grip go more and more, the five shot was another kind of key. It might not open anything but could close it. Bang and black.

It was a breathless marathon. Would heroic JJ reach the hidden land before crazy caught him? Yesterday in Malibu, he felt crazy close. He had just dropped a twenty in a street fiddler's hat because the guy was far from shore on *Ashokan Farewell*, when a big dude tugged his sleeve and asked for the time. It had brought him back hard and angry from the sweetness, and he had walked away, and looking back couldn't remember whether he had said or thought, got no time for you, motherfucker. Looking back, he saw the big dude watching him with a hard expression. He could go back and ask, did I speak to you just now? He felt the world go soft and drifty. He could turn and walk back and get involved with the guy. You barged into my head, you insensitive motherfucker! He kept walking. Crazy could catch him. That could happen.

But something was up in the waiting room. There was more light in the waiting room. He could sometimes see people clearer as long as they didn't burst in like the got-the-time dude, but entered like his mother, slowly opening the door, poking in her sad, saggy, begging bowl face, which said, *I have always suspected about the basement and my abnormal brother and my tasty sons.*

People were still ghosts in a fog, but he saw them clearer now, saw them waver up in their drownedness and gill-gasping need, saw their fear, their anger, like what-the-fuck-man Carlos, so funny, and funny was good, like cool water, better than hot hatred, so change there too, from hate to humor. Hate was waste, like burning ants. You had to burn the world to get them all. Hate was like poisoning yourself and expecting your enemy to die. He had read that on the internet and memorized it, a billboard inside his forehead until he tore it down because it was just words. Words were part of the enemy's tricky kit. Words were a chatty guy in a nice suit, the maître d' whose job it is to keep you from the food.

So let hate blow by. Turn sideways in the hurricane, and let it blow by and no flinch because clean and courageous. He had learned clean and courageous in martial arts, and he had practiced it in combat, putting his head up over the parapets to aim in while the Iraqi death blossoms flew by. The Iraqis were wild scared shooters but could still catch you lucky in the forehead, or the leg, or in the shoulder and out the spine, like with teenage, crook-tooth Ned, his first battle buddy. They were on a roof, taking long range fire from two sides, low angle and so far harmless. Then three bad guys reached a high roof and got a machine gun up there. His guys returned fire but only by holding their M4s over the parapet and spraying, Iraqi style. He was squad sergeant now, shouting, "Aim in, motherfuckers, aim in." He found two of the bad guys in his six power scope and hit them in the head, and eventually his squad came up with him, and after the machine gunner went down, he turned to find Ned beside him with his spine blown out. Old Ned was back in Kentucky now dying of bed sores. JJ emailed him every week and had sent many boxes of videos. He had killed him. He had made him braver than he could be, braver than smart. On the rooftop he had heard Ned crash through a magazine, then heard him eject and reload and felt him staying up and not ducking, staying up in the bullet rain like his brave, careful-aiming battle buddy. JJ had the machine gunner pinned, trying to nick a forearm or smash the gun, at the same time thinking but not saying, little Ned, motherfucker, duck while you work. But too bad, a bullet from one of the far off side shooters caught Ned just over chest Kevlar, and he went down, JJ thinking, at last he ducked, and found him shot to shit.

They ended that firefight with tanks, the way they ended most of the Fallujah firefights, 120 millimeter cannons against AK47s. They blew the town apart in a week, a third of the buildings rubble, the streets full of corpse-gorging cats and dogs. Then the generals came in with the reporters, and the generals wore starchy uniforms and grave sympathetic faces and medals for the cameras, but a day before, on the last day of battle, JJ killed the kid, and he limped into line without shaving and without rinsing or even scraping his blood-crusted uniform and helmet, and his eyes were drifty. Captain Hediger got him out of line before the generals got to him and sent him to Germany on medical, using the shrapnel in his ass as a ticket. Besides all the campaign medals, he ended up with two purple hearts, one for his grenaded ass, one for his shot-through calf, and two bronze stars. Both stars were with *V* device for heroism, and one could have silver if he had had a better attitude. He did another six months in Afghanistan, and after he got home he threw the medals onto the freeway and watched them ricochet under the wheels of a semi. He got medals and Ned got bed sores and the generals got cameras, and the Washington guys spoke to handsome reporters in measured tones. He had sneaked a look at his file way back in crazy school and read that the counselor thought he might be a sociopath, but now he knew that everybody was a sociopath, and the trick was hiding it. You could hide it with hoo-has and hajji hatred like his army buddies, or with camera-grave faces like the politicians, but when you shot a kid and saw his face so soft and loving, and felt his spirit zoom through you, and you couldn't get your next breath for almost thirty seconds until Corporal Tooley said, "Sarge, Sarge!" and you left the house drunk and hadn't sobered up yet, not really, in all these long years—then it was hard to hide the space in your chest with nothing in it. And it was easy to see everyone else had the same space, like a secret stomach you couldn't get food to, and all the hamburgers you crammed in, and all the pussy you jammed in, and all the money you rammed in couldn't reach that stomach. Everybody on earth was hollowed out like zombies, or else why poverty, why war, why my stuff instead of our stuff? And the guys that got up front, the guys on TV and in the movies, and the generals, and the politicians, were the snappy smoothtalking zombies, big time graffiti taggers whose job was spraying happy faces on the world.

And sometimes there was El, who he had spoken to only twice, and she had spoken to him only once really, meeting his eyes and saying, we are both on the side of animals. And he had almost burst into tears and swung the shovel to bump her back and keep from crazy. Now when she came back in his head, lying on her back on the water of his mind, gently backstroking across the water of his mind, gazing into his inside eyes and smiling, he would close his outer eyes and let her swim, and his breathing would slow, and did her lips move a little, was she whispering a little? Some good kind thing, like, *how I love the animals. How I love them. I do love them. I love them. I love. I love.* And he could feel his inside stomach where there wasn't anything start to churn, and sometimes he would groan and sometimes had to snap his eyes open and fight off a surge of combat panic.

He hadn't looked at her video yet, except when he saved it on his drive, making sure the hat cam got it. He would finish the Carlos clip this morning, then post it around the web. High chance of going viral. If the money flowed, he would send it to Carlos. *Something for little Juanita's college, bro, what chu tink 'bout dat?*

Then he would open the El video, see what he had. It wouldn't be the dreamscape in his mind. It would fade the dreamscape into truth. Which was right. Let it fade, but slow and kind. Get *Little Jenny Dow* by Bill Frisell on the speakers, strong and loud, put on the video, no dialogue at first, get across the room, watch it play on a loop with his eyes half open, through an eyelash screen. Then slowly trim Frisell and amp the dialogue, hear their conversation, slowly open his eyes, let reality emerge. There were no hands in his heart, was the thing. A stump-armed heart, cut off sometime before the fourth grade, so he bumped the world and could not touch it. So turn Frisell down slowly, slowly swell the dialogue, hear what he coldly said, what she said sweetly. See if fingers would emerge from the stumps.

9

The sun was low, and a rosy light spread across the grassland and vineyards. The entire crew had gone cage by cage through the feeding and cleaning, three making notes while El and Bluey worked. The squeeze walls moved the animals to the side while they raked for dung, filled water containers, opened the feed doors to leave precise quantities of pellets, biscuits, fruit, hay, thawed chicken and mice, or slab meat. Later, there would be prescribed days of fasting for some of the animals, all designated on a laminated schedule taped on the freezers. When they were done, the carts were stowed in the rear tandem in slots beside the feed bins.

They took a break. Annie said dinner would be ready in an hour. Roger and Dawson went to their vehicles while El and Bluey walked the compound, a last inspection. Bluey told her about the Hispanic guys wanting to buy the tiger. He said, "According to Haley, he emits the lost chord."

"I can't wait to hear it. Have you heard him yet?"

"Haley says it's a nighttime event."

"Did you bring that book, by the way?"

"It's in my truck."

"Well, can I borrow it, or are you gonna read it?"

Bluey said, "You read it. Tell me what you think."

"You're sure? You hesitated there—"

He said again, "You read it."

"Annie said Rosa was a Baba lover. Is that where you got the book?"

"Yes."

"Well, I'll be careful with it."

"Thanks."

"I'll look for that mast. What was the name of that village?"

"Hardeva."

"Right. So what do you think so far?"

"I think I'm lucky. We have a fine crew. How are you and Annie?"

"She's great. She told her harrowing story about the money. We laugh a good bit. She said—" She was about to mention Annie's fear that Dawson would fall in love with her, but why clutter? They stopped before the tall cage of Sibyl the African gray parrot, whose head flicked up and down, back and forth, appraising them.

"What?"

She said, "She said Dawson hates her."

Behind them, they heard a scuff, looked back. It was Dawson, ten feet away, a halo over his long hair and thin shoulders from the lowering sun.

El was stricken, but relieved she had not mentioned the love bit.

Dawson smirked. When he heard El's comment, he was in sudden pain, as if naked in a dream. He thought of turning back, but they noticed him. He said, "I don't hate her. She just currently irritates me."

Bluey felt a bolt of good will. His nephew had not mentioned the lost college fund. He said, "Well, she's irritated me for longer, and I still love her."

Dawson said, "I was thinking about our talk, and I had some ideas."

El said, "I'll let you guys talk. I can help Annie."

"Well, since you're here, and you're one of the honchos, I wouldn't mind getting your feedback."

This directness and use of the word honcho reminded El of Annie, and she saw in his golden outline the wraith of his mother. She said, "Come out of the sun. We can't see you." She moved to the side, ushered him to a between position so that sunlight gleamed his face.

Dawson became faintly dreamy, partly from her touch, partly from their direct attention. He gave himself to intelligence. He began enumerating—the exuberant logo, the magnetic signs for the trucks, banners for the web. He said, "We set up a photography area where kids can get their pictures taken with an animal, so they're right in the cage. We use a green screen to subtract the background. Charge a few bucks, print them right there, and off they go. They got their arms around a tiger or a bear. Sell them a frame with our logo. Plus, we can set up a live cam on the website, so people can see how things are going with their favorite animal. You could hire some SEO, which is search engine optimization, but that's expensive and any-way the best way is to get newspapers and online sites to post stories about us, which will get the web built. Plus it's not phonied up like most SEO, and it's cheap. Plus, there's cool modeling software which can model stuff in 3-D. Then you can print it on a 3-D printer. I could make all the animals and get them printed in wax, then cast in pewter or send them to China and get them cast in resin and get them painted. Or cast in bronze. I can use the actual animals we have and put their names on a base plate. And have a club for kids. If you join you get an animal, if you do something else, you get another one, like a badge for something. Maybe hook up with the boy scouts or brownies. Or just sell them in the souvenir booth. Those are my ideas so far. I'm thinking about four thousand, maybe five, leaving out the 3-D animals. That's an expensive program, but you can get the student edition for cheap. Also, I'd have to learn the software." He saw them watching him and felt suddenly inappropriate, a stranger at the wrong threshold with a cornucopia of junk.

Bluey said, "What do you think, El?"

El was drifting back from the spell of Dawson's speech, made so incisively and clearly, but with an odd irritated detachment. The thought had come that Annie was right—she could have a dalliance here. But also right about the cliff ahead. Then let him be a bright little brother.

She said, "Well, if you're going to toss out any of those ideas, I'd like to know which ones, since they all sound great to me." And she felt, to her dismay, that she had emitted a shine, an irrepressible female signal that she liked this bright boy's style.

Bluey said evenly, "I like these ideas. The money is no problem. I will give full license and a credit card when you need it. But step by step so I can see you can do it, and so we can think it through. Where to start? How about the logo? When can you have something to look at?" He already had an agency working on that, but they were backed up and it would be a few weeks before they had art to review. If he could get something good from Dawson, he would cancel, pay a fee if he had to. Give it all to this fellow, if he could perform. If he couldn't, then woe betide, a wounded spirit loosed among them.

Dawson could feel his pulse throbbing in his neck. He blinked emphatically several times. He said, "I can get you a glimpse by the morning. I can do the first letter of the logo at least. Maybe the whole thing. The printing is simple, just email the file and pick it up."

"Get some sleep though. We have to drive tomorrow."

"I will." He walked away toward the van.

Bluey said, "Dawson."

Dawson stopped, turned.

"I appreciate it."

"Okay." He moved off.

"Bye," said El. She had made her tone formal, which felt stupidly cruel. She watched his slender form move across the bronze sky, repented again the flirt she had emitted. In case he fell in love with her, she would train him to friendship. She said, "Pretty good ideas. Are they new?"

Bluey raised his eyebrows. He was in contact with several charter school consortia, and he and the national director of the Boy Scouts had discussed a badge earning system for the ecopark. Also, his advertising agency had proposed a web cam. But he said, "Some, but it's all new for him, and he thought of it in a few hours. But, in general, what do you think? About our setup. What to do?"

"Bluey, it works. The systems are right, up and down fast, a place for everything. I know you're not wanting a load of praise here, but just in case there's some little guy in there waiting for appreciation, then I hereby bestow it."

"The little guy is dancing."

"I was thinking, by the way, about a skit. You know, shout, come one come all and get a little crowd. I was thinking, well, we have Sybil, and then I saw Annie in her head scarf looking like a pirate, so I thought, a pirate skit with a parrot. We'll get Sybil to say something piratey—"

"You will get Sybil to speak?"

"Well, it's worth a try. God, Bluey, I really feel happy. See how the sun hits the enclosures? Like gold plate. I need to keep my camera with me, that's one thing. That zoo cam is a good idea. Thank you, thank you." Then she stepped forward and put her arms around his solid width. She said to his chest, "You can be our gorilla, since we don't have one."

He patted her back, and they released, both turning toward the last of the sun. But there was more in her that wanted expression. She laughed out a gust of joy, then turned quickly to hammer him solidly on the sternum, crying, as she hammered one two three times, "Good, good, good!"

"Ow," he said.

•

As they ate, they emitted a chorus of compliments on Annie's concoction, spaghetti from jars but with a sausage meatball kicker. Also salad and oven toasted garlic bread.

Annie said, "I have no idea how much food to cook. We have three skinny ones and two king-sized ones, and I'll just have to learn. So I just made a lot this time. Also, I have decided there will be one day of fasting. Complete fasting, to give me a break. I'll make coffee, but that's it. Just kidding. Roger, you looked worried."

"I *was* worried." He was working through a football sized mound of pasta and sauce.

They were seated at the settee, Bluey at the end on a folding chair. Patti and Goose lay together between the front seats, heads on paws, watching. Bluey gave a short talk, the day's summation, first promising not to bring work into the meals in future, ladies, then remarking on what they had learned, tomorrow's schedule and destination, and ending with a short catalog of Dawson's ideas. Annie beamed.

When they were finished, Roger and Annie took the first stint at washing up. Dawson, Bluey, and El descended the steps of the RV. A carpet of sharp stars had emerged in the dry air, and a fat moon sat the horizon. With one mind they moved away from the RV into the thicker dark. The zoo was quiet now, without chittering, chuffing, or sounds of movement. A moment later, the glowing belt of galaxy emerged above them.

Dawson said, *so long*, and moved off toward his van, waving his hand to acknowledge their good nights. He had thought to make a more sociable comment, mention the stars maybe, but resisted—small talk was false—and so ended with his familiar bluntness. It was abrupt, but the urge to correct it was embarrassing, and besides he was walking off.

The stars were amazingly dense. You could wave your hand through them. Light years old light. What did Einstein figure out? Supposedly hard to understand. But if it was true, it had to be simple, and everything built from that. If you could be super tiny and walk around in the atoms and electrons, you would say, I get this. Or if you could be a giant and span the universe with your arms spread, you would say, damn, this light is slow. A million years to go between fingertips. Hubba hubba, light. It's zippy for the tiny people on the planets, but for me it's like molasses dripping through space. What God would say. He should note that somewhere, then forgot as he entered the van and opened his laptop to inspect his logo, which he had worked on an hour before dinner and which was getting there fast and sweet.

•

Bluey and El stood for a moment in silence. It had been dark for an hour, and the tiger had not begun to purr. They could see its faint form erect in its cage, facing them.

El said, "I'm gonna bug you about that book again."

Bluey felt the request like a sting. He said, "Sure." They started toward the flatbed. He had not opened the book, and now this energetic child would read it before he did. His reticence had left him outside something.

He cranked open the door, retrieved the book from the front seat, handed it to her.

"Were you reading it?" she said. "It was right on the seat. Because I can—"

"No, I just had it handy."

El said, "I will be very careful with this book. I will know where it is at all times."

They talked for a moment about the schedule. Tomorrow would be a long day of driving, then the set-up.

El said, "You think Bhajan will purr?"

"I've been listening."

"Me too. See you in the morning."

As he watched her slender form slip away in the starlight, he felt the book moving with her, and some elastic band in his heart stretching, unable to release.

El met Roger walking along the perimeter of the zoo in the dark. His head was down.

"Hey, Roger."

"Hey. Didn't see you." They stopped between the guanacos and the Somali wild ass. He said, "You walk like a panther." Pumper and Nickel came to the front of their enclosure, listened placidly, chewing. Charlie woke from a drowse, flicked his ears, and ignored them.

She said, "Well, first day impressions. How do you like your new job? Since your mom's not here to ask you."

"It's my dream job, Mother."

"Really?"

"You know what would make this a good job?"

"What?"

"If it turned out I liked animals."

"Is that a deep comment? Like, do I like myself? To quote Dawson."

"I was watching you guys during the feeding. You guys like animals. And I was thinking, maybe there's a chance for me too. Gosh."

El laughed. "You *are* a dumbass jock." She felt something heavy under his lightness. A full moon was rising, and she tried to make out his expression, but they were facing away from it, and the starlight was faint on his face. She had not wanted conversation, wanted to get to the RV and open the book, which she was holding double-armed against her chest. But something in him drew her. She said, "Here's what Bluey says. You don't start by loving animals. You start by recognizing them.

That's a big theme with him, in case you ever want to know what his big themes are."

"Which means what?"

"I see you want a free education." She lightly backhanded his chest, more to connect than frisk. He waited. She said, "It means they're in us. In biology, they have this thing called recapitulation theory, which everyone argues about because the Nazis used it, but essentially it means that higher forms of life were built from lower forms, and their embryos show that—for instance, human embryos have gill slits at one stage. So they have this theory in the social sciences too, which the Nazis used to be good racists. Anyway, I'm going off. But it's just that, when you feel an animal, when you recognize it and feel it, it's because you have that in you too, the psyche evolved like the body and animals are a deep layer in us. Sometimes, not so deep. Like in war, or just in bickering. That makes it sounds just negative, which it's not. It's basal, is the main thing." She spoke prosaically—"*The basal layer of consciousness from which the higher layers emerge and on which they are invisibly rooted.* A line from my class notes. So when Dawson said that, about liking animals and liking yourself, that was right. He's super bright, by the way."

"I thought you just met him."

"He has his IQ tattooed on his wrist. It's too dark to see if my jokes are getting through."

"Ha ha."

"That's better. No, he came up with all this stuff—you heard Bluey going on. I was there. He's just got this smart kid way of talking, you can tell. Annie says he can really draw, too, so we'll see. Also, she says he's brilliant and mothers never lie."

"Ha ha."

"Now we're working together." She rapped his chest again. "Roger, I'm getting moody signals, and I never want to leave a moody guy, but I need to get going. Are you moody?"

"Not really. I'm just getting used to where I am."

"Out here under the stars with your long lost cousin."

"Planet earth."

She said, "In case you're moody, here's a hug." She held the book aside and embraced him with one arm. He patted her back. They released. She said, "I'm not going to tell Bluey about your criminal past, by the way. Maybe later. Or you can tell him sometime."

"Okay."

"Good night. See you in the morning."

"See you."

She watched him move off toward his truck, slightly hunched, as if against rain. She could have asked if he wanted to play cards or something, in the RV, with Annie, a cheery session of fellow feeling. She didn't have any cards though. And she would have been distracted, with the mast book lying there waiting. Which Bluey had never read. She headed for the RV, passed the tiger cage, felt Bhajan's quiet attention. He had eaten his chicken in four or five bites. She would come out before bed, see if he actually did purr.

Annie was sitting at the settee smoking her electronic cigarette when El entered. "Hallo, mate," she said, putting on a heavy Australian accent. "Just having a toke. Harmless, they say. I mean for second hand smoke. Been reading?"

El put the book on the table. "No, I got this from Bluey. Remember I told you about the tiger and the mast? This is the book."

Annie held the book, looked at the cover, but did not open it. "Rosa gave this to Bluey?"

"Right."

"I stayed with her for a month at the end. Then Bluey took a sabbatical to be with her, and I said my goodbyes. She gave me a book too. The *Discourses* by Baba."

"Did you read it?"

A look of impatience flashed across Annie's face. "I read it to her. She would say, read the about the qualifications of the aspirant, I think you would like that one. Basically it was a way to get me to read the book. I was caring for her body, and she was caring for my soul." She tossed her head, looked away an irked expression. After the cleanup with Roger, Annie had fallen into a sulk, alone in an RV, burdened with chores, among strangers, no TV, no man, nothing but a cookbook to read, nothing coming up. She did not want conversation, unless it was about how exactly and precisely you could set sail for a fun future of greener pastures.

El said, “So who was Meher Baba?”

“Basically he was a guru, the king of the gurus, according to him. He was Jesus Christ come again, and Krishna, and Buddha, and everyone. Mohammed too. The avatar. So that's a bump in the road, isn't it? A wall really. You have to get over that wall, the I-am-god wall. But if you're just shopping around in the smorgasbord of spirituality, I have to say, the *Discourses* are pretty good. Except for that wall. The warden comes out to meet you and says, you ready to come in here and hear the gate clank? That's what I told Rosa, I didn't want to hear that clank.”

“And what did she say?”

“She laughed. Look I can hardly bear to hold a conversation right now. It’s like summer camp, and I'm homesick, except I don't have one. You're gonna get pretty tired of me. I'm gonna go for a stroll.” She rose, moved toward the door, then turned. “You know why people hate religion, even if they're religious, they hate it, secretly and for good reason. They have to leave everything at the door and deny themselves down to their very core. No more ice cream for you, you glutton. And what do you get back? Self-righteousness and a ticket to heaven. If there is a god, and you can buy your way in with that farce, then he's a gullible incompetent. For all I know you're a Mormon.”

“I'm not. Just out of curiosity though, did you tell Rosa that?”

“Yes. No, not with that force. She was dying. People soften when they die. Like babies. If there is another world it must be soft, where you go when you die and where babies come from. I'm going for a walk.” She pointed her electronic cigarette at El like a wand, started to speak again. Then her face clutched, and she turned, opened the door, and rapidly descended the steps.

Annie inhaled the cool night air. El's calm curiosity, so far unstained by prejudice or experience, was purity really, and had clanged against her irascibility. She had not wanted to talk, but had talked anyway. There was something about the girl that received her, something she could pour herself into, like a wide bowl. She flashed that she could lie naked with El, and kiss her, which she had never done with a woman. But she could with that young girl, hold her and pour herself into the deep bowl of El. Be Dawson's rival. Had she brought Dawson up with El for that, her sneaky snake mind using Dawson to worm toward sex? No, that was mother love. She had lost his money, permitted it anyway, black black. But people got over being betrayed, or else no one could stand anyone.

She snapped the cap onto her cigarette, stowed it in her jeans. She would stroll around the zoo, murmur to the animals like her brother.

She crossed through the stockade gap, then crossed past the dark tiger to the entry gate with its arch and umbrellaed booth. Which was her station. The smiling ticket lady. She entered the booth. She smiled and sold a ticket to an imaginary man. She could say, rescue me, sir! They have kidnapped me!

She left the booth to stroll. Ballyhoo the binturong was in his little wooden cabin. Dark in dark. Quanna the bonobo was a black hump of fur in her cage's corner. She had seen a documentary about bonobos, knew they loved sex, sex as release, sex as truce. Across the stockade, she could see the lights in Bluey and Roger's cabs. Roger and she had done the clean-up together, he the dishes, she the gathering and drying. Twice he had bumped his head on the air conditioner. A polite, well-coached football playing giant. She had not bothered to engage him, and he had not bothered either, beyond, *I like your accent.* What did he see, an older gal? No, his boss's sister. She could flirt him into bed. Pass the time like bonobos. Bonobo sex was idle and exterior though, not like sex with El would be, sweet and deep and pouring out. She glanced toward the RV, but her view was blocked by the big tiger cage. She could see the tiger on his haunches in the starlight. Was he looking at her? She crossed the grass, stood before him. He was looking straight at her.

She said, "Hummmm, hummm. I'm not edible. I'm friendly."

Then she heard a deep drone, which for an instant she thought was an airplane, then realized it was coming from the tiger, who had begun to purr.

•

El had seated herself at the settee with the book before her. When Annie left the RV, El had the urge to accompany her. They could walk somewhere, let Annie walk beside her, ease her fire in a friend's cool cloud. Annie had been suddenly hot about religion. A wound there? Or just loneliness. She had left abruptly, not permitting an offer, and El experienced reluctant relief. She had the book in front of her now, after two weeks of wanting. The cover showed Meher Baba in middle age with his arm around a dark slender man, a mast probably.

She felt a surge of depression, and Howie Barnard popped into her mind. Howie had been her first lay, how she had mooned for him, hours of that, and then finally in his father's car, she had opened her treasure, and he had entered and finished, and she had been instantly depressed, not floating on romance but crashed on it, unable even to blame Howie, a simplehearted beast following his nature. She had broken up with him a week later, which crushed him, too bad, and learned a lesson, don't build things up in your head. Now here was this book, built up in her head, with a tiger and a mast and Haley's story and Howie Barnard popping up.

She had a thought then, actually glanced around the room looking for a broomstick, thinking, she could open the book with a broomstick from four feet away. She opened the book to page 261, where there was a two inch column of text under the heading *Description.* There were other headings, *Place, Map Ref., Known as, Date of Contact.* She read, "A very high mast in a majzoob-like state, between the sixth plane and the seventh. For twenty-five years, Nanga Baba sat in a squatting position, quite naked, on a hilltop." Then stuff about the village where he lived, naked in the rain and snow, eating a mixture of wood, stone, and dry bread prepared by the villagers. Then read, "A short while after Baba and his men had reached there, they were sitting before Nanga Baba, and the latter, pointing to Baba, said, 'He is my elder brother; he adjusts and protects the whole world.'"

She thumbed through more pages, read bits and pieces—

"An advanced pilgrim, aged eighteen, who had been, Baba explained, a yogi in a past life."

"A bearded man, looking like a Muslim, who stood smartly to attention when Baba and his party of mandali passed by in their bus. Baba pointed him out as the spiritual chargeman of Aligarh."

"Shanti Bai, a good mastani, much revered, who keeps five or six dogs always about her...like all masts and mastanis who keep dogs about them, she feeds these dogs before she herself eats."

There were photographs too, of raggedy men and women in the streets and countryside of India, sometimes being embraced by a beaming Baba, sometimes staring dazedly into the camera.

She closed the book, suddenly impatient. She thought of Annie's impatience and the prison wall, but this was not that. This was like reading the history of another race on another planet in another galaxy when what you wanted was information about your own people and your own being. Which was what Annie was feeling after all, what everyone felt when they looked into spirituality—a room of golden visions, then a door in the face. Not for you, dear. For you, corn flakes, talk, and church on Sundays.

She held the book between her hands, squeezed it tightly. She thought, either crush it out of existence or absorb it, refuse it or be transformed. Human beings were only where they were, sealed off from whatever these masts saw. It came to her then, that moment, that she *did* think the masts saw something, and that the book was not a trick. If it was an account of life on a distant planet, at least, she thought, I don't doubt the planet, or the life. She moved her hands slowly and purposefully apart. She felt the book slide coolly across her palms, then fingers, then come to rest on the table. And when she heard the faint *clump* as it fell from her fingertips, she felt calm come like a presence. Something in her became resistless, and she let the presence be. She thought, well, this is probably God.

Something in her came up to meet the presence, and she thought, *it's Pearl, my childhood fairy, and you came back, with your joy and love.* Her eyes overflowed. Two cool tears raced down to tickle her chin.

Then the presence was gone, like a mirage blinking off. She tried to think it back, but that was like gripping air. Where the presence had been there was now an ache, a hole in her heart like the one Packer made, only a good hole. Which was how it worked. God made a hole in you so he could poke through. It was simple and ordinary. You waited by the hole, and trusted by the hole. Go within, they said, and that was right. Into love.

She put her hands gently over the book, and a sigh quivered from her breast. Her cheeks were cold, and she stroked the tears away with her palms. She had had a spiritual experience. Joy and love erupting up and out, joy and love, just so.

She said, "Oh, oh," to hear her voice, the voice of El Chastain, in an RV, traveling zoo, planet earth. She looked at the photo on the book cover, Meher Baba and the mast. Was he that? The king of the gurus? And if he was, then what? He had come and gone. She sighed again, expressing still some remnant of joy. She drew her fingers across her eyes, wiped them on her shirt. She felt a surge of sudden restlessness. She wanted to get near Annie, get a dose of exasperation.

As she slid from the booth, the RV door opened, and Annie poked her head in. She said, "That tiger's purring up a storm."

10

Dawson completed the word *exotic* in the logo in an hour and a half. The shading was still crude, but from three feet away looked excellent. He had the meerkat and peacock bending down, peering through the *e* and *c*, and had spider monkey tail-hanging from the cross of the *t*, a dance of color and cheer. He had gotten the animal images from the net, then tweaked them into high texture cartoons in Photoshop. He thought of heading for Bluey's truck with the laptop, but no, immature, so he started on *animal*, thinking, maybe the sun bear with its legs crossed, sitting on the *m*, hardly see the *m*, sitting up like a person, and it's got the parrot on its shoulder. And maybe the okapi poking its long neck up behind and angled out, a single central group, for contrast with the spread out *exotic*.

He started the browser to get some sun bear images when he saw shadows moving on the road, looked up, and saw a group of figures walking past on the road, headed for the caravan perimeter. They were dark against dark, six or eight of them, walking fast, no talk. He closed his computer, switched off the side sconce. They faded into the dark, and he felt a sudden clutch. He had parked his van twenty yards off the road and about fifty yards from the other vehicles and the zoo, a place to concentrate. He was closest to the tandem, Roger's house, and maybe he should go over and alert the bouncer, which is how he thought of Roger. Maybe childish though. But what if it was some sort of thugs? Stupid was worse than childish. He got up, eased open his side door. He listened. Nothing. He got out his phone, dialed 911, put his thumb on *send* to be ready, and trotted the fifty yards across the long grass to the tandem. There was a faint light glowing from the window of the living compartment. He jumped up and gave it a couple of fast raps. In a moment, the silhouette of Roger's head blocked the light.

"Who's that?" said the bouncer.

"Dawson. I just saw some guys coming up here, a bunch of them. So—" He made a face. Yeah, probably childish.

"So maybe they mean us harm?"

He pushed through, fuck it. "Maybe."

"Stay there." Roger's head disappeared and ten seconds later he opened the truck door and descended. He was wearing boxer shorts and a t-shirt, barefooted. He reached behind the seat and extracted a two foot truck iron. He said, "All right. Let's go get'em."

Dawson snorted. This bouncer wasn't bad. "I have no idea where they are though. They just scooted past my van. I'm out on the road there."

"Let's go see Bluey, see what's up."

"Okay."

They crossed the grass toward the flatbed, a hundred feet away. Halfway there, they heard voices in mild conversation. Roger lifted the truck iron above his head and threw it hard down into the grass where it stuck with a thump. "Try not to fall on that," he said. Dawson was starting a blush when Roger the bouncer clapped him on the back and said, "Let's go to the meeting."

In the light from Bluey's cab window they saw Bluey in a white T-shirt and jeans and several men in a circle, talking. They stopped outside the circle, and when the talking stopped to acknowledge them, Roger said, "Hey, dudes. Me and Dawson are out riding the fences." And Dawson felt, this bouncer is unexpectedly cool. Big all his life.

"Hey, guys," said Bluey. "We're having a confab about the new tiger. Seems like these guys love to hear him purr, and he's purring, if you listen. Which is unusual, since tigers are not known to purr. They chuff and roar but don't purr." The visitors nodded, partly at acknowledgment of this kindly discourse, partly to signal they were not off put by Bluey's reinforcements. It was Haley and his crew of Latinos. Bluey said,

"These guys want to park for the night beside the tiger, as I understand it. I see you brought your blankets with you. Seems like you'll get dewed on though."

Haley said, "Well, we might. That's all right."

"You plan to stay all night?"

"If you don't mind. We'll be quiet as a mouse."

"Okay. But this is strange, Tom."

Haley chuckled. "I know it."

Bluey said, "Well, a tiger purring is strange too. You guys go get comfortable. I'll be out in a minute. I think I have some plastic to cover you with."

"We don't want to be any trouble."

"No trouble."

Haley and his crew slushed off through the grass.

Bluey said, "Roger, do one thing. There's roll of plastic in—"

"I saw it. I'll get it."

"I appreciate it."

"This dude here got me out of bed, said we were under attack." He nudged Dawson with his elbow.

Dawson completed the blush he had started earlier. He said, "These guys want to stay up all night to listen to the tiger purr?"

Bluey said, "It seems they do. I'll get dressed. I was about the make the last rounds."

"I'll get the plastic," said Roger.

Bluey vanished inside his cab house. Roger trudged back through the grass, and Dawson saw him jerk the truck iron from the sod. Then he became aware of the low drone from the tiger, like a faraway engine. He headed toward the zoo, walking softly, listening. Those guys must be thinking, a purring tiger is rare, therefore we must listen. Like that guy he came across an hour ago on the net who ate a car piece by piece and had millions of hits, since few eat cars.

He entered the stockade and moved quietly with don't-wake-the-animals consideration between two big cages. On his left, something made a fast pained sound and banged the zoo link. Dawson darted sideways. His elbow struck the corner of a cage and flashed pain. "Fuck!" Something in the banged-into cage thumped, and zoo link rattled.

Dawson said, "Damn, guys." He rubbed his elbow. It hurt massively, right on the bone. He crossed the grass toward the tiger cage. The Latinos and Haley had settled in a semi-circle on their blankets. The pain in his elbow drained as he neared the cage, and when he stood behind the men, the pain had faded to forgotten. He could see the giant form of the tiger, crested with silver from the fat low moon, sitting up on his haunches, ears erect, facing away from him and the seated men. The purring droned, quite loud now, oddly loud, amplified almost, with hardly a pause between inhalations and exhalations.

Dawson thought, why did they sit behind the tiger? Why not on the other side where they could see him from the front, with moonlight. He thought to go around the cage, get a good look at the tiger's face, see if his mouth was open, but then the tiger rose, still purring, turned, and settled again on its haunches, now facing Dawson and the semi-circle of men, his head lowered beneath the moon. The Latinos murmured appreciatively. The tiger lifted his head, and the purr rose clear and emphatic. The whiskers and ears and massive head blocked the moon, and a silver halo shimmered, so that Dawson saw a vision of sudden glory and moving splendor. The tiger's head lowered, and the vision was gone. Dawson's mouth opened. He sat down, then laid down on the grass. He closed his eyes, tried to print the vision in memory. He could use it. That could be a graphic for the zoo. He knew a paint program he could use. Or learn to paint with paint. No wonder people liked to paint. The grass was soft and sweet-smelling, and he grew groggy, lying on the soft, sweet-smelling grass, the purr buzzing like a massive bee, zooming around inside him, spreading nectar, a friendly bee. He fell asleep.

•

Roger slid the truck iron back behind the driver's seat, hoisted himself into the cab, then crouched through to his bedroom. He had unpacked his clothes into the little cupboards, everything tidy and folded, even the socks, and he planned to keep it that way, sleep in an orderly room for once in his life, drive the truck, unload and feed animals, shovel shit, run with feed bags, be dedicated. He needed something for his arms and chest though. Pushups and chinups for a start, but for bulk he needed weights. Maybe get Dawson to hit a sporting goods store. That was a pretty good kid, took his teasing, stood his ground. He would have skittered like a mouse in a high school hallway though.

When Dawson rapped on his window, Roger was into an email to a girl in Oklahoma, who was attractive from her pic on the dating site. How did you know it was really her, of course, or if it was a pic she got somewhere on the web, and she's fooling around. But he blocked suspicion. He had opened his cab's side windows and heard the purr's drone, but didn't know what it was until Bluey told them. He had sailed into personal revealment, letting her hear about his checkered past and his hopes for the future and his present job of hauling wild animals. He had no idea he could express himself so easily, his actual self, what he was feeling and hoping. He told about his breakup with Sue Chen and his being cut from the pros and his lack of football fire, which he planned to get to the bottom of and correct and be stronger in body and mind. He said he knew he was being personal maybe too early, and *so sorry if it was too much, but in case it wasn't, in case you might be needing to get interested in someone, then this is the guy you'd be interested in. I think I'm being personal to be nice, so you'll know who I am.*

Now he tapped the space bar on his laptop to wake it and reread his entry while he slipped on his jeans and shoes. He got fast back into the mood, tied one shoe, and then started typing again—*Well, I have to go. I have to get a roll of plastic for some guys. Our tiger is purring and people have come to listen, which is odd, that he purrs and that they want to listen. I had to get dressed again. Who knows, I could be writing to my future wife! Don't worry, I'm joking. But it's true, also. Or I might never hear from you again, oh well."* He almost stopped, feeling pressed to get going, then added—*"You're really pretty from your pic, and what I liked is you're only giving out a half smile, sort of a let's-just-see-what-happens smile, which I liked. I think that's what sparked me and made me write to you. See you.*

He reread. He was fairly pleased. Possibly his email was too out there, but if he were this girl in Oklahoma and got this letter, he would email it to his best friend, say, *read this, you won't believe it.* And the friend would say, *Dori*—her name was Doris Statemen—*what a catch.*

He got the cursor over send, then bent down to tie his other tennis shoe. His heart hammered. He finished tying the shoe, put his finger over the mouse pad, thinking, like a bombardier ready to drop, change things forever. He hesitated, felt the silence in the little cab begin to pulse, heard the faint drone of the tiger. He had to get that plastic. He circled his finger over the mouse pad like a miniature hawk, looking for signs. He double-tapped.

•

As Annie and El approached the tiger cage, they saw Haley and the Latinos sitting on spread blankets in a half circle, one of the group behind and lying in the shadows face up on the grass. The tiger faced away from them, erect in the moonlight, mouth slightly open, the purr around him like a cloud of sound. Haley rose when he saw them and came forward.

He spoke in a half-whisper. "We talked to Bluey, got his okay to pay our last respects, so to speak. Hope we won't be disturbing you."

El said, "No, it's fine. You're right, he really purrs. So loud."

She couldn't see Haley's face well, but could see his form, cupped forward in the shadows like a man restraining a hug. She wanted to question him. What was their fascination with the purr, all these guys, like pilgrims? And also ask about the mast he had seen in India, get his name or description, try to find him in the book. But she hesitated, couldn't select a thought. The purr drummed at her, and there was something odd, what?

Now Haley was bowing away, saying, "We're just going to miss this tiger. We won't make a peep." She caught the gleam of his soft smile as he made a hush hush down-patting motion with his hands, retreating five yards all the way back to his spot in the semi-circle, then turned to Bhajan and sat down.

He hadn't limped, that was the oddness. He had sprung up and made two fast steps to meet them, no limp. She waved her hand, a slack salute, farewell, Haley. She would have liked him in a bright room, clear questions, the mast, the tiger, the limp even, but the desire vagued away. She was aware of the purr thrumming in her, delicate as a child's hands.

Annie and El sat together on the other side of the cage. The tiger faced them, erect on its haunches. They could hear the purr full and deep and loud, hardly changing tones, inbreath and out, emerging from the tiger's center chest or throat or behind his chest or in their chests or between them or behind them. They stretched their legs, arms back, basking while the tiger watched. They glanced at each other and their faces opened with laughter, like girls.

•

Bluey pulled his socks on, slipped into his pull-on boots. His interview with Haley and his workmen had left him uneasy. Something off there. Had Haley and his hombres formed some scheme to steal the tiger back, for Christ's sake? Haley had talked about the lost chord. Now he arrives with a crowd. Well, they couldn't get a fork lift in without waking everyone. If they planned to lead the tiger away, they could get somebody killed.

He stood, his mouth open, thinking. How had he followed worry so far? Unlike him. That had been Rosa's playful complaint, that he could not empathize with her worries since he did not worry. Untrue though. He worried, but quickly, then planned, a quality that had made him successful and even before his inheritance, fairly wealthy. He needed to concentrate on the project. He needed sleep. They weren't ready for the public. Though he had anticipated and accepted this unreadiness, it bothered him. It was not the planning or equipment. He had had months to think out systems, supervise construction, rethink. In zoos, it was almost always keeper error that brought trouble. A cage uncleaned, or god forbid, left open. An injury or illness unnoticed, an animal improperly fed or unfed or injured by the fork lift or unsecured in the trucks. Something left undone, something to come unraveled. The crew, thrown together more by fate than selection, were indispensable, irreplaceable, and untrained, all weaknesses. He was like a general cornered into battle with recruits. But hadn't that always been the plan, a weakness inevitable but momentary? So why this fret and clutch? Unlike him, and bad in a keeper, since it would be absorbed by the animals, and by the crew too. So accept imperfection, buckle your belt (he buckled it), stick on your safari hat (he stuck it on), slip on the treat jacket (he slipped into his pellet-and-seed-filled treat jacket), and make the rounds.

He unplugged his rechargeable lantern and slipped it into a pocket, then slid from the sleeping compartment into the driver's seat. The stockade blocked his view, and he could see only the top section of the tiger's cage, its stainless steel gleaming in the moonlight.

A wave of nausea swept through him, and he needed an expulsion of breath to fight it. He inhaled, and again needed to blow his breath hard out. He cranked open the door, wanting motion, and as he swung out on the handrail to descend the steps heard something swish in the grass beneath his boot. A shadowed figure moved under the cab.

He said, "Ho, Goose."

There was no response. Before placing his foot down, he thumbed on the lantern and inspected the grass. Nothing. He stepped down, then directed the lantern's mirror under the truck. Staring unblinking into the light, unmoving, her belly on the grass, was Patti, Annie's dog. She had been just outside his door, under the steps. She continued to gaze into the light without blinking or moving, without response. He put his left hand in front of the lantern so the dog could see it, swept it twice, made a *shhh shhh* sound. Patti rose with slow mechanical precision, turned, and padded away into the dark.

His nausea dissipated. He became aware of the tiger's smooth drone. He pushed the flatbed's door closed, crossed through the stockade gap between Cloe and Demijohn, both at the front of their cages, the lion haunch down, the okapi head up and alert, both facing the tiger. Ahead of him, he saw Roger slouching toward the tiger, a dark burden across his shoulder, the plastic, no doubt. Had he thought to bring scissors? Bluey blew out his breath, expelling worry. Across the dark grass he saw the semi-circle of visitors, their blankets bundled behind them, or was one of them lying down—

He stopped, watched Roger approach the visitors, then began his rounds with Demijohn. The lion swung his head away from the lantern light, then swung it back, blinking. He cocked his head to one side, then the other, again, and again, slowly rocking it, like someone at the edge of a dance floor.

Bluey began with the smooth incantation he used with animals. "Ho, Demijohn, old friend, you are a great fine beast, and I am pleased with you." He removed a carnivore pellet from his jacket, tapped it through the zoo link. It thumped on the metal floor. Demijohn continued to rock his head in the glow, ominous in the upward light, moving gracefully. He ignored the pellet, and also ignored Bluey. "All right, dear Demijohn, may you pass a night of restful sleep, and I will see you in the mañana." He would have given him a couplet from Shakespeare, or the lovely word music from Fern Hill which he had recently memorized, but the lion was elsewhere.

Next was Nubia, the hyena, up on his haunches, alert. Nubia swung his head to the light, swung it back, became still again.

Bluey said, "A tasty pellet for you, Nubia, to top off your evening meal." He pushed the pellet through the wire, saw it fall unnoticed between the hyena's paws. "You too, my friend, are distracted? You have heard a purr in the dark. It's our new companion, Bhajan the tiger, safely kept, I promise you, under the dingle starry, as poet Thomas says. I am not wanted? I bid you good evening, dear Nubia. Eat your pellet when you may."

Then Clark, the puma, up on his haunches, then Lobo, the dhole, on his haunches too, then Bump, the sun bear, Paris, the Siberian lynx, Alfie, the African wild dog, on his haunches, but also, with his forepaws aloft and held against the zoo link, and then Kip, the caracal, on his haunches. All alert, all facing the tiger cage, listening.

Next came the tandem animals, the honey badger (Toohey), the raccoon (Chortle), the mandrill baboon (Thane), the binturong (Ballyhoo), the bonobo (Quanna), the guenon (Taj), the spider monkey (Shindig), the meerkat (Oz), the African gray parrot, (Sibyl), the peacock, (Spectra), the ostrich, (Bart), the bharal (Phoenix), the guanacos (Pumper and Nickel), the wild ass (Charlie), the okapi (Cloe).

All were at the front of their cages, even the binturong, out of its night enclosure, and Sibyl the parrot, clinging to her zoo link by beak and talon, unmoving. The pellets and seeds fell ignored on the cage floors. Bluey had ceased his incantation. He moved from cage to cage, automatically noting fur, eyes, noses, bedding, water, dung, and always behind him the mellow drone of the tiger, even and clear and penetrating. A memory woke and floated clear and bright, himself alone in the bush, sitting above Lake Matilda, the cattle spoked about him, their broad noses swaying, his face wet from tongues, some fundament in himself abiding with welcome.

He closed his eyes, willed urgency to calm so that an explanation might rise. Here was a tiger purring, which was unnatural. Here were beasts unnaturally mesmerized. He inhaled, expelled breath luxuriantly until his chest was empty, waited in the droning silence. No thought rose. He ran his hands over his short white hair, laced them together behind his neck. Something was hidden. He would wait and watch.

He turned to the tiger cage. The tiger was lying on his belly, parallel to the cage, paws outstretched, head erect. El and Annie sat cross-legged on the grass in front of him. They smiled up at Bluey as he approached.

El said, "How's everybody?"

"They're listening to the tiger, just like you guys. In fact, they're all at the front of their cages, and none of them were interested in treats."

"Poor baby," said Annie. He had squatted beside Annie, bushman style, and Annie leaned forward and kissed his knee.

El stood. She said, "I'll be back." She walked to the zoo perimeter and begin a fast tour.

Annie tugged at his cuff. "Sit with us." She moved over, spread her hands over the grass. "Right here in this nice spot which I have warmed for you."

Bluey remained in his squat. "I have some emails."

"Did you see those guys on the other side there?"

"They stopped by my truck to ask permission."

"Should I feed them?"

"No. They brought coffee."

"El informs me the tiger is a member of the class Panthera and does not purr. As a rule. Because the hyoid bone in their throat is only partially ossified. You have educated this girl well."

"They used to divide cats into purrers and roarers. And that's right, we thought it was the hyoid bone. But that's an open issue again."

El returned, collapsed into a cross-legged position beside Bluey. Her rag doll agility sent a shiver of delight through Annie.

El said, "My god, this is sort of spectacular. The whole zoo is hypnotized. And us too. It's like sun bathing or something. We've been purr bathing." She had been experiencing the odd sensation of being twin selves, her inside spirit self and her front self. When Annie appeared at the RV door, excited about the purr, they went out to hear it, and it was loud and constant and made thinking hard, like talking in a wind, so she had chatted, been blithe, and the twinness made her ache. It was like the TV show, *The Millionaire*, which her parents talked about, where you got a million dollars on the front lawn and went back inside the house to your life, with your parents and your bedroom, and everything's the same on the outside, but now you're a brand new person, rich and free. She had been talking to Annie, telling what she remembered about the mechanism of purring, and that was her outside person, the chatty, make-a-nice-impression person, while her inside person had an armful of money, which is this case was divinity, a handful at least, or a pinch, which was enough, since it was the secret substance. You didn't get your million all at once with divinity. But you located the bank.

Annie said, "El was going to tell me about NASA but couldn't remember."

Bluey said, "They've been experimenting with purring to stop bone degeneration in space. Working with various frequencies."

"Ah, I remember," said El. "Then I bet we all get very strong bones." She thought of Haley's limp. But talking was an effort.

Bluey said, "I noticed Haley's limp is better."

"I was just going to mention that." To Annie, El said, "He got bitten by a grizzly bear and had a limp. Now he doesn't limp."

Annie said, "Well, somebody should call NASA."

El said, "You know how the sound of the ocean is so soothing? I'm very soothed right now. Aren't we all soothed? So maybe it's like the sound of the ocean, some home sound. And then also maybe it heals bones as an extra good thing." She laughed. "That's all I got. Sit down, want to? You look so scrunched, you outback bloke."

Bluey smiled. He lifted one of El's hands, kissed it, lifted one of Annie's, kissed it. Their faces opened with pleasure.

"I'm going to bed. You guys should too." After the hand kissing, duty made a mild clang. He said, "We have a long drive tomorrow."

"That's true," said El.

Annie bumped his knee with her elbow. "You are correct, my captain."

Bluey rose. El was up swiftly beside him, then Annie, languidly.

El said, "We should probably say so long to Haley and his guys."

Annie squared herself to Bluey, found his eyes, embraced him briefly, then gazed soberly into his face. She said, "You are my captain. You have rescued me from a desert island."

She walked swiftly away toward the RV before he could reply. She raised her hands above her head for a moment, swung them down. She shouted, "Don't expect perfection! Goddammit!"

El said, "Family life."

Bluey and El went around the tiger cage, found the workers and Haley, and behind them, Dawson, still asleep. Roger was standing, his arms folded across his chest. Dawson lay on the grass, on his back, his mouth open in an *o*, like a baby, deeply sleeping. He was covered with a sheet of plastic. Bluey noted that behind Haley's guys Roger had stretched another sheet of plastic.

Roger jerked his chin toward them. "Hey, guys."

Bluey looked down at Dawson, then up at Roger. "Are you standing guard?"

"I guess so. I can't make up my mind whether to leave him here or wake him up."

Bluey smiled. "So you're thinking about it."

"I'm giving it a long think." Roger felt at rest and easygoing. After stretching the plastic and covering Dawson, he stood above him watching him sleep and listening to the loud tiger. He thought of returning to his cab to bed, but stayed. What to do with Dawson? He could carry him, which would embarrass him, if he woke, which he would. He could let him lie in the dew, get a cold maybe. He could wake him, but see how he was sleeping, so all gone and collapsed. So he stood with his arms folded, thinking about sleep, that it would be good to sleep like

Dawson was sleeping, deep down, all gone, touching base, as he listened to the purr and watched Dawson.

Bluey squatted and rocked Dawson's shoulder. Dawson's eyes popped open. He swept off the plastic and got swiftly to his feet. He made a sleepy stagger, and Roger clamped him, chest and back.

Bluey rose, said, "Sorry to wake you. We start early tomorrow. Long drive."

"Right. Okay. I had a dream. Hey—" His face opened with enthusiasm, then closed. He had started to mention the monkey-draped logo to Bluey, but stopped. The impulse clashed with something, the dream, the feeling in the dream. He said, "Goodnight." He walked away toward his van.

El watched his thin shoulders bob, wanted to stop him, ask about his dream. What was your dream? Let's sit in a circle and hear the dream.

Haley rose and approached. He said to Bluey, his tone warm and direct with the courage of good manners. "Thanks for plastic. I already thanked Roger here." He nodded up to Roger, standing behind Bluey and El.

Roger tipped his head, smiled no sweat.

Bluey said, "I see what you mean about this purr. It's got the whole menagerie alerted."

"Really?" Haley peered toward the perimeter. "Well. What do you make of it?"

Bluey shook his head. "Maybe it's making them edgy, big tiger in the night." He did not believe that though. Something else, still elusive. Behind him, he felt Roger move away into the dark toward the perimeter. He said, "El says maybe it's the sound of ocean, the cradle of life."

El said, "By the way, do you know that mast's name?"

"I don't recall. If I ever did know."

"I wonder if Fuad would know."

"He might. Are you wanting to google that mast? I doubt he'd be in google."

"No, it's that Bluey lent me this book. It's all about the masts of India."

"Well, I'll ask him. I'll email you what he says. I forgot you had a book. What does it say about a mast?"

Both Bluey and Haley looked at her. She hesitated, felt her eyes wet unexpectedly. Then she found her earlier thought. She said, "It's sort of like reading the history of another planet, so different from our lives." That was sensible. She felt her tears retreat. She saw she had not satisfied them, but only made a waiting half-smile.

Haley said, "What was the name of that book?"

El said, "*The Wayfarers.* By William Donkin. You can probably find it on the web."

"Thank you." Haley hesitated, seemed ready to bow away again and retreat.

El said, "I wanted to ask you, that mast in India? What was he like? What did he look like?"

"Well, he was naked. And his hair was wild. He had a beard. He was sort of short. He was old, no idea how old. His hair was white, but dirty. It had stuff in it, like bark or twigs. That's about it. I didn't get that close to him. I didn't want him to catch me with that brush. That's about it. Oh, for god's sake, he had bangles. He had all these bangles on, rusty metal, looked like, or else tarnished, if it was brass. On his arms and on his legs too. So look for a guy with lots of bangles. When was this book written?"

"Late forties."

"Well, let's see. This was a year ago, so that's what, around sixty years, so if they ran into him in the book then he'd be really old today. Hard to say how old he was though."

El said, "In the book, some of them were really old, like 120 years." She noted to herself that this statement signaled her acceptance of the book, that it was facts and not fraud. She had the impulse to correct the record, issue a writ of skepticism, but let that die. She became aware of the purr again. She looked at the tiger. He was on his haunches again, facing them, his face a blot of shadow, crowned by moonlight, delicately gorgeous. She squinted, trying to make out the direction of his gaze, but the eyes were lost in shadow. He was looking at her though, she felt that. She desired that.

Haley said, "Well, I better—"

El stopped him again. "Just one thing, what was the name of that village?"

"Hardeva."

"And where was it again? Because there's a bunch of maps in the book."

"Well, we flew into Calcutta and then drove, I believe northeast, but Fuad would know. A couple of hundred miles, I bet. The roads are bad, and you can't go fast. I'll talk to Fuad and let you know."

"That's good of you, Mr. Haley. Thanks a lot."

He offered his hand to her, and they shook. He shook with Bluey. "I will email you. I want to keep in touch, if you don't mind."

Bluey said, "Good. I'll email you back. It looks like we'll have a webcam up on the internet. So you can peek in from time to time."

"I definitely will. Good luck on your travels."

Haley raised his hand to Roger, who had appeared again behind El and Bluey. He bowed away and returned to his place among his workers.

Roger, who had been inspecting the animals, heard something about an old man with iron bangles as he approached. He had begun thinking about Dori Stateman and whether she had written back. Now he listened to his kind cousin as she included him—a village, a naked holy man with a tiger, Bluey's synchronous book. As her voice picked through the story, he felt her generosity in the sleepy night, catching him up. He wanted to wrap her in his arms and say, it doesn't matter, but let her finish, something about a book about a mast she would search for a mast in. He nodded. It was a possible Dori had already written.

Bluey said, "Let's hit the hay, guys. We'll be ten hours on the road."

They said their goodnights. El went toward the RV until they vanished, then detoured back to Bump, where she started a brief tour of the perimeter again, murmuring to the animals, *ho, Bumpy Bear, sweetheart Lobo, Clark, my main man,* then fell silent as she was ignored. She swept along the perimeter, daunted, but charmed. As she approached the last cage, the raccoon turned toward her, then turned in a full circle. As he came about to face her again, he made a quiet chitter, tossed his head, sat on his haunches, and again gazed toward the tiger cage.

She entered the RV quietly in case Annie was in bed, but Annie was coming out of the bathroom, bunching a white towel around her hair, dressed in blue satin pajamas and fuzzy blue slippers.

El said, "You look like you live here."

"Have you seen Patti? I couldn't find her. She's probably off somewhere listening to that purr. Yes, I've made myself at home with my nice pajamas and my shower."

"I haven't seen her. She'll probably come whimper at the door. I don't have nice pajamas, darn it. Or any pajamas. Can I go ahead and make my bed?"

They folded down the wall bed. It was already made up, the blankets and sheet neatly tucked and stretched over the pillow.

El said, "Oh, Annie, you made my bed." She poured Annie a fond look.

Annie said, "It's pretty comfy too, if you like firm, which I hope you do. The big bed is too. Pretty firm." And Annie thought, *I'm chattering. Next thing, I'll flirt.*

El said, "Well, thanks, that's super sweet. And look, we don't need to be switching back and forth. This is a perfect little place for me. It's right out in the main room, so I'll have to be tidy, which is good, since I tend to splat out if I get the chance."

Annie said, "Well, we'll see. I forgot to pee."

She went into the bathroom. She had already peed, but needed to breathe away flutters. She stood now looking at herself in the mirror, her hands on the sink, head cocked. She saw the towel burnoose needed a tweak, and she straightened it, made a tuck. There. She noted the faint smile creases, the deltas beside her eyes. Still attractive, even make-up-less, those proud cheekbones, sleek nose, mouth (she pursed her mouth) friendly and delicious. But fading.

She opened the spun glass louvers and looked into the dark. She felt night air drift delicate on her face and neck. The tiger was still purring. She turned to the mirror again, stared at her face. I spent my life dealing in the drug of beauty. Beneath her, she felt, was a pool of tears, but she could not immerse herself. She said to the mirror, "You will be good, Annie. This is your vow." She gave the burnoose another tuck, checked the buttons on her pajamas, looked again at the mirror. She said, "Keep on trucking." She started to open the door, then turned and flushed the toilet.

El had undressed, was sitting in the passenger seat in a long brown T-shirt, legs crossed, thumbing through a book.

Annie said, "I need a book too. I should probably read *The Joy of Cooking*, but ugh."

"Well, I have three books. I have an Elmore Leonard, *Get Shorty*, and then I have *Salt*, which is the history of salt, which my dad liked. And then I have the complete Emily Dickinson, just in case." She had left out *The Wayfarers*. That book was not part of the lending library.

"In case of what?"

"Well, in case you're in the mood. I mean with poetry, I always think, even with Emily Dickinson, you usually have to hike a ways before you come across a vista. So if you can stand a hike—"

"Hike for vistas."

"Good vistas in Emily Dickinson though."

Annie said, "I know they made the movie, *Get Shorty*. Is the book good?"

El said, "I haven't read it, but Leonard's good. A master of pace and lowlife ne'er-do-wells."

"Well, there you go," said Annie, giving her hands a flip.

El swung out of the passenger seat and moved past Annie, Annie stepping back so there would be no contact between her loins and El's compact butt. El stepped on the settee, sprang onto her bed, opened a cupboard, removed a paperback, lofted herself back onto the carpet in a silky move. She handed the book to Annie. She said, "My library is always open to you, madam."

"Great," said Annie, faintly numb with the effort to repress her attraction to this nimble bouncy sprite. "Well, good night," she said. She started toward the rear compartment, then turned. "You know what? I have to get up early tomorrow. Bluey wants me to have breakfast ready by seven. So damn, here you are sleeping in here. No, we'll just have to switch, El. I mean permanently. Because, look, I'll be banging around every morning. I'll wake you."

"No, no. When I saw you had taken your shower, I thought, okay good. She takes a shower at night. I do in the morning. I'll just get up and take my shower. I get up early anyway."

Annie said, "Really?"

"Absolutely really."

"Okay, then. Good night, sleep tight. If you hear a whimper, wake me up."

"Good night."

Annie closed her door behind her, tossed the paperback onto the bed. Her heart was beating, and she felt herself faintly quaking. Her bed-switching altruism had been deflected, fairly and simply. It had been a handhold against the wind of her attraction and had been neatly knocked away by this effortless siren. But she had thought of it, and had offered it sincerely, and had freed herself for that moment from the clutch of love. That's how you do it. You keep on trucking, old Annie. She made a bank of pillows and got into bed, looking forward to reading about rascals.

•

El washed her face, gave her hair a fast brush, brushed her teeth. She had lied about her shower time. She was a night showerer, but could not bear to turn Annie out of luxury, and the lie popped helpfully out. Well, she could shower in the morning, and if she got sticky she could wipe down. Pajamas would be good though, since then you didn't stick to yourself. She could mention pajamas to her mother and get some sent, which her mother would do in a flash, kind helpful mother, and El had not called them, which she would do tomorrow. She plugged in her phone, turned off the RV porchlight and interior lamps, then made a slope of pillows and tucked in with the mast book under the reading sconce. As she stilled and silence took hold, she became aware of the tiger's drone, faithfully underscoring the quiet. She turned on the overhead vent fan, and the purr vanished.

She found a map of India glued to the rear cover of the book, colored by hand it looked like, and without much detail, but with the names of villages and cities, some with notes and dates. A record of mast hunting. After several minutes of study, and thumbing back and forth in the book, she figured out how it worked, the first chapters given to five central masts, the five favorites they were called, and some essays about masts too, and the supplement arranged alphabetically by village and city. She studied the area around Calcutta on one of the maps for several inches. There was no mention of Hardeva, and no mention in the supplement either. Then look for a mast with iron bangles, and she began to flip around, reading here and there, mostly in the supplement, since that's where you could blaze through, one odd filthy eccentric personality after another, on this plane or that, naked or wearing seven coats, living at a train station or cemetery or public urinal, surrounded by disciples or dogs or alone, tea-drinking or chain-smoking, or not.

Finally she came across Saiyad Qadir Badshah, with only a short description—"A mahbubi mast, with bangles on his arms, who is always in a happy mood." Bangles! He was from Madras though, far south. But the clue was mahbubi. What was a mahbubi mast?

Eventually she found a chapter entitled *Spiritually Advanced Souls,* and there was the mahbubi mast, a type three mast, who was feminine and sometimes wore a few bangles. They were fairly common, damn. But the next type of mast was the ittefaqi mast, type four, and here was the mother lode. The ittefaqi mast wore iron rings on his arms and legs and had pieces of iron *here and there* on his body! So the Hardeva mast was ittefaqi. There were lots of them too, it seemed, and they waved their arms, talked nonsense, roamed around, and also they had not been seekers for God before getting intoxicated by divine love. There were examples of three of them at the end of the ittefaqi section, Narain Baba of Beawar, Sabbal Bua of Mandla, and Lohewala Baba of Chanda.

So off to the Beawar section in the supplement, and then Mandla and then Chanda. The Beawar guy was the most promising. He was young and wore a loin cloth in town but in the countryside went naked. That could be their tiger mast. No pictures though. Disappointing partly, but partly not, since otherwise she would have had to get dressed and see if Haley was still out there to show him the picture. She would have done it, but was feeling cozy in her high bed snuggery, detecting away in a field of clues. The Mandla and Chanda guys were possibles too, the Mandla guy naked, except he had all kinds of stuff hanging off him, sickles, chains, wires, locks, and a crowbar, called a sabbal, which was how he got his name. Age not given, but probably older than the Beawar guy, since he had been a messenger in the local court. The Chanda guy though was described as middle-aged, and only half-naked.

He hoarded iron, didn't seem to wear it so much, and people would find train wheels hoisted to the tops of trees where he lived and wonder how he got them up there. Also, Chanda was in the central provinces, it said, so she opened the map again and started to hunt. She found Chanda in the middle, a thousand miles probably from Calcutta, and shoot, there was Beawar in the west and a little south of Delhi. Mandla she couldn't find and was getting sleepy. She had to get up, in what—she looked at her phone—six hours.

She closed the book. She had been in a fascinated fever, detecting away in a field of clues. Now she lay on her back and held the book as she had held it before, at the settee, recalling she had squeezed it in frustration and had been flooded with love. Then the love vanished, and she had gone outside with Annie, glad of her crisp emphatic presence. That was fine, to leave the settee, it was mature even, to get up from a delicious meal of love and go about your life and not sit groping in the empty air.

She squeezed the book now, thinking, if you could squeeze out love whenever you wanted. She thought of Packer in Dubai, whom she had lived with for a year and gotten used to. She had held the reins in that relationship. He had been a kind of audience and had unexpectedly left the theater and had broken her heart a little but her pride a lot. Just what he should have done, gotten free from someone who did not need him truly. We should say, I need you, we must marry, not I love you. Now he was in Dubai, and she felt a pulse of love and forgiveness and apology, and sent it out, like a radio wave. Maybe he would feel it, morning over there, eating his falafel and dates or whatever. She lay the book on the shelf beside her head. Love had come, blooming up from inside somewhere. There was a hole in her heart. She could almost touch it, right there, a precious sore spot. In her right ear, like a whisper, she heard the fan. Inside its sound would be the purr. She plumped her pillow and was asleep in a few seconds.

•

Dawson shed grogginess as he walked back to his van. His dream came vividly back, bright and technicolor. He bent in through the side door, slid it closed, popped open the roof vent. The vent breathed cool night air. He got undressed, washed his face and brushed his teeth at the little sink, using a glass to rinse, since the van held only twenty gallons of water. He hit the spacebar on the laptop, saw the logo pop up from black. An hour ago, or two, he had been working on it, lost in detail. He studied it, imagined the logo discovered in a Paleolithic cave, 20,000 year old art. Whoever had done this was talented. What spell had gripped to make him descend to this depth and work alone in the dark, animals clambering on letters? What could it mean? He closed the laptop, turned off the overhead light, and darkness fell in his van cave. He felt his way to the loft bed, hoisted himself aboard, pulled up the blanket, lay back on his hands, and thought of his dream.

He had been walking a road in an green Oz-like countryside, with smooth bushes and trees, and the light brown road smooth too and winding like a river. Then on the horizon, not far off, at the crest of a hill, a troupe of animals descended toward him on the road, bright and cartoonishly untextured like his logo animals, giraffes, rhinos, baboons, buffalo, zebra, gazelle, colorful and without facial features, but instead smooth-faced and without expression. And in the front, leading them, a massive faceless lion. So friend or foe? How to tell? The troupe advanced resolutely along the road, winding toward him to stop ten feet from him. Then the lion detached itself from the group and came forward and in a fluid motion offered his paw in friendship.

And Bluey had shaken him awake. It was his best dream ever, a perfect clear bright colorful dream, without dream drippiness or murk. But what did it mean? He was in a traveling zoo with lots of animals, so he would become friends with animals? The animals would like him? If they did, that was news because he had hardly noticed them. He drew them, but not them really, but ones he found on the net. So was it, Dawson, notice the animals? Were dreams instructions? That was a friendly lion. Had he taken that offered paw? Bluey had woken him. If he ever saw that lion again, he would take the paw, definitely. He fell asleep, his hands behind his head, the breath of night across his face.

•

Roger cranked open his truck door, swung up the three steps, and entered his compartment. He wanted to get to his computer, but first set his phone alarm for six, fifteen minutes before first light according to the weather app. He would be sweaty after his feed bag jog, and they wouldn't want him at the breakfast table.

He watched the computer boot. If she hadn't written back, he was going to be disappointed. If she had, then what, she hung out at the computer all day?

The screen flicked on, and as the browser came up, a nausea ball rolled up from his stomach held near his heart. He groaned and went outside.

The night air was crisp against his skin, and stars were a splash of glistening light. He walked twenty feet away from the cab and opened his fly. As he urinated, the pain drained. He breathed, pushing something out with several long exhalations until he felt clearer. If she was working on the computer, or if she heard an email ding, she might have written back right away. It would be only ten, her time. As he turned back toward the truck, he felt the pain ball reemerge and thicken his middle with another surge of nausea.

There was movement in the darkness under the truck, a soft glisten, like a snake. And his feet were bare. He stretched forward to open the door and retrieved the flashlight from the plastic pocket. He beamed the light under the truck. Annie's dog peered up at him.

"You look like a snake," he said.

The dog did not move. The wave of nausea pulsed. He felt a fierce distaste for this dog.

"Go on," he said. He jerked the light, waved his free hand. The dog rose and walked languidly toward the stockade. What was that dog's name? They should call him snake.

He climbed into the compartment, woke the computer again, and clicked to his bookmarked profile on the dating site. His email was highlighted. He thought of exercising patience, opening her response tomorrow. But then he wouldn't sleep. Don't make it a thing. He clicked the message, thinking, could be my wife, first contact, hey, hey.

The message came up—"Thank you for writing. I liked your letter, but can't respond just now. Will soon though."

He read it three times, the third time through noting that she could have said *really liked*, but said *liked*, and had said *just now* instead of *right now*, and had said *will soon though* instead of *I will soon though*. And the impression he got was, smart person, busy, active, courteous. She had left out that *really* though. Or maybe she had written it and then deleted it, going slow. And she had written even though she was busy, not able to finish but wanting to get something out. Did that show thoughtfulness or need? Thoughtfulness. Need would have put in the *really*. Good sign then. What I will tell our kids about. He closed the computer and lay down on his bed. He became aware then of something buzzing, and almost got up to look for a mosquito before he realized it was the tireless tiger. He went to sleep without covering himself, glowing in the cool night air.

•

Bluey's truck was older, and in the sleeping compartment there was no water or sink, so he brushed his teeth in the field, rinsed with a gallon jug, then splashed his face and scrubbed it fresh with a towel. In his youth, he had done that, bottle washing in the bush for weeks during the yearly muster.

Goose had settled on the passenger seat, and as Bluey entered through the driver's door, he squatted for a moment between the seats to lay his hand on the dog's head. Finally, he gave the muzzle a squeeze and wiggle, entered the compartment, and got into bed.

He had set his alarm for five thirty, so he wouldn't get much sleep, but he wanted to welcome the beasts as the light came, this is our life now, here I am. He would get Dawson those cameras he wanted, put the purring on the web, interest the public, have night gatherings. Money must flow. He had a year, maybe two, to make it work. Tomorrow they would drive, then set up, a long day. Then the public. He had a fine crew. His speed demon sister had embraced and thanked him. Roger was diligent and dry. Dawson was honest and intense and bright. El was a spirit. He was lucky, hoist on the shoulders of karma.

He could hear the purr, like a distant engine. Every beast alert. The explanations—one, something with the mast; two, a tiger in the night;

three—there was no three. And one meant something improbably occult. So two, a tiger in the night, provoking alarm, and Haley and his pilgrims drunk on placebos. He was the tiger expert, the one they flew in. Tomorrow he would send emails, which he had been too tired to send tonight. Get his colleagues tuned in, get Samuelson and Lee Chin apprised, see what they thought. Ever heard of a tiger purring? Send them video, get Dawson the camera. Long drive. First full day for beasts and crew. Where was sleep? Eventually he slept and dreamed many dreams, the last one about a tiger that moaned in a dark forest and could not be seen.

11

Annie had been to the bathroom twice during the night, unusual for her and each time hard to get back to sleep, since each time she stopped in the hallway to listen for El's breathing. The first time she couldn't hear it, but the second, around four, she could.

She stood for a moment on the bathroom threshold, listening. The fan had been turned off, and the tiger's purr had stopped. The silence closed loneliness around her like a cool vise. Something savage surged. She had made a vow the evening before not to trouble this girl, and it had been simple then in the bathroom before the mirror, after the soothing purr, like a vow to diet after a big meal. But here was love gently breathing in the night. Love had always saved her. She felt herself sway in the darkness, as if prodded by invisible hands to El's bedside. She could say, "Oh sorry, I couldn't sleep. I thought you were awake. Sorry."

Revulsion swept her. Love could not save her. It had never saved her. Love was tawdry with sharp rock beneath soft water. She let self-loathing penetrate. She heard El's relentless breath. She willed herself calm. She let loneliness come, and it came like a mist and embalmed her. She absorbed it. She heard El's breathing, softly calling with slow inhalations and exhalations, and there formed in her heart a quiet firm hopeless no, and she let love go.

And felt love come. It entered delicately, like dawn, elegant and familiar and common as water. It spread through her chest and stomach.

Outside her, she heard the call of El's soft breath, which was the mask and fraud of love, and inside love bloomed, actual love, which was the soul then, Bluey's thing. It was hidden, and you couldn't see it until you did because you felt it. She felt her body soft in a glow. She felt her feet rooting. Love was around and in her like a presence.

She felt an urge to act, to embody kindness, to struggle up and against and immerse herself in kindness. She found the doorjamb in the dark and touched it, first her right hand, her fingers like caressing antennas, then both hands on both sides of the door, touching gently the cool creases of plastic with the sides of her fingers, here, where I am, this place, which I am given. But the plastic was inert and unresponsive. She moved her hands, stroking. Something immediately went bad. Sensuality pulsed, and her loins distinctly pulsed. Love vanished, a mirage into dry sand. Loneliness surged back, faded Annie, alone.

She had been delivered back to herself. Love had projected her being in a flash film. She had feared starvation and eaten chalk. Then love blew in and all the dust away. Then gone.

But love had left a footprint and a memory, and the memory was a candle. She had rubbed a doorjamb, and stupid sex went off, and love vanished. Well then, no doorjamb rubbing! Trembles fluttered through her. She breathed them out. She wiped her eyes with the sides of her fingers. No fucking doorjamb rubbing. That was a test. Love could not mind a bit of fun swearing. It didn't.

She heard a whimper then and felt her way to the front door. She opened it, and her dog, Patti, came up the metal steps with a clicking scuffle. Annie held the door, winced, listened. El did not stir. She carefully closed the door, then waved Patti before her into the back bedroom. She got her empty coffee cup from the shelf, went to the bathroom, filled it with water, and returned to the bedroom, closing the door silently behind her. Patti was on the bed, turning in a small circle, preparing to settle. Annie held the cup out and Patti slurped it dry. She gave a suggestive push, and the dog thumped to the carpet and curled beside the headboard. Annie found a half-eaten granola bar in the drawer and held it out, felt it taken by gentle dog lips, heard it crunched. She said, "I will be a better mother tomorrow." Dawson's face flashed in her mind, and she felt a sudden fierce ache. He was hungry too, but hard to feed. She would be a better mother. She fell asleep.

•

Dawson woke before six and went outside in his underwear and T-shirt to relieve himself. The dew was cold on his bare feet, and his mind brightened. Behind him, the sky was starting to faintly pale, which meant the sun had gone around the world and was coming back, making day. *Here comes the sun, and I say*— He went back inside to start work, thinking, I'll try to get out there when it just peeks up. I could sit on top of the van, wipe it off with a towel. Have a towel just for that. What I daily do.

•

Roger sat up, swung his thick legs over the bed, toed into his tennis shoes. He had slept like a drunk. His laptop lay folded on the shelf, yearning. But wait a full long day until evening. Don't be a puppy.

He heard low talking and recognized Bluey's baritone, then saw the top of him across the stockade, moving around like a big penguin. He heard the rhythmic incantation of poetry, and a thought depressively dawned—he had left out the good part.

He had several gardens as a kid and so took horticulture in college, but had surrounded it with paper-only athlete courses, since he was going to be a football millionaire. Then he wasn't.

He went to the west facing window to see if Dawson's van was lighted yet, and saw Dawson sitting on the roof, his arms wrapped around his knees, facing the sun. He felt again depression faintly fuming. He had left out the good part.

He had an urge to talk to El. El, who didn't tell on him, who told him in a nice way about the science of animals. El, what should I do with my life? And there's this girl in Oklahoma City I'm in love with. He pulled his shorts on over his tennis shoes, a session of tug. He had to get out and under that feed bag, which wasn't going to be fun. And might not be satisfying.

•

"And see, dear Demijohn, where the morn in russet mantle clad walks o'er the dew of yon high eastward hill." The lion was lying on his side, his eyes lazily open, watching Bluey's face as he spoke. The carnivore pellet from last night lay where it had fallen, and now Bluey added one more through the zoo link. The lion rolled onto his back, arching, pawed the air indifferently, then rolled up onto his belly and inhaled the two pellets. He gazed at Bluey, chewed briefly, swallowed, then stared across Bluey's shoulder at the tiger.

Sometime during the night, the Latinos and Haley had departed. Bhajan was sleeping, lying on his side, a ten foot sprawl of orange and black. Below the cage, the crushed grass where the men had nested shown pale yellow in the sunlighted dew, and in the center of the depression Goose twisted furiously on his back, then rolled up and shook, producing a pale fan of rainbow. Seven crows perched on the cage top, swiveling their heads as they stared around, pacing and fluttering. An eighth crow was inside the cage, clutching the rim of the tiger's drinking trough, energetically dipping its beak and tossing water over its feathers. As Bluey watched, the tiger's eyes opened and his tail lashed through the air five feet from the crow. The crow ignored it. The tiger lifted its head, seemed to study the bird, then let his head fall back. Bluey had seen tigers kill vultures, and his science mind idly churned, odd bird behavior, unlikely to seed genes, a fadeaway variant. Then another crow fluttered though the bars, landed on the trough and began to toss water. The remaining crows rose skyward in ones and twos, leaving their chums to their fates.

Goose raced across the grass, did a pouncing dance about Bluey's legs, then sat, nose expectantly aloft. Bluey squatted and worked the dog's ears, watching the tiger and crows, expecting, and faintly ready to enjoy, the thrill of confrontation. Both crows hopped from the water trough to the cage floor, toddled to the bars, and fluttered up again to the cage top. One flew and then the other. Bhajan had ignored them.

The hyena lay on his stomach, watching Bluey approach with flat bright eyes. As he slid a pellet into the cage, Bluey began Fern Hill—

"Now as I was young and easy, Nubia, under the apple boughs about the lilting house—" Nubia's eyes followed him without malice or fondness or much interest.

He heard scuffling from the tandem trailer and crossed to the stockade gap to find Roger descending the ramp in shorts and a T-shirt. A feed bag was slumped on his head.

"Good morning. Thought I'd go for a run."

Bluey smiled. "I thought you were swiping the stores."

"Ha! But the thing is, should I be helping? I thought we were going to feed and clean after breakfast."

"We are. Right now I'm just saying good morning to the beasts."

"Also, I'm gonna be pretty sweaty. I mean for breakfast."

"Will you stink?"

"I could. I use deodorant though."

"We'll see how it goes. Hate to fix you a to-go breakfast, and you'll miss all the small talk."

"Ha. That's true." He adjusted the feed bag, shaking it into balance. "Great for the neck."

Bluey watched the muscle in Roger's neck bunch. "Go easy. I can't afford to lose you."

"This one's only fifty pounds. See you for breakfast."

He turned and trotted across the compound, headed toward the road. The bag flounced once or twice, then settled and rode smoothly as if on wheels.

Bluey continued his rounds, nursing *Fern Hill* to make it last. At the raccoon cage, he turned to the zoo and shouted, opening his arms, "You are my band of brothers! I welcome you."

This provoked a chorus of bleats, hoots, chuffs, chirps, and grunts. They were up and alert. All were defecating, all fur in good repair, moods unsullen, eyes clear. Ready for prosperous sessions of public display.

He headed across the compound toward the flatbed. He could get those emails off before breakfast, let them have the day to think. He could smell coffee.

•

El finished her shower and stepped out of the tiny stall into the roomier bathroom to dry off. Dream fragments circled but would not coalesce. Something about a flood, and her parents were there. As she soaped up, she felt for the dream, but it had drifted away.

She flew the brush through her hair a few times. In an hour it would dry and flounce, and she could finger comb it. She had good hair, like her mother, who she had to call today. They would be wondering. In the mirror, she glanced fast over her face, breasts, shoulders, hips, pubis, legs. A flush of pride, and she closed her eyes to clear it. Her mood was so bright. She was perched, like a bird, high up. An image of one of the masts in the book flashed, Coca-Cola Baba or something. They were there in India now, she supposed, walking the lanes and lying in hovels. Meher Baba was long gone, and his followers too she supposed. But wouldn't there be a steady crop of masts?

She had accepted the book. Had she? Yes, it lay in the quiet of herself, under worry. She had been gripping the book when love came through a hole in her heart. Now the book had made an unobtrusive nest and was nesting nicely near the heart hole. She closed her eyes, worked imaginary fingers around the book nest and thought, do I toss this nest, or do I tolerate it? She released the nest. Toleration of course. And watch for eggs, ha.

She pulled on her underwear and jeans, then her sports bra and her much-loved T-shirt, white with a big bright parrot. She planned to work with Sybil today, maybe in the RV while Annie drove. She would develop the pirate theme. She imagined a crowd of people crowding in to get a look, and she would signal, and Sybil would say, "Back, you devils, back!" She could wear an eyepatch and burnoose, a quick fun show, then perch Sybil on her shoulder and lead a tour and talk animal welfare. The problem was Sybil, who was mute.

As she opened the bathroom door, Annie's door opened, and they stared at each other, El pert, Annie drowsy. El laughed, the sheer fun of a drowsy Annie. She said, "Good morning, Annie. Perfect timing."

Annie made a faint nod, entered the bathroom. El went into the kitchen, figured out the coffeemaker, and made the maximum.

•

Annie had waked and lay for a moment on her side, waiting to wake more. She had been flying, and you had to steer with your mind. You had to concentrate, or you would start descending. It wasn't that hard, but you had to concentrate. Nobody crashed though. She and her fellow fliers were covering lots of countryside, farms and little villages. They were learning to fly. It was fun, but focus or down you went. It was dusk and hard to see. She had worried about radio towers but never saw any.

Part way through her make-up she stopped and gazed at herself. A handsome, lived-in face. El had brightly laughed at her. The night before, she had said, the history of salt, a book my father liked. And Leonard, a master of pace and ne'er-do-wells. Neat, efficient reviews. She offered what you needed. Take this candy I have, just one, not two, neat and delicious. So measured empathy, which came from heart. A smart loving attractive young person. Who wouldn't want that? The four o'clock experience came back in a rush. She had given love up, and love had come.

I will never touch that girl in a suggestive way. Never ever.

She packed up her make-up and smiled at the mirror, making her face beautiful. She had carried her face like a flag. Here comes pretty Annie! She could give that up. She would have to anyway, forty-three years old. There should be a shop, and you say, how much for an ounce of love? Three quarts of pride, dear. Who wouldn't make that trade?

The bathroom was suddenly too small and white and stiff. She liked wooden things, not plastic things, and she had rubbed that plastic last night and felt her loins go off and her heart go blank. Well, that was good information. Avoid plastic! She could send Dawson for some wood, and they could plate the bathroom. She was going crazy on purpose, amusing herself, but that was how you did go crazy. You couldn't get love, so you found a hammer and nails and covered everything with wood.

She thought, these are rich thoughts for little Annie. Because love had left a footprint.

She cranked open the louvered window to let in the morning light. And there was her brother, across the grass, not thirty feet away. He raised his hands and shouted, "You are my band of brothers! I welcome you."

She began to shout something back about sisters, but didn't. She watched him move past the tiger cage, speak something to the tiger. She was aware of the coffee smell then and almost shouted to him that, hey, coffee's ready! But she let him go. If he came too late for this pot, she would make a fresh one. He disappeared through the stockade, a small grief. He would be back though, and she would have fresh coffee for him.

•

Annie served the breakfast, toast and scrambled eggs, with cheese and a can of chilies. Roger had arrived panting and looking rained on, but had thought to bring a small towel, which he scrubbed himself with from time to time. He did not stink, but glistened, and kept his forearms off the table. When everyone was eating, Annie joined them on the folding chair.

Bluey outlined a schedule of showers. He described sailor showers to preserve water, get wet, turn the water off, soap up, water on to rinse. He estimated they had a three day capacity before they had to dump waste water and refill with fresh, but would need to be strict. Kitchen cleanup would be handled by Dawson and Annie, while he and El and Roger cleaned cages and handled the loading if they were moving, which today they were. They had to set up and feed that evening.

El said, "I want to have Sybil in the RV. I have some ideas for a show."

"Tell us."

El related her idea about the burnoose and eyepatch and *back, you devils, back*. If anyone had a good idea, tell her.

Bluey said, "If you can get Sybil to cooperate."

"Well, she's an African Gray, so high hopes. If she doesn't, maybe we can get a Mina Bird."

"And have parrot stew," said Roger, and when no one laughed, blushed, lifted his coffee before his face.

El poked his shoulder carefully so his coffee wouldn't slop. She said, "Back, you devil, back." Then she turned to Dawson. "You said you had a dream last night. Can you tell it? Unless it's too private. I love dreams."

Dawson told briefly about the parade of faceless animals, the lion offering his paw.

El said, "Wow. That is no ordinary dream. Or is it?"

Dawson said, "No, I don't dream a lot."

Annie noted El's forward lean, Dawson's resistance to being interesting, and his helpless leaks of pleasure. She willed El to lean back.

Annie said, "You used to dream about dinosaurs."

Dawson half-smiled, made his face straight. Input from a mother, thought Annie, away away, because mothers were betrayers. They spawned and continued dancing while the babes ached, and the child ached, and the young man ached. She said, "And you know how you stopped? I told you to think about all the scary dinosaurs you could before you went to sleep so your mind would be used them. And you did, and you never dreamed of them again."

Dawson smiled. "That's right. That was good advice."

Annie got up, clattering her coffee cup purposely against her plate. Her eyes had wet. She said, "Just leave the plates on the table. We don't have room to stack."

The men stood. Bluey said, "Trouble with this whole setup is, this is the gal's home, and us guys are going to be in their hair every day. No help for it."

El said formally, "Do not give it a second thought, sir. This area is our mutual home, and all are welcome."

Outside on the grass, Dawson said, "Uncle Bluey. I finished that logo. When you have time."

Bluey turned. "Already?"

Dawson flash-frowned pride. "I've been working on it. I finished it this morning."

"Well, let's have a look."

"It's on my computer."

"Okay. Help Annie clean up, then get your computer and find me."

"Okay." He started up the RV stairs, then stepped back as El came down.

She smiled, poked him in the stomach with a finger, said, "Dream on."

He made a mouth smile, glanced behind at her trim rear under loose jeans, bright parrot T-shirt over slim shoulders. Was she coming on to him?

In the kitchen, Annie ran water into a sudsy plastic basin and began dumping dishes into it.

She said, "If you wash, I'll rinse and dry and put things up. We can't put them in the drainer because there's too many."

"Okay." He stationed himself at the basin and began rapidly sponging dishes and sliding them into the water-filled second sink.

Annie sloshed and dried, making stacks. She said, "You were always a great dish washer."

"Yep." Then, to break the frost that gripped him with his mother, he said, "It has never truly tested me."

Annie moved behind him, opened a cabinet over his head, and rattled in a stack of dishes. The cabinet closed, and he heard no movement. Then he felt hands light on his waist, and the soft pressure of her head against his back. He continued to sponge, silent, but did not lean away from the pressure.

•

El and Roger worked together cleaning cages. Bluey had trundled out the food cart. It was a moving day, and he would feed, but lightly, in case some of the animals could not handle motion.

In the tandem beside the freezers was a four hundred gallon water tank and a two hundred foot hose, which Roger handled along with the dung bucket. El used the squeeze wall of each enclosure to ease the animals to the side, then opened the small access door to use the flat shovel and broom. When the dung had been separated from the floor litter, it was deposited in the bucket, and the straw and wood chips were swept to the side. Roger sprayed the floor with a spray bottle of disinfectant, then swept it with water, and the bedding was spread again. They started with Kip the caracal, a carnivore cat, but small so kept in the tandem. Then Tooey the honey badger, Chortle, the raccoon and their only

American, Thane the Mandrill baboon. El kept up a soft-voiced running commentary.

Ballyhoo the binturong. "She's a sweetie, aren't you Ballyhoo. She loves fruit, and if you're not watching, she'll jump on your back and make a nest on your head."

Quanna the Bonobo. "Bonobos are really smart. And Quanna is brilliant. See, she moves to the side, very sweet and lets me scoop the poop. Thank you, Quanna."

Taj the De Brazza guenon. "Taj is a hard core, straight up male monkey. Cheek pouches, long tail, eats everything, including lizards. Can you show your teeth? Chi chi chi! See his teeth."

Then Shindig the spider monkey, Oz the meerkat, and Sybil the African Gray parrot. "Sybil is mute, but I hope to fix that. African grays are famous talkers. They can imitate a person's voice even, can't you, Sybil? Can you say, back, you devils, back? Back, you devils, back!"

Then Spectra the peacock, Bart the ostrich, Phoenix the Himalayan blue sheep, Pumper and Nickel, the wild llamas, called guanacos, Charlie the Somali wild ass, and Cloe the okapi, a lovely giraffe-like forest antelope.

They went around again, this time working the larger carnivore cages. El explained that these were the kill-you animals. They were powerful and had big teeth and claws. So alert and careful was the deal here.

Alfie the African wild dog. "Alfie likes to run in packs, and he thinks, what am I doing here? Which I wonder too, Alfie, lots of times."

Roger, who had been looking for an opportunity to speak, almost did, but El had moved to Paris. "The Siberian is the biggest lynx. He's a lurker in the night, and now he's in prison. We're all in prison though. Sentenced to life. That's philosophical."

Bump the sun bear. "Hello, Bump. I see you have become friends with Goose." Goose lay in the shadow at the end of Bump's cage and lifted his head at the sound of his name. "Goose, this is Bump the lump, my second year buddy."

Lobo the Dhole. "Lobo is a wild dog from Asia. Genghis Khan probably saw a lot of them. One day we'll have a pack, won't we Lobo, and you can whistle at the girls again. They whistle when they hunt."

Then Clark the puma, her other second year animal, then Nubia the spotted hyena and Demijohn the lion.

Then Bhajan, whose cage did not have a squeeze wall. His pile of dung, however, was conveniently near the access opening. El unlatched the small door and pulled the dung into the bucket with the tip of the shovel. She said, "You are a considerate fellow, Bhajan, sir. We enjoyed your purring last night."

Bhajan rose and padded slowly across the cage toward them, flickering orange and black behind the vertical bars. He turned as he neared them, then stopped and gazed into El's face, then turned his head slightly and gazed at Roger.

Roger said, "That's some direct attention. He's thinking, if I ever get out of here, I'll eat the big guy first."

The tiger lowered his head and moved forward until the top of his head was pressed into the bars. El raised her hand without thinking, put a hand on the tiger's head between two bars and stroked the fur. Roger lifted his hand. El said, "No no. Well, okay, go ahead. But just this one time, okay? Never do this. Look at him. I've never seen that."

Roger scrubbed the fur with a single forefinger.

El said, "A rare treat. But never do this again, okay?"

Bhajan stepped back, lifting his head. His eyes flicked back and forth between them. He paced away to the other end of his cage and lay down with a rolling thump.

El looked behind her for Bluey. He was standing beside the binturong cage near the big-wheeled food cart, holding a laptop and talking to Dawson.

She said, "Bluey's the tiger expert. Annie said he was still purring at two this morning. I told you his history, with the mast and all that."

Roger nodded, recalling something about a holy man and a village, but what he wanted mostly was get El into a different mood, into a sitting-by-the-river mood and tell her his cooped up thoughts.

El said, "You can roll the hose. But tell me this." She smiled directly into his face now, laying her hand on his forearm. "Last night you wondered if you liked animals. Have you decided?"

Her touch and smile made something bloom, and it was the sitting-by-the-river moment. He said, "Yes, I like them." Then he added,

"Now that I'm here." The words, *now that I'm here*, rang inside him like a bell.

"Well, good. I was worried about you."

He said, "You're a nice cousin. So you get a sweaty hug." He pulled her briefly against his damp shirt, making quick contact and releasing her. He was faintly chagrined. He puffed laughter and half-smiled.

She laughed. She said, "I can take another shower." She saw that his half smile was sweet. He was sweeter.

He began looping the hose across his forearm, following it toward the water tank in the tandem. He looked over his shoulder. "I do like the animals," he said. Then loudly, almost a shout, "Now that I'm here!"

•

Dawson said, "We should get out of the sun. You can't see the screen in sunlight."

They moved into the shade of the binturong cage, and Dawson opened the laptop and touched a few keys. The screen sprang up with the animal-festooned logo, "Exotic Animal Caravan," each letter a bright color, each animal a lithe cartoon.

Bluey said, "Well, damn. This is just what we need, which I didn't know myself. And I don't have to hurt the feelings of my nephew." He smiled, saw Dawson's gathered-in expression, saw his comment had omitted gush. He said, "This is an amazing piece of work. I had no idea this was in your kit."

Dawson frowned away pleasure.

Bluey said, "Can we make it big? Like ten feet?"

"Yes. It's algorithms, not pixels."

"Well, Dawson, thank you. Did you get any sleep, for Christ's sake."

"Yeah."

Bluey waited for more but nothing followed. He said, "So now how to use it?" He fell silent, inviting Dawson.

"Well, first thing, have a hard sign made. Laminate it to sign board and put it right above the entrance. Also make magnetic signs for the trucks. Get all the letters and envelopes made with it. Put it on the web-site. Also, I have this idea for around the stockade. We make some giant plastic posters of life-sized people, from behind, like they're looking in through cracks in the bamboo at something. The poster matches the bamboo, which I can do. So when people come up, they see, hey, something cool's going on in there, everybody's looking through the cracks. They know it's a poster, but it's cool. Someone went to some trouble."

"That's good. I thought you were a computer major. Are you taking marketing?"

"I did a lot of graphics in high school. People would hear about me." Dawson's face flickered with irritated intelligence.

Bluey said, his voice kind but flat, "What else have you been thinking about?"

Dawson blinked. "Okay. Remember I said I could do the live cam for the website? I made an equipment list. Also, I looked at the website. It's sort of—"

"Mediocre."

"Yeah. And remember I said we could do pictures of people with the animals using a green screen? I mean, kids can take a pic of themselves petting a tiger, or riding it. So that. And I can make an equipment list for that. It's all cheap, sort of. And then I was in the tandem trailer this morning because you said you had signs for the cages, and I found them in the bin in there. They're okay, but—"

"They need the logo."

"Well, right, and I can do better maps too if you want. Put the logo maybe up the side, sideways, kind of cool, redo the drawing so it's like the logo, put everything in the same graphic package so they'll say, hey, these guys have got something going on. I better join the eco club, send my kids to eco camp. If you have a club and a camp. And we should get all the printing together and gets bids. There are big companies on the internet that will bid. It'll be cheaper than some local outfit. I saw your pin system on the side there, how the signs attach to the cages. That'll work."

Bluey made a resolute face, smiled. "You mean I've done something right?"

Dawson smiled back. His intensity cheerily relented. He laid his arm across Bluey's thick shoulder. He said, "You have earned my approval, Uncle Bluey."

They both laughed. Dawson dropped his arm, and his expression in-gathered again.

Bluey said, "Okay, that's a bit of work. So here's your schedule. Every morning, after the cleanup, you help me feed and inspect the beasts. We make our rounds, just like now, after the cages are cleaned. You can cut fruits and vegetables, which will speed things up. Then you retreat to your van, and you work. Here's what we discussed. One, you make the logo sign for the front gate and for the trucks. Two, you make the posters for the stockade. Three, you redo the cage signs. Show me one first before you do all the rest. Four, redesign the website, and show me as you go. Five, give me an equipment list for the webcam and green screen, with prices. Okay? Same page?"

Dawson nodded. "Same page."

"I do have a club and camp, by the way. We'll talk it over, get your thoughts."

Dawson kept his face straight. He had been admitted to the council.

Bluey said, "There's a box of fruit under the curtain. Slide your laptop in there beside it. Here's your knife. It's razor sharp, and we mean to feed our friends fruit, not fingers. Quarter the oranges, halve the pears and apples. This is Quanna, our bonobo. Her relatives are from the Congo, but Quanna is from San Diego. Now here's some advice for you, young nephew. Whenever you walk by one of these cages, let your heart break a little. If it already does, good. If not, let it break. Quanna will feel it. And your uncle will appreciate it."

Dawson picked up the knife and began slicing orange on the white plastic cutting board. Without looking up, he said, "What if it doesn't break?"

Bluey gathered orange quarters. He said, "The right question, young sir. It means, pay better attention. Now then, working with me, you'll hear poetry. And today is Fern Hill day." He put the orange quarters on a metal plate and slid them into Quanna's cage through the feed door, then slid in two primate biscuits. He gazed fondly at Quanna, who stood watching, her crumpled black face pressed against the zoo link. "Now as I was young and easy, Quanna, under the apple boughs—"

•

The RV kitchen was quite shippy, with its locking cupboards and smooth drawers that thumped when you closed them. It made Annie think of the *Argosy*, a sailboat she had lived on for almost a year, taking a break between her junior and senior years in college. It had been her boyfriend Jack's boat, his dad's boat actually, and when Jack had to go home to Melbourne because of mononucleosis, she lived alone for a month until Smitty moved in. And then of course here comes Jack back, free of bugs, and discovers Smitty in his underwear. Smitty was way rougher than Jack, so no fist fight, but lots of anger and angst from Jack, the college man, along with smirks from Smitty, the marina knock-about whose highlights were trips to Greece and Florida crewing yachts.

She had gone back to college afterward, but for quite a while thought of Jack's torment and got letters from him. She made up thought experiments to help her digest things, and then wrote them up for two papers in psychology, her minor. The first paper she entitled "Sexual Jealousy—History and Evolution" and the second, which she had to get permission for since it was the same thing expanded, she jokily called "The Further Evolution of Sexual Jealousy." Everyone liked to discuss sex, especially with a pretty girl, even the girls it turned out, so research was easy, students and professors, working people and professional people. She talked to Chinese, Arabs, Indonesians, Indians, and of course whites from everywhere. It was fun. She began with animals and apes, talking lots to her big brother, Mr. World Zooman himself, then moved to Paleolithic man, Neolithic man, Sumerian man, Greek and Roman man, on and on to modern man. She had a pile of material and could have written a book, and still could, since all her taped conversation and notes were in storage, but in the end it would have been a book just like the papers, a long gab without a core, because neither she, nor anyone she talked to, and none of the books she read, understood the elusive subject of sex and sexual jealousy. Annie herself was not immune to sexual jealousy, but it sat lightly on her, almost indifferently, which was why Jack's agony tormented her. Perhaps it was a kind of strength, since she was freer, but it was abnormal, and maybe why she had never married, though she had married three times. She could wrap her arms and legs around husbands, but when they wanted to go, or she did, she undid them, oh, we're done? At best, she was flexible. At worst, uninvolved. She had a missing bone. But her lightness made her good company for men, witty and funny, and—lucky her—she had beauty.

And now she had felt true love.

Patti had finished eating and lay on the kitchen floor, staring. Annie opened the RV door, said, "Go on. Go go go." Patti rose with a snort and linoleum clicks and padded down the stairs. She was a not especially likeable dog. She was a character-building dog, which seemed to be Annie's current phase, give up love and fun, and as that thought came, a swift racing pain zoomed down her front.

The RV door opened again. It was Roger with a towel and an apologetic smile.

Annie put her hands on her hips and said, "What the hell do you think you're doing?"

Roger's face opened with a good-natured laugh. "How's it going?" He climbed the steps, and stood stooping.

She moved to him, turned him toward the bathroom, gave a small shove, her hands small against his moist brawn. She said, "El was right. This is your home. Come in whenever you want. Unless we're in our underwear or something. Just come in."

"Okay," said Roger. "Thanks." He disappeared into the bathroom.

That was the thing with character-building, thought Annie, who had noted his pleasant heft under her hands and had slipped in that underwear comment, if you traded in love and fun, you better get something back. You better.

•

Haley and his Latinos arrived in time to see the tiger and carnivores loaded onto the flatbed and the long tarp unfurl and enclose them. They stood in a group with sober faces. Several of the Latinos crossed themselves.

Bluey locked the tarp in place. He said to Haley, "We're about to roll. I want to thank you for the use of the land, much appreciated. And thank Fuad for me too."

"I will. I talked to him last night. He said to tell you that he wishes you well. I emailed you this morning so you'd have my email address.

Tell El that Fuad doesn't recall the mast's name, by the way. I couldn't remember any more about him, but those iron bangles are a tip off. He's likely dead though."

"Probably."

"I ordered the book, two of them, one for Fuad. Not used either. It's in print. So there's some interest in masts, I guess. Never know what's going in this big world until you look. And then not either."

Bluey felt sudden affection for this man, who had before seemed so soldierly and bluff, and now seemed easy and self-deprecating. An impulse came. He asked, "How's the limp?"

Haley smiled, laid his hand over Bluey's shoulder. "Gone with the wind, Dr. Macintosh." He dropped his hand, started to say something else, but only slightly shook his head.

Bluey said, "Is Fuad going to get another Bengal?"

"Sure. Got his feelers out. Not from a mast though." He found Bluey's eyes with a straight gaze. "Now then, you haven't asked what all these hombres are doing here, gathered up around your tiger. You're either polite or afraid we're nuts."

Bluey said, "I don't understand it, that's true." Haley watched him. Silence spread for a moment. Bluey said, "But I do know one thing—the best part of everything is invisible."

Haley nodded, then bowed his head a fraction. "Well, you got my number. You call me if you need me for any damn thing. And get that webcam up and running. I'll be checking the website."

They shook hands, and ten minutes later the Exotic Safari Caravan was on the road.

12

Dawson brought up the rear. At a dump station, they had emptied the RV's waste tanks and filled up with water, diesel, and gas. Now it was ten hours on the road, then more setting up.

He could see the RV ahead and thought of passing them, get a rise out of the women. But the impulse only flickered. There was a charge in him circling. When it came it filled him with energy, and he had to calm, then it came again, and he would think of Bluey numbering out his tasks, one through five, after he had told him the ideas only once. He was hooked to a locomotive, and it was Uncle Bluey, whom he had loved as a child, whose love he had longed for as a boy. Whose advice was that he should let his heart break. El had gently poked his stomach and laughed and said *dream on*. In the kitchen, his mother's delicate hug. To Bluey, he had made a typical reply, *what if it doesn't break?* But behind his eyes he could feel tears waiting.

He had brought his favorite Bill Frisell disk, with his current favorite tune, *Little Jenny Dow*. He could put that in the player. Instead, he put in his earplug and began listening to Bluey explaining animals.

•

El sat in the settee with Sybil's cage on the table, giving Sybil a rhythmic dose of *back, you devils, back,* but the pressure of not being buckled into a seatbelt, and also of ignoring Annie up in the cockpit, got too strong, so she rummaged for her rattiest T-shirt and made a shoulder perch. She took a mild beaking on the thumb as she transferred the bird to her shoulder, but no blood, and after a few exploratory paces Sybil got her claws settled and her weight balanced, and El slid carefully into the passenger seat, a two foot bird riding alongside her left ear like a gray torpedo.

She held an orange bird treat up with her right hand, circled it before Sybil's revolving head. "Back, you devils, back," she said. She lowered the bird treat, palmed it out of sight. "I hope this is not going to drive you crazy."

"Not at all," said Annie. "I hope you're not going to be too disappointed if this bird doesn't cooperate."

"Well, I'm going to be very disappointed, aren't I, Sybil? Bitterly disappointed, so be a good parrot. And back, you devils, back." And she circled the treat.

Sybil said, "Back, you devils, back."

Annie glanced over. The parrot had imitated El's voice, but the sound had come from a slightly higher location. "Did she just say that?"

El held the treat on the palm of her hand, let Sybil beak it up. She said, "She did. Because she's a talking parrot, aren't you, Sybil." She paused, rummaging in the treat box in her lap, making an *umm umm* sound, then held up another treat. She said, "Back, you devils, back."

Sybil said, "Back, you devils, back," and ate the treat.

Annie said, "You should radio Bluey."

El raised her hand and pinned the bird lightly between her cheek and palm. "What an excellent lovely girl who can speak so sweetly. How about this—when we stop for lunch, I'll say, hey, guys, come here. And Sybil will say, back, you devils, back."

And that's what they did, in two hours, and by that time Sybil had learned the whispered cue word, *back*, and could perform with merely a throat stroke as reward.

They pulled into a rest stop, lining the three trucks abreast in the truck area. Roger and Dawson opened the RV's pullout awning. Bluey set up the folding table and chairs. As Annie spread the sandwich fixings, the men gathered behind her in a fortuitous grouping. El, watching through the window, emerged from the RV with Sybil balanced on her shoulder.

She said, "Hey, guys, come here a sec. I got something."

The men moved forward perfectly together. El murmured, "Back," and Sybil said satisfyingly, "Back, you devils, back!"

"Ho!" said Roger, and did a fast athletic rumba as he approached.

"Wow, you did it," said Dawson.

Bluey stroked the parrot's neck with side of a forefinger. He said, "Did I hear a cue word?"

"B-A-C-K," said El. "And I swear, maybe twenty reps, and she had it. And then how long, Annie, and she had the cue word? An hour maybe?"

Annie said, "About. This girl's an expert, I'll say that."

"Oh, god, no," said El. "Sybil's the star, aren't you, dear?" She pursed her lips, and Sybil gave them a light beak tap.

Dawson said, "Did you teach her to kiss too?"

"No, she just does. It's like she woke up and said, hey, why not be a chum?"

El replaced Sybil in her cage and hung it from the awning's strut. They sat in shade, each concocting a ham sandwich—Roger two—from the spread of tomatoes, lettuce, thin-sliced onion, and chow-chow. A bag of chips was passed, and Annie poured five glasses of the sun tea she had brewed in the RV cockpit. Patti and Goose lay hopefully under the table. Sybil swiveled her elegant head from time to time as the conversation proceeded.

El asked for suggestions. She needed a routine, some sort of vaudeville type act. *Back, you devils, back* was a good start, but then what? Think about it, everybody, and we'll see what Sybil can do. Keep it to short phrases. Something piratey. Any ideas? Well, think about it.

Dawson said, "After *back, you devils, back,* you tell the parrot, hey, you still sound like a pirate. We're not pirates anymore."

The group perked. Here was something.

Dawson said, "You say, we're not going to rob these people, we're going to educate them, about animal welfare or whatever. And Sybil says, then why is he picking pockets? Can she say that?"

"Maybe. Probably. What's—"

"And Roger's standing there with an eyepatch and a pirate scarf around his head. Big giant in among them. And he says, what, we're not picking pockets, what am I supposed to do with these? And he holds up a bag of wallets. A plastic bag so you can see it's a bunch of wallets."

Roger said, "I can do that. Cool."

El reached both hands across the table to Dawson, drawing one of his hands toward hers as if by magnetism. They shook. "What a gem," said El, and it was unclear to Annie, and to Dawson, whether the gem was Dawson or his idea.

While the lunch was cleared, Bluey went to the tandem. He raised the sliding door and strolled among the cages, sniffing for vomit, but there was none. After five silent years, the bird had spoken. Perhaps his colleagues had responded by email. He would call them if they hadn't. A purring tiger, an Indian holy man, and Sybil speaks. He yearned to conclude—but could not.

He slid the lock onto the hasp and turned to find El approaching.

He said, "Damn, hunh?"

She said, "I'm just effervescing. And isn't that a great little skit from Dawson? What I was thinking, I'll write it up, and put in stuff about the ecopark. We can develop it, and then maybe add some more. Maybe Dawson can—well, we'll see. I don't want to pressure him. That was quick though, that pirate skit."

"Pressure him. I have a feeling that's good for him."

"All right. I won't start with Sybil until we have it down. Maybe we got lucky, who knows. Maybe all she can ever say is *back, you devils.*"

"I have a good feeling about that parrot."

"Me too."

He snapped the lock shut. He said, "Did you take a look at that book?"

"Yes, I did. It's really interesting." She had made her voice careless. But carelessness was false. She looked intently at him. "I felt—well—" Her expression invited him to presume.

He said, "A spiritual feeling?"

Her face opened. She said, "I did, Bluey." She was easy suddenly and thought of telling him about Pearl and her youthful yearning, but they had to drive, and anyway a conversation would be better somewhere calm and unhurried. She laughed. "I do want to tell you about it. Maybe we can have a talk. Would that be okay?"

"Sure."

She wanted to ask him why he had not read the book. Did he think it was a fraud? The book given by Rosa? But the question seemed intrusive.

They started toward the RV, where Dawson and Roger were closing the belly hatch.

Bluey said, "Let's roll, guys."

Roger, in a guttural pirate voice, said, "What, we're not picking pockets! What am I supposed to do with these wallets!"

They laughed. His pirate was incredulous and charming.

El said, "You're hired." Then to Dawson—"So let us know if anything comes after the bag of wallets."

Dawson made a mild scowl.

El said, "Once we get it nailed down, I can start with Sybil. I don't want to have to revise." Dawson remained silent. She could not catch his eye. She said, "We can brainstorm at dinner tonight. Okay, later, dudes." She opened the RV door and climbed the steps.

Dawson began walking toward his van, thinking. Guy says, *what about this bag of wallets?* El says, *Roger, you have to give them back.* The parrot says, *no way, we need the booty!* Lame. She says, *Roger, you have to give those wallets back.* Roger says, *Okay, okay, I'm giving them back.* He finds some kid. *Here's your wallet, kid. Sorry I stole your wallet.* The kid takes the wallet. The parrot says, *That's not his wallet!* Roger takes the wallet back, says, *What are you, a pirate?* The parrot says, *You want a job!*

He had to write it down, then thought of telling El now, turning back to the RV and telling her, which would create delay, so don't, and then turned back, went to the RV and up the steps. Annie was settling into the driver's seat and turned. El was adjusting the parrot on her T-shirt padded shoulder.

Dawson repeated the skit, ending with the parrot's question, *You want a job?* He said, "That's the crowd warmer. Maybe you do a little curtsy. Sort of cue applause, and then get into your spiel. So that's four things the parrot needs to learn, and she's learned one already." He stopped, frowned, waited.

"Well," said El. "I think it's perfect. It gets the crowd involved, which is really cool. And you heard Roger. He can do it. You have a pen and paper?"

"No, that's why I wanted to—" He stopped mid-lie. He could have remembered it. He had come to the RV to impress El.

Annie said, "I'll get one." She clambered out of the seat, went to her room. El spoke into the handset, "Bluey, hold up a second. You read me?"

After a moment, Bluey's voice came back, "Go ahead."

"Dawson had an idea, and we're gonna write it down. It's really good." Then she said, "You were right."

Annie returned with a pad and pen.

Dawson said, "So you got Roger, El, and Sybil. R, E, S." And he went through the skit again as Annie wrote, and thought, what had Bluey been right about? It was something about him. They had talked about him.

Annie finished. El said, "Great. I have a bird on my shoulder, or I'd hug you. This will be so much fun, won't it Sybil, sweetie?"

Dawson stood, descended one step, then stood on the step, turned and said, "What was Bluey right about?"

El, bird-perched, turned slowly to her left and looked at Dawson around Sybil's flank. She said, "Bluey said I should just ask you what happens next. I said I didn't want to pressure you, but he said to just go ahead, you're good under pressure. So I told him he was right."

She had used a plain-toned evenness and direct gaze. He felt a bolt of pleasure and went fast out of the RV without speaking.

•

Roger followed the flatbed, trying to keep the distance about a hundred feet to keep from getting cut off. They had laughed at his pirate riff, with that big buffoon baffled feeling, *What, no wallets*? In grade school Roger had sometimes acted in front of the bathroom mirror, usually backing some dude down, or practicing something to say to a girl.

It was possible he could actually act and become an actor, with his unusual body size as a calling card. But that was a sideways move, not toward football, which was where he was headed now. And where he hadn't been headed before.

In tryouts, he had been pretending to block. He was acting, like a kid in front of a mirror, not someone actually out on a field with no-mercy killers, which is what the pros were, which is what Bosco James was, a big-bellied black guy with arms like thighs, a pro bowl veteran. He would line up, rattling trash, like—"Sorry to kill your dreams, kid." Like—"Are you a girl, dog? I can't feel you." Like—"Here I come again, Mr. Tender." The coach had put him up to it, a harden-the-rookie strategy. On runs, Bosco was slippery with spins and swims, and on passing plays he narrowed the pocket, now and then even got through. The coaches saw. After the third pre-season game, they cut him, sorry kid, try us again next year. After he emptied his locker, he had to pass Bosco, naked on a locker bench, like a big black Buddha. Bosco offered him a fist bump, said, "Peace out, dog." That was what he thought about when he ran with the bag of zoo food that morning, Bosco's fist bump, Bosco's deep voice coming at him not with pity, not with respect, not with apology, but with something else, it is what it is, dog. Peace out. Bosco's natural man-up with a guy he had sent down. I won, you lost, I don't joy, it is what it is. That was a quality he lacked, that Bosco had, that gave him license to get in your head on the football field, and no-mercy kill you if you let him. Bosco did his job, sent the kid home. And what if football wasn't Roger's job, and that was it? What if he was big and strong, but that was just clothes he had to look past to see his real self, which was what? A truck driver? Or get a day job from one of those felon programs? Get out on the employment racetrack with speedsters like Dawson? If he had money he could start a nursery, but forty thousand wasn't money. Money was a hundred at least, for a truck, tools, a skid steer. After a few years of pro ball, he would have money.

He needed maturity, a settling in, which was what Bosco had, plus those big weird arms. Besides, in training camp, he hadn't been in top shape. He had fallen in with his high school guys, smoked toot, played video games, gorged on chips and pop. His mother slouched in the doorway and said, "Shouldn't you be training or something?" Puffing away on her Newports. Nobody there to encourage him. Nobody like El. He had said, *I'm good, now that I'm here*, and something rang in him like a bell. On his way to put up the hose, he shouted it again, *Now that I'm here.*

He gripped the wheel and thought of Bosco, and thought of dumping him, standing over him, give him a hand up, no joy, then set up again, see what happened. Hell no, he wasn't going to quit football. He was going to train. Besides, there was the no-money problem, and the felony problem. But that was fearful, downward thinking. Upward thinking was, *Here comes Mr. Tender, Fatso.*

•

Dawson had a college friend, Mike Puck, whose rhymable name they spun tirelessly into lame jokes, who fell in love with Sara Millerman. She was a slim girl desirable to many, and so Puck, brilliant but layered with baby fat, was last in line. When he did finally get a date, he walked her from her dorm to a student production of The Cherry Orchard, then to the union for a beer, then back to her dorm. And that fucker Puck won her heart, and they dated for three more months, working out in the gym together—new for Puck—and using her car to see far away drive-in movies and neck, until Puck fell out of love and broke it off. She wouldn't put out due to her religion, which was one thing, especially at the end, but mostly she was seamlessly polite. Seamlessly! Puck would shout after it was over. Polite without seams! Love was hypnosis, he would say. Like being hypnotized into liking liver. You might like it under hypnosis, but then you wake up. Christ, that's liver! What was memorable to Dawson about Puck's adventure in wooing though, was that he did woo. He was their famous tongue twister of a friend, that pudgy fucker Puck, whose teeth and eyes were small, whose nose was large, who was pudgy, but who wooed with courage, and had war stories. Dawson was a virgin and unable to woo with courage. Dawson's idea of wooing would be to drive the van up by the RV and wave, give a thumbs up, fall back again. Or get her on the radio, say, *How's the training coming?* He had almost done that a couple of times, actually reaching for the radio and holding his finger over the talk button, but didn't, partly from cowardice, partly because the skit, which he had gone over several times in his mind, had become mortifyingly corny. Puck could have done it probably. He would nerd through, say, Puck here, to check the progress on my fantastic skit. She had looked at him across the parrot in a steady way and eased his mistrust. *Yes, Bluey and I discussed you. It was this way and that way and see?—harmless.* Anyway, he had performed, and they wrote it down. So what next, if you couldn't nerd along like Puck? He could call Puck, which he should do anyway, since they had roomed together and were buds. Puck was in computers too, the other darling of the department beside Dawson, and would one day be a millionaire, probably, which may have attracted Sara Millerman. Puck could say, here's what you do, Dawson, you say—

He fished his phone from his front pocket, hit two on the speed dial. Puck was a late sleeper, so he let the phone ring. After seven rings, Puck answered.

"This is Puck, you dumb fuck. It's four o'clock in the morning."

Dawson deepened his voice. "This is Professor Simpson, Mr. Puck, and it's almost noon."

"Dawson, dude. You got to hide your number to run tricks. What's up? Where are you?"

"I'm on the interstate, driving a van, working for the zoo. We're heading up to Oregon. Guess what? In six months I'll have fifty grand. That's my salary."

"No shit. So no loans, you fucker."

"No loans, Puck."

"Anyway, don't worry. You'll always have a job working for me."

"You always get that backwards. So what's new?"

They shot the shit about their friends, about Puck's robotic project, a terrain walking crane, about Puck's new girlfriend, Karen.

Then Dawson said, "Guess what? I have a strong attraction to this girl who's in the zoo. She's my uncle's student. She's good-looking too."

"Oh Jesus. You want the Puck's advice, right?"

"I'm thinking, I should just be myself, declare my feelings."

That got a guffaw. "Christ, Dawson, prepare to have your skinny heart broken. That's the best I can do. And don't kill yourself."

"Well, that's good advice. Really though. Give me a line. Just one line."

"Okay. Here's the line. You say, very sincerely—what's her name?"

"El."

"Okay, you say El, you certainly look nice today in those pants you have on. And see, that gets her thinking about her pants, and how she could take those pants off. And that's what you're looking for."

Dawson laughed. "I might even use that line."

"Well, fuck it, I got nothing for you, dude. If you like this girl, and you're around her, she'll know it. You're a good emotion hider, but that shit leaks, or else nobody ever gets laid, and the world ends. So no sweat, Dawson dude. Invite me to the wedding, and if not, don't kill yourself."

"So long, Puck, you fuck."

"Call me again when you need another line. I got a bunch of them."

They hung up. He could radio her, "El, I noticed you're wearing nice pants today." He smiled. He could say, "El, you seem kind and honest. El, please acquaint me with the animals as I heard you doing with Roger. El, do you want cream and sugar in your coffee?" Then he could say, "And now take off those pants." And suddenly he was aflame with desire and had a powerful urge to masturbate, and would have right there behind the wheel, except that it would have been chancy and messy.

•

El worked with Sybil for an hour, waiting between signals sometimes for ten minutes, chatting to Annie about Dawson's skit, her plan to segue into animal conservation and the ecopark, lead a tour. Did Annie want to lead tours? Why not, said Annie. Throw on a burnoose, big smile, say things.

Then El would whisper—"Back."

And reliable Sybil said, "Back, you devils, back," and was kissed and stroked and much loved.

El had thought of moving to the next phrases but didn't want to jam the bird and besides wanted to relieve Annie at the wheel, and then move the conversation to the *Discourses* of Meher Baba. What did she remember? What did Meher Baba say about everything? What was the universe? What was God? Get an informative conversation going. Maybe tell Annie about the hole in her heart. Or not, depending on the mood.

When she mentioned driving, Annie said, no, no, happy to drive all day, you're working, but El insisted. She said, "I have to stop with Sybil anyway. I don't want to overload her, poor baby."

So Annie relented. They radioed Bluey that they would pull off briefly to change drivers, which they did, and also reinstalled Sybil in her cage, placing it on the floor beside Patti, who had nested under the settee. El drove, a little faster now, catching back up, and pretty soon there was Dawson's van. El slowed and radioed that they were back in line.

She glanced at Annie to get a feel for her mood and saw Annie's face sober and thought-absorbed. El hesitated. A familiar thought settled on her like old clothes, and she became absorbed herself. It was a thought she had first in high school and a lot since, and had much manicured, that her life, and everyone else's life, was a zooming train, and all were passengers. I see you get on, you sit, you get off. Annie had gotten on her train, and she had gotten on Annie's, and Packer had gotten off. The old got off for good, and the young became old and got off, and the train zoomed. Many corollaries—bad track, rich trains, poor trains, trains full of pretty people or angry people, trains on separate tracks, never to meet. Many questions—who was the engineer and could you meet him (*no*), could you get him to speed up or slow down (*no*), could you guide the train by leaning (*a track, you fool!*), did the old, by chance, by lovely happenstance, get off and then on an invisible train bound for glory, or did they get off into oblivion? She could tell Annie her train thoughts, but that felt frivolous. Annie had gotten on her train, and the mast book had gotten on, and a purring tiger, and love had gotten on, coming up from the bottom of her heart like a ghost. Annie, five feet away, was a fellow passenger who knew about Meher Baba, king of the masts.

El said, "I want to ask you something sometime. You may not be in the mood to talk."

Annie wagged her head, made a smile. "I'll talk."

"You sure? I can definitely wait."

"You know what I'm thinking about?"

El thought, it would be Dawson and her, the coming love affair and broken heart. She made her tone unguilty. "What?"

"You and Dawson, of course."

The *of course* convicted her. She said, "Well, Annie, I don't know what—"

"Oh, it's just life happening. We're all cooped up in a little circus and here's goes life. You have fascinated him, which I'm sure you see. Permit me to be a smidgeon moody. Soon I will cut these underground cables, which are thick cables, between me and Dawson. I will set him free to fly or fall. Anyway, I've had my mood and now forget it."

El started to mention her train thought but saw that was an impulse toward guilty blitheness. Yes, she had felt Dawson's pained attraction, but she had not encouraged and definitely not flirted. She had lived though, right out in front of him. She had been herself and taken his hands with enthusiasm when his skit popped out. Was she supposed to be mean? But that was self-justification. She had not flirted, but she had lived out in front of him, had seen him leaning, and lived anyway, unkind and bad to do. Like enjoying ice cream in a famine. Can't I live! You cannot. To live out front is sometimes wrong and don't be simple. She would speak to Dawson. Would that be bad? It might be. He could say, what are you talking about?

Annie said, "So ask me."

El focused through her discomposure. She said, "Well, Bluey gave me this book last night which I started to read. I just looked into it really. It's about the masts in India. Who are people who are lost in the inner world, on the way to God. And Meher Baba and his people went around to them and helped them. *The Wayfarers* by William Donkin. Have you heard of it?"

"It's probably Rosa's book."

"It was. Anyway, I started reading it, jumping around. It was really interesting." And I had a spiritual experience, and I want to know about God. But she said, "So I wanted to ask you about Meher Baba."

"Like was he deluded? Or a fraud?"

"I guess, if you think he was. But really about what he said."

"Believe it or not, I was thinking last night when I got up to pee of getting that book again, the one Rosa had me read, the *Discourses.*"

"Really—"

Annie thought, because I had a spiritual experience after giving up sex with you.

The radio crackled on and Dawson's voice said, "Hey, if you guys want to get up ahead of me again, I'll fade back and let you in."

El pressed talk. "Sounds good," she said and thought, why does it matter?

El pulled into the left lane and slowly passed the van. Through Annie's window, Dawson and Annie exchanged finger waves. El let the van dwindle behind her, then pulled ahead of it and back into line. She said, "So you were thinking of getting the book—"

"I was. We could have a book club."

"Do you remember what he said?"

"I was trying to remember last night. It was extremely high-minded. God is everything, and we're all going back to God. Don't worry, be happy. That's from him. And Meher Baba is the avatar, which is God who comes down to earth now and then to sort of clear the debris. But for me mainly it was Rosa. I would read, and she would pay perfect attention and beam, and I would be a little envious, which I would hide, from myself at least, but I'm sure I didn't hide it from her. She would say, all right, dear, that's enough. Enough of this spiritual business. Let's have tea. Which was really the spiritual business. She was being kind and setting me free. She had love, and I didn't." She could say, until last night. Then she could say everything. She let the words be for a moment. Then she said, "Until last night."

"Last night?" El felt a flash tingle. "What happened?"

"Last night, around four when I got up to pee—" Would she tell it all? She might. She said, "I had quite a—I had a spiritual experience. And it had to do with you." Now the rest might come. Make a rubble. Or not.

"Really? Can you tell me?"

Annie had been looking through the window at the speeding freeway. Now she glanced at El. She said, "I can tell you. I fell in love with you, and I wanted to seduce you last night." She flushed, and her heart started. "I'm not a lesbian, far from it. But I fell in love with you for some reason. Are you shocked?" It was out. Annie's tension drained.

"Well—a little bit."

"There you go. It's a little shocking, but so what? I do like you, and if we got naked, well well, wouldn't that be sweet, and no, I'm not trying to seduce you. My spiritual experience was, I gave you up. I gave up that type of love, which is the love I know about. And then, better love came. Shining love, from a faraway land. I wanted to crawl into bed with you, and that was too tawdry and mean, And I gave it up. And then—room in my heart! I'm still sort of hallucinating. So that's the tale of Annie's spiritual experience. Have I shocked you into silence?"

El said, "Oh, Annie. I had no idea you were feeling any of that. We're so ignorant of each other. I mean everybody is. It's just great you told me all that though. Give me your hand. Let me just—"

Annie reached her hand across, and they clasped tightly, both looking ahead through the window with the same contented smile. A final squeeze, and they released.

El said, "So last night I was sitting at the settee, just after you sort of stormed out. Remember? You went out and came back in to say Bhajan was purring?"

"I remember."

"And guess what? I also had a spiritual experience."

"Really?"

"Yes. I felt love too, like fresh water. Just sweeping in. I'm not sure why though. I didn't give something up like you did. No, I did. I sort of did. I started reading about those masts, and it was like a foreign language or something. And I wanted so much to *know.* What did they experience? The pictures in that book were very stirring. Meher Baba and the masts. And the things they said too. And I couldn't— Oops, I'm going to cry. Oops oops." She brushed the sides of her eyes and shook her head. "So that's when I had my spiritual experience. I felt so outcast from that, you could say. Yes, I felt outcast. And then, somehow I had an experience. Now I remember. I was holding the book and let it go. I sort of relinquished it. I accepted that some people could have something I couldn't. And a little hole opened in my heart, and love flooded in. Damn, I wish we weren't driving so we could hug. Which might turn you on though, so that'd be bad."

Neither bothered to laugh. They looked at each other and smiled. They reached their hands simultaneously and clasped them again, holding them for a long moment before releasing.

Annie said, "Well, it's an amazing coincidence, or else it's that tiger. Have you thought of that?"

•

Lee Chin answered on the second ring. "Bluey?"

Bluey pushed the earbuds in tighter and spoke over the diesel roar. "Lee, got a minute?"

"Yeah. I got your email. Hey, big news here. Kati had twins this morning." Lee was a curator of cats at the National zoo. Kati was the zoo's five year old Sumatran tiger. Lee and Bluey had met more than twenty years ago in China.

"Wonderful. Everybody good?"

"Everybody's good. She batted the first one by accident, and we thought it was a goner, but it's moving around again. Then out pops the second one. We haven't been able to separate her from them yet, so we haven't examined them, but they look good."

Bluey and Chin had not talked for several months, and Bluey spent a patient moment inquiring about Lee's family, two daughters in college, and a wife employed as a congressional staff member, and another moment answering Lee's questions about the progress of the caravan. Because of his long association with and respect for Bluey, Lee was a supporter.

Then Lee said, "Okay, about your tiger. How long he purrs?"

"Probably six hours. From ten til four in the morning."

"Okay, that's one thing. And you say all the other animals are at rigid attention."

"Right. I could not distract them with treats."

"Okay. Well, that's nothing, man. That used to happen all the time back home."

"Really—"

"Hell, no. I'm joking. I wish you take a photo of that. You tape the purr?"

"Not yet. But I'll begin documenting shortly. We haven't got the cameras yet."

"Okay. You send it to me, okay? And one thing—your animals have chips embedded?"

"None of them."

"Well, goddamn. That was my brilliant contribution. I could have constructed something elaborate as hell from chips. The purring makes a sonic vibration, disturbs something. I was ready to write my paper."

"Sorry."

"Then best guess for me, check the water. That's the only common thing ingested, right? And the bedding. What you using, cedar?"

"Right."

"Well, that's the first thing, which I know you thought about. Change the water, call the company that makes the tanks and the chips. Put fresh water, fresh bedding. Clean the cages. That's all I got. But that tiger was purring before, right? I mean he was purring for that guy Haley, right? What does Haley say about his population? They all rigid?"

"He had the tiger quarantined in a shed, over a hundred yards away. So there was no reaction."

"You said you wrote Samuelson. You talk to him yet?"

"Just before you. He said chips too."

"He did?"

"He did."

"Well, I guess I'm not the only smartest guy in the room. That's all I got, Bluey. Get that camera up and give us a peek though. Pretty interesting."

"Give those babies a kiss for me."

"I will. Email me when the cameras are up."

They hung up, and Bluey tucked the earbuds into a console pocket. Goose lifted his head, gave matters a brief consideration, dropped it again, closed his eyes. Bluey leaned right, laid a hand on Goose's brow for a long moment. Goose huffed. His eyes remained closed.

Bluey had expected nothing and had gotten it, but the outreach was obligatory. At the last stop, he had drained and refilled the drinking water tank. But that was a forlorn hope. He could conceive of no causal mechanism, other than psychic, that could account for the behavior he had witnessed. So be there with that thought. Give way to that thought. Something psychic. A purring tiger, utterly unknown before. Mesmerized beasts. And a mast. He had given El the book. He would need it.

•

El said, "I spent an hour last night searching that book for the mast that raised him. Which I didn't find."

Annie said, "And then you have the head keeper and his guys camping out. So it's the tiger, with his NASA vibrations. I guess that would be sort of disappointing. I mean if the purr was like LSD or something."

"But the love wasn't."

"No."

They were silent for a moment. El said, "You know how with a card trick, you're amazed? For some reason, I'm not very amazed."

"It's sort of an effort to be amazed, isn't it?"

"It is."

Annie said, "How could we ever know, anyway? I mean if it *is* the tiger? That's how religions start. Somebody feels something and next thing, you can't eat fish. So being hardheaded, can a tiger inject you with love? Hmmm. So it's a coincidence. We're both going through changes and having to let go of stuff. That's what makes sense. And by the way there happens to be a tiger over there purring. You're a scientist. What does a scientist say?"

"Well first, we should just call science careful thinking. But thinking carefully? I have no idea."

Annie said, "By the way, just for the record, I'm free of sexual feeling toward you. Last night I was in a state. I was mad as hell and got passionate. And there you were, sweet child. I'm not saying it couldn't come back, but if it does, I will struggle with it in private."

"We could have a code word. If you say *pumpkin* that means you feel a twinge of attraction. Then I fart."

"Ha! Okay, pumpkin."

El again reached her hand across the space separating them, and they clasped quietly for a moment.

El said, "Boy oh boy. See how we do that? We just want to touch. That's friendship, Annie, not sex. So try not to forget that!"

Annie laughed. "That's the story of my life. I couldn't separate friendship and sex."

El said, "Well, let me just admit that I'm excited. I mean what if the universe *is* divine? A deep sense of that just came over me last night. And I thought, we're all in God's stomach, and we're slowing digesting. And the masts are almost digested! Actually, I think I believe that. I have an urge to get up and go back in the bedroom and cry, but we'd crash."

"Want me to drive?"

"No no. I'll cry right here at the wheel. I'm not. I want to see what I'm like after a few days. That's why I wanted to read Meher Baba's books. Calm down and get some thoughts."

They were silent for a moment. Annie said, "Now I will tell the story of Lucas Morningstar."

"Okay."

"Lucas was a little aboriginal guy who worked for my dad. He was the cook for the hands. He taught me to cook. He was a sweet guy, but slow talking, slow walking, very methodical. I used to drag him outside to play basketball with me. He was a bit round, and I thought he could use the exercise. In radio school, you don't have any kids around. Anyway, one of us would shoot, and there'd be a rebound, and I almost always got it. Because Lucas would not jump. He would just stand there, and I could just jump up and grab it right on top on his head. Which was fine with merciless teenage me. But finally I said, Lucas, why don't you jump? And he said, very serious—" Annie made her voice low and slow. "Because, Annie, I might not get it."

"Ha!"

"But the strange thing is, he meant it. That was inside him, a profound reluctance to hope. But he was very steady, super dependable, and a good cook."

"But a bad rebounder."

"Yes. Rebounders must hope. He would cook the same thing every week. I took the *Joy of Cooking* out to the cook shack and made him try new things, but it was hard work. Anyway, Lucas is many years gone, poor Yorick. He was sort of like a cow, how a cow crosses a field, just nodding its head and rolling along, not bothered by hope. Not that his attitude was admirable. He hadn't gotten past hope. He just hadn't gotten to it. Why am I telling you this?"

"Because I am hoping?"

"Yes, because you are hoping. And I am hoping, and every time I hope, I get pissed."

"You do?"

"Yes, and I think I feel anger stirring right now. Yes, there it is. My old friend. Last night I felt something. Great. I'm grateful, but I'm still mad. Because say it's a let's-all-go-back-to-God universe, and we're all digesting, as you say, then why is everything so goddamn vague? Every day we are just swimming in vague. If God is so loving, and it's all a game of hide and seek, why doesn't he play a game we all like? At least one we can understand. Or let us know how we're doing? Send an angel now and then. Instead, fifty thousand people die in an earthquake, and I'm supposed to give up having a good time so I can get right with the guy that engineered that? Well, I'm back to my normal self. Now I see the benefit of fasting, or at least shutting up. Meher Baba was silent for forty years. So, Annie, take a lesson, and shut up."

El said, "You're a fighter. You even want to pick a fight with God. I remember after 9-11 Billy Graham came on the radio and said, gee, I still can't figure out where evil comes from. Over here is love, and over there earthquakes and angry people. I don't mean you exactly."

"Well, it's true. I'm pissed when it comes to God. When they drag me out of the courtroom, I'll be shouting, goddammit, I'm innocent! Vagueness is atheism's best argument."

"Put up or shut up."

"Yes."

"Then again, you had a spiritual experience."

"Oh lord, it's true." She removed her phone from her shirt pocket, fitted an earbud into her ear. "Can we stop for a while? I'm starting to drift. Dawson set me up with that tape of Bluey's talk. I have to become an animal expert." She closed her eyes and switched on Blue's emphatic discourse. She tried to listen, but for a long time it was only sound.

•

Roger had bought one cheese cracker packet at the truck stop. It was open now and stacked on the console, a little four-layer cake of bad nutrition for a guy in training. Nutrition was a big thing in the league now. Not so much organics but definitely nutrient density and proper portions of carbs, proteins, and fat. Older guys were stoked about the benefits. Every team had a staff nutritionist ready to jump you if you strolled in with a big mac. No nutritionist currently aboard the Peterbuilt though.

He had come out of the bathroom at the truck stop, and the cash register guy was free and looking at him, and there was the carton of cheese crackers open on the counter, so one those, please, and it was in his shirt pocket before self-discipline could get through the door. Now self-discipline was frowning at the crackers. He wasn't going to eat them, pretty sure. He had stacked them for drama. He turned on the radio and put it on AM scan and got five seconds of everything from indie pop to pleading preachers, then back again, round and round. After four passes, he turned off the radio and let the cheese cracker stack pulse its invitation. How about eat one cracker and toss the rest? Or eat them all to celebrate a never-again resolution? How about toss them all, then buy a whole carton at the next stop, cram it down in a bathroom stall? How not to be the bathroom stall guy? How to be the big black Buddha like Bosco James instead of wrestling crazy? Bosco would say, why you making a mess, son?

Eventually he rolled down the window to toss the crackers, then thought, El and Annie will see them sailing by and think I'm littering. Still, one by one, he zipped them into the blasting air. The cracker shrine was gone. He had a hollow feeling.

•

El had gotten another thought and wanted to express it, but Annie had fallen into an open-mouthed doze. Then Annie woke and stared moodily out of the window. So El thought, no, enough for one day.

They were an hour into Oregon and would be there soon enough. That would get them interacting.

The thought that had come was two girls in a flower field. They have felt love and find themselves in a field of flowers with beautiful flowers everywhere. But there are also giant flowers that tower over their heads, and which they can't appreciate, because they are too short. Annie might say, maybe they are sour flowers, like the corpse flower. And El would say, we must grow tall and see.

El thought—for some reason I have a good opinion of all flowers, even giant ones. Because I have heard reports from the tall people. If the tall people are lying, why is the lie always about love?

•

Dawson was going over Bluey's points and using the voice recognition feature of his phone to send himself email notes. Now and then he would take a break and do a game he liked, which was speaking emphatic gibberish into the phone to see how the interpreter handled it, emailing good ones to himself. So far his best one was *will cause high good she hugged Joel Courtney yell him up hung up a titty bar hardcore teen shot of Holland kidding me Quran good shooting guard.* So titty bar and hardcore teen, connected. And Quran and Holland, wasn't there some sort of Holland-Quran stabbing thing in the news? So the interpreter was contextualizing. Go to work for Google, be a thing to do. Free place with free food and ping pong. Solve puzzles all day in an office. What he was fit for with his rocket brain. Or weld all day. Or chop wood. Something all day every day.

Then his thoughts drifted back to El. He had finally found something to say on the radio that wasn't exactly stupid—*Come up ahead again, and I'll fall back.* Anal, on second thought, but too late. When they passed, he saw she was driving. She glanced at him, gave him a chin jab.

There was something wrong with his attitude. She had snuck inside him and gotten on a throne. She was glowing, and he couldn't see her in the glow. He tried corrective thoughts. She was a human being, a bag of pus and blood and goo and shit. An animated bag though. And the animation was charming and thoughtful and kind and slim and pretty. He felt his penis thicken, thought of pus and blood and felt it wilt. What if he really did sometime put his penis in her? What then? He would look at her face, and slowly lightly press her face against his neck, and say, oh El, my penis is in you! Yes, dear, now move. And up and down he would move, with healthy surging ups and downs. Call that pudgy Puck, say, Pudgy Puck, I did the fuck.

No! Never tell, ever tell.

Can you fuck someone so gently that they hardly feel it?

13

JJ was shooting with a 4K camera in an underwater housing at 2000 frames a second, so on playback the wave crests frayed in fat juicy drops, and the surfers skidded toward him with slow insane patience. Earlier that morning, he caught a surfboard fin across his left trapezius, and it had gone through the body glove into the meat. He went back to his SUV, wiped off with peroxide, then superglued the gap, and strapped duct tape over a pad of paper towels. It might be seeping though. When he kicked down to the two fifty pound barbell weights he had pulled out to the break, he looked for sharks.

He was shooting a San Diego preliminary for the juniors, so it was lots of mom and pops on the beach with binoculars. When they saw him with the camera and barbell weights they flocked, and he promised to hand out cards when he finished so they could order. A couple of dads even helped him haul the weights out until the waves drove them off. He had a spare air can on his dive belt but hadn't needed it yet, not even to get the weights out to the break. He could hold his breath for two minutes, even with activity, and three if he was hovering.

The golden morning sun was gone. The light was high center now, no photographer's favorite, but the dark boards overhead were haloed with sparkles, and twice he had bounced up inside a curl and captured a fracturing crystal pipe, the second time with a grinning kid skimming toward him inside it, which is how he got his shoulder split. It was worth it, since his 4K slomo was brand new, latest tech, and could make two second shots into beauty-aching minutes.

He was making beauty-aching minutes at home too, not with slomo but with his hat cam El footage, blowing her voice out of the frame into an *I love* voiceover, fading and panning stills which started into motion, stopped, then moved again, syncing each frame to *Little Jenny Dow*. It was hard work, and harder now since his mother saw her shrink twice a week, getting pep talks, then returned home to slip JJ solemn straight-backed glances. She cooked meals and left them in the fridge with notes. She made his bed and cleaned his bathroom when he left the house. Once she stopped at his doorway in her robe and said, *I know those cameras in the basement aren't for security, JJ.* She was groping toward something she couldn't see, building courage. But she was building the way the world was built, in the night, without light, toward nothing.

The tide was high when he started the barbell weights back toward the beach, pulling down his rope leash fourteen feet to pace the weights beachward twenty steps before breaking back to the surface. The effort opened his cut, and he saw it feather stain the water when he lifted. The second kick down he saw the shark, a ten footer, cutting past and turning, feeling for decision. He unzipped his body glove so he could get to his Gerber. When he reached the break, his mask blew down around his neck. He didn't bother to reset it, but let the world foam white above and murky green beneath and once felt the shark's body or tail bump past his waist. He pulled down the rope to the sand, paced the weights, kicked up to breathe, then down to pace the weights, then was in the shallows, and the fathers came to help and saw the blood on his chest and sympathetically exclaimed.

At his SUV, he handed out cards to moms and pops. He felt black lost sorrow. He could have ended in a satisfying shark fight.

14

Charles Garrell, chairman of the county commission, said, "When you get off the freeway you'll see the Holiday Inn. I got a guy in a white county van on the side of the road. He's going to lead you in. You got about three miles after that. You're going to be in a hotspot between the chickens and cows. I expect we'll put thirty thousand past your gate every day. I ran three hoses out to you, and electric, and you'll see the dumpster. You can move it with your forklift if you need to."

Bluey said, "Wonderful. By the way, did a package arrive for me?"

"Yes, and for some damn reason it got opened. It's a box of uniform shirts. I put it on top of the dumpster. Sorry it got opened."

"No problem. I feel well cared for and many thanks."

"I can't wait to experience the thrilling menagerie."

They ended the call, and Bluey radioed that their turn was approaching, that they would follow a white van, please respond. A crackle of acknowledgments—"Right, okay, ten-four."

Bluey did math—thirty thousand, give him ten percent, three thousand times five, fifteen grand a day, five days, seventy-five grand, less twenty percent for the county, sixty grand. If five percent, thirty grand. His per day expenses, best guess, salaries included, would average $2,500. Travel time was dead, so the caravan would be open to the public only three fourths of the time. Take a fourth from thirty, twenty-three about, deduct expenses, net ten grand per show. Profit was possible. Which meant the ecopark might prosper and not, like public zoos, teeter from year to year on uncertain budgets. But if one percent, then six grand and a loss. But surely more than one percent. The exit came up, and the county van pulled onto the road in front of him.

They drove past plowed greening fields into the Willamette valley. As they crossed a swift river, the Ferris wheel came into view, then the midway, the permanent buildings, the big tents. They drove past the site, then turned onto a gravel road and entered the rear of the fair grounds. Behind two hangar-sized rectangular buildings in a grassy field, a short round man stood beside a dumpster, Charles Garrell, fair director and welcoming committee. He was a bluntnosed man with a horseshoe of wooly hair around a smooth head. He beamed and offered his hand.

"Honored to meet you, Dr. Bluey Macintosh."

"Honored to be here."

"We put you in an NPR radio ad. It'll be on today and the whole five days. Oh, you're gonna be a draw. You'll get traffic." Garrell pointed to a gate in the chain link fence. Beyond it, a road led between the flanks of the buildings. "There's your gate. Setup like you want, but that's the access. They come out of the chickens and turkeys smack into you before they hit the cows. Anybody likes chickens bound to like a lion." He handed Bluey a card. "My cell's on there. Call me when you get to your first problem. I'll be on the grounds all five days conducting this orchestra. By the way, if you need extra help, I got two teenage sons, and they're halfway responsible."

•

The stockade and hip level crowd fencing were in place in under an hour. Bluey sent Dawson to the RV to shower, then began a stroll through the grounds. Toohey and Thane had vomited again. Now the routine on moving days would be to feed those two in the evening after the move.

The sun was low, the horizon rosy, the air cool. A morning fog would likely roll up from the river but be gone when the fair opened at nine the next morning. The forecast was for sunshine.

Bluey passed around the perimeter between the crowd fence and the enclosures, speaking each animal's name as he passed—"Ho, Quanna. Ho, Kip." When he finished the round, he crossed to the zoo's center to help El assemble the oval of locking crowd fence around the tiger. She had already installed the signage, each sign velcroed to the right side of the cages, five foot tall white slabs of weatherproof plastic with each animal's name, description, and habitat, an immense dashed white line to direct and inform. She had changed into gym shorts.

She said, "I'll be the sign person if that's all right. We don't want them battered-looking."

"You are hereafter the sign walla."

There was the unspoken promise of talk between them, but the smell of meat loaf was in the air, and they would be called soon. El said, "Annie and I had a nice ride together and talked of many things. She said you were a mystic. You owe me a talk. Remember?"

"I remember."

"Annie also experienced something. Of a spiritual nature." Was that a violation of confidence? It involved her sensual love of El, so yes. She said, "Maybe I shouldn't have mentioned that. Annie thinks Dawson is attracted to me." She paused, got a slow nod. "Do you think he is?"

"Why not? Try not to make a mess."

"God, no. Anyway, I'm four years older. Annie said, maybe it's the tiger. All this love. There's Haley and his guys too."

Bhajan lay on his side ten feet away, his head against a mound of cedar chips. He met their gazes, then rolled onto his feet, shuddering chips from his shoulders. He held their gaze for a moment, then swung away, crossed to his water trough, and began lapping tonguefulls of water. When he was done, he crossed the cage to face them, held them in an impassive gaze, then lowered his head and pressed his forehead against the bars.

El approached. Across her shoulder, she said, "He did that this morning, Bluey, with Roger and me." She laid her hand on his head, stroked the orange fur. "I let Roger touch him, but I told him never to do it again. Now I'm doing it."

Bluey said, "El, come away."

She stepped back. Bhajan raised his head, turned and crashed gently back onto the cedar chips. He head lolled, and his eyes closed.

El said, "Don't worry, I remember all the crazy keeper stories. But this is an extremely attractive tiger. Let's just admit that." She shuddered, and her arms and shoulders shook spasmodically. "God, that was a super shiver. I need to go for a run. Bluey, something is happening here. Maybe it hasn't gotten into you yet, but it has me. I'm about to pop. We're done, right? I want to run. Tell Annie I won't be long if she calls us for dinner. I don't want to run on a full stomach. Maybe we could walk around the fairgrounds and have a talk after supper. If you have time." She broke into a run, waved briefly over her head, and disappeared through the compound entrance into the fairgrounds.

Goose sprinted into view from the rear gap in the stockade, made a fast circuit around the tiger cage and stopped in front of Bluey, head high. Bluey bent, bestowed a quick ear scrub. Patti emerged from the stockade gap, approached slowly, and dropped to her stomach in the grass behind Goose. Bluey watched the tiger breathe, saw its long flat flank rise and fall.

He said, "Bhajan."

The tiger continued to breathe.

He said loudly, "Bhajan!"

Goose alerted, stood, glanced fast about. The tiger gave no notice.

Bluey made another rounds, then started back to his truck to check email. As he passed the RV, the door opened, and Dawson descended the steps with his shaving kit, towel across his shoulder, barefoot, hair wet and straight-combed, his tennis shoes in his hand.

Dawson said, "Hey, man. I was thinking. Remember those banners I was talking about. On the stockade. The people all looking in at something? I was thinking, that's pretty high priority. That's a crowd magnet. So maybe after the logo, that's the next thing."

"Good."

"By the way, I need the address of the ecopark, and phone if you want to put that. I mean for the trucks and stationary."

"I'll email it."

"And I was thinking, for the stockade, a kind of a Norman Rockwell thing. Little kids and strollers, everybody pressed forward, except one or two little kids are too short and no one's holding them up, and they're looking back."

"Good." A pause. Their moods did not match, Bluey's thoughtful, Dawson's eager. Bluey made his tone interested. "Let me see a sketch before you commit."

This kindness could not halt Dawson's quick chagrin as he understood his imposition. He said, "Mom says dinner in ten minutes." He padded around the RV toward his van, parked some hundred yards away by the river.

Bluey felt for some easing comment, but Dawson's self-consciousness repelled solace. Annie opened the RV door, dinner bell in hand, saw her absorbed brother, and halted. She rang the bell, but softly.

He turned.

"Dinner," she said, and laughed. She said, "Have I recalled you from the deep?"

He entered the RV and seated himself at the settee. Annie had arranged silverware, plates, and napkins.

He said, "You seem happy."

"Off and on. Presently on, since my son was here and did not scorn me."

"El is running and apologizes if she's late."

"You want some tea? I made iced tea, and then I thought, it'll keep us up with the caffeine. But that's all we have for now. We need a grocery run already. I made a calendar of meals too. You want some?"

"Yes, thanks." As Annie began to gather tea things, he said, "Now you must tell me your theory of why our parents were glancers."

"Oh, it's just a thought. It's that after a big war, and that was the biggest war ever, World War Two, there are so many souls needing bodies again you have to take pot luck, and maybe you're not deeply connected to the family you get. I know a lot of people that feel that way, that they were born to glancers."

"Interesting thought. El said you talked of many things. And that you had an experience, which might be private, and she's sorry she mentioned it."

"Oh, god." Annie brought glasses and a plastic pitcher to the table, removed the lid, poured. The rumble and clank of ice remarked the silence. She felt—the others will be coming. But tell. Tell until they come.

She said, "Yes, I had a little experience. Of a spiritual nature, you might say." She saw his face shift and soften, and some inner keystone inside her slipped. She slid abruptly into the settee, sloshing a lurp of tea onto Bluey's knuckles. Sobs cascaded up and out. Tears dripped onto the settee, making crystal glimmers. After a moment, her sobs began to mix with laughter. Then that was gone. A fifteen second tear-joy locomotive. She raised her head, saw Bluey's benign half smile. He seemed unbaffled and content. She laid her hands against her cheeks, reentering her face, then reached for Bluey's cheeks. He leaned slightly forward, offering them. She laid her hands on the white stubble and briefly pressed. As she took her hands away, she flicked his nose with a forefinger. She smiled. She said, "Can't you be a little surprised?"

His mouth opened, but no words came.

She said, "I fell in love with El and then renounced her. My fastest love affair ever. I woke up at four and thought about getting into bed with her." She dabbed his tea-wet hand with a napkin. "But something entered me, and I didn't. I felt a transport of divine love. What you have always wanted for me. So stop hoping. The transformation has begun." Her grimace did not erase that truth. Let that truth exist. She scrubbed her teary face with the damp napkin. Through the RV window, she saw El and Dawson walking across the field of grass. "El also had an experience, did she tell you? So maybe it's that tiger and his hyoid bone. Boy, did I just cry and laugh? I think I'm levitating. Doesn't it have to be the tiger?"

She got up to ring the dinner bell in earnest.

•

Roger lay on his bed with his laptop open. She had written back. He read—"It was a pleasure to read your nice letter, and I think it would be fun to meet you. Why does that sound so shallow! Oh, well. Your letter was nice, and it would hopefully be fun to get together. That is about all you can get from a letter. Relationships are pretty darn slow. I could say damn or goddamn, by the way, but darn is about as much as I wanted right there. I think your directness has inspired me. So who am I? God knows. I was a cheerleader in high school which I point out because you play football. So we have sports in common. I played volleyball in college as well. I was an average striker, but I could dig and pass quite well. I am not trying to impress you. I'm just being straightforward and happy to talk. I am trying to say candid things and get us off to a good start, which is what you did. I work in a coffee shop. Actually, I run the coffee roaster which supplies five shops. Well, it was fun to write to you. You are on the west coast! It's like a flower and a bee. I am putting a little perfume in the air to see if you buzz over from way out there in California or wherever you are just now. That sounds conceited, but I am letting it stand. If you are a mass murderer, please do not write back! I just reread this. What will you think! I have to wait and see! Send!"

Partly way through the dinner bell rang, and he ignored it. He had been rapt. His heart beat, and he closed his eyes. A sigh rinsed through him. He reread her letter, and it was like on a dance floor, and she dances over and says, can you dance? Holding out her hand. Definitely he could dance. He could put his arm around her waist and turn her round and round. He would write later. He reread the letter once more. He could come home to this girl, who danced so friendly and free. He closed the laptop and with both hands brought it slightly forward, keeping its edge neatly aligned with the edge of the desk, just so.

•

Dawson sat on the edge of the van's open sliding door, wiped his feet with a dirty T-shirt, then put on socks and high-top tennis shoes, leaving them unlaced. He combed his hair, then snagged it into a pony tail, got a rubber band around it and shook it until finger-sized strands fell down his temples. Without a border his face was like a blade. He had parked away from the others again, pulling across the grass and stopping beside a dirt brown path along the river. When he turned off the engine, he could hear a river rapids hushing through the tree screen.

Good white noise for sleep. Except if guys came out early to fish if that's what the path was.

He turned, put a knee on the floor mat, and checked his face in the mirror above the sink. He had good skin, but had felt a zit coming, and there it was, left corner of his mouth, a pink sore bump, so he had that to look forward to, two or three days of swelling, screwing with it toward the end, trying to get it to pop, then a day or two of healing. Sitting across from El and eating dinner. He could get Clearasil, or put a little round band-aid on it, and say, I cut myself shaving. Or he could actually do that, nick it with his razor, a shaving cut which, yes, happens to be on my unsightly pimple, so what?

Then there was the girl herself, jogging out of the trees along the path in her blue shorts. She had sweated semicircles under her arms and a big one across the parrots in front, and pieces of hair were stuck to her shining brow. He got out onto the grass, rolled the van door closed, used the clicker to lock it. She jogged up, danced a few steps before stopping, one hand shoving hair back, the other akimbo, blowing breath and smiling.

She said, "You got a good spot here. There's a path down to the river back there. Really pretty."

He said, "Good." She was really pretty too, and healthy. He could go for a run with her. Except he would probably faint. He needed something to say and almost stupidly said that. Then he remembered the dinner bell. He said, "The dinner bell rang. I was just heading up there." He added, "You can jog on if you want."

"Well, I probably—no, I'll walk with you. I can wipe off later."

They started across the grass which was unmowed and knee high. She said, "My mother always talks about chiggers. She grew up in Louisiana and one time had almost five hundred chigger bites. She got them in tall grass on a bird-watching trip."

"What's a chigger?"

"Oh, it's a tiny bug, and its bite swells up like a little pimple and itches. She got a fever and had to go to the hospital."

He could say, you saw my pimple, didn't you? You're bringing up chiggers to fuck with me. A breathy *ha* came out.

She said, "What?"

"Nothing. Just chiggers. Good we don't have them."

She said, "I always think of the civil war and all those guys having to camp out. They have ticks all over the south too."

"And people shooting at you."

"That too."

She bent forward, still walking, and peripherally he saw her lift the front of her shirt and dry her face. He kept his gaze forward. He caught her sweaty clean scent. He could say, one day I want to try a jog. He could say, I would like to know more about chiggers in the civil war. Or—those are nice shorts you have on, El. He didn't say anything.

She said, "I haven't called my parents yet. I definitely have to call them tonight. And Packer too, who's probably getting a grudge. Packer's my boyfriend. He's in Dubai."

That stabbed him center-chest. Of course she would have a boyfriend, you small blind person. The center-chest pain was his badge. It was justice.

They walked together, kicking down the tall grass. He saw her head fall forward a little and her slim shoulders rise as if she had hunkered on a thought. She was slightly ahead now, so that he could peripherally see the flank of her body. She seemed innocent of her allure which sharpened his pain. He could reach and touch her but wouldn't, of course. Rapists did. They went wild with isolation. How if some day he stopped her in the grass, held her gently by the shoulders, said, *El, I am here and he is not. Ignore my pimple.* He stopped a laugh. She forged through the grass. As they passed the big trucks and neared the RV, he tried to think of some easy-going thing to say. But she was ahead of him on the mowed grass now and speeding up, and he would have to scurry to reach her, and, anyway, nothing came.

•

Dinner was two pans of meat loaf, baked potatoes, and a salad. Bluey assessed the day's performance—excellent—and described tomorrow, Annie at the gate, he and El mingling, Roger monitoring the crowd and cleaning if necessary, Dawson off for groceries and errands, then to work in his van. The uniform shirts were stacked on the passenger seat, two for everyone.

Roger, who was seated next to El on the settee, said, "El, you are sweaty. Please keep your sweaty forearms away from me."

She obliged him with a halfhearted elbow. He said, "By the way, I'm gonna run every morning, in case you want to run with someone."

El said, "Would I have to carry a bag of feed?"

"It would not be fair to make me carry all the feed."

This got a smile, a slight arch of the neck. But she didn't reply. She methodically forked her meat loaf into small pieces.

Roger looked at Bluey, who was seated beside Dawson. "Bluey, I'm going to work hard here and be on the ball. But a year from now, I hope to be playing football in the NFL."

"We hate to lose you."

"So the thing is, I need to be in the best shape of my life in six months. I was thinking, I could get some of those exercise bands, you know? But then, that's for toning, and I need bulk. So what I really want—and it won't get in the way of any of my work, that's for sure—I need weights. There's lots of room in the trucks for them. The thing is, I want to get about three hundred pounds, which is a lot to carry, so I could chip in for the diesel. They wouldn't be in the way."

Bluey said, "How much will you be willing to chip in?" Then, as Roger considered this with an open mouth, he laughed. He said, "I'm teasing. I will inflict no fee for the transport of your weights. I admire your ambition."

"Well, I really thank you. But the thing is, how can I get the weights?" He glanced at Dawson.

Dawson was staring out of the window. He felt Roger's glance and said absently, "I can get them at Walmart." He turned to Bluey, "There's a Best Buy in Eugene too. I should get the stuff we talked about, right?"

Bluey said, "Let's go over it one more time. But yes, get the stuff."

Dawson returned his face to the window, where the sun yellowed a ribbed sky. He would spend the evening working on the logo. He would hear the river and work. That would feel flat. The world had become wide and smooth, and he was a dot in the middle. He heard his mother say, "I have a grocery list too, by the way."

He said to the window, “No problem.”

Roger said, “Okay, last thing, since you'll be at Walmart—”

Dawson said, “Protein powder.”

“That's right! They've got this protein powder I used to get. How did you guess that?”

Dawson made a trifle shrug. He thought, because Mother mentioned food and that reminded you. He thought—like the web. It's all a thought web. Different than the internet, made of mind. He should think about that, but it went away.

Annie, who was seated on the folding chair at the table's end, rose, brought the remaining pan of meat loaf from the stove top and spatulaed the remainder onto Roger's plate. She said, “Can you consume that?”

He said, “I can and I will. I see where Dawson gets his mind-reading ability.”

Bluey said, “Everyone can read minds.” He felt them waiting. He said, “We register each other's moods and intentions using the tiniest clues because we see the mind behind the face. The questions comes, is empathy interpretation, or is there a force in the mind of another that impresses us and is not wholly dependent on clues? Is it possible to read minds without seeing the face? Various views on that.”

This tidy conundrum left a wake of silence. Then Dawson turned from the window. He said, “It can't be just interpretation. Because how would we know what we're seeing? I mean how do we know what frustration looks like? Or irony? We don't study ourselves in the mirror and memorize that. We knew that before there were mirrors.”

Bluey said, “We call it instinct, but that's just naming the mystery.” He laid his thick hand on Dawson's for a brief second. He said, “If this conversation continues, we will dissolve into light.”

•

El tucked her phone into her jeans and left the RV. The sun was down and the temperature had dropped, and the coolness of night came up from the river. Her hair was still damp from the shower, which today she had squeezed in before Annie's, and she felt a cap of chill. She scrubbed her scalp, then flounced. Now it was either down to the river to make the call, or head into the carnival and find the carousel she had seen earlier. The river meant a flashlight. And she would have to pass Dawson's van. Carnival then.

She crossed the zoo grounds. Most of the animals were in a contented digestive doze. Bhajan sprawled full length, eyes closed. As she reached the entrance gate, Goose rose from his spot beside the sun bear and padded after her. She heard his pant, turned.

"Coming? Please come. I want you, Goose."

Earlier, she had run through the midway. There were carts and dollies everywhere, everybody setting up, and she had gotten looks, a health jogger in the working world. But before heading off down the road, then down the path through the trees, she had seen the carousel at the end of a lane of booths.

Goose fell into place at her side, and they entered the fairgrounds. They walked up the lane along the manure-musty chicken building, past a stand selling dipped apples, past the buffalo burgers, then into the midway. It was empty now, everyone off to the RV camp she had seen at the edge of the fair. The exuberant neon was off, and the wide-spaced security lights made a cold gloom. Way better than the river, which would have been, why so blue amid this beauty? This was, come one, come all, get your gloom on in dead town.

She took a lane into the ride grounds, went past the Fireball, a flashy train on a giant loop, past a second-hand looking Ferris wheel and Octopus, then the Tilt-a-Whirl, and had they moved the carousel? No. There it still was, down another lane, and behind it, like a beacon, a low swollen moon.

She slid onto the giraffe bench, patted the plastic seat beside her. Goose popped up and laid his head on her lap. She woke her phone, held one on the dialer.

Her Mother answered. "El, dear?"

"It's me."

"Well, your father will be upset. He's teaching a pottery class at the Y."

"Tell him I love him."

"I will. Where are you?"

El gave a brief synopsis—the Heavenly Vineyards set up and take down, the drive, the thrilling inaugural speech of Sybil the parrot, the skit, Annie, Roger, Bluey, Dawson.

"Gosh, that sounds like fun. How are you? I'm catching an undertone."

"Well—"

"Is it Packer?"

"No, it's not Packer." It would be a labor to tell. But tell. She said, "What happened, it's Dawson. He's nineteen. He's a very smart loner type. And he's attracted to me, and it feels awful. Annie predicted it would happen. And so I lied to him, and I said I had a boyfriend. Named Packer. So I'm getting some mileage there. I said I had to call my boyfriend. And just then, dammit, I got blue. Like I hit a switch somewhere. So that's it. I'm not guilty, I just—"

"You must like him."

"Yes! I like him! So it's too bad." She had not mentioned her spiritual experience. She hadn't even mentioned Bhajan. She said, "Also, I forgot the main thing, there's this tiger who purrs. A Bengal tiger, and tigers don't purr, except for this one." She could say, *It could be affecting us.* But that was an effort. She said, "Anyway. I could go on. Pretend I just went on for twenty minutes about my sad feelings. Any Sacramento murders, by the way, to get your career going?"

"Not yet. Fingers crossed. You know where I am right now?"

"Where?"

"I'm sitting in dad's green chair, and in front of me I have a steaming cup of mint tea. It's steeping, and it's probably just about right. I'm taking out the teabag and sipping. Yes. It's very tasty. Also, I have a cookie. Dippy is somewhere. Dippy? There he is. He's coming from the kitchen. Dip, come up. Now he's on my lap. Lay down. No, that's my cookie. I'm giving him a one-handed ear scratch, and he's going into happy land. I have taped a masterpiece theater, but I've forgotten which one. That's the evening plan. So think of me scratching Dip, sipping tea, and enjoying a nice murder. Can you think of that?"

"Yes, I can. Thanks, Mom. You have made me cry. Well, good. I'm also scratching a dog's head. His name is Goose. I'm sitting on a carousel in the fairgrounds. Now I better get off the phone, because I'm about to get arrested by a security guard."

"Is it all right? Should I worry?"

"No. He's just walking by. We're waving to each other. He says, thieves do not bring dogs and talk on cell phones. Off he goes. All the lights are off mostly."

"I love you, sweetie."

"I love you right back. Give dad a kiss for me. I mean really do."

"I'll meet him at the door with a giant smacker."

El heard a smacking sound. Her mother said, "And that's a kiss from him."

"Bye, Mom."

"Bye, sweetheart."

•

Dawson stopped and turned to his mother. He said, "You want me to have feelings, and I don't. You can't go get them off a tree, you know."

He and Annie had finished the dishes, and she had walked halfway with him in the cooling darkness toward his van. She had stopped them in the tall grass and said, try not to be mad, I know you have a right but what a waste, what can I do?

Her face was shadowed, and he couldn't see her expression. It would be grieved, set with pleading. Forgive me, I insist. But he had found something true to say. Feelings don't grow on trees.

She said, "No, they don't."

He felt her softness but wanted to be away, in his van, and not yield. He folded his arms and shifted his feet. She touched his forearm.

She said, "Did you know your uncle was a poet?"

"No."

"Well, he is. A private one, for his friends. He sent me a poem years ago that I love. Here it is—

Man's love is fire and pits itself against the night.
Water is a woman's love. It finds the lowest place and stills.

Isn't that lovely?"

"Say it again."

She did.

He said, "That's nice. Email it to me, will you?"

"I will. Anyway, that's how I'm feeling. I have become still, at least stiller, down here in the lowest place. Maybe I'm loving myself. Forgiving myself anyway, even if I shouldn't. I was reckless. I let a bastard into our lives and didn't watch him, and I should have. I can't take it back. Or be sorrier than I am. But I *am* sorry, about many things." There was a silence. She said, "So anyway, sweet dreams."

She gave his arm a last touch as she walked away.

He said, "Send that poem."

"I will."

He stood and listened for a while to the sigh of grass her passage made. She had untied her end of some tether between them, and he felt it slacken. Maturity would be, all right, Mother, let it be in the past. But something in him could not rise. He headed for the van, and the river murmur came up over the whisper of grass. He stopped at the van door and turned to the river and listened. He thought, it's like an old language no one understands anymore.

•

Annie passed through the gap in the stockade, thinking to browse the beasts, give them presence, as Bluey would put it. As she passed between the lion and okapi cages, she stopped. Bluey had erected a halogen on a pole above one end of the tiger cage, and Roger was stretched on the grass under it doing push-ups. She counted. He trembled up the last one at twenty-three, but some before too, so pretty good for a giant. She could say, next time let me sit on your shoulders. When she was twenty she would have said it, and done it too. The old young Annie. Now the new old Annie. Her speech to Dawson had surprised her. Remorse, not guilt. In remorse was hope. She had not embraced him though. She had kept her pain, and as they parted felt her heart tear. You could wait out that pain. Or rodeo it away on someone's shoulders.

Roger had gotten to his feet and was doing twists as she approached. She said, "What position did you play?"

"Offensive lineman. You know what that is?"

She said, "Sure. My first husband drug me to Forty-niners' games. You're the guy that has to stop those tricky defensive guys. And protect that precious boy in the back."

She saw his broad face gladden. "You're right. Those guys are major tricky."

"Hard on the body. And the head too, is what we hear these days."

Roger only nodded.

She said, "Well, I'll let you get back to it."

"I'm just finishing up. Don't want to get sweaty."

Did he want to talk? But she didn't. She said, "See you." She turned back toward the RV, forgetting her planned rounds, and her eyes swept the tiger, upright and watching. An impulse of sympathy turned her back. "Hey, this tiger will probably purr again. I'm going to make some tea when he starts and put a blanket down. So if you want some tea. It has caffeine, but I'll make it weak."

He said, "Cool."

•

Bluey was rereading his colleague Samuelson's long email detailing his research into the hyoid bone, vibration frequencies, and harmonics. He heard a soft voice under his compartment window.

"Bluey?"

"El? What's up?"

"Nothing. Just wondered if you had a minute. Later is okay."

"I'm coming out. Let me get my shoes on."

He pulled a sweatshirt over his head, slipped his bare feet into the coolness of rubber shoes, then shrugged into the cargo jacket. He got down through the passenger door. El stood, hands in her jeans pockets. In the flash of cab light before the door closed, he caught her expression—determined, apprehensive.

He said, "You wanted to have a talk."

"I do. But maybe this is not the time. I mean we have a big day tomorrow."

"We do. But we're ready. So we can have a talk. Let's find a spot."

"Also, Bhajan is going to purr and the animals will begin behaving. So—"

"C'mon. We'll find a place we won't be interrupted."

He led them through the stockade to a spot between Oz the meerkat and Sybil. Bluey sat on the grass and leaned against the bamboo. El stopped at Sybil's cage. She said, "Hello, sweetie. Soon a treat will come. Now I'm going to give you a little test. Are you ready for my test?"

Sybil was perched on one of her cross members looking forward toward the center of the zoo and the tiger cage.

El said, "Back!"

Sybil swiveled her head toward El, then back. She said, "Back, you devil's, back."

"Thank you, sweetie. That was super duper. That's all for today. We'll just be back here talking and don't mind us. Thank you, sweetie."

She sat a yard from Bluey, facing him, legs folded under her. She said, "That is so exciting, Sybil speaking. Isn't it?"

"It is."

"Oh, you're not excited. That's okay. I just talked to my mother, which was great. She got me out of a mood." She flash-considered telling about the Dawson lie, but no, superfluous. She said, "So I wanted to ask you about something. This could be personal, I'm not sure. Well, it is personal. I said I had a spiritual experience. I felt a brand new, very distinct, very sweet feeling. In my heart. It was love, of all things. I'm super grateful. But who am I grateful to? Does it have to be God? I mean I'm sort of into the new atheists. Annie says you're a mystic. I really don't know what I'm asking. But *The Wayfarers* is a fantastic book if it's true. And we have a tiger that was raised by one of those guys. If it's not true, then it's a super detailed lie. But if you pulled a gun and made me guess, I would guess it's true. My dad says that, by the way, about the gun. Also, if he were here, he'd say, hey, you're using my material. So." She peered at him. He was hunched, grass-staring, immobile. "Now I offer you, Bluey Macintosh, my full attention. I have no idea what I'm asking. But maybe my life just got super interesting. And extremely deeply meaningful. Boy, that feels good to say. All right, I'm shutting up. If you don't have a comment, I completely accept that."

Bluey lifted his head. He had been feeling for a beginning and had come to—put a dipper anywhere in the river, it's all water. He said, "You picked up a scent, and you want to know if anyone else smells something."

"Yes."

"And people might say, what? I don't smell anything. Or they might talk about the types of scent, Indian, Chinese, this and that. Do they know something? Do they have a map to find the source of the scent? And why are there so many opinions? Why don't they agree? So I'll start there. Here's a thought I have always loved—if any two people are determined to be honest and patient, they are compelled, by the nature of existence itself, to agree about everything. It's a simple thought, but deep. And true. Because that's how honesty works. It's a kind of surrender, and, if you have patience, it leads past opinion to wonder. But you might say, well, so what if they agree about the nature of the world? They'll still fight to get what they want. But they won't, because in the end honesty reveals commonality. Oneness, to say it plainly. That's what you come to when honesty begins to work. You see that we're all—well, we may not be in the same boat, but we're all in the same ocean. I've started with big thoughts because big thoughts straighten out the little ones. Little thoughts like to tangle. Here's the central big thought—everything is a divine effulgence, and the purpose of life is to discover that and get home. And how to do it? Inside your heart, there's a furnace, and that furnace is need, and it's love, and it's the soul catching the scent of where it came from, which is love, which is oneness. And all the pettiness and disappointment and pride you feel can be fed piece by piece into that furnace. You burn yourself up, and you find out that fire keeps you warmer than all your philosophy ever did. That's it."

"Oh, that's perfect. That's so excellent." She wrapped her arms around her chest. She said, "Annie said atheism's best argument was vagueness. It's a good point. If you saw that effulgence everywhere all the time, it would be simple. But then last night I did see it. A little bit. Love came, out of a hole in my heart, is how I thought about it. It's the furnace really. So do I suddenly believe in God? I remember you told me it's not what you believe, it's what you feel. Faith is different. Maybe that's all you need. It's definitely different than belief." She reached forward and softly touched both of her hands to his, then withdrew. She said, "You are a true Bluey. Thank you for telling me those excellent thoughts. Also, as far as I can tell, Meher Baba says just about that too." She gave him a tentative glance.

"So why did I not respond to him? Why did I not read the book?"

"Well, if it's too personal—"

"You said it just now. You must feel something."

"And you didn't?"

"I didn't."

"That must have hurt Rosa." She shook her head. "Oh, right there is something too personal. Don't answer."

"It did hurt her. But for me, not for her."

El's face opened with a thought. "You know why she gave you that book, Bluey? That was her smart kindness. Because it's not a book of spiritual topics or something, which for you would be old hat. It's a book of facts. But for some reason it didn't interest you. I'm so nosy. But here's the main thing. What if Meher Baba really was God? Would it help if you thought that? Would believing that help you feel God? Or would it just be naming the furnace and not make any difference?"

"That deserves thought."

"Anyway, I read about Meher Baba on the net. There's probably fifty websites. Plus we have a tiger that's maybe connected to him. I'm going to get his book called the *Discourses*."

"He has another one called *God Speaks*."

"Oh god, really? Well, if he was God, I guess that's what he would say. I was thinking, if you were like a baker in Jerusalem, I mean back then, and your friend says, hey, that Jesus guy is coming to town, let's check him out. What would you do? I mean, would you put down your pastry dough and pack a lunch? Or would you say, Jees, not another one. I mean, if you believe in Jesus, you're lucky two thousand years have gone by, and he has all this cred. Because back then, hey, there he is, that scrawny guy on a donkey. They killed him, after all. I guess I'm packing a lunch though. Also, and this is probably the main thing, I had my spiritual experience over one of Meher Baba's books. A book about him, anyway."

Blue listened, fascinated. He wanted to embrace her, but let the urge pass. He said, "Let me know what you find."

•

Roger made a fast circuit around the cages, creating breeze to dry the sweat bloomed by his pushups. He passed the ostrich cage, then the peacock, heard voices, and slowed. As he came abreast of the parrot cage, he saw through the links, past Sybil's sleek form, Bluey and El seated on the grass beside the bamboo, El talking. He made a pivot and started back the other way. Her tone was intent and private, and besides he didn't want to greet and be greeted. He was concentrating on the upcoming challenge of composing his letter to Dori. He had the first sentence mind-written, *I loved your letter*, but after that, doing pushups and walking, he had flashed on himself at his laptop, fearing. What would be the next sentence? He had gotten infected with fantasies, which he couldn't write. The fantasies were about him and Dori in a garden, reaching up for okra, bending down for cabbage, a scoop of compost here, snag a weed there. He comes up behind her and slaps her butt. She says, pretend insulted, *hey, mister*, and stands up, and they are face to face, and he picks her up and lays her between the tomatoes with their musty tomato leaf smell and pulls her pants down, and she can hardly stop kissing him, and they have intercourse in the tomatoes and flow and flow.

If he wrote that, and she read that, she would probably call the police. In a month he could write that, when they were friends. Here's a vegetable garden fantasy I had when we first met. I realize sex in a bed is more normal and is fine. But she says, no, I like garden sex, sex in beautiful nature. And into his mind as he made his brisk sweat-evaporating walk comes Dori and Roger in the water by a waterfall, and she lifts her legs to fit with him, their bodies skin to skin, her head against his chest, and they flow.

So to get from here, where she was wild imagination, to there, where they loved each other and felt free. There were steps, like the steps to the NFL, pushups and feed bags. The next step with Dori was a calm letter with a particular tone, a perfect right mature tone that wouldn't alarm her or be childish or mention sex. If he wrote right now, in his current mood, he would write formally, to prove he wasn't a sex addict, or in love with a letter and a picture. And formal would be awful, like drinking dirt, and lovingly would be wrong. So then some kind of invented tone that would convince her he was normal. Dori, your letter caught my attention, and I would like to get to know you. Perhaps we can arrange a meeting and have coffee? Fine, she writes back, we'll have coffee, just coffee, I mean it, and don't try to get me into the tomatoes. They would definitely joke around. He could make her laugh. If she were right now with him, he could lead her from cage to cage. This is Kip the caracal, who lives in distant somewhere, this is Toohey, the honey badger, who will fight a lion. If she were beside him now, he would fold her in his arms, and they would flow.

•

For two straight hours, Dawson had used the gradient map tool in Illustrator to shade animals and letters, getting into it, little tweak here, a fold there, so that when he finally came up from his concentration daze, he sunk back on his seat like a freed prisoner. The electronic pen fell out of his hand and clattered on the floorboards. He closed his eyes. When he opened them again, the logo would be fresh. Splash it into his head, see if he had something, or if it was a gaudy corny nothing.

He felt tension drain in the black, and thought, like a pond draining. On the pond bottom, a muddy car, a rusty bed, the bottom me. That was the self, always underneath. No matter what you filled it with, the mud me underneath.

He opened his eyes just before the screen blinked black and screensaver flowers bloomed. But he had seen the logo for an instant, a perfect sighting, a flash of color and jolt of beauty. Gratitude rushed. It was good. He could rest. He could get out the car manual, check amp hours in the van batteries, compute all about laptop batteries and phone batteries and what chance he could drain the juice. He could take a walk, listen for the tiger in case it purred, see if El was there, sit beside her, have a chat. She had become harmless, because unattainable, a pain to be gotten used to, like a limp. They could chat. You say this, I say that.

Poor fellow, who must all alone endure the lonely fire of loneliness. Unrequited love was a famous theme, said Mrs. Harrow in high school English. He could email her, *Oh Mrs. Harrow, how right you were*! Dawson? I remember you. You didn't say one word in class, did you? How does it feel now, buddy boy! His phone vibrated, his mother's number.

"Hello."

"Dawson, you want to come up for a bit? We're going to have tiger tea."

•

Annie laid a blanket in front of Bhajan's cage, then in the blanket center placed the baking pan with the mugs and the tea steeping in a lidded pot. She brought a ladle and paper towels to pour it through and had added teapot to her list, and a strainer and crock pot, and a laptop and printer for the calendar and recipes and for searching the net, all of which Bluey had okayed. Dawson had informed her that she could find more recipes and food ideas online than in any book. She had an aversion to the internet, partly because her last asshole had gambled away the last of their money there, and because Dawson had used it to hack, but also because it was a time-wasting neon emptiness. But as an info store, she could use it. She was in a taking-on mood. Taking on the cooking and the food organization, but also taking on her new situation without whining. She had led whining to a corner, now you just sit there and when you want to join the rest of us, you'll be welcome. Her stern self in charge. Which so far never lasted. Her stern self had a tendency to shrug and join the party when things got tough, tough being lonely. But something in her was hawk high. Her sternness felt kinder.

She had wept earlier at the settee with Bluey, confessing her crazy heat for El and her release. He had gently covered her hands, making his thick hands into feather hands, and had not interrupted the tears with consolation. She rinsed herself out, so that later, with Dawson, she had found an unguilty place to take her stand and say, darn it, Dawson, about everything. Which was her gentle sternness.

The tea was ready to pour, but so far it was just her and the tiger, who lay on his side, head against the chips, watching her. It was about time for him to purr, if he was going to. She scissored across the boundary fence. She leaned her left shoulder against the bars a yard from his massive head, thinking, if he were quick, he could get a claw into my deltoid, thinking, go ahead, I'm quick too. She stood away. What in the world was she doing? Those claws could probably get to the bone. She wanted to touch the tiger, was the truth. She gripped the bars beside his head and held them. Whether he would react in some way, any slight way? Bhajan watched indifferently.

She removed her hands, dusted them together, finished with tiger teasing. She folded her arms, then unfolded them. She put her right hand six inches through the bars at the bottom of the cage and extended her index finger. Bhajan rolled onto his back and stretched, still holding her in his gaze. She jerked her hand back. Then she extended the finger again. Bhajan's stretch elongated his body, twelve feet of tiger, and then, on his back, he began to twist so that the huge black paw pads, big as silver dollars, moved towards her extended finger, closer, then a foot away, then a few inches, moving with slow indifferent coincidence, until the front of the paw, where the orange brown fur joined the leather and where the thumb-sized talons were half concealed in their sheathes, came gently into contact with her finger, leather to fingertip, then brushed indifferently past. She stepped away, looked around. Oh my. The tiger had touched her on purpose.

She heard the door of the RV open and close. She turned, and a moment later El came through the stockade, spinning a yellow shawl around her shoulders.

Annie said, "El, come here, come here."

Annie stepped back across the crowd barrier, and El approached, her face lifted in inquiry. Annie was taken by a surge of affection and embraced her, then held her at arm's length. She said, "You look just like a flower with your beautiful shawl. You'll never guess what just happened. Shall we sit?" They sat. "Well, I shouldn't tell you, now that I think about it." She looked at El's easy waiting face and said, "Oh, I will. This strange tiger just touched me." And she related Bhajan's slow stretch, the curving toward her finger, the touch. She looked at Bhajan, who lay on his side now, eyes closed. "He meant to do it. It was extremely exciting." El's face had become intent. Her forehead creased.

Annie said, "Oh, I know it was bad. It was just an experiment. I won't do it again, I promise. Was it really bad?"

El said, "Yes, definitely bad, Annie. It was really bad. It's amazing, of course. But never do it again, no matter what."

And they both understood she was saying the right thing if the world was normal, but the world might not be normal. But obey rules. Be normal until you couldn't.

El stood. She said, "I'm going to make a quick rounds."

•

Roger sat before his laptop and stared at the screen. His fingers rotated over the keyboard. He scratched his cheek, bobbed his head. He had written, "I loved your letter." The sentence glared at him. He thought, I want to know more about you and about the coffee shop. He could not type that, due to lameness. If he wrote from his dirt clod self, she would see. She would say, it was nice to meet you, you seem nice. I don't go out with dirt clods. He could type, I feel like a dirt clod. How come you wrote that nice letter to me? What's going on here? Are you a guy?

"Roger?"

Roger pivoted gratefully from his laptop, parted the curtains, and slid open his window. Dawson peered up at him in a hooded sweatshirt.

Roger said, "Hey, man."

"Hey. Mom called, and she has some tea laid out by the tiger."

"Oh, yeah. I'm coming out."

Roger closed his laptop with a grateful *clump.* He would clear his head, come back later and be better. Then he thought, google it. Google love letters! There would be thousands of love letter examples, introductory love letters, first date thank yous. It would be awful, but he would do it. He grabbed his denim jacket from the closet and got down from the cab. Dawson was coming around the truck's front.

Roger said, "Hey, man."

"Hey."

They started toward the stockade gap. Then Roger touched Dawson's arm, stopping him. Roger said, "Hey, just a second."

"Okay."

"I want to ask you something. You can write, right? El says you have a high IQ."

"Really? Well, that doesn't mean I can write."

"Well, better than me probably. I wondered if you could maybe take a look at something I'm writing."

"What?"

"Well, what it is, it's a letter to a girl. I got on this dating site, and this girl wrote to me, and she wrote a really good letter, and now I have to write back. And I'll write it. I'm not asking you to write it. But to read it and maybe edit it. In case it needs something."

"Okay."

"Really? Thanks, man." There was a pause in the dark. Neither could see the other's face. Roger said, "It's pretty hard, writing to someone you have no idea who it is. It's the first time I did this. Well, the second, because I wrote one already, which wasn't bad actually, but now I'm stuck."

Dawson said, "Sounds like it would be pretty hard. Since you don't know them and can't see them."

"Exactly. And who knows really who it is? Even if it's really a girl, instead of a joker, which has happened, right? To a football player too, by the way."

"I remember that." There was a pause. Dawson began to turn toward the stockade gap, but was stopped when the dark form of Roger raised its hands and folded them behind his head. Dawson waited.

Roger said, "I felt bad for that guy. Basically, he just wanted a girlfriend, and it's pretty hard to get one, especially when you get out of school. You can go a bar, which I always hated, to tell you the truth, like shopping. Or she could actually be a hooker, which has actually happened to me. I couldn't do hookers."

"You don't know what you're missing."

Roger snorted a laugh. "Anyway. You got a girlfriend?"

"No. I'm still in school though, so maybe I'll get lucky."

"That was funny, right?"

"That was me being funny."

"Hey, you know what would be good? I'll write this letter and you read it, but before you read it, you read her letter, so you can sort of see what's going on. How would that be?"

Dawson did not reply.

Roger said, "Not good?"

"I don't know, Roger. Sounds like Cyrano de Bergerac." There was a silence. Dawson said, "Which was about a guy that wrote love letters for another guy."

"Well, I'll write it for sure. But just read her letter and see if it sounds like a letter someone might send. Sort of a check."

"In case it's a joker."

"Right. I don't think it's a joker really. Actually, I'm attracted to this person."

"And you want me to tell you if you're nuts."

"Sort of. Yeah, actually."

"All right. I'll read it right now. You want me to?"

"That'd be great." Roger climbed back inside his truck, and a moment later returned with the laptop displaying Dori's letter. He left the passenger door open and set the computer on the truck seat. He said, "Okay, this is her letter back to me. You could read my first one too, I don't care, but my next one is the main one, which I haven't written. Which I will write tonight. Anyway, there it is. Thanks for doing this." Roger laid his large hand on Dawson's shoulder. He said, "Hey, maybe she's got a sister, never know."

This move from supplicant to condescension was off-putting for both of them. A silence followed. Roger backed away two steps, said, "Okay. Read away. Just lock the door when you're done. I've got the keys. Thanks, man. This is great."

Roger turned and passed through the gap in the stockade. As his hand touched the bamboo, he heard a solid thump and felt the bamboo vibrate. Had someone thrown something? To his right, Cloe, the okapi, made a soft bleat. Roger stopped, hand on the bamboo. He listened. He heard faintly a few fast pants, then another vibrating thump. He bent, and under the lion cage, he saw the snake dog, Patti, turning in a small circle. Then she lowered her head and rocketed forward into the bamboo. Thump.

He said, "Hey. Hey, dog!"

Patti had begun circling again and now stopped. She turned her short muzzle to Roger for a second, then wheeled, trotted away down the perimeter of cages into the gloom.

Roger considered turning back to tell Dawson what he had just seen, but the dog had vanished, and besides, Dawson was reading, and definitely don't disturb him. But Jesus, the dog had rammed his head into the bamboo. He had felt the shock in his hand. Way outside normal. Maybe rabies. He would tell Bluey.

As he stepped over the thigh-high crowd fence into the grounds, Bhajan began to purr.

15

Bluey leaned against the stockade, listening to the rustle and murmur of beasts, letting the residue of his conversation with El dissipate. She had left some minutes before, back to the RV and the book. He had spoken of spirituality well and clearly, but beneath his clarity he sensed the faint pressure of hypocrisy. Her youthful simplicity was an accusation. She was clear. She was not disappointed. She yearned and was free. Through the years, his own need had become a habit of pain, held in front like honor, like armor. From time to time love returned, but faintly, like a memory. Equanimity had become a refuge. He recalled a line he had written years ago—*dignity made mean, worn out by emptiness.*

He heard the metal rattle of utensils on ceramic, Annie at tea, then heard the purr begin and the zoo grow quiet. He stood, and the purr came up louder, unobstructed by the parrot cage. He heard voices, smooth and blurred in the purr's white noise. He started toward the tiger. Eventually the book would return to him. He would consider it.

•

Annie had things nicely arranged on the tea tray when the purr began. Five mugs, two spoons in one of them, honey bear, ladle, steeping pot, and a pint of half and half. Now she lifted and dropped the spoons into the mug for the summoning clatter. She had expressed herself first by orienting the teacups with their handles turned inward, like spokes, then saw that would make them harder to grasp, and turned them outward, like rays, which was better, sunlike and more joyful. She had called Dawson, and the whereabouts of the rest were noted, and all were free to come and soon would come and be with her on the blanket. She would content them with tea. When the purr began it entered smoothly into her mood so that one moment, silence, then, as she guided the mugs into their sunny disposition, like a far off, closer-coming engine, the purr. When she finished, she raised her face to the tiger. He watched her with his giant languid passivity, a half inch space between the black leather of his lips, so that the yellow shafts of his canines gleamed. The purr moved through her body as if she were a conductor passing its current into the earth.

When she looked back to the tea things, she had an clear vibrant impression—the world had become three dimensional. Her wheel of mugs, the golden honey bear, the X of spoons, all radiant and clear, like putting on the special glasses in a movie, and the world glimmers. She extended her arms and waved her hands. The three dimensionality remained, immune to scrubbing. A psychedelic flashback maybe, from the mescaline that guy had slipped into her beer twenty years ago in a Melbourne bar, only it wasn't electric. This was steady and lower grade. You couldn't wave your hand and make things twinkle. This was steady and behind the glimmer something else. Wellbeing was the word for it. Being well in being. She was in being and being was well and be well in this, which shined and was lovely, everything where I put it, waiting for the coming company, glimmering and faithfully waiting, the spoons reposing in their mug, the wheel of mugs, the ripply blanket, the sweet green smell of cut green grass, the spicy good-natured scent of dung.

She turned to the tiger, still watching her with his intent single-minded indifference. She said, "Watch this, my friend!"

And she began the vaudeville dance she had learned for a movie fifteen years ago, an arm pumping, bowlegged sideways strut, which carried her past the tiger to the cage's end, then back along the tiger to the other end, the tiger head-rotating with her, then back and forth again, and she was back to stand breathlessly in front of him. She strummed the bars with the fingers of her right hand, and the thrumming of flesh on metal dissolved in purr, and the purr made being well.

She was three feet from the tiger and now she stepped closer and laid her face and arms wide spread against the bars and pressed, and the tiger was two feet beyond, watching and immobilely purring, and she bathed.

"Annie!"

It was Bluey, her brother, master of the caravan, come to scold, away, away, disobedient person!

She said softly to the tiger, "They're coming for me." She lightly thrust away, and when she turned to her brother, coming up fast and intent, she saw the world's glimmer had gone, and coming was a session of apology and promise, to which she would earnestly submit, and soothe and promise and serve all tea from the nicely laid out blanket of tea things, which she saw were all still in place and patiently waiting, still well in being.

She held her hands aloft, slightly bowed her head. She said, "How wrong it was for me to do that. I could have made such trouble. I'm very very sorry."

Bluey received this open-mouthed. He said "Why did you do it?"

She said, "That purr put a spell on me, Bluey, dear." She moved forward and embraced his solidity. She laid her head on his chest. She felt his hands against her back. She said, "I've made some tea."

She sat and Bluey squatted, his thickness riding oddly nimbly along his out-cocked thighs. He was silent while she ladled, his and hers, added a spoon of honey, no milk for either, moving methodically under his gaze, and, as she imagined, his gathering thought. It would not be opprobrium, she saw. He had moved to patience.

He said, "What do you mean, a spell?"

As she talked, Roger came up, and she ladled him tea, and El came up, and she ladled tea. "I'm explaining to Bluey why I did a foolish thing—I laid my face against the bars of Bhajan's cage. Bhajan means the song of God, or song to God, or something. And I was fixing these tea things when the purr started up, right in my face. And then—" Now she must describe the world of wellbeing. And how to do it, without saying words which were not that and away from it? But they were waiting, and she had begun, and Bluey was attending with grave patience, holding his tea and not sipping, calm and alert and waiting. Faintly at first, then more fervently, she began to shiver, and when she stirred the honey into El's tea the spoon rattled. She stood and held her hands to El, pulled her to her feet. She said, "Can you dance, El? Do you like to dance? I do."

El said, a soft smile, "I saw you."

"Maybe it could be part of the skit or something," said Annie. "Now do this." She placed El beside her and pumped her arms, and El pumped hers, and they matched nicely, two slim same-heighted women, arm-pumping, then the first step sideways, El neatly following with her soft half smile, understanding, like Bluey, some force in Annie compelled, and to submit was right. El followed and with instant nimble expertise made four bowlegged sideways arm-pumping steps, four steps in reverse, then back again, and back again, then Annie foretold the finish with eyebrows and a head tilt and ended them with an arm-curving low-bowing *ta da*, and El, an instant later, made a graceful dancer's parenthesis.

Roger applauded, "That was great. For the skit, really. At the end. Annie just pops out and hey, a dance, why not?"

The two women embraced. El rocked her head slowly, smiling. Annie shrugged and slumped. Both sat.

Dawson had come up to stand in the penumbra of the halogen at the end of the tiger cage. He had read Dori's letter. Her spirited pep had churned a mix of jealousy and joy, and when he turned into the circle of light to find the two women, his mother and his heartache, stepping nimbly in the grass, he smiled, then laughed, a short humming reluctant laugh that blended into the purr, laughing at the beautiful persistent plaguing truth that there was never anywhere to hide in all of life ever.

Annie saw him then and inquired with eyebrows. He approached past the sprawled tiger, whom he ignored but felt like pressure against his right side. He knelt on the blanket. Annie ladled a cup of tea, handed him the honey bear and a spoon.

Annie said, "I was just telling about a violation I committed. For some reason, I pressed myself against the bars of the tiger cage. I'll never do it again, that's for sure. I promise." Here she looked at Bluey, made her face firm. The firmness was a lie. She might open that cage and teach that tiger a dance step. If she got in that glorious mood again.

Bluey said, "This tiger seems to have a property which affects the beasts and probably us. Haley said we would discover that, and it seems we have. My colleagues and I are considering the matter." He looked at Annie. "In the meantime, we must try not to go insane."

El said, "Also, Annie and I had sort of spiritual experiences." Roger and Dawson, who had begun to look around at the circle of cages and the rapt animals, turned to her. She said, "Not a ball of fire or anything, at least for me." She set herself. "A really big kindness came around me."

"A kindness came around you?" said Annie. She laughed. "That's just what must happen. A kindness must come around us." She folded El into her arms, spoke in her ear. "Pumpkin pumpkin. Just kidding. That's an affectionate pumpkin."

El said, "So jumping to a conclusion, the mast gave the tiger's hyoid bone a tweak so he can purr. Which makes you want to dance. For some reason." Her voice altered, and she added intently, "But absolutely Annie, never go near the bars. That is so bad. If you knew the stories, you would freak out." Then kindly—"No matter what, sweetie."

Annie said, "No, I know. I definitely won't." This time she thought she meant it and said, "I won't," again, as insurance.

Dawson said, "What's a mast?"

Bluey made a quick disquisition, Haley and Fuad in India, the bamboo cage, the god-intoxicated.

Dawson said, "So this is a magic tiger?"

Roger said, "By the way, here's a weird thing. I was coming through the stockade a minute ago and your dog—what's her name?"

Annie said, "Patti."

"She was ramming her head into the stockade, like a bull. Bang. She did it three times. I couldn't see very well, but I heard it, and then I saw her do it the last time. Sort of back off and run straight in, bang. She must be sick."

Annie's mouth opened. She looked at Bluey.

Bluey said, "I'll find her when I make the rounds." Bluey whistled a shrill ascending note. "Goose!" Goose emerged from the shadows beside the sun bear cage, trotted to Bluey, accepted an ear scrub, slumped beside him, then rose again as Bluey stood.

Annie's glance sorted through the shadowy perimeter of cages. She called, "Patti!" Then—"I'm not sure she even knows her name. Could it be rabies?"

Bluey said, "We'll find her. Let's make the rounds together, you and me. Then I better get my shower so I don't keep you girls up."

El said, "You go, Annie. I'll get this cleared up."

Bluey said, "Breakfast at seven sharp, guys. Then feed and clean, and the public at nine. We'll learn a lot."

Bluey and Annie started the rounds. Goose loped ahead of them, trotted past a few cages, then back and around them, then ahead again. The animals, as before, were at the front of their cages, all alert, all erect. Bluey did not bother with treats. From time to time, Annie called to her dog. They passed through the stockade to look near the caravan vehicles and found her near her food and water bowls, under the rear bumper of the RV, belly-sprawled. She watched them placidly.

Annie bent. "Patti, come. Come on, dear. Come." Annie patted her thighs. The dog upgathered and paced forward into the RV porchlight, stood, head lowered. Goose circled, sniffed. Bluey bent and passed a hand across the dog's broad head.

He said, "It's spongey." He tapped the swelling over the dog's eyes. The dog stood unblinking, without flinching. He pushed the dog's head sideways, grunted dismissal, and Patti reestablished her sphinx pose on the matted grass. Bluey looked at Annie. He said, "No idea."

Annie said, "Bluey dear, what in the world, right? Don't you think that? What in the world?"

"I'm waiting to see what I think."

"You didn't go crazy when you saw me up against that cage."

"I went a little crazy."

"Not very crazy, Bluey. And now Patti. This is an odd zoo."

"It is."

"So the tiger and the mast, something with that."

Bluey pursed his lips, did not reply.

"You're waiting, I get it. You were always good at that. A stone is good at waiting too. What if I do that again? Something comes over me."

"You think you might?"

"I could, Bluey. I got in a state. Remember on your eighteenth birthday you had that experience, something was holding the water flat, you said, and the universe was alive. It was like that, sort of. Everything was existing. I looked away and then looked back and there it was, all the same. It's always like that, I know. But I could see it this time. Like the universe was friendly, saying, don't worry, I'm keeping everything in place. El said, a great kindness, and that was it exactly."

Bluey said, "*Though I have broken my vows a hundred times not once has this flowing toward me ceased or slowed.* That's from Rumi."

"Have you felt something?"

"You have, and El has." He gestured to the cages. "And they have. So I'm listening."

"And Bhajan came to Fuad in a dream. I'm trying to get you to feel a little surprised. So you can be normal."

Bluey said, "In the meantime, young lady—and this is your very own master speaking—I issue you this strict and absolute order—never go near the tiger that way again. Have you got it?"

"Yes. I do have it."

He drew her to him and held her, one hand on her hair, one on her back. He said, "I feel something, not to worry."

Annie found Bluey's hand, felt a familiar flashing incongruity, his blocky hand, his sensitivity. She kissed the hand, laid it against her cheek.

"Come for your shower," she said.

•

Roger and Dawson went through the gap into the darkness beyond the stockade, then stopped together, facing each other.

Dawson said, "I read it. I left the laptop on the seat."

"Thanks."

"So if you want me to read your letter, I can do that."

"Well, I was thinking. I don't know, man—"

"You have become shy."

"Naw. Well, maybe. Here's the thing—I'm thinking it would be—I don't want to be—"

"Deceptive."

"Right. That's right. I mean even to show someone else the letter— It's probably okay, but maybe not. Like I'm hatching a plot. I'm a crappy writer is what I'm worried about."

"But then if you hide that—"

"Right, should I hide that? That's what I've been thinking about. I would have this whole fake thing I'm starting out with."

"What you do, you get a fruit jar and fart into it and send that to her. You say, this is the real me."

"So you're saying what? I should put up a front?"

"No, I'm just making it complicated. What you do, you send the jar but don't fart in it, and you tell her we had this talk about putting up a front. And you say the jar is a gift, in case you might need a jar." Dawson exploded into high pitched laughter, then felt the searing revulsion of inappropriateness. He said, "Go fall in love, man. I recommend it." He could say, I'm in love with your cousin. But he had a front. The front was, I look down. Now he was looking across the darkness to the dim outline of a soft-natured giant, who stood with arms in a protective fold, and the giant's tone was soft, and if he could see the giant's face it would be soft too. He could reach across the dark and touch the folded arms, he could say something kind. He couldn't. He said, "Here's my deep dark secret. I'm in love with your cousin." There was silence. Dawson said, "This cannot be told to man nor beast."

"Really? With El?"

"No, your other cousin."

"You're in love with her? Did you know her before?"

"No. I have an instantaneous love response."

"Well, Jees. And you don't want me to—"

"Tell her? Definitely not. She has a boyfriend anyway."

"Really? I thought she just broke up."

"No, she— She did?"

"Well, that's what I heard. They were living together, and the guy went overseas. My aunt told my mother."

"He went to Dubai, and his name is Packer."

"Okay. And she said they were back on, hunh?"

Dawson said, "I guess. I got to go." He was a pinned grub on the public whiteboard. She had manipulated him, and the world knew.

So—the hot light of exposure, a drenching pain rain. Then—gone. Almost gone. What she would naturally do, what anyone would do to protect herself from a lovelorn child. He made a great puff of breath, indifferent that it was audible, that it disclosed him. He said, "You know what? Dori wrote you a great letter back. So you must have written a great letter to get her to do that. So stop worrying. Who knows, man. I see long arms extending. Where's she from?"

"Oklahoma City."

"Yeah, her long arms reaching out from Oklahoma City, and you're reaching out from Oregon, and you'll hold hands over, where would that be? Utah or Nebraska or something. Get married in Nebraska. I'll bring the jar."

Roger laughed. "Okay, man. And don't worry—"

"I know, my secret's safe. I fell out of love anyway." Dawson reached forward, lightly pounded one of Roger's forearms. "Go write. See you."

"See you. Thanks, man."

Dawson paced into the tall grass, felt within the impulse to slump, but a countering impulse prevailed, and as he walked he came more and more erect, and when he reached his van, dimly glowing under the starlight and a round belly of moon, he began to hear the river's mumble, and the last fifty feet he had no thoughts.

•

Roger typed. *I just got back from having tea with the crew right beneath the tiger cage. Our tiger is called Bhajan, and he purrs, which is unusual in a tiger, since they do not purr usually. So he is unique. Well, I tried to write to you earlier and just stared at the screen. I couldn't make up my mind what to say. I was afraid of screwing it up. It's very hard to get to know someone through email, as you mentioned.*

Roger sat for another moment waiting for an idea, then felt bladder pressure and got up, crouched through the passage, and went outside to relieve himself. He started in front of the truck, then clenched—he had seen Dawson earlier in bare feet—and paced twenty steps diagonal into the grass and finished. The night was moonlit and with no bug noise or wind. Dori's picture from the web came up in his mind, all he knew of her except her letter and its happy tone. She had seen his picture and read his letter, and that was all she knew too, way different from the caveman days, which he sometimes thought about, and now saw himself as a caveman coming into the cave after a hunt, and Dori says, hey, where's the zebra meat? Oh, that zebra got away, he says. She says, a big fellow like you lets a zebra get away? But she's smiling. He says, I'd like to see you try to kill a zebra. She says, okay, I'm coming with you tomorrow. Which is great because it's lonely on the hunt. So they're out there, and there's the zebra, and they have a conference, and she gives him the spear, because he's the big fellow, and he follows the plan and gets the zebra. They cut him up and take the meat back to the cave, and they did a fun thing together, with good planning, and they sit at the cave entrance (spear nearby in case of bears) and watch the sun go down, two happy cave people.

He could put that in the letter. Except start it when he walks by her dad's cave, and she makes fun of him about not getting a zebra, and he says, let's see you do better, and so on. Then they sit and watch the sun and think, we make a good team, let's be together.

He went back inside the truck and tried to write it up, but it turned artificial and wouldn't come. He despaired. Then a current came. He wrote—"If I saw you at a football game, and you were a hundred people away, say, and we saw each other and started making our way to meet each other, sort of bouncing off people and having trouble and getting distracted and then looking up, and there she is, only fifty people away now, and we are coming closer and closer. But instead email."

He reread and deleted it. Then he wrote, continuing his *It's hard to get to know someone via email* sentence—"What I would really like to do, I would like to see you in Oklahoma City and have coffee with you at your coffee shop. Then we go for a walk, along a street or anywhere, and walk all around the city and talk and hear all about each other's lives. Then we start walking out into the suburbs, and we tell how we feel about various things, and finally we end up somewhere out in the country walking along by a stream, and maybe we don't even talk very much and maybe we hold hands. That could be seen as sentimental, but it seems to me that's how people do get to know each other, by starting out together with other people, and then they're more and more off by themselves, and they find out they're happy together. It would be great to be happy with you, as far as I can tell so far, which sounds like a bold thing to say, I know. For some reason I have an instinct to speak out. Well, I do want to ask about your life and about the coffee shop and whether your feet get tired and do you have to smile too much, though I'm not sure you meet the public, if you're the roaster. Your comment about the serial killer was funny, by the way. Well, that's it for this letter, I think." He stopped and then added, "If this was the caveman days, I would certainly rather be walking past your dad's cave and seeing you in there by the fire rather than emailing you! But I will have to take what I can get. Roger."

He read the letter again, put in a few commas, considered deleting the caveman bit, didn't, and hit send. And he thought, now there's a nice chunk of zebra meat.

The letter had only taken a half hour or so, and Dawson would still be up. He could zip across the grass and read it to him. But that would be frantic feeling. That part about walking out of the city, and then the stream. What would she hear? No doubt he was making her up in his mind, the ideal girl who would read his letter and swell with affection the way he had swelled writing it. Maybe she would write back something confusing or worried or about some shallow thing that happened to her. He would still have the affection though. Affection had come out strong in the letter and strong in his chest, a good sign for the future. He might get disappointed pretty soon. But he had affection and could carry it around until it fit somebody. But it might fit Dori, which would be excellent and wonderful.

•

Bluey had finished his shower and toilet in the tiny RV bathroom and now hopped-slipped into his jeans and sweatshirt. He would have to change again back in his cab, and it would have been more convenient to have brought his Lycra pajamas, but he had been diffident to appear in them before El, delicacy for her, but pride too, her leader in domestic array. He was smiling at this as he opened the bathroom door.

El, nested in her bunk under the light cone of a sconce, laid *The Wayfarers* against her breast. She said, "What's so funny, buddy?"

He didn't bother to reply. He said, "Where are you now?"

"I'm still skipping around. I can't help myself. This supplement is a bunch of super interesting anecdotes. But I'll start it pretty soon and be a scholar."

"Read one."

"Read an anecdote? I just read this one. This is the story of Mastani Mai, who was from Lahore. So quote—'A very good mastani who, for twenty-five years, sat in one place opposite the railway station. Those about her said she had been there before the present shops were built, and in 1941, there was a garage immediately behind the place where she sat. Over her head she wore a shawl that was quite stiff with mud and dust; it was so ingrained with dirt that it looked almost like cardboard. Her face was covered by this shawl. One evening, Baba took Norina (this was on the bus trip from Jaipur to Quetta) to see her, and he lifted the shawl away from her face. She had a very dark countenance with strange, light-bluish eyes, and she looked up adoringly at Baba, put her hands together, and said, *Allah.*'"

Bluey nodded.

El said, "Bluey, what if it's all true? That God was here and going around to all these strange people in India, and all the while history went on. It's hard to believe. But it's also hard to disbelieve."

"This brings to mind a story. I'll tell you tomorrow, because you are nicely tucked in, and it's time for bed."

"That's just the time for a story, when I'm tucked in. Sit and tell. Is it too long?"

Annie, who had been listening from the kitchen, dried her hands and sat at the settee. She said, "A bedtime story. We'll want one every night."

Bluey sat across from Annie. He said, "This story holds a revered place in all the stories I know, because it marks out a key point I like to remember. The story is, a certain saint, I forget who, call him Latif, is standing in the desert, gazing intently at a pool of water. Another saint, call him Hakeem, happens by. Hakeem says, what are you doing, Latif, standing here looking at the water? Latif says, I came across the desert and have great thirst, and I found this pool. I know that many springs hereabouts are poisoned, so I'm waiting to see which shall prevail, knowledge or certainty. And of course, if certainty prevails, I will have to bind my thirst and seek for water elsewhere. And Hakeem said, Latif, I see you are advancing on the way."

El said, "Wait. He said, if certainty prevails he won't drink?"

"Right. The story doesn't tell us what the other side is, what knowledge is, but it marks out certainty as a fraud. That's why I thought of the story, when you were wondering about the authenticity of that book. We never have certainty. All we get is a ladder, and it's lost in the clouds. But you can sense if the ladder goes up."

El said, "You know what? Right at this moment, I'm just bursting with happiness!" She leaned forward and held out her hand, which Bluey took. Tears came loose and rolled down her cheeks. She released his hand and jabbed them away. She said, "Well, how about that?"

"Group hug," said Annie. But no one moved.

Bluey rose. "Good night. We must sleep. Tomorrow we learn how to operate a traveling zoo. Hakeem says, trust in God, but tie your camel. Tomorrow we tie the camel."

They said good night. Bluey left the RV and passed into the crisp night. Goose trotted up, circled him, then fell in at his side. He decided to make a last rounds and passed through the stockade into the zoo perimeter. He turned right, passed the okapi, the Somali ass, the guanacos. All were rapt and ignored him. Then, as he passed the cage of Phoenix, the Himalayan blue sheep, he heard a tinny thump and turned. Phoenix had laid one of her short horns laterally against the wire, and in the halogen light he could see her eyes twisted up towards him. He laid his hand along the cold metal lattice, felt the cool horn and fur of her cheek. He said, "Ho, Phoenix. Ho, girl." He felt a light pressure against his ankle—Goose, on all fours, but leaning and still. He gave it ten seconds, then withdrew his hand, breaking the connection.

Phoenix backed away, then seemed to stagger. She bumped into the opposite side of her cage, then, abruptly collapsed, dropping with a double thump, belly and then head, onto the wood chips. Bluey went fast to the cage's end, flipped up the lock cover and felt for the combination keys with his fingertips. He entered the first three numbers, five-five-

five, and was feeling for the eight, when Phoenix lifted her head, swiveled it several times, orienting, then rose quickly and stood. Bluey found the eight, pushed it, heard the lock tick. But he did not open the cage. Phoenix had again become quiet and attentive. He opened the cage and closed it to reset the lock. It made a crisp metallic click. Phoenix gave no notice.

Bluey continued through the herbivores, past the entry gate, then along the carnivores. As he passed the puma, he raised his arms wide, felt the motion of cool air, passed Nubia the hyena and Demijohn the lion, then stopped, arms spread, before the stockade gap and turned finally to face Bhajan, who he had saved for last. On the top rail of the tiger cage, two crows gleamed in the halogen. They could be different from the morning crows. But would not be.

The tiger was a prone shadow. The head was erect, facing him. Bluey said loudly, "I'm interested! I am interested!" He ran his hands across his face, held cool fingertips for a long moment against his eyelids. He opened his eyes, interlaced his fingers, and gripped. He said, "I'm interested." The tiger's head fell onto the wood chips. From the shadow, the tireless purr continued.

•

Dawson opened his laptop but instead of the jolt of beauty he had gotten earlier, it had gone flat, a colorful so-what. But he knew the impression was moody and dismissed it. He closed the computer, and the interior fell into darkness. He had left the sliding door open and swiveled in his chair to face the river, letting his feet dangle in space. He could feel its moist chill like a presence. He had written songs in his short-lived guitar-learning days, and his best line came back to him, *Standing on the sidewalk, sometimes I want to shout, What about this loneliness, no one talks about.* He cradled the air guitar, hunched his shoulders, thought of stomping into the vocal, but the desire fell away, and the guitar vanished. He couldn't recall the tune anyway, something punkish and pissed. He had been an irritated youth. He still was. He objected to the world. Your honor, I object. Nothing is true.

He swung over to the sink, hunched, and brushed his teeth in a trickle of water. He splashed his face, scrubbed it with wet hands, then dried on the hand towel.

He was hard awake. He should climb into the bed and lay in the dark. But the bed did not invite. Maybe he could carry a pillow and blanket back to the zoo and sleep under the tiger cage. The purr would be white noise. He couldn't do that though, because what would they think. Also it would be—I slink in from my vigil. On the other hand—lie down under the tiger and deeply sleep.

•

After her shower, Annie went outside to the front of the RV and called—"Patti! Patti!"

The dog padded slowly forward from the gloom beneath the RV, head down. She stood impassively while Annie tied one end of a nylon rope to a tow loop under the bumper and knotted the other to her collar. Annie scooted the water and food bowls toward the dog, who ignored them and ignored Annie.

"I'll be just inside. If you need me, just give a little bark. Okay?" She stroked the flat swollen head, then, with her fingertips, delivered a light dabbling tickle under the dog's chin. Patti did not respond. She considered a more vigorous two-handed ruffing, but was afraid. Perhaps the dog was ill and dangerous. She had wanted a feelingful companion and had bravely walked the cages of the San Mateo pound until she found a dog she thought others unlikely to choose. She had bestowed life and was now afflicted with an unsociable burden. Who might be sick, who might bite her if she made a mistake.. Tomorrow they would find a vet. There would be one somewhere in the fair with all these animals.

She stood, went to the RV front, fished her electronic cigarette from her robe, leaned into the front bumper. She could hear the purr faint through the stockade. She switched the cigarette on, took a deep pull, felt the comforting flush of nicotine. That was an interesting difference, those two, the purr and the nicotine. Both were solace, but the nicotine up front, the purr somewhere behind. She closed her eyes. She took another pull and felt again the nicotine's charge of wellbeing, but now felt it as obtrusive. She could let it go, and she did let it go. The words came in her mind, *I have quit.* She gave it a few seconds and saw it was true. She tried to snap the device in two, but it was strongly made. But she needed action. She walked a hundred steps around the zoo to the fair fence where the chicken building reared thirty feet into the night. She could make that throw and did, the electronic cigarette uttering three tinny dings on the corrugated roof, ding ding done.

•

El awoke at two in the morning, bright-minded. She finished in the bathroom, then stood beside her bed, considering. If she climbed back in, she would likely lie awake. She could read the book, but that would start her mind even more. She could read Emily Dickinson, but that was work. She could take a walk, but that would also wake her more. But she was bright awake, accept it. So take a fresh fast walk around the zoo, say, here I am, don't worry, then crash back to bed, try to get three more hours before six. She listened for the purr, but could only hear the ventilation fan. She swung the blanket off the bed. It was a puffy synthetic and would be warm. She caped it around her shoulders, slipped into her clogs, and went outside.

As she came through the stockade, she heard the purr and saw Bhajan on his side, head down, his body long and shadowed, like a horizon of hills. She started around the carnivore side, Demijohn, Nubia, Clark, all rapt and oblivious. She felt cool damp dart under the blanket and swipe chill up her bare legs and onto her pelvis. She could move those legs as she had with Annie, and she did, trying to reinvent the dance, a sideways hoppy strut, and couldn't quite, but invented something close and did that, putting in some energy half kicks. Her bare legs puffed the blanket, making a chill tussle between cool air and trapped heat. She danced past three more cages, the dhole and lynx and wild dog. The animals were still alert but now in resting poses, on bellies or butts, facing the tiger. Maybe she herself had picked that alertness up, a psychic current from thirty yards away, right through stockade and RV wall. All were rapt and, except a slight head shift toward her from the wild dog, all ignored her, listening to the tiger, whom she had not yet faced.

She stopped the dance, breathing deeply now. She threw one side of the blanket over her shoulder to capture heat and began a determined circuit. She had fallen asleep fast after Bluey's story because of happiness. Because her heart and mind had been poured together by Bluey's story about the two saints, and because earlier he had told her about spirituality with his quiet centered clarity and about the inner furnace and that honest people must agree. It made good simple sense and settled in her and flowed her pieces together into existence happiness.

Plus there had been the dancing, which was hypnotic. She had right away found Annie's tricky step and followed and sailed and been exhilarated. Halfway through, she noticed Dawson standing at the end of the tiger cage, watching with dead pan fascination, and she wanted to retreat into demurral but also to accompany Annie and do the last perky step, and did, and then saw Dawson come steadfastly onto the blanket to receive his tea. Whatever he felt, his outside showed brave composure. She was grateful. They hadn't spoken, saying only, see you, when they parted, but his *see you* had been kind and released her, so that when Bluey came out of the shower and found her reading, she had been happy.

As she passed Chortle the raccoon's cage, he reached his left arm through the wire, opened his hand and held it still, and she willingly laid her index finger across the hand's cool palm, which closed and held. She brought her other index finger close, and he reached with his right hand and enfolded the finger, so that now they made a circle. The circle held for ten seconds. Then Chortle released with both hands simultaneously and grasped the wire. His head rocked once, twice, and was still. She was between him and the tiger, but he seemed to be looking through her. He had forgotten her.

She continued past the remaining cages, then turned to the tiger and approached. Bhajan was standing now, head erect, watching her. She stopped five feet away, and they gazed, his head lowered below his shoulders, so that their eyes were level, a friendly stalemate. The purr continued, like a motor in his throat, with no change in tone, in breath and out. Annie had pressed herself against the bars. El could do that if she let go, if she spread her arms and held the bars and laid her head against the metal and trusted.

Definitely don't, no matter what.

And she thought, what if it's an evolutionary move, and a strong certain-feeling thought cascade came, a tiger with a hypnotizing purr, a prey catcher, like the fleshy stalk some fish dangled near their mouth. The purr numbs prey. A mutation of the mysterious hyoid bone. Which NASA knew about and was researching. And the tiger is thinking, I'm standing right here purring hard, and why hasn't this girl succumbed? That was a whole other way to think than sacred mast-raised tigers, the evolution-science way.

She said loudly, to hear herself above the purr, "Bhajan, are you trying to hypnotize me?"

"Hunh!"

She started. The voice, which was Dawson's, had come from beneath the tiger cage. She bent to peer, and there he was, wrapped in a blanket cocoon, head lifted but looking the wrong way.

She said, "Hi, Dawson." Now he rolled toward her and squinted. She would be in shadow, so she said, "It's El."

"Oh. Hi."

"Sleeping under the tiger cage, I see."

"Yeah."

"Sorry to wake you. Go back to sleep."

"What are you doing? What time is it?"

"Just checking things out. It's still night, time to sleep."

"Oh." Then—"Is sleeping here okay?"

"Why not." She thought of saying, I'll like to try it too, but didn't. "Good night."

"Good night."

She had to leave and not disturb him, but she hadn't finished her science thought. She could make a check-out round, which would be natural in case he noticed. She reversed course, went past the raccoon again, offered a finger, was ignored.

So the theory so far—a new type of tiger mesmerizes prey by purring.

The idea ached. It did not include. It sat outside the way science always did. It was plastered-on. It left out the dancing and Annie's intoxication and existence happiness and masts, whom she had read about now, and who sat patiently off to the side of her mind. Who are we, they wondered to her. Who is Meher Baba, that came to see us? And what is this tiger doing in the middle of our zoo purring up a storm and obsessing our animals?

She had come to the gap in the stockade, and she could go through and leave the purr behind and get into her bed in the RV. But she stopped. She was behind the okapi cage and could smell the faint tang of Cloe's dung. The separation between her science thought and her happiness had produced an unpleasant feeling, a flutter of nausea, and now she sank to her knees, which was good, just the right thing, then rolled onto her blanket, kicking and shaking the end down past her feet, and curled her legs up and rolled the blanket over herself, pulled it over her head so that she was in a cocoon where she could be and experience existence and not think. In a moment she was asleep.

16

Annie woke to her alarm at five thirty. As she left the bathroom, she noticed El's empty bed. There was no blanket. Was she making the morning rounds in a blanket? And then thought, she went visit Dawson in the night, and felt a flutter of jealousy. But it fled without a push.

She had to get breakfast moving, but first went outside to untie her dog. She moved to the rear of the RV and called, "Patti, Patti." The rope tailed away under the chassis, and she began to pull, expecting the dog's weight. In a moment, she came to the chewed-off end.

"Patti! Patti!"

A moment later, she heard the stir of grass as Patti, trailing a foot of rope, walked from under the RV and stood beside her. She untied the rope from the collar. She would add a chain to Dawson's list. Then she noticed the water pan was empty, but the dog food had not been touched. She would tell Bluey. She felt a throb of premonition.

•

El woke, realized where she was, and lay still for a moment. The blanket covered her shoulders and head, and when she opened her eyes she could see its gray blue folds in the morning light. She had slept on her stomach and now rolled onto her side. The ground was solid beneath her, but she wasn't stiff. She tried to think if she had dreamed. There was nothing.

Then a fast charge of energy roused her. She stood, saraped the blanket around her body and started toward the RV. She glanced back toward the tiger and Dawson. He was gone. Bhajan lay full length, asleep. As she walked to the RV, she saw between Roger's tandem and the flatbed a slim blanketed figure on the glistened grass. He disappeared inside the van. He must have passed her a moment before. Perhaps his passage had waked her. Her face was covered, but he would have guessed, that's El, since he had seen her in the blanket.

At the RV steps she could hear Annie's breakfast clatter inside and the muted voice of the radio. She would enter in a moment, but first turned toward the sun, which was shooting brokenly through a horizon of fair rides. She, felt the light bright and cold on her face. The restlessness of the evolutionary science thought had gone, but the background feeling, existence happiness, was there, like a pulse.

She entered the RV, gathering the blanket into the cabin before closing the door. Annie switched off the radio. She turned from the stove where she was frying French toast, making a mound, and said, "You don't have to tell me."

El smiled, said, "Good." Then— "Of course, I'll tell you. I was outside sleeping on the grass. I couldn't sleep and went for a walk and just sort of folded up and slept. And guess who was out there and gave me a scare? Your son, right under the tiger cage."

"He was? What in the world was he doing?"

"Sleeping. I accidentally woke him up. This was around two. Then I just plopped on the grass and was out."

"How did he scare you?"

"He said, *hunh* or something. And there he was, under the tiger cage."

"Bhajan was purring?"

"He was."

"So how did you sleep?"

"Super duper. I saw Dawson heading back to his van this morning." She bent, rummaged through the drawer under her bed for a T-shirt and underwear, then swept the blanket across the bed and stepped into the bathroom.

Annie put the mound of cooked bread into the warmed oven and began cracking eggs. She went back to the thought train El had interrupted, all about the word *nigger*. Before El had come in, she had been listening to the radio, NPR, and the story had been about someone prominent who had used the N-word, as the news reader put it. Annie had been saying the word to herself, *nigger, nigger,* seeing what was there, and it was hatred and superiority and contempt and maybe, if the mind worked that way, a whole load of historical inhumanity, all packed in and capped off with prohibition, which was how we did it, packing hate into a minefield of certain words. The man who used it—actually only referring to the word, saying, hey, they say *nigger* all the time—was maybe inspired to shake off his bonds, accept the truth of his hatred and repent, except no, he was an irked white guy with a southern accent and not feeling his way toward freedom and fellow feeling, but toward the freedom to hate, which was freedom for him, bottled up in the south with black people all over downtown now. She saw it all clearly, the news reader's false objectivity, the southerner's bold gamble at the microphone, his hopeful betrayed expression and wild trapped pride. She imagined him entering a black church, savage for his rights, and a sea of black faces turns and silently inquires, and he shouts, *nigger! nigger! nigger!* But they laugh, say, *praise Jesus*, and his hatred drains. He laughs too, and the preacher calls them out to barbeque, and the white guy is limp and happy and eats and weeps.

Annie was suddenly filled with yearning. She finished cracking eggs and took up the oily spatula to cut a section of butter, and the spatula moved as if magnetized to her breast, and she dipped her head over it as if it were a child, needing to let love flow, and it did flow, but the spatula was metal and could not hold the love, and she was holding an oily spatula against her breast and would now have to change shirts. She drew a breath deeply in and trembled it out, then uttered a puff of laughter. She had an urge to sink to her knees in a prayer posture and bow down, but something resisted, embarrassment faintly, but more, that there was something of demand in that, of special marking and difference from her normal self, and prayer should be an ordinary thing, what happens in the heart from time to time, what happens when you live a life. Still, she put the spatula down and went to the settee and sat, and now she was lower than standing, and it was a halfway measure, but also halfway satisfying, and the urge to go further was there, and gradually, watching herself for false notes, she let herself slip off the settee onto her knees, then let herself bow forward until her head touched the linoleum, and that satisfied. Then she was quickly up, dusting palms on knees. The RV door opened.

Dawson said, "Did you lose something?"

She turned, gladness sweeping embarrassment, and enveloped him, kissed his forehead under his turned-around baseball cap.

She said, "Good morning, merry sunshine," and felt his reluctant pleasure.

He said, "What were you doing?"

She said, "Oh. What was it? I think I dropped a spoon." She cupped his cheeks briefly and returned to her eggs and before he could pursue it, said, "El says she found you under the tiger cage."

"Most definitely."

"How was that?"

"Fine."

Annie brought a cup of coffee, the pint of half and half, the sugar bowl, and a spoon.

He lifted the spoon. "Is this the one you dropped?"

She lifted his hat, smoothed back his hair, then with two hands jammed it on sideways. She returned to the stove and cut a chunk of butter into the frying pan. She said, "Why did you sleep under the tiger cage?"

He reset his hat, bill forward, stirred half and half and sugar into his coffee. "It seemed like a good idea."

The bathroom door opened and a towel-wrapped El poked her head out, modestly surveying, then stood straight, wrapped the towel a notch tighter, and stepped out. Dawson, back to El, did not look around.

El said, "Good morning, Dawson."

Now he turned, saw her bare legs, and swiveled back. "Good morning."

"Annie, can I use your room to change?"

"Of course"

El gathered jeans and socks, and went into Annie's room, closed the door. Her voice came through the louvers. "Guess what, Dawson? I slept in the zoo too."

"Really?" He had passed her that morning and the *really* felt vaguely like a lie. He did not bother to untell it.

El said, "I did. After I left you, I sort of wandered around and pretty soon I just sort of slumped down. These blankets are great, aren't they?"

"Yes."

"The dew got me a little. I bet it didn't get you though, did it?"

"No, I was under there."

Dawson waited, hoping the conversation had ended because the talk, first with his mother, and now with El, was invasive and burdened the monolithic feeling he had waked to. He had come awake under the tiger cage into a glow, as if he were a child waking into warmth. It was required that he wake more, but he could do that without hurry. He could drift quietly from warmth into the world, which was first a slow stroll past the sleeping El, then to his van to shave and wash and brush his teeth, drifting more and more awake, reluctant and assenting, and noting idly that his pimple had vanished overnight. He sat now with dark rich coffee, given by his mother, who moved with purpose in the kitchen, and behind the louvers El rustled as she dressed. He was coming away from the waking warmth of the child self. He must grant that distance but also saw that he might, if he were simple and quiet, bend forward again over himself and the cradle of himself, and if he concentrated he might contact his child self again, down in the folds of being.

Annie said, "Well, a penny for your thoughts."

He looked up at his mother who was gazing at him with fond hip-cocked curiosity.

She said, "You are drifting somewhere, and I shouldn't molest you, but I'm just stupid with love." She turned to the stove to stir the scrambled eggs.

He could rise and embrace her and saw himself doing that but didn't. Soon he would tumble into life, but not yet. He sipped his coffee and noted its perfect taste. He wanted nothing. He drained his coffee, feeling the pebbles of grounds enter his mouth. He swallowed them as sacrament. He said, with slow spell-breaking volume, "Mighty good java, darling Mother."

Annie gazed with benign regard, and then with the spatula she catapulted a yellow fleck of egg across the room. It spatted and tumbled on the settee top. They looked at each other with half smiles. Annie turned back to her eggs. With an index finger, delicately and thoroughly, Dawson wiped the egg from the tabletop and scraped it into the empty coffee mug. And he noticed and felt and simply felt that he was clean of grievance and had forgiven his mother, who, like him, was bound in a self and set out like a single tree on a plain.

•

That morning Bluey woke early and spent a half hour answering emails, one from his neighbor George, who would arrive tomorrow, as promised, with a one man tent, a fishing pole, and interest in Annie. Then he found the number for the Los Angeles Baba group and entered it in his phone. Perhaps they would know the number of Ellen Auster, Rosa's Baba contact, who he might call and speak with, who would be over eighty now, and who had met Meher Baba. Through his cab window, he saw Roger jog past with his feed bag, and a moment later watched Dawson, a moving bundle of blanket, cross the field to his van. That Dawson had slept in the zoo he noted but did not consider. Opening day had arrived.

On his morning rounds he found every animal asleep, even the birds. He stopped at Bhajan's cage. The tiger was sprawled full length, eyes closed, slowly breathing. A deposit of feces lay near the feed door. He drew his breath deeply in, let it slowly emit, matching his breath to the tiger's, watching the wide flank rise, hesitate, then patiently deflate, then rise again. He yearned to the tiger—open your eyes, offer confirmation.

He heard steps and turned. It was Garrell, the round bellied fair director, and behind him, two round bellied young men. All three faces were gathered and intent.

Garrell said, "Dr. Macintosh, we got a situation here."

Bluey said, "What happened?"

"Did any of your animals escape last night?" Garrell shifted his weight, and his face creased.

Bluey said, "They did not. Tell me what happened."

"Something got into the bird building and tore up the turkeys. We got five dead turkeys. Now that's never happened before. So here I come to talk to you."

"I understand."

Bluey walked with them to the bird building. Something had found the single open window in the building, pushed through the screen, and had entered three separate cages by leaping over five foot high fencing. Five headless turkeys lay in a wheelbarrow.

Garrell said, "It could be coyote. And we've got wolves coming back around here. It could be a cougar. It tore the screen off the only open window. That's smart, don't you think."

Bluey agreed it was smart. He assured Garrell again that his cages were secure.

Garrell said, "Well, I'm not accusing. I wonder if it's a weasel. I hear weasel will kill for joy. These birds were not eaten. A turkey's a big damn bird though, for a weasel."

He and the two young men, whom he introduced as his sons, accompanied Bluey back to the entrance of the zoo. He said, "If it comes that you need a hand today, call my cell. These guys are both football referees and have that much to recommend them. I am too, by the way. We're a family of referees."

Bluey said he would keep that it mind. He noted that Garrell's suspicion had diminished. His own had only been parked. As he neared the rear exit, he heard huffing behind him and turned.

Roger chugged to a halt, hauled the feed bag from his shoulders and swung it onto the grass. He said, "Morning, Bluey."

Bluey's gaze enveloped the big man, his heaving breath, his soaked T-shirt, the rivulets streaking his large face. He said, "You're a mess."

Roger said, "I was running in the fair, only flat place. Kind of cool."

Bluey said, "I want to mention a thought I had about you."

Roger seemed to sturdy up, prepare for weather. He said, "Okay."

"I was thinking about your football career."

"Ah. Did you read about me?"

"Not about you in particular. You were an offensive lineman?"

"Yes."

"In high school and in college?"

"Right."

"That's where a lot of the battle is done, isn't it? I read that linemen sometimes get hit so hard their hair gets rubbed off."

"I bet you read about chronic traumatic encephalopathy, right? CTE."

"I did. The evidence is mounting. In rugby too. So I thought I would mention it, see what your thoughts were."

There was a moment of silence. Bluey's sobriety had stilled them. Roger said, "I know I'm gambling." Another pause. He added, "I may already have it, is one thing."

"Have you noticed symptoms?"

"No, but it's possible."

"Is it discussed in the locker room?"

"Not much. It's like, why talk about it? And in the pros, there's money. And more rah rah. But, right, it's a gamble."

Bluey said mildly, "In my day, on the rugby pitch, we were ignorant, so it was just fun and manly glory. You are not so fortunate."

Roger's mouth opened. He looked away. It was time for another subject.

Bluey said, "C'mon to breakfast. You need a towel."

"I know it. I got to get my clothes. I'll be there in a minute." He turned away, then back. "And thanks, you know? I *am* thinking about it, of course. But look at me. I'm built for football. It's the main thing I can do."

Bluey nodded. "Well, things can have more than one use, like a knife, for murder or carrots."

Roger's face brightened. "Very true, sir!" He extended his hand, and they shook, Roger raising his eyebrows, putting recognition into a firm grip.

•

Bluey found Annie emerging from the RV with the bell in hand. He raised a finger to forestall her.

He said, "Where's Patti?"

Annie frowned. "She's under the RV. Did something happen?" She told him about the chewed-through rope. He told her about the turkeys.

"Oh, for god's sake," said Annie. They went to the RV rear. Bluey knelt and chuck-chucked. Patti rose and walked slowly forward and stood while Bluey inspected her mouth, then the grass beneath the RV. No blood or feathers. The forehead was still swollen. He said, "I doubt this dog could jump a five foot fence. But we're going to put her in the tandem for today until Dawson gets back from town with a chain."

•

At breakfast, each time Roger wiped his face with his hand towel, sweat beads rebloomed. Dawson said he looked like he was eating habaneros, sniffed him for odors, then stuffed his nose with shreds of napkin which Annie and El removed.

Bluey outlined the day and tasks—Roger and El to clean cages, Dawson and Bluey to feed, then Dawson off to town with lists. The gate opened at nine. Smile and wear your shirt. He and El to stroll and talk, Annie to man the gate, Roger to monitor the crowd for fence-crossing, animal feeding or teasing.

After clean-up, El stopped Dawson as he started toward his RV. She said, "I saw those lists. Busy day. But I'm going to bug you for something too. If you see a used bookstore, or any bookstore, see if they have a copy of Meher Baba's *Discourses*. I'll pay whatever."

"Who's Meher Baba?"

"A spiritual master from India. Bluey lent me a book about him and the masts."

"Is that mast in the book? The one that raised—"

"I don't know. I've been looking, but we don't know his name. By the way, how was it sleeping under the tiger? Did you dream again?"

"No dreams."

"How was it?"

"I became a little child."

"Really?"

"Sort of. By the way, you don't have to worry about me."

"I don't?"

"I admit I got infatuated with you. But now I'm good."

"Really?"

They gazed together for a moment. Dawson said, "You can hug me. I won't hug back."

"Oh, I do want to hug you." She did, drawing him onto her and enveloping him. He did not hug back. Then he lifted his hands and lightly patted her back. She stepped away.

He said, "Pretty good, hunh?"

"Pretty good."

"I better get going."

"Me too."

"I'll look for the book."

"Thanks."

•

A half mile of cars lined up on the county road for the fair's inaugural day. Sheriff's deputies with blue-flashing roof racks manned the intersections. Dawson passed car after car of families and couples, fathers tilting for a look out the window, the backseat jostle of kids, distracted mothers, texting teenagers. He squinted, making the cars into a column of weary refugees. They were fleeing a disaster in the city. Was it war? They fled emptiness. They rushed to the fair's tinsel wonderland to spectate and forget.

In Dawson, the detachment and inside clearing had persisted even after the joshing with Roger and encounter with El. It was calm, call it that. A deep seat. And when the fear came that it was a mood merely and would evaporate, and he would be a refugee again himself, as he had always been, fleeing unconfidence toward academic and artistic glory, the calm persisted. Fear stopped outside its perimeter like a wolf beyond firelight. The calm was a force, a true thing that was, not willed but accepted. Something born and beneath. And he thought, God starts here, plain God. They should tell you about it very early, in school.

Don't worry, little children. Be patient in the refugee line. Something is important. Plain God is possible.

Eventually the calm did weaken, replaced in time by memory—he had wiped his mother's egg from the table and forgiven her. He had been brave with El. The memories seemed rich and unfit for his life, and yet they were his, what he had done and been.

As he neared Eugene, he pulled into a service station to fill up with Bluey's credit card. He set his phone's map for the computer store, asked a woman at the next pump the name of the best supermarket. Then he found a used bookstore on the phone. 8:25. Maybe open, probably not. Still he would swing by since the computer store didn't open until nine, and he wanted to hit the grocery store last for freshness. And he had Walmart for the weights and dog chain and stuff for his mother, plus a pair of pajamas for El his mother had given him two twenties to pay for. And protein powder.

He balanced the phone on his knee and followed the GPS map through Eugene, a pleasant tree-planted town. He parked in front of Coffee Sally's and went up two store fronts to the bookstore, which was in fact closed. But inside there was thin white-haired guy behind a raised book-stacked counter, like a book castle, maybe Mr. Smith himself, since it was the Smith Family Bookstore. He rapped the glass door, began a series of apologetic gestures. The man tapped his wrist. Dawson continued gesturing. Finally the man descended the book fortress and made a patient, gliding walk to the door. He held a hand to his ear and waited.

Dawson said loudly through the glass, "I need a special book. The *Discourses* by Meher Baba. Sorry to bug you, but I—"

The guy fiddled the lock and opened the door. He said, "There must be a seminar."

"Why?"

"I sold that book yesterday. I do not have another and had that one for seven years."

"Really? No, there's not a seminar. But it's an interesting coincidence."

"You can buy a new one online which, foolish me, I should never say."

"Okay. Thanks for talking to me."

"Come at nine, and we will talk more."

Dawson went back to his van. He was pleased with the encounter, which had been kindly, on the old guy's part but on his too. The old guy had said, come again, and we will talk. He could say, try this book I liked.

8:45. He went into Coffee Sally's. A scatter of wooden tables and chairs, a young couple, two guys and one woman with laptops at separate tables along the window. He ordered a latte from the Asian man behind the counter. Then, because odd excited energy was surging, he worked up a ditty to amuse himself, and as the man handed him the latte, he had it—*China man in coffee shop. This is very wrong. Coffee be for Smith. It not be for Wong.* Dawson emitted a goofy guffaw and said to the man's inquiring face, "Sorry. I just thought of something."

He crossed to the condiment bar, repeating the ditty, and at *It not be for Wong*, again emitted a laugh. The nearest laptop guy gave him a head-cocked glance, then went back to his screen. There were two books in front of the laptop and on the spine of the bottom book the title *Discourses* was visible. After sugaring his coffee, Dawson crossed the room, stood before the table.

The laptop guy looked up. He said, "Are you gonna tell me a joke" He was fiftyish, square-shouldered, thin sandy hair combed straight back.

"No, but I saw you had the *Discourses*. Did you buy it yesterday at the bookstore?"

"Have you been following me?"

"Ha! No, but the guy told me he sold one yesterday, and here you are. I was looking for one."

The man folded his hands beneath his chin, then flipped them forward in a ten-fingered X, indicating the chair opposite. "Sit, and we will discuss."

"You want to sell it?"

The man gestured again and Dawson sat. The man said, "This is a very valuable book. I would not want to part with it."

"But you would for the right price?"

"Yes, I would. How strong is your interest?"

"Well, I better conceal that. Anyway, it's not for me. A friend asked me to look for it."

"Nice."

"That's true, actually."

The man regarded him with sober amusement. "How strong is your friend's interest?"

"Fairly strong."

"Fifty dollars strong?"

Dawson let a moment pass. He said, "Yes."

"Done." The man reached around the laptop and lifted both books onto his lap. "You may think, well, he lives around here, and this is his customary coffee shop. But it is not. I was in Smith's yesterday and did not have time for coffee but wanted one, since Sally's coffee is good. You have not tasted yours."

Dawson tasted his latte. "Good."

"So I came back to fulfill a desire, but perhaps instead, in a hocus pocus way, to meet you and satisfy your friend."

Dawson said, "And earn fifty bucks."

"There's that."

Dawson rummaged in his wallet, withdrew one of his four fifties, scissored it between fingers. The man plucked it and brought it to his lap. He said, "This book is the avatar's flypaper."

"You've read it?"

"Many times, but I'm due for a tune up. I lent my last copy, and it never came back." He handed the book across the table. "I release it with good will."

Dawson took the book, stood. "Thanks."

The man's face, which before had seemed privately amused by the encounter, now softened. He touched Dawson's arm. He said, "By the way, in case you might be interested, all of Baba's books are now available online. Google Meher Baba books and look for the Meher Trust."

"Now you tell me."

The man smiled. He said, "Good luck to you and your friend." He turned to his laptop.

On the way to his van, Dawson glanced at the book's cover, a black and white photo of Meher Baba, an intent long-haired man in his thirties, a beautiful man really, in a white shirt, a broad mustache. 8:52. The bookstore opened in a few minutes, and he could browse the spiritual books, but he would have to browse the computer store too, and then Walmart and the grocery store, and it was the Exotic Animal Caravan's first day, and he should be there, not screwing around. Anyway he had the *Discourses,* the main thing. And there was the online site the guy mentioned.

As he got into his van, he thought of returning to the coffee shop, getting the guy's email address. That would be odd. He wanted it though. The guy had an appealing offhand confidence, and that last move, that arm touch and the soft look, had affected him. He almost returned to the coffee shop but didn't. But he felt he had parted from a friend without saying goodbye.

He spent two hours in the computer store, reading reviews on his phone, going back and forth, finally got everything, including a laptop and printer for his mother. They didn't have a green screen, but he would get that online. He hit Walmart next, got a pair of pink pajamas with blue hippos, plus a dog chain, protein powder, a teapot, crock pot, and tea strainer, then carted three hundred pounds of weights out to the van. At the grocery store, his mother's list came to fourteen sacks of food and two newspapers. As he was checking out, Bluey called his cell and asked him to get fifty landscape spikes at a hardware store. Dawson asked how the show was going, but Bluey had hung up. He stopped at the big box hardware store across the street, then headed for the fairgrounds.

The line of cars had shrunk, but not by much. The parking lots were overflowing, and cars were being parked along the roads, with lines of families trooping in from several hundred yards away. He was wearing his Exotic Animal Caravan shirt, and the deputy let him leave the main road and enter from behind the zoo again. He parked in front of the RV, and when he turned off the van immediately heard silence and had an instant premonition—opening day had been a bust.

He entered through the rear stockade gap. A circle of people four and five deep was gathered at the crowd fencing. He spotted Bluey in the carnivore section beside the hyena cage, chatting with a section of the crowd, which seemed oddly hushed, like a museum crowd, or an audience waiting for a performance to begin. Some lifted children, moved into gaps. Many held cameras and smart phones.

Roger, strolling between the fencing and cages, saw Dawson behind the lion cage. He said, "C'mon, dude. We need you. We're walking the perimeter, just being a presence. We're the police."

Dawson said, "What's going on?"

Roger opened his mouth to rely, but stopped, held up one hand. There had been a sound like a cough, a deep chuff. Immediately a cacophony began, a chorus of shrieks, roars, hoots, chitters. Hooves, paws, and nails clicked and banged on metal cage bottoms like discordant drums. Then the vocalizations steadied, gathered, finally became a single resonant chord. Five seconds later the cry ceased. The dhole made a series of piercing yips in the silence.

Dawson said, "Jesus fucking Christ! Was that the tiger? Did the tiger start that?" Dawson jumped, using Roger's shoulder as a hoist, and looked over the crowd. The tiger cage was surrounded by a dense crowd. He caught a glimpse of El inside the crowd fence perimeter, the parrot on her shoulder, a red burnoose wrapped around her head.

He followed Roger on a circuit between the cages and fencing. Roger said, "We got to keep moving. Did you get the spikes?"

"In the van."

"They keep pushing the fence in, so tonight we're gonna spike it."

"Roger, motherfucker, what is this?"

"Okay, yeah, about every five minutes, or every two minutes, it kind of varies, the tiger chuffs and they make that note. Some guy told me it was a perfect fifth, F and C."

"How long has it been going on?"

"Right when the gates opened, man. It kind of goes in cycles. It's fucking amazing, dude."

"And the tiger is the signal?"

"Right. They wait for the tiger."

"Jesus fucking Christ. What does Bluey say?"

"He smiles and shrugs." Then he leaned closer and said, "Your mom already gave me a money bag to put in the RV. It was fat, dude. I hid it in the trash can."

They met Bluey, approaching from the other direction. He said to Dawson, "Get everything?"

"Yeah. I have to get it unloaded. This is an amazing phenomenon, right?"

"It is. Can you unload by yourself? We have to keep circling. Then come back, and you can help."

"No problem. I mean this is more than amazing, right? So what's the explanation? What's the cause of this?"

They were standing beside the raccoon cage. Chortle emitted a high chitter and thrust his arm through the fencing, opened his hand. Bluey enfolded the hand with his own. He put his other hand on Dawson's shoulder and said, "I don't have an explanation."

"You don't?"

"No. I'm just like a baby."

"Really? God, man—" Then Dawson gasped. Some internal force had erupted, pushing up from his belly and through his throat. He gasped again, and fat tears ran down his cheeks. He began to tremble. He wobbled.

Roger clasped him around the waist. He said, "Dude, man. Are you sick?"

Bluey said, "He's not sick. Take him to the RV."

"No, no," said Dawson. "I'm okay. I'm okay." He was seized then with a violent shudder and convulsed with sobs. He covered his face. He held out his hands, backed two steps. Between sobs, he said, "I'm okay, I'm okay," then turned and trotted away through a gauntlet of stares from the crowd.

Roger turned to Bluey, his hands up and spread. "What the fuck, man. What is happening? I may have to quit this job." His hands were trembling. Bluey grasped them tightly in his own and held them until Roger's trembling subsided. He said, "It's not bad, Roger. It's not bad."

•

As El circled the perimeter, the tiger circled with her, giving the appearance of a fearsome stalker. Above her, on the top rail of the cage, two crows perched, now and then hop-flapping from rail to rail to follow El's progress. The crows, the stalking tiger, and the tiger's intermittent chuff, which catalyzed the chorus, were great crowd-pleasers. Around the tiger, people were packed eight deep, with dozens of smart phones stalked up like periscopes. When a section of fencing began to move inward from the pressure, El murmured to the parrot riding the towel across her shoulder, and Sybil obligingly squawked, "Back, you devils, back!" This was another crowd-pleaser, but it still took considerable air-patting and kindly grimacing to make much dent in the press of bodies, first here, then there, like fighting tide. Then a chuff from Bhajan and the chorus of cries, including Sybil's raucous screech directly into her ear. The crowd laughed and exclaimed and rotated their smart phone periscopes. Then more policing, squawking, and air-patting.

Bluey had called her cell a half hour ago and informed her that he and Garrell were devising some sort of whistle system, so that the crowd could be let in for twenty minutes with instructions to leave when the whistle sounded. She was losing the fence fight badly now and longing for the whistle, and thought probably they had abandoned the idea, then heard it, twenty feet away. She seized a corner bar of the cage and stepped onto the protruding surface so she could see over the crowd. It was Garrell, standing near the end of the tiger cage wearing a referee's striped shirt, a whistle around his neck. He bellowed, "Thank you, folks. Thank you. Let's give the next group a chance. Thank you, folks. Thank you."

His friendly command began to disperse the crowd, which started to exit past the ticket booth and a line of waiting customers. El repositioned the fence, then trotted through the crowd to the booth, where she had seen Annie heading back up the line. Annie carried a zippered bank bag and roll of red tickets.

Annie said, "I went down the line to sell tickets so we could get them in faster. You okay?"

"I'm fine. I thought I could work the line with you."

"With your bird? I about got a quota anyway. Bluey wants two hundred at a time. You better get back. I think he's ready to blow that whistle."

The whistle blew. Annie swung the gate open and began plucking the proffered tickets as the crowd fanned into the grounds. El returned to the tiger enclosure, scissoring across the crowd fence. Bhajan lay on his belly, regarding her. She had been busy all day and like all of the crew, had skipped lunch and had had no time to consider explanations, which would have been like ash anyway, light and useless. As the crowd gathered behind her, she gazed into Bhajan's eyes. Then, carefully erect, since Sybil rode her shoulder, she did a slow sideways dance step, finishing with a silent *ta da*. As if on cue, Sybil flap-hopped from her shoulder, seized the bars with talons and beak, and in an instant plopped through and onto the cage floor. Bhajan stood, watched the bird flounder across the wood chips past his head, which turned to follow her progress. With a supreme frenzy of flapping, Sybil began to claw and beak her way up the rear haunch, finally reaching the tiger's motionless back. She paced forward, wings spread and flailing for balance, until she reached the shoulder blades, where her talons curled into the fur. El began circling again, and the tiger paced behind, his rolling shoulders creating a graceful glide so that Sybil seemed to be surfing on a rolling orange sea. The smart phone periscopes recorded it all.

17

JJ bought twenty videos, mostly shoot-em-ups, but also five dramas, give Ned a little altitude even if it bored him. Ned would be gone soon, was maybe gone now, since it was an any day deal. His sister told JJ she could see the white bone of the pelvis. They were using maggots too, which they called medical maggots, which yesterday Ned had tried to joke about on the phone—I'm getting used to being dead, man. Then in querulous despair—*fuck me, man, fuck me.* JJ had sent ten grand to the sister so she could stay with him. Sometimes when he called though, the nurse answered, didn't know where the sister was. Oh well. Send the money, send the videos, forget it. Everybody forgets everything. The head nurse asks the attendant, did you turn the patient in room 567? Yes, ma'am, I did. The head nurse is satisfied, and the attendant is satisfied he has satisfied the head nurse, and Ned is not turned, at least not enough because the pressure ulcers start. Or maybe would start anyway. JJ had an idea for a paraplegic bed, a robotic bed with continually moving rollers and sent emails to the ten top medical device companies, offering the idea for free, but hadn't heard from any of them. Maybe they were all inventing away, rushing to market. At the news conference—*Where did this idea come from, doctor?* An email from some dude. *Which dude was that?* No idea, we didn't write back. *Really, you didn't write to the originator of your marvelous invention!* Sad but true. Because everyone forgets everything.

He carried his basket of videos past the electronic gadgets, inspecting for anything new, saw nothing, and got in line behind a middle-aged black woman with an old fashioned afro. He had two hours to get to the airport, where he and his realtor were going up in a helicopter. She had a list of nine properties and was excited, first time in a chopper.

He was moving out of the basement house. A week ago, his shrink-inspired mother had summoned him to Delmarco's by the Sea, a five star that might subdue screaming, for a big this-is-it meeting. She had started strong with a list of bullet points, probably practiced with her shrink, lift the stones, free the bugs. You and Trey may have been abused, I may have known but didn't know I knew, I too may have been abused, your uncle too, but now we must live and try to heal and forgive, and then she was weeping, and after that shouting, *I know you have that pistol, and you could kill us both, why don't you! Just pull it out and shoot us now, right now, for god's sake, please just shoot us now.* The cry of *pistol* was like a gunshot itself. The restaurant cleared. The waiters vanished. The cops would come. JJ left his mother weeping on the tablecloth. At home, he left a note on the coffeepot, *I've called a realtor.* She would read it trembling, in shock, needing a fix of shrink. In his mind, he saw her lift it, read it, go instantly sleepy. She staggers back to her bedroom and falls onto the bed and sleeps for days. Everyone forgets everything.

Twenty feet ahead the CNN logo dance came up on fifty TV screens, and a pretty girl behind the news desk mouthed the intro to a puff piece, throwing off shrugs and archy eyebrows before the cutaway to a round pinkfaced reporter in *Eugene, Oregon*, said the caption, obviously a local news guy, standing in a crowd at an entrance gate, and above the gate, a sign—The *Exotic Animal Caravan.*

JJ put his basket on the counter, getting an arch is-that-appropriate glance from the afro woman, and went to the TVs. On the screen, the gates opened and crowd surged, the fat reporter leading, beckoning to the camera, talking fast. A flash of cages in a circle with brown animals moving, then a bigger cage coming up and a fence, and a tiger in the cage looking into the camera, which zoomed up and back and El was there, smiling, tilting her head, raising her eyebrows in a jolly deprecating way, listening to the round reporter, answering, gesturing, swinging her hands like brushes, as if she were painting the world, which she was, toning the world with delicate shades of love and gracious kindness.

JJ looked for a volume control. Nothing worked. He shouted, "Hey! Hey!"

The shouted-at clerk, a short thin kid, frowned JJ's way.

JJ said, "I need the volume, man, quick."

The kid slouched over, reached behind the screens, turned something. The volume came up. He said, "Can't turn it up much, because—"

JJ flicked a stopping palm, and the kid slouched away.

El said, "—a chuff. Tigers make a chuff. It's sort of a grunt. And that's the signal. And no, this is not part of any training. We've just begun our tour. We're on the way to the Exotic Animal Ecopark in Tennessee, which will be a model for future—"

Behind her, the tiger uttered a chesty boom. El nodded, shrugged. Off camera, a rising chorus of animal sound. The camera lifted and panned the crowd, the brown figures in the cages yipping, hooting, pounding, the sound resolving finally into a long resonant note. The camera zoomed to Spectra, tail-fanned and shrieking. It panned to Demijohn, then Nubia, both open-mouthed and roaring, then to Cloe the okapi, pounding her metal cage bottom with one hoof. Then abrupt quiet. The camera returned to smiling El. She said, "Okay. That's it. I have to go."

The reporter said, "So no explanation?"

El said, waving, "No explanation." She turned away, then turned back and said, "The Exotic Animal Ecopark in Tennessee," waved again, and was gone.

JJ's phone vibrated in his front pocket. He looked, expecting the realtor, but it was Greta Delay, his date that night, no doubt needing the hotel. Greta was an escort, clean and pretty, keeping herself in college, she said. He slipped the phone back into his pocket. He would call her later. He would cancel, eat the fee. He would cancel with the realtor. A plan had come. He would mail the videos, gear up, then head to Eugene. He would be their videographer, gratis. He would make a documentary. He felt a golden glow. There was management in the universe, him at the counter, her face on fifty screens, her deeply medicinal face, her grace, her kindness to the dumpy reporter, her bold promotion of the ecopark, her life's purpose, to help animals, to help others, to be a kind person. There was management. He would do anything.

18

The gates closed at six, and the zoo fell silent. Sometime during the afternoon, Dawson had unpacked the van, even leaving Roger's weights beside his cab, but did not arrive for supper and did not answer his cell or radio when Annie called. They had been isolated from each other all day, and when they gathered spent a moment in exclamation and report.

When this faded, El said to Bluey, "So what's going on," and they waited.

He nodded. He said he understood their expectation but could not satisfy it. He said the miraculous is obedience to a higher law. He said beneath the tissue of every explanation there is something breathing.

He said, "Let's give whatever is coming toward us time to arrive. That's my counsel. Now then, I have hundreds of emails to attend to, and three national news crews to coordinate with for tomorrow. The website crashed, by the way. And, happy to announce, we earned over twenty thousand dollars."

•

Bluey stood beside his truck. Across the field he could see the fog-blurred light from Dawson's van. If he didn't arrive for the evening purr, someone would have to make the walk. He inhaled cool air, willed himself to slow. He was duty-pressed to enter the cab and begin answering emails—from colleagues, from friends, from strangers—but wanted first a portion of calm. He closed his eyes, but immediately opened them. He had heard a heavy step.

Roger said, "Hey, man."

"Hey."

Roger stopped in front of him. "Annie wants me to check on Dawson, so that's where I'm heading."

Bluey said, "Good."

Roger shifted, raised his hands to the back of his head, then slung them from his neck. He said, "You ready for something?"

"Shoot."

Roger laced his hands, reverse flexed them at his waist. He said, "Hell, you're not going to care. I'm pretty sure. I got a felony record."

"You mean the drug thing?"

"El told you?"

"No, I looked you up."

"I should have told you, I guess."

"You're strategy was, let him get to know me."

"Right."

"Well, you're fired anyway."

"Ha. I just realized you wouldn't care. Pretty weird. A couple of days ago, I was worried as shit. Now here's this other deal. Maybe you'll care about this. I got on this dating site, and I've been writing to this girl in Oklahoma City." Roger ran both hands over his close-cropped skull, stretched his arms wide. "Now guess what? She's flying out here tomorrow. She saw me on the internet. She saw us all. You know we're going viral, right? Anyway, she emailed. When you said we have to wait for what's coming, I thought, man, he's talking to me. Her name is Dori. She's flying in around two. She'll get a motel and take a cab out here. So what do you think? Bad move?"

"Two days ago, maybe. Now, who knows."

•

Through the tree screen, Roger could hear the rapids, and now and then glimpsed a fleece of silver fog. When he reached the van, he saw

Dawson sitting up on his bunk, crossed-legged, reading intently under the goose-necked light. Roger rapped.

Dawson's head snapped up. Roger slid open the door. He said, "You okay? Your mom said dinner's getting cold."

"I'm fine. Come in, sit down." Roger hoisted himself into the small space, sat in the swivel chair. Dawson said, "You're worried about me, right? I burst into tears, right? Did you tell my mother?"

"No," said Roger.

"Well, that's good. You know what? That purr is having an effect on us. Not just the animals. Do you feel any different?"

"Yes, but there's a new woman in my life, so I would." Roger told him the developments. He said, "You think I'm crazy?"

"No. Of course, maybe she just wants to see this cool zoo."

"Probably."

"See, that's extraordinary, isn't it? It's not in the normal line of things that happen. So that's what I'm saying, about the purr. You seem pretty calm, by the way, for a guy that's falling in love. Are you calm?"

Roger considered. "Yes, I am. I'm a little worried. You know, you're supposed to meet someone for coffee or something. But here she comes. She'll be here tomorrow afternoon."

"Here's my advice." Dawson smiled. "Lead with your heart."

"Yeah?"

"Definitely."

"Okay." Roger's voice had slightly thickened.

"You know I'm sort of joking, and still you choke up. I think that's the purr. It's affecting us. I've been absorbed in this book, which I just got for El. You know the deal with the tiger right, raised by a holy man?"

Roger drew a long deep breath, head-bounced a nod.

Dawson said, "This has all been raining down on me. Don't go. Do you have to go?"

Roger smiled. "At some point I will have to go."

"Ha! This book is called the *Discourses*, and it's by Meher Baba, who spent a lot of time traveling in India to see these masts, which our tiger was raised by, which you know, right? Anyway, Meher Baba says he's the divine avatar. Which is either giantly egotistical, or true, and just what God would say. It's like one of those logic puzzles with the Washingtons and Longfellows. Do you know those?"

"No."

"Doesn't matter. But Longfellows always lie and Washingtons always tell the truth, so they would both say I'm a Washington, if that was the question. That's not a proof, just an interesting preliminary consideration as we begin to grapple with this difficult subject. I'm being funny."

"That was really funny."

"Sometimes I get this fantastic nausea. It's because I'm way the fuck off. Anyway, the purpose of life, you may say, Roger, that it is a divine game of hide and seek, God seeking himself, looking through our eyes for himself. And what is the glue, Roger, that binds all this stuff together? It's love. Which is what God is. Do you notice I just used your name? I have this terrific urge right now to give you a hug. I really do. A strong urge. Good, the urge is dying because I talked about it, because it would have been physically awkward in this tiny space. I'm sort of trembling. I had this neat thought about the two lists of God. My head is majorly buzzing."

Roger stood, his massive frame hunkered, reached and squeezed Dawson's bare foot with one hand. "That's your hug, dude, in case the hug urge has not gone away." He sat again. "Go ahead. I'm listening. Tell me about the two lists of God."

"When you die you come up in front of God, and he reads you two lists. First list, all the mean shit you did. A long list, very humiliating. Then he pulls out another list, and that's a list of all the good shit you didn't do. That's way longer. Actually it's an infinite list. You say, but God, I didn't know about that stuff. He says, that's right, because you are small-hearted. Now go back and learn something. That's why we have to reincarnate. We're all second-listers. That's why we fall in love, because we are questing for God, who is the immense wet ocean. It's a super inclusive idea. For some reason, I'm feeling super tiny, like a way high eagle. I feel nauseous."

"You gonna throw up?"

"I might. I should probably eat something. Here's the main thing. It's all a distraction. All these thoughts. Because you know what, here we are. We are always trapped right here. And all these thoughts, they're like scaffolding or something. You think they're holding up the world, but really they're just in the way. Damn. A wave of just immense nausea rolled through."

Roger cranked open the sliding door. He said, "C'mon out."

Dawson slid down from his bunk and stepped onto the grass, then reached back for his blanket, slung it around his shoulders. Then he reached in again and retrieved the book from his bunk and the sack of Walmart pajamas.

Roger said, "Shoes?"

"Barefoot is good."

"You okay?"

"Yes, I'm okay." Roger's great flank of body stood before him. He handed Roger the book. then wrapped his arms around Roger's waist and laid his head against the chest. He felt Roger's free hand softly at his back. He stepped away, took the book back.

He said, "So there's your hug."

•

Annie vaguely ached. Now and then as she and El cleaned the kitchen, she bent to peer through the window and across the grass toward Dawson's van. It had been fifteen minutes since Roger left. Then she looked through the window again, and there they were, striding across the grass in what Annie thought happily was a non-reluctant way, Dawson blanket-wrapped and slightly behind and small-seeming. She went to the microwave, pressed start, and heard the engine's excellent whir.

El was seated at the settee and looked up, then out of the window. "Ah," she said. "He likes that blanket. I think he's barefoot."

Annie looked again, finally saw a flash of foot. "He certainly is. El, do one thing. Google hookworms in California."

El, who had just set up Annie's new laptop and was browsing the news, entered *hookworms in CA* in the search box. She had seen the book in Dawson's hand, perhaps the *Discourses.* The last time she had seen him, Dawson had invited her to hug him and stood slimly harmless.

That moment, his arms-down harmlessness, came back from time to time during the day as she crowd-wrangled.

She announced, "Hookworms can be a problem in California. Brought here perhaps by the Chinese. Or Hindus. Preliminary impressions only."

Annie filled the teapot and put it on the stove to heat. She crossed to the door then and opened it to Roger.

Roger said, "He was reading."

Annie said, "Come in, come in."

Roger stepped aside, and Dawson started up the steps. Roger said, "I better get moving."

"No, please, Roger. You must come in. I've made tea. Spend a moment with us."

Roger turned. On the walk back, he had begun mind-composing a letter to Dori about God and the two lists. But Annie's voice was like a spread blanket. He said, "Okay."

Dawson handed the pajama sack to his mother, then slid into the settee across from El. Roger sat beside him. Dawson pushed the book across to her.

She said, "I saw you carrying it. I was hoping."

Dawson briefly recounted speaking to the old guy at the door of the closed bookstore, then stopping at the coffee shop. "I get my coffee, and I'm putting sugar, and I look over, and there on this guy's table I see the *Discourses*. So I say, did you buy that book yesterday? He said, have you been following me? And he sold it to me."

El said, "That's amazing. How much do I owe you?"

"It's a gift."

"Really? No—"

"No, it's a gift. I read it a little. By the way, the guy told me it was on the web now."

El began sorting through the pages. She said, "Well, thanks a bunch. That's so nice. What do you think of it?"

Dawson bit his hamburger. It was delicious and warming. He said from the side of his mouth, "I liked it." They were all around him, two women and the big fellow, hung out in space around him, seeing him eat, hearing the crushing slushes of his chewing, seeing him and seeing each other. It was all there was. It was golden.

El stopped fanning the book. Her fingers tweezed between the pages and removed a fifty dollar bill. She said, "Wow. Fifty bucks."

Dawson reached, plucked the bill. He put his fork down and with two hands pressed the bill against his forehead for a moment. He returned it to El, who held it aloft, like evidence. She said, "You gave him fifty bucks, and he gave it back."

Dawson nodded.

Roger said, "Ahhhh—"

El said, "I can't keep it, of course."

She placed the bill beside Dawson's plate. He fished his wallet from his front pocket, placed the bill inside, thrust back the wallet. El said, "You didn't get his name or anything, did you?"

Something was surging inside Dawson. He forked cheesy beans into his mouth until his mouth was puffy full, and he began to rhythmically tap the fork against his lips while he worked the food down. He thought of immediately getting up, no explanation, excuse me, excuse me, and going out to the long grass in the field and rolling. He could roll and roll and get tired. They were looking at him, waiting for an answer, because El had asked a question—what had she asked?—and they were seeing that he had been taken in a vortex and ate strangely, and they kept their faces polite. His mother was looking over from the stove because he had not answered El's question. He bent his head, then recalled the question and said, emitting normal, "I almost went back and got his name."

They nodded. He had spoken plainly. He felt their gratitude.

The last of the cheesy beans vanished from his mouth. He sighed a slow secret sigh. He held his fork between his two hands. He said, "They say some people can bend forks. Mentally. Why would you do that though? There are seven planes, and that's the path. And on the first four you get more and more power over energy. But you would never bend forks. You would see something so bright up ahead, you wouldn't think of bending forks." They were watching him. He stared at the fork. There was flickering at the edge of his vision, like vague sparklers, colored ones, which would vanish if you looked, but something flickering definitely, which might be good or bad, but maybe bad, some pulled-loose wire spraying color.

El said, "It sounds like you read of lot of the book. I can't wait to get to it. But maybe you should keep it for a while."

Dawson said, "It's on the web. Yes, I read a lot. There's a huge amount of stuff on the web about the spirit world, and it's all different, so it's guesses and hopes. You just google, and everybody loads you up. I've been thinking about information. Can I talk? It might be interesting." He received silent attention and a murmured *go* from El. He said, "Like if you could be a tiny person and walk around inside the human body and see everything working, all the molecules and mitochondria, there goes a blood cell, there goes a carbon atom, just have complete information, even be small enough to see quarks. It would still be a spectator sport, like watching a football game. You wouldn't know the rules. You could guess them, but that's it. And you would have to constantly revise your guesses, which is what science is. And even let's say if you could see the world from the point of view of every particle, be a quark, zip here and there, and every time you got near a muon this happens or that happens, and if you could have the total information of what's in everybody's mind at any moment, and in every quark, if quarks have consciousness, let's say they do, or if they don't at least you have perfect quark empathy, then what would you have? What! What!" Dawson's face had become grieved, his tone feverish. His hands slapped the tabletop. Annie, watching from the kitchen, met El's eyes, and they exchanged worry.

Dawson said, "And even, let's say, you figure out all the rules, what only quarks feel, but now you feel the rules too. And you say, oh, there's an energetic force in these quarks and when you press your nose up close and have this perfect empathy you say, but what's that force? What makes that force causal? What's manifesting that? That's good to realize! It means, if you want to know the truth, you can't find out by knowing things. That's a very appealing thought. Do you mind letting me out?" He touched Roger's shoulder, then patted it lightly. Roger got to his feet, standing bent under the air conditioner. Dawson stood beside him, patted Roger's chest. "Do you think we are the same species? Ha!"

Annie brought a tray of teacups and tea boxes and placed it on the table. She said, "Where are you going? You must stay for tea at least. We have all had a quite a day. I want us to gather a little and be together and give our impressions. So will you stay a bit?"

"Okay." He gathered his plate from the table. "Let me wash this. Let me stamp." He stamped his feet in baby steps to the kitchen sink, scraped the leftovers into the garbage.

El said, "Why is that an appealing thought, that if you knew what quarks were feeling you still wouldn't know the truth?" Annie delivered her a reproving glance. El made a frown apology.

Dawson put his plate into the sink, then turned, swooped his hands upward as if throwing something invisible into the air. "Here's why—because at the very last detail of matter and energy, where the very tiniest particle is spinning, and you knock on that tiny particle's door and say, why are you behaving this way? What can the particle say? It will say, that's my nature. I obey the rule. And then you ask the rule, oh rule, why do you impel this poor particle to behave this way? And also, what are you, what is a rule? And the last rule must shrug. You say, but you're the invisible guidance that makes everything dance, and you shrug? Yes, the rule says. I'm just a rule, and I must shrug, since I am in ignorant bondage to my nature! So thought has to shrug too. Thought poops out. That's appealing to me. Very appealing. You know why? You know why!" Here Dawson pressed his palms against his temples and grimaced.

Annie laid her hands against his wrists, slowly guided his hands downward, then drew him into her chest, felt his body rigid and unyielding. She said, "What kind of tea. Peppermint?"

"I'm okay. Yes, peppermint. Am I not making sense?"

Annie released him. "You're making wonderful sense. And I am listening—we all are—with delight, aren't we?" She swept the table with a glance.

El said, "Definitely."

Roger said, "The last rule shrugs. I like it."

Annie said, "I'm sure there will be more. But first, we must have tea. We must nourish and soothe all our particles and rules. El has googled something interesting which I want to get to." She invited El with raised eyebrows.

El said, "Your mother saw your bare feet and thought of hookworms, which are definitely in California."

Dawson smiled, moved his head side to side in an Indian wag.

Annie poured hot water into four mugs. She said, "It's a point though."

El said, "Also, a side note. Hookworms can prevent certain allergies. Various ones are wrangling about it."

Annie made four peppermint teas, added honey, distributed them. She crossed to the counter and removed the pajamas from the Walmart sack. She said, "Good lord, what did you get? Pink with hippos. You were thinking zoo, no doubt. These are for you, dear."

El held them forth. "Oh my. I love them. These are so perfect, Dawson. Thank you, Annie."

Dawson said, "The change is in the bag."

"I'm paying you back, of course," El said.

Annie said, "Oh, hush, young girl." She lifted a section of the newspaper from the kitchen counter. She said, "I've saved the jumble. When he was home, Dawson and I always did the jumble." She pressed her hand against Dawson's chest. "Now come sit." She slid into the settee, patted the seat. Dawson, who had slouched against the counter, now bucked away and slouched into the settee across from Roger.

Annie said, "Okay, first one. Shoot, no pencils. Roger, will you—"

But Dawson was up. "I'll get them."

Annie said, "Kitchen drawer on the right."

Dawson brought two pens and two pencils, reslouched into the settee. Annie tore the newspaper into pieces, giving everyone a scratchpad. She said, "First word. I-n-y-a-r. Inyar. I write them in a circle, which helps break it up. And when you have it, just—"

Roger, who had been scribbling, said, "Rainy."

"Ah, rainy," said Annie. "Very good. But next time just announce that you have it. At least, that's how we play. Because if we don't, it would not be fun, since Dawson is too quick. Dawson, did you get that?"

Dawson, who had not written anything, said, "Yes."

Roger tapped Dawson gently on the forehead with his pencil. He said, "No, we are not the same species."

Annie said, "T-e-c-o-t. Tecot."

Scribbling began. Dawson folded his arms, closed his eyes, lowered his head.

Annie said, "Sometimes I think we shouldn't play this together. It's fun, but I can't play without being competitive. Which is why it's fun to play Dawson, who I can't beat so I don't have to worry. Does anyone have it?"

"I think I do," said El. She looked at Dawson. "Do you have it?"

He said "Ta ta ta ta! Ta ta ta ta!"

El nodded.

Roger said, "Is that a hint?"

El said, "Yep."

"Okay," Roger said. "Crappy hint though."

Annie said, "Think music."

Roger said, "You have it?"

Annie said, "Think music."

"What does it start with?

"O."

Roger said, "Ah, okay. Octet."

Dawson said, "Wow."

Roger said, "Hey, I got *rainy* first."

Dawson said, "No, I mean hints are so cool. That we can hint."

Annie said, "*E-w-t-i-n-g. Ewting.*"

They scribbled. Dawson's mouth opened. He drummed fingers against his lips. Then he stood. He bent forward, let his arms dangle in front of him. He flipped his hands outward as if pleading. He cocked his head.

Roger said, "Is that a hint?"

"No. I'm just—it could be actually. But no. You know why we can hint? You know what the secret of hinting is? It's because everything is connected. It's because ideas have this shadow around them, which is other ideas. And there's no—" Dawson's face went white. His eyes drifted, then closed. His body crumpled. Roger moved his bulk from the settee with instant speed, caught Dawson neatly under his armpits.

Annie said, "Oh, god, what happened?"

Roger said, "He fainted." He hoisted Dawson limp body against his chest. Dawson's face was slack and open-mouthed.

Annie said, "Oh, god. Put him in my room, on the bed." Roger hoisted Dawson higher, backed into the rear room. Annie followed, her hands on Dawson face, his hair, his neck.

El watched, unalarmed, which she absently noted. She was trying the circle technique Annie mentioned, jumbling the letters randomly. Now she read them clockwise silently, *t-n-i-w-e-g*. Dawson said his posture might be a hint, or that hand flipping gesture. He flipped his hands, and now El flipped hers, open and outward, then had it instantly, *twinge*. She could hear muffled sounds as they arranged Dawson on the bed. She could go look, see his gone-away expression. She had seen his arms hang long and loose, had seen his face slacken and whiten and loosen, and his consciousness fall away as he fell, and Roger move like a cat to catch him. He had asked, how can we hint, and had said, there's a shadow, and fainted. She got that right away, that things in the mind had to be connected if you could hint from one to another, which meant there was a web, and that's what he saw, or felt with some other place than his front mind, and his front mind whited out. She felt a deep good feeling, a trembling solid deep good feeling. She could go out to the tiger and open the cage and probably have a nice tiger ride. That would be a crowd-pleaser.

She got up and went into the bedroom. Roger stood grief-faced, his hands laced behind his head, his elbows near the ceiling. Annie sat on the bed, head bowed, a hand on Dawson's cheek. She glanced up as El entered, her face half pleading, half full of love. She said, "It's okay, I think. Isn't it?"

El said, "I think it is."

•

Bluey dialed the number of Ellen Auster, pushed *send*, and watched the screen as the phone went through its routine. It was past eight, nearly time for the purr, but he had saved time for the call. He had been answering emails from colleagues, many from the US, Haley included, several from Australia and China, a few from Africa. He pasted in a boiler plate reply—the indefatigable purr, the animal behavior, and now the periodic vocalization inspired by the tiger's chuff. He ended, "And finally, there is—however subjective a phenomenon it may be—an undeniable ebullience in my heart and in the hearts of my staff, and not merely, I think, the response of delighted wonder at this unusual event. I might say it this way—a deep satisfaction has descended on us, or welled up within us, and we are, each in his own way, enough infected with this satisfaction that a neuroscientist could likely find alterations in our brain patterns sufficient to impress the skeptical." Each email called also for a personal touch, a remembrance here, a particular answer there, the task took over an hour. At one point his friend George called, full of questions, and with the news that he was arriving the next afternoon for a long weekend, but without his son, Charlie, who could not get off after all, which Bluey already knew, having received and answered Charlie's email.

"Hellooo." The greeting was sung in an elderly female voice.

Bluey said, "Hello. Am I speaking to Ellen?"

"Yes, this is Ellen."

"My name is Bluey Macintosh. You knew my wife Rosa some years ago."

"Yes, I did. I knew you also."

"That's right. It's not too late, I hope. I got your number from the Los Angeles Baba center, and they didn't know what time you—"

"I'm wide awake. I'm reading. I was back home in Cornwall during the war. Mentally. I'm reading *The Last Lion*, the Churchill biography. Nice to hear your voice."

"Do I remember you knew Churchill?"

"I did. My parents mainly, but he liked me too. He was an immense vitality. A required one."

"You will wonder why I'm calling. Or do you know?"

"Oh, lord. Because I'm psychic?"

"Yes. I don't ask, but I'm fool enough to wonder."

"Oh, I don't mind. But no, I hadn't thought of it. And you see, you must think of it, even if you're psychic."

"I don't know how that works. I've often wondered."

"But you didn't call to learn that."

"No." Bluey briefly recounted the tiger, the mast, the purr, the animal behavior, the furor on the internet. "I don't suppose you have been watching the news?"

"No, but I will now. They have a TV in the meeting area here. Someone will know and fill me in. If I tell them you called, what a fuss. I would have to give a talk. But I'm afraid I can't tell you anything about the masts, anything more than what is in *The Wayfarers* anyway. Have you read that book?"

"No. But I have it."

"I know you have it. Rosa asked me to buy it. I think a week or so before she died. And deliver it in secret."

"I didn't know that."

"Oh, yes. We conspired. I wanted to wrap it, but she said, no, she must wrap it herself. Did she?"

"She did."

"Oh, yes." There was a silence, tactfully observed by both to let Bluey's emotion dissipate. Ellen said, "So you did not call to learn about masts?"

"I called to ask you about Meher Baba. Who I believe you knew."

"I was in his presence. None of us knew him, of course."

"No."

There was another silence.

Ellen said, "You know, Baba once said about proselytizing—someone asked him, I think. That from our mouth to someone's ear can be our business, if we like, but from the ear to the heart is his business. Rosa, of course, understood that. She was perplexed by you though. How could a loving old soul not recognize the avatar? And so the conspiracy of *The Wayfarers.* And now it has come to this, and you have called me. And a mysterious mast too!" She laughed. "You know, if Baba were here, I can just see his face. He would show such amazement. Really? A tiger? A mast? Amazing! Of course, I don't know. But when you arrived to meet him, he would always ask, how was the trip, where are you staying, are you comfortable, just as if he knew nothing at all. Otherwise, of course, we would have all been frozen in self-consciousness. Well, I'm prattling. And I have a feeling that you called with a particular need. You have a question to ask."

"I do, I think. I'm not sure what it is though."

"You have called, I think, to learn what use Meher Baba might be to a seeker."

"Yes. That's what it is."

"Well, it's the central question. The simplest answer of course is that love is a game of catch and takes two. But let me tell a story. I don't recall where I heard it, but here it is. Two philosophers stop in the desert before a date palm. The first wonders if the tree is a mirage and cannot bring himself to eat. The second is also suspicious and munches a date while he considers the problem."

"Ha! So try the dates?"

"Well, from the ear to the heart, you see. But my testimony is that Baba's dates are delicious. He left us so much. Film, a biography, so many books."

"Well, would it be wrong to ask you to—"

"Psychically investigate your tiger? No, dear. I might have done it thirty years ago. I am not so presumptuous now. And say I did. Say I was able to penetrate something and give you information and say it was even conclusively true. For instance if I revealed the tiger was a special type of being or deva and had a special mark on his left paw. Don't look, because he doesn't, as far as I know. Or if I could tell you who that mast was. You can collect as many facts as you want and psychics might pile on their bit too, and it's still outside you, and you have no more love or longing than you did. And that's all we're trying to accomplish, isn't it? Does this strike home?"

"It does."

"I have this image at times of a little man, modern man, and a long line of dump trucks, and they are dumping information on him, on and on, and he is lonely and lost and completely buried and thinks if only he could sort through it all he could find the answer to life. But information is all of a kind—outside. You know this, but I think it's good to hear it out loud from time to time, from a friend."

"Yes, it is."

"But you have asked me the most important question. What is the use of Meher Baba? I take that to heart, and I want to tell you something. I don't know what it might be, but I may be the right person to ask. I wrote books too, you know. I was a philosophy professor. For me, a tedious undertaking. A two thousand year old conversation that ends—well, it ends with the little man, still lonely, still buried. You and I, though, can speak in shorthand. We have not come to the same date palm, perhaps, but we have tasted dates. You know, so many are attracted to Baba, young and old, and they say his name and look at his picture and talk about him, and it's often fairly empty and bit desperate, and they know it, and still they do it, because it's the process. This spirituality business is so shadowy at first, and we are impatient to nail it down. And what use is the avatar in that? His work, you know, was inner, the twiddling of his fingers and all that. Have you heard of that? He twiddled his fingers while working on the inner planes. And that work was the chief work he did, to give the world a push. But now what use? Today, as we are talking, what use is he? And here is your answer, Dr. Macintosh. It has come to me quite brightly. Everything is a species of imagination, and God, through his manifestation as the avatar, and through his photos and films and books and his name itself, reaches across the veils that separate us from him and draws us on a little. And when we awake a little, that name and photo begin to come more alive. Or say it this way—they gather deeper and deeper layers of imagination around them because they are true, which means they issue from the very bottommost being, and our lives become well-organized. Like a great stack of things, and if the bottommost layer is well-placed and foundational, then the topmost layer will not teeter. Well, isn't that a handy thought—consciousness is a stack of layers, and the avatar slides under our stack to give us a nice foundation. I like it. Baba would say, hold onto my daaman, which was the hem of his sadhra. I think that's the use of Meher Baba."

"I understand. I understand that."

"Now that's enough from an old woman. You have lots to do, and I must go watch the TV news. Who knows, I may chat up the old folks and enjoy a bit of fame. I have become part of an adventure."

"Thank you, Ellen."

"I send you love, Bluey."

"Thank you."

"Goodbye. Call again if you like."

"I will. Goodbye."

He ended the call. He sat for a moment, letting the thickness in his chest disperse. He closed his eyes, and Rosa's image wavered into his mind. He felt the familiar spikes of need and grief, but did not respond. He opened his eyes and stood. He opened his hands, as if to catch light, and felt that he did catch light. He felt a rain of gladness. Then in his mouth, with hallucinatory vividness, was the taste of dates. He laughed out loud.

19

Dawson opened his eyes. His mother sat sideways at the end of the bed, staring out of the window in an alert pose. He closed his eyes. He had been in the kitchen, on the settee. They had been playing jumble. They asked for a hint. He had had that insight, that ideas are connected. And something flashed through him like current, and it was a ladder or pyramid, and flashed fast and bright, one thing inside another inside another, like flower petals opening, and there was a bright white center. Then he woke. He opened his eyes again. He was lying on his back, on pillows. He moved his hand to see it move, across his face, back and forth, in a slow arc.

Annie's head snapped toward him, then her body turned, and he saw her worry, her willed calm.

He said, "I'm fine."

"You fainted. Roger caught you."

"I was saying there was a penumbra, wasn't I? Around everything."

"Well, you might have. But you know, I wondered if you have been drinking enough water. You never drink enough. And here I have a glass right here ready for you."

She got up, came close to his side, and sat. She handed him a glass of water from the headboard.

He took it. He drank. "That's so good, Mother. That is just what I wanted."

Annie gave him a deprecating smile. "Hardly."

He handed the water back. He said, "What time is it?"

"Eight about."

"Bhajan will begin to purr pretty soon."

"Well, you know, we've pretty much concluded that tiger—well, I'm thinking, let's take a break. I mean, you fainted. And you were rambling on about particles and rules. Which was interesting. But I do think—I think of Icarus. You know Icarus, who fell to earth when his wings melted? Well—"

"May I get up?"

She stood, and he swung his legs off the bed. He stood straight. He stood nicely tall. He touched his mother's arm, and she was there at the end of his fingers, wanting to embrace him and holding her need regardfully away. He thought, I am here, in my body. And it came to him that there was a central issue in all of life, and now he knew it. Be home. Feel.

Annie saw humor move across his thinking face and waited.

He smiled. He said, "Knock."

She said, "Who's there."

And he lifted his arm, inviting her, and she came into him, laying her cheek on his chest. He said clearly in four distinct syllables, "No i-de-a,"

And it was clear the joke had ended.

•

El made a fast circuit of the zoo and found every animal asleep. Even the birds did not stir as she passed. She crossed to Bhajan. He was sprawled on cedar chips, his head tucked toward his shoulder. His flank rose slowly, hesitated, slowly fell. She checked her phone. It was almost nine. Time for the purr, or nearly, though she wasn't sure.

She had come away from the RV to be alone and to read and had brought her tiny flashlight. The fairgrounds were closed, but she could hear a raised voice from time to time across the stockade, the cleaning crew or somebody in their food booth. She could return to the carousel but would be out of place in the busyness. Besides, the purr would start soon.

She wanted to call her parents, to hear their stable voices. They would be calling soon in any case, once the zoo news got to them. But what to tell them? Well, Dawson fainted, and we're all half drunk on a purr, and there's a mystery about a holy man, and an insane parrot. But I'm safe, on an adventure, don't worry. She would call them but later, maybe wait until they called, which might be inconsiderate if they watched TV, so call them, but later. Right now she wanted to get somewhere and read.

She found a place between the spider monkey and meerkat and sat with her back against the bamboo and flicked on the flashlight. Earlier at the settee with Dawson, she had hardly glanced at the book. She had found the fifty dollars, which had switched Dawson on, and he fainted, and she hadn't read even one complete sentence. She craved to read a sentence and get the flavor of the book, which had come down to her on a mystical track, the mast, *The Wayfarers*, the tiger, the purr—don't forget Fuad's dream—and then Dawson and the coffee shop guy as a fantastical finale. Or a bunch of coincidences, and the book would be dull or facile and Meher Baba a moneygrubber guru. Which she should be open to.

She opened the *Discourses* to anywhere, giving chance a chance, and it was middle book, and there was subhead, *The Journey of the Soul to the Oversoul.* Her heart was thumping, and her mind strobing, and she read the first sentence twice—"*Atma*, or the soul, is in reality identical with *Paramatma*, or the Oversoul."

It was not going in. It was an okay sentence but not going in because her nerves were lit. She felt a jumpy current in her chest and flicks of pulse in her throat. She had a quick frantic impulse—tear the page out and stuff it into her mouth and chew it up, chew chew chew, and get it all down. Then close her eyes and that would do for that book and for all books until she cooled.

She did close her eyes. Atma was Paramatma, an old time thought. Her soul was identical to God's soul. A true-seeming thought, but instead of the smug clamp of mind-rightness, she felt a bright course of unhappiness run through her center, through her mind and heart and bowels, a hot unhappiness, like depression, a whole street of it, flowing down down, and it pulled. She pulled in reverse, and it came to her then, bright and clear, that what she wanted, all she wanted, was the purr, to sit near Bhajan as he purred and float up out of her body.

She closed the book and switched off the flashlight. Perhaps it was a good helpful book. She would read it when she cooled. It would say, you are on the way to God and maybe have pointers, but mainly that. Maybe some nice details to think about. She held the book to her breast and felt its sobriety, but did not want to read it, and would not read it for a while, and the relief of that reprieved her. The depression closed. She would read it sometime if this love ever stopped coming, which was coming again strong, coming up and pushing out in sighs, which ungulped from her chest in heavy heaves. Dawson had fainted. Annie said, I will try to keep him here, away from the tiger. But don't, Annie. Bring him to the tiger. Make him a bed beneath the tiger cage and say, sleep deeply, nothing is wrong.

The tiger began to purr.

•

Roger unwrapped his weights and packed them neatly into one of the underside cargo compartments of the front tandem. He needed a bench for bench presses, which he had forgotten, but maybe could rig something. It wasn't important though. The weights weren't important either.

He got his high beam flashlight from cab door and threaded his way down to the river, picking through bushes and rocks until he found a place just down from the rapids. He butt-scrunched into the cool gravel and wrapped his arms around his knees. He could hear the rapids' flushing, tried to spot water with the high beam, but fog was forming, and the light went white in vapor. He switched the light off. A ten-foot-away frog creaked an approving croak.

He had been thinking. He concluded and admitted that his first letter to Dori, the one that had gotten things going, had been written under the influence of the purr. Which could make it a fake letter, in a sense. And the next letter too, and really his whole mood about Dori. That was one way of thinking. The other way was that it had uncapped the real him, and he flowed out, and he was realer now than he was a week ago. That would make the purr like medicine though. If you stopped taking it, you could cork up and be a clod again. But why would you have to? If it was more of the real him, even if he never heard the purr again, there could still be more of the real him. The purr was a flashlight, and you got to see more of your whole wide simple self, and it was not a side trip like you got with weed. What was attractive about him was really him, if he could keep being it, and why not, so forget this glump of unconfidence and admit the gladness that was forming up inside him like a cupped hand, way down, holding everything up, even his Dori-nervous self and doubtful football future. A cupped hand. He shouldn't forget that.

He said it out loud to the river, "A cupped hand." Then changed *a* to *the* and said that out loud.

"The cupped hand."

It was a sort of poem. Shout in the locker room, *Guys listen up*! I'm going to recite a short poem. Silence and waiting faces. Then—*The cupped hand*. The locker room goes off in guffaws. They had been his brothers in high school, and in college too, though there was talk of money even from the first and some were stars with expectations, and some had no expectations, and it wasn't really brotherhood. Listen up, guys, listen up—*The cupped hand*. The locker room faded. The river glimmered through moonlighted fog. Tomorrow he would wake in his cubby and dress and throw on his feedbag saddle and run. Toward Bosco James. Be a professional with an even steady mind. Take your talent seriously. In training camp, something in him said, maybe not. Since high school, really, but size concealed it. But now stand straight, take aim. But what if you aimed at something you didn't want? What did he want? He stared at the river, obediently flowing, and felt the world obediently waiting for his decision. There was one clear thing he wanted, and it was Dori. He wanted her to come into his life.

An image popped into his mind. It was two sections of puzzle pieces moving toward each other, bumping, nudging, feeling for fit along their fronts. It was like a vision or a symbol, and it popped in automatically. It was him and Dori, who hardly knew each other, but something was pushing them, or drawing them, and they would meet along their puzzle fronts, and their ins and outs would nudge and mold and join. He felt flutters, like pregame jitters, that he had an image, and that it was him and Dori, a sign pointing toward the future. He could play football. He could play it from the inside out, like Bosco James, a realistic man with a wife and family. Maybe he and Dori wouldn't fit, but take the chance. She was taking the chance. It was a worth-it chance.

His phone vibrated in his front pocket, and he thought, it's Dori. He stretched, fished the phone up. He had entered her number in his contacts and saw her name green lit on the screen.

"Hello."

"Hi. Is this Roger?"

"Yes. Dori?"

"Right. So this is what we sound like."

"Right."

"Is it too late? I know you have to get up."

"No, it's not too late. I'm sitting by the river."

"Really? That must be nice. You must have had a busy day. You're on the national news, you know."

"I heard that."

"So what's going on with your animals?"

"Well—we don't know. Not even Bluey. They just start singing. It's something with our tiger, we're pretty sure. He's—extremely unique."

"Well, I can't wait to meet him."

"I can't wait to meet you."

"Really?"

"I was sitting by the river thinking about you."

"What were you thinking?"

He could tell her about the puzzle image, but it would be a lot of words. He said, "That I hope it works out."

"That's nice."

"Where are you?"

"You want to picture me? Picture me in a tree house. You have to climb the tree to get up here. It's dark, but I could do it blindfolded. The ladder's somewhere. My dad made it for us when we were little."

"Who's us? I mean, your brothers and sisters?"

"A brother. He's a year younger. Look, I have to tell you something, so I'm just going to come right out with it. I've been feeling bad all day because I lied to you. I said I had an aunt in Eugene which was totally false. God, I just pushed a weight off me. Well, there it is. Why did I lie? It's because I wanted to come out and meet you, and I thought I needed an excuse, and it couldn't just be I saw you on TV, which is what it was, but I thought, well, that's too impulsive. So I made up an aunt which was very wormy and based on fear. Anyway, I felt crappy right away."

"Well, shoot. I wanted to meet her."

"Ha! Well, don't worry, I have plenty of aunts for you to meet. I got them all over. God, that's a forward thing to say, talking about introducing you to my aunts. I swear."

"I hope I get to meet them." Then Roger followed an urge. He said, "I was sitting here thinking about how people get to know each other, and I thought, it's like—you know when you put one of those thousand piece puzzles together, and say you put two big bunches of pieces together first and then try to join them, and you have to sort of get them to fit all along their fronts. I don't know—"

"No, it's cool. I get that."

"Really? It flashed into my head like that. Because you have to be careful and gentle, you know, because the pieces will flip up, and, you know, you have to carefully move them around."

"Wow. And not lie."

"Well, and when you lie, which is like a piece flipping up let's say, you just gently tap it back down. And everything's fine."

"Well, you're forgiving me. That's great. That's immensely great. Well, I'm coming. I should be out at the fairgrounds around three. I rented a car. You'll be working. That's fine."

"We close the gates at six."

"Well, I've packed my little green suitcase. I have a hotel room. I'm not coming out there for sex, by the way. Maybe I shouldn't mention that."

"Well—I'm glad you did."

"Really? Don't make a joke. If you were going to. Were you?"

"No. It would be on my list eventually. But not at the top."

"That's a good way of putting it." Then—"Did you mean for this trip?"

"No. Just on the list."

"Okay. Wow. We're getting a lot said."

"You know I—well—" He had a wild inspiration, tell her the poem, the cupped hand. He smiled the impulse away.

She said, "What?"

"I'm just glad you said that. That's pretty brave."

"Wow. That's cool. I tell you one thing, my dad would like you. He calls me brave too. Plus he's a big Cowboys fan, so you could talk football. God, now I'm going to introduce you to my dad."

"Well, since I don't get to meet your aunt."

"Ha! Oh, god. I better get off the phone. I'm might bawl or something. Do you mind? It was really great talking to you. I'll see you tomorrow."

"No, that's fine. Bye."

"I look forward to meeting you. Well, we've already met. Bye."

She was gone. She had flashed on, like a light, and then off. But he was still bright. Earlier he had thought, I could cork up and be a clod, but you just followed your feelings. People say, I want to be loved, but they were mixed up. They want to love. As they talked he had felt love flowing out of him and felt her uncertainties and braveries and himself catching them, like catching something delicate, like falling ash, in a cupped hand, the cupped hand.

He got to his feet, brushed his butt, flicked on the flashlight. The purr would probably be going, and he wanted to get a good dose before bed.

•

Bluey heard a knock. He poked his head through the curtain. It was Annie. He clambered out onto the cool grass, barefoot.

She said, "God, is everybody going barefoot? Dawson was too. He and El are out there soaking up the purr. But listen, something happened." And she told him about Dawson's faint and his rambling discourse about particles. "I told him, hey, young man, too much purr, but he's out there. He's gonna sleep there again. So I want you to forbid it. I'm thinking he could have a breakdown or something."

"Really?"

"Well, he fainted, for god's sake. He was out for almost an hour."

"Wasn't that sleeping?"

"Well, you don't start a nap by fainting. He just went white. You can say all you want about we just have to wait and see, but someone has fainted now. If Roger hadn't caught him, he could have been really hurt. By the way, Patti got away. I opened the tandem to chain her up, and she scampered past me. We didn't get a vet either. Do you think we should? You'll have to catch her."

"Let's go see." Bluey touched her back, and they started together toward the stockade gap.

Annie said, "There might be hookworms here. You should wear shoes."

•

Bhajan lay on his stomach, purring, his slightly cocked head resting on one paw. Before him, on the blanket, Dawson and Roger had made a tower, Dawson with his bare right foot on top of Roger's head, his left leg flailing for balance. El watched, her arms instinctively half-raised, concerned and delighted. She had arrived at the tiger cage to find Dawson spreading a blanket. Roger had arrived at the same time, up from the river.

Dawson had embraced him. He said, "You caught me? What a guy. You're a mountain. I could climb you. Should I? That would be great, to climb Mount Roger."

And so in the gusto of the purr, with glad rapt ardor, they had tried their skill. Roger locked his elbows akimbo and stood straddle-legged and Dawson climbed, ending with his feet on Roger's shoulders, holding onto his head, then released the head and gradually straightened, both finding balance and keeping it. Then Dawson placed his single bare foot on the burred hair, and so stood, atop Mount Roger, wavering in perilous victory.

"Can you catch me? I'm gonna drop right in front of you like a cheerleader."

"No!" said Annie, who had appeared with Bluey.

"It's okay," said Roger. "I got him, no doubt. Any time, dude." He was eyeballing up, arms out.

Dawson made an awkward windmill, then kipped, folded in the air, and dropped neatly into Roger's arms. Roger tossed him forward, and he scampered across the grass. He slapped hands with Roger, then went to his mother.

"That was safe. Come sit."

"Oh, god, that was not safe" She went to stand before Bhajan, who lifted his head slightly. She said, "Are you responsible for this?"

Bhajan, purring, rolled onto his back, toward her, his body thumping as he came around. His huge right paw ended against the cage bars. Annie, with two hands, seized it, pulled herself into the bars and held the paw's furred back hard against her breast. Bhajan did not stir. The purr continued. Annie reflexively glanced at Bluey, who stood for a moment, then came forward. Gently, he pulled Annie's hands from the paw. He said, "All right. All right."

Annie walked around the perimeter of the blanket, pulling the wrinkles out. She said, "Come sit, everyone. What will happen next? Roger's head will explode, and we'll all say, gosh. Nothing really is extraordinary if it happens, is it? Bluey says we must accept. That's good advice. Although, never stand on Roger's head again. Roger, do not permit that."

They had seated themselves in a semi-circle, Annie in the center, Roger and Bluey at the ends. Bhajan had rolled upright again. His purr bathed them.

Roger said, "That was amazing though. That's harder than it looks."

Annie said, "Well, maybe not. It looked hard." She scrubbed the air. "But wait. I have a philosophical thought which I want to express, and it's about how we should live, but I can't quite get it. This damn purr makes it hard to think." She pressed her hands into her face, slid them, ending palms together under her chin, prayer-like and open-mouthed. She said, "Here's the question—what should we do? No, what *can* we do? I mean, how should humanity live? I've always thought about that. What's the best possible world? That's what liberals and conservative fight about. Everybody's selfish, so conservative say, just accept that. And liberals say, no, make people better. But really, something awful has closed around each one of us and keeps us separate. We don't trust, and if you don't trust me, I don't trust you. If someone suddenly could trust—but it's not trust, it's love. Trust is just easier to believe in. It's like love at arm's length. We don't love, which is an old boring fact, but it's the central thing anyway. We should all be banging on our cages just like our beautiful singing animals, saying, let me out. That's all anyone should say. I want to get out and see my neighbor and say, fine day. And be among friends. That's my amazing idea for curing the world's problems. We must build a civilization that makes us feel connected. And we will see that love is better than hate. The end."

She rose quickly and went to the tiger cage. "I'm not going to do anything, Bluey, don't worry. Though I can hardly keep my hands off him. Sweet Bhajan, don't roll over again, for Bluey's sake. I'm having a really odd sensation. I'm depressed and happy at the same time. You, my dear tiger, are putting us through our paces, aren't you? Does anyone else feel that? The discourse has ended. Now, dear Bhajan, you may subtract my head, as I think you have been trying to do."

Dawson said, "You know—"

They looked at him. Annie said, "What?"

"I had an idea. I have to think about it."

Bluey rose. He said, "I'm going to make the rounds. Dawson, how about coming with me. I have to give you my anti-fainting speech."

Annie said, "Yes, you must have it, Dawson."

Dawson rose, and he and Bluey started around the perimeter. The animals were rapt and ignored them. Goose emerged from beside the sun bear cage, circled them, then resettled.

Bluey said, "So what happened?"

"I'm not sure I can tell you. We we're playing jumble, where you—"

"The scrambled word game."

"Right. And I gave them a hint. And then I thought, why can we hint? You know, ideas are invisible, which is important to realize, because that's most of what we are, and we can't see them. Anyway, if you can hint from one idea to another, then ideas are connected, and if I say roots and leaves and bark you think of a tree because those ideas surround tree, and if they went away then tree would go away too because tree is like a space that the other ideas make when they form around it.

Don't worry, I'm not going to faint. But then, in the RV, I just spun up automatically into some sort of lightball. I felt myself going through levels or something. And then I woke up. I'm sure it was Bhajan and his freaky hyoid bone or whatever. But I consider it good and not bad. It was not a nightmare. It was a vision. I have no idea what of, but it started with the jumble. So if anything, no more jumble. But I still do want to sleep under the tiger cage. I'm fine."

"Well, at least don't climb Roger again."

"No, I won't. So can I sleep under Bhajan?"

"You can. Did you dream?"

"No. Not last night anyway. We could all sleep there. There's plenty of room. I have this idea. Can we sit?" They had come halfway around the carnivores to Alfie, the wild dog. Bluey squatted. Dawson sat with his legs folded. Dawson said, "You know, you told me, when we started, the reason for preserving the animals, and it was so people would not lose their connection to the deeper layers of life. So you're making a model for the world, the new animal thing, which is great, which I get. But basically you love animals."

Bluey smiled. He tapped a forefinger against Dawson's knee. He said, "You have found me out."

"So here's my idea, based on what Mother said, which is that we should find a way to be connected. You know, not just come out of our houses and go back in, or go to a movie or a restaurant. So you have a big dome, and it's about a hundred yards across, and really high, a geodesic dome, and there are no walls in it. Which is super important, so there's a hum of people under the same sky. Maybe paint it blue. Or there are walls, but just like seven foot movable walls that you can rearrange. And people meet there. You know what? Everything is already connected, but we don't see it. That's how I whited out. We are all completely connected, and it's just like ideas, not one of us could disappear without screwing everything up. It would make a hole which would destroy the entire fabric of the universe. That's a very important idea. So there could be a gourmet club with a kitchen, and they make snacks for the chess club or the book club or movie club, and there's outdoor clubs and just every kind of interest group can meet there. And connect there. And a debate club or free speech forum and as soon as you get angry you have to shut up. And that's what you do instead of go to movies, you go out and mingle with people. You can still see movies, but then you get to have a good discussion afterward. Or you play cards or do crafts or tutor kids or learn to program. And there's lots of communication between the groups, and you can wander around, join any group you want, and the thing is, it's a dome, and covers everybody, and there is a hum of humanity which you don't try to silence but encourage, and everybody is under there playing together, even if they're not in the same group. Maybe they make little businesses and that funds the dome. I mean, wouldn't people want to go to the dome instead of just sit in a movie and go home?"

"They would."

"Really? You think so?"

"I do."

"So the trouble could be, say you got some hacker kid who was into his video games or something, which the world has a lot of, or say it's the top athlete guy who feels superior to everyone. They would not fit in, so maybe you have classes—"

"How to be a dome person."

"Right. And the important thing would be the person that leads the class would have to be a soaked-in dome person. An actual honest loving person and model that. Right away, you see how it could all fall to shit. If you couldn't find somebody like that. And also you could have factions and all that. So you have dome meetings once a week and air things out. You know what, it would all depend of the mood of the world. You couldn't have domes in a world of mad power-mongering. Domes are for utopias."

"Or maybe for the transition to utopia, to model domeness."

"Which is what you're doing, isn't it?"

"It is."

"Which is what Mother was saying really. We need a place to practice. And domes would be that. So how would I start?"

"Really?"

"Yeah."

"You write it up and present it to people who can fund it. You understand as you begin that your chief work is persuasion, and that you must be circumspect so that objections are anticipated and overcome, and that if you can get through the initial resistance and inspire, you might succeed."

"Did you do that?"

"I had money. But I will have to do it soon."

"Bhajan is going to help."

"He will."

"You have a one-step-at-a-time attitude, don't you?"

"I probably do."

"It's a good attitude. I need that. You think a dome could work?"

"Well, I think if there was a dome, many people would want to go."

"So one step at a time. I'll write something up. Will you—"

"Of course, I'll read it."

"You know, if it is the tiger—which it is, of course—it might end, which I worry about actually."

"That you'll spring back to the old Dawson."

"Right."

"We do remember and forget, no doubt. But spirituality reveals, it doesn't create. What is revealed can be forgotten, but not if we want to remember it. Need love, and you'll be safe."

"That is super deeply true. Very domey. Bluey. You are my number one recruit."

"I'm honored."

•

There was a service station across the road from the country fair, but the clerk had not heard of any exotic animal caravan. When he returned to his SUV, there was an elderly farmer-type guy filling his pickup, and he pointed it out across the parking fields beside a bundle of buildings. He said, "See the brown fence. That's bamboo. That's them. They got the parrot that rides the tiger."

JJ said he had heard that. He pulled his SUV past the lone diesel pump and parked behind the station. He had been falling asleep at the wheel for the last hour and thought maybe he could catch a fast nap before reconnoitering. Or he could sit awake until the darkness thickened. He slept.

He woke at ten. He hadn't eaten since morning but clamped hunger. He had driven around the fairgrounds earlier and gotten a picture of the layout and security, guys at the gates mainly. The lot was empty, so now probably only a few rovers, maybe motor rovers too. He got out, rested his thirty power binoculars against the SUV roof and scanned. Five hundred yards away they had a pole light inside the bamboo. He could make out the gleam of an RV and a couple of big trucks outside the fence. That would be their vehicles. He could wait until morning, be part of the crowd. But he wanted to go now. He wanted to get close and be just outside sight but close, and unseen, and join them that way, what he had done in the war a few times, in Ramadi, and then in Fallujah, at night, letting the watch know he was going beyond the perimeter, moving to find a spot, out-patienting the bad guy sentries, moving deeper. One night in Fallujah, he had gotten through their perimeter, and settled for an hour across from a house with two pickups. A couple of hours from dawn he had heard them wake, saw their faces through his six power as they passed a match. Young and whiskered. His squad had found the beheading room the day before, where they made the videos. Maybe these guys. He could shoot the brains out of one of them, watch the other two freak. But probably not these guys. Beheaders would be older, with a crust. Or he could throw a grenade and try to get them all, which had the advantage of not giving up his position. He saw his retreat route bright in his mind, down the alley, through two houses, across a street, suppress the sentry with a burst, shout *JJ coming through,* home free. He could hear their soft voices, see their cigarette tips dance in the dark. He would not kill them. The tanks would kill them tomorrow probably. Probably they had been friends before the Americans came and had played soccer in the playground where the tanks and strykers parked. If you were inside the enemy lines and stopped being scared and found a place to think, you couldn't be a good solder. The next day JJ killed the kid, and that was it for him anyway.

The plan was, head down the fence line, a guy strolling, get to those buildings where the fairground fence met the bamboo. He would get close and see. Make a peek. He had seen the zoo layout on TV, a circle of cages inside the bamboo with a tiger in the middle. He had been in the computer store when she appeared on fifty televisions, an amazing surprise, and the natural thing was to jump in the SUV and drive. On the drive he had done over eighty and planned. Walk in, say, hey, saw you guys on TV. I make videos. Let's do a deal. El, you can be the star. Remember me? Creeping was not the plan. That came because it was night and silent, and he could do it and was drawn to do it.

Across the street from the buildings there was a stand of woods, and as he turned along the fairgrounds fence he felt that as his retreat in case. If a rover spotted him, better to vanish than have to bullshit, particularly since he had the five shot in his front pocket. He felt tension grow like battle joy. He concentrated, tried to snuff it. Tension triggered flashbacks. And then one came anyway, frying pan daddy, of course, flashing angry in his mind like a strobe, with his bloody chest and mangled son and mean mute account-for-me expression. Frying pan daddy is upset. You must account.

JJ stopped, knelt, closed his eyes, breathed. Frying pan daddy paled away. When he opened his eyes, he was looking at a dog.

The dog was mostly shadows, but he could see its big flat head and round-muscled shoulders. It was standing, watching him from five feet away. It was saying, I could have bitten off your face, but that's not the kind of dog I am.

JJ made a go-away gesture, said softly, "Shhhh—"

The dog dropped his head, walked fast past JJ's boots, stopped five feet behind him, turned, still standing.

JJ said, "Shhh. Shhh."

The dog watched without moving. As JJ continued toward the bamboo, the dog followed, stiff-legged, like a horse. It was odd but good, the dog close and powerful but not nervy or barky, simply following. Odd and good.

He reached the junction of the zoo stockade with the fairground fence, saw they had plastic tied the bamboo into a fairground gate to make the zoo entrance. He was trespassing already, lurking the parking lot, but that was only a low misdemeanor. They would warn, not prosecute, and anyway he could run. Entering the fairgrounds would be different. He could cut the ties with his Gerber knife and slip through and be inside unseen. That would be a high misdemeanor, maybe a low felony, since he was armed. There would be a fence between him and the woods too, so no longer a straight sprint, instead a stop and noisy clamber, then the run. The dog was slightly to his side now, standing in a gleam. He could see its flat white-streaked gray forehead and had the impression the fur was finger-painted, like war paint. The dog was waiting. The dog said, *Cut those ties. I'm with you.* He slipped the Gerber from the band under his shirt, inserted the blade. He cut one tie. The phrase, *cut ties,* lit through his mind and expressed courage and truth and the courage for truth. The battle knife felt strong in his hand like a sword. He cut another tie. He pressed into the stockade, eased it away. A gap formed. He slipped a leg through, then his trunk, then the other leg. He was in the fairgrounds. The dog watched.

JJ popped the bottom tie, toed the bamboo away from the pole. The dog wedged his head into the opening, pushed, stutter-stepped briefly, and was through. The dog trotted five feet, turned, nose-pointed again toward JJ. JJ had the impulse to touch it, see if it was a robot. He squatted. He waved his Gerber slowly in front of the dog's face. The dog ignored the blade. JJ was pressed against the fence, in shadow, but the dog had found the gleam again and stood exposed. JJ gestured with the knife, move in, and the dog sidled stiffly toward the shadowed bamboo. That was unreal, that the dog obeyed. It was true and not true. The dog waited. The dog expected.

JJ sheathed the Gerber under his T-shirt. He knelt and moved forward on his hands and knees toward the bamboo gate. He flutter-thought that this was odd and dangerous, creeping on strangers in the night, armed, but that awareness was indifferent and useless, a shrug in a lynch mob, and he continued, looking down and back, and there was the dog a foot from his heels, faithfully following.

He reached the bamboo archway and recognized the banner sign he had seen on the news, which he couldn't read since it was directly above him but which would say the *Exotic Animal Caravan.* And what the fuck, there were two big black crows perched up there, and one of them appeared to be wagging his head and giving him the eye. They were his sentries. They said, we watch, you creep. The bamboo halves of the gate were connected by a chain, and he could move forward and peek the gap, but he was at the edge of a shadow bank, and ahead the bamboo was softly lit by a security light. He dropped to his belly. He felt cool grass along his belly and thighs. He clamped his arms to his sides, pressed his face into the grass, breathed in the scent of grass and soil. Humiliation flickered but did not penetrate. He was a belly down intruder. Be that then. He lifted his face and undulated and that way moved, an inch, three inches, five. He left the shadows and moved into the light, feeling the light on his head and shoulders like eyes. Now he was at the gap and looked for the first time into the zoo and became aware for the first time of a deep buzzing sound, like a generator or insect or animal.

He felt a charge enter his loins. He felt his penis thicken. He heard the murmur of voices. With his forehead, he pushed the gate slightly more open and saw two shapes beside a cage fifty feet away, one sitting with folded legs, speaking rapidly, gesturing, the other squatting. It was Bluey squatting, his back to the gate, his head tilted as he listened. The fast talker stopped. Both heads turned, looked up. A slender dark-haired woman approached, murmured. They listened. She bent, kissed the top of the talker's head, playfully pushed his head, put her face into Bluey's hands, received his kiss. She turned and came directly toward JJ. She made a walking pirouette, spoke again to the two figures, and came on. As she turned, JJ lowered his face into the grass to hide his skin. He slowly pushed back. If she came to the gate and looked down he was caught. Panic flushed.

The woman's voice sounded commandingly, now ten feet away—"Patti! Patti!"

Behind him, a swish of grass, and the flank of the dog was at his temple. The dog nosed into the gap. The chain tinked. The dog pushed through.

"There you are. All right. Come. Come-come."

Now it was quiet. He undulated again and looked through the gap. Bluey and the talker had vanished.

On the way back to his SUV, he tried to calm, and it was like coming back from the enemy line, the deep rinsing of relief, but also, far back, and spreading, the flatness. He had crept their perimeter. That was done. Now he would eat and find a hotel and turn the TV on, and there was a mad tight ache because El was behind him, and the gap was growing. He had not seen her. Maybe she had been in the RV, which he could creep. As that thought hit he spun, walked backward two steps, spun again, continued toward the SUV. That would be mad foolish and risky, and pointless also. But he had just done it. It had seemed natural and ordinary with the robot dog beside him, the robot dog saying cut those ties and creep, then stepping up to save him at the last minute. It was not ordinary though. Ordinary people were gliders and couldn't do what they wanted or know what they wanted. He wanted clearly. He wanted El, not to fuck her, but to El bathe, which he had thought of on the drive down as his central desire, and now couldn't do tonight. Unless he creeped the RV, and again he spun in step, continued toward his SUV. You had to park want and wait, and not be insane and skip steps, like kidnap her and take her to a cabin in Canada, which would be insane, and also get him caught and prison, which for sure don't do, no matter what thoughts you get. The steps would be—appear professionally at the zoo, with gear and solid professional long-term relaxed interest in making a video for the welfare of the zoo. Sell the idea and exhibit dignity. You have a fine zoo. I'd love to help you. How about El is my star, with her passion for animals and good looks? But only eventually say that. At first say, Bluey, you are the star, with your neat gray beard and confidence and long term ways. But you don't say it. You observe and *mean* it out to him, long term to long term.

His foodless belly rumbled. He might not eat though. The pleasure of food would distract. He had lived through all his life to be here, outside this door, her door. He had come from the black basement, through his furious youth, through the war's slaughter. Now he must inhale deeply. He must not skip steps. He must be prepared. He was not prepared.

20

On the other side of the stockade, Dawson heard the chain thrash and his mother make inquisitive doggy comments and heard Bluey murmuring to the animals as he continued his rounds. Dawson had stopped twenty feet from the tiger, thinking to present his dome idea to El and Roger, get the youth view, then saw Roger rolled like a burrito in one end of the blanket, squirming for comfort, and El on her cell, talking into a hand cave. He stopped in shadow. He thought, I'm off stage, preparing to enter. He thought, I have an attitude for everyone, a character to be. With El, lovelorn and fatalistic, but newly friendly! With Roger the precocious younger brother. He was in the play. He had been written in. That was the dome idea, in a way. A place for everyone to be in the play and have attitudes. Then say he was in a venture capitalist's office, in a suit and tie—*Sir, I want to make a place where humanity can gather and have attitudes.* He sobered off a smile. You had to be serious to pull down something from the heights and push it into the street, where people went fretful and broke, where they would turn a little, if they caught the scent, if you could create a scent, and they come a little into the dome and look it over, and someone says, *Do you like paper airplanes? Come over here*, and there would be the head paper airplane guy in the state, and he helps you make a fantastic airplane that soars. And next time you bring your wife, who likes to make beer or play rook, and the kids come and learn to play the guitar. And why it wouldn't work would be no love and no hope because there were no people with love and hope. Unless they caught the scent. Unless they said, we forgot how good it is to live and play our parts. And they say to their friends, we hope someday you'll join us, and the world can live as one. It was ridiculous and true, and if Lennon only saw the ridiculous side there wouldn't be that song which everyone liked. So be serious and have heart and not be deep down doubtful. Deep down be sober.

The tiger was standing in his cage, head up, facing him, purring like a geyser, like a light in the dark, like the moon on a lake, and he had the impression as he approached that the tiger's purr laid a silver moon path before him.

He kicked Roger's butt through the blankets.

Roger made a mild muffled murmur, "Hey."

El, still on the phone, lifted her free hand and twiddled fingers at him. He sat between them. The tiger had come around to face him, and now thumped onto his belly, head up for a moment, then lowered his head to his paws. His large eyes closed and opened, a slow blink.

El ended her call, extended her arms behind her, leaned back, her legs forward, straight out, ankles crossed. She said, "That was my folks. They saw me on the news."

Dawson said, "What did you tell them?" He had a nice impression. The purr had gone from a moonbeam to a moon fluid, and had encapsulated him and El's legs and the side of her face with its soft half smile and her thoughts of her parents whom she loved and had said goodbye to out of regard for his entry on the stage. He had a strong desire to pull her toward him and embrace her, but above the waist, to leave his male parts behind and move across the space and take her gently over and hold her for a moment, then release her. Release her, but be with her, be the soft mild curious kindness of her. You could do that without embracing her. You could do that from here, where you were, where you sat.

El shook her head with light deprecation. She smiled. She said, "I told them—" and went on about what she had told them, the purr, the abnormal vocalizations, the crowds.

He felt himself embracing her from within, felt her feel it as she noticed it through her thought stream, felt her slacken and glide in the fun of friendliness, and grow a little animated, and a little jokey, a girl with girls, and he thought, why marry anyone, you can marry them all.

Roger said from inside his burrito, "I have to call my folks too."

"Yes, you do," said Dawson.

Roger rolled until he reached Dawson's side, then bumped him, rolled away. He said, "They left messages on my phone. If I call them I will have to hear their voices. If I hear their voices, I will experience pain."

Dawson leaned, laid his forearms across Roger's thick shoulder, gave him a light pound. He said, "Tell us more."

Roger said, "El, should I tell more?"

El said, "Yes."

Roger said, "Do you experience pain when you talk to your parents?"

"Well, maybe. Well, no, not really."

Roger said, "I do. Always painful."

El said, "Oh, shoot. Why?"

"This blanket is helping me think. I think that's what I'll do from now on when I need a good long think. I'll roll up in a blanket. And become helpless. If you had a grudge against me, you could get me now."

Dawson rose, stood on Roger's butt, lightly bounced. "I do have a grudge, you fucker."

El said, "So why do you feel pain."

Dawson continued to bounce on Roger's butt. El smiled, shook her head. Dawson stepped onto the grass, sat.

Roger said, "I feel pain when I talk to anyone, actually. When I think about it. Unless I have some role. Like in a grocery store. Then me and the cashier get along fine. But as soon as you get outside, like if you were just walking along? Well, you still have your citizen role, but you don't say to some guy at a bus stop, hello, citizen. Right now my role is, I'm wrapped in a blanket, telling the truth of my pain. Because of this purr. Here's my pain—I wanted my parents to love me, and I could tell they didn't. Which hurt my feelings. In an underneath way. Not like getting hit. Like breathing in something bad. They say they love you, but they hardly notice you, and that's what you realize. If I ever have a child the first thing I'll do every morning is to go to the child and notice him. Because if you don't it will hurt his feelings, in a slow way."

Roger seemed to have stopped. El said, "We're listening."

Dawson said, "Definitely."

Roger said, "Then you say, well, no one noticed my parents either. Which is true. Children live in the land of giants. I'm going to unroll from this blanket eventually and don't look at me for a while. The magic blanket is speaking. I stayed at my father's house on the way down from Oregon. We're not really friends, and right now I am feeling sorry for him because he missed being his own child's friend, which I'm sure is hard for him to think about when he's quiet. My mother is—like if there was some loose paint, my mother would cross the room to chip at it. I'm part of the loose paint. But this is about my poor father, who right now is running for state representative. He's found this district of hard-ass farmers, and their basic philosophy is, don't give my stuff to lazy people. So I said, dad, what is it, all the lazy people move to ghettos where they can be lazy? We don't talk that much, about anything really, but we got onto politics that night because I got busted and hurt his political career. But just a minute ago I thought of what I should have said. I should have said, Dad, say there's an eighteen year old kid. A black kid, and he's got low pants and tattoos, and he's hanging in the hood, dealing dope. So say this kid is on the corner, and you drive by and naturally you feel hostile hatred. Look at him, low pants fucker. But think of him when he was seventeen. Pants not quite so low maybe, maybe he's strolling with his homeys. Then he's sixteen, then fourteen, then he's ten, and he's playing basketball somewhere. He's drinking a coke. Maybe you don't hate him so much, maybe you just say, man, that kid is on a bad road. And drive on. Then he's eight, then he's six, then he's three. When he's finally three, what a cute little kid. He's toddling along. You don't hate him at all. You say, that's a cute sweet little kid. Then he starts growing. He's four, then he's five. Pretty soon, he's all the way back to eighteen, and you hate him. So when did that start? I mean if you had to watch him all the time, every second, and you loved him when he was three, what second do you start loving him less, even a tiny bit less? How does that happen? It happens because you look away. You stop noticing him, and just as soon as you stop noticing him, hate jumps into you, and when you turn back to notice him again, it's too late. You took your eye off him, and now you hate him a little. And the more you take your eye off him the more you hate him. You can't hate what you notice. That's why God can't hate anyone, because he never looks away. You could say this is about me and my dad, and it is, but really it's way too sad to be just about Roger and his poor dad. Who I will call tonight. I'll call my mother too, the paint-chipping loner. Every one of us was three once. I'm going to unroll now and be Roger again, the big giant. But don't look at me for a while."

El rose now and lay on top of him, stretching full out across the blanket. She said, "No no, don't unroll yet. Not yet. Pretty soon you can." Tears had streaked her face. "Oh, Roger, we must never look away. That's the secret. You have found it out. My goodness. Don't you think?" This last was spoken to Dawson, who was breathing heavily, mouth open. El saw his need and expectation and rolled off Roger. She patted Roger's back invitingly. She said, "Come lay down here."

Dawson did, stretching himself full out across Roger's body. When he and El locked gazes, they both laughed out loud.

After a moment, Roger said, "Okay. I'm unrolling. I'm a little nervous, so don't exactly look at me for about an hour. Okay?"

Both said okay.

•

El had told him of a path beside the river and a gravel bar, so Bluey laced on his high top boots, pocketed a flashlight in case the moon didn't penetrate the trees, and set out across the grassy field. Goose loped ahead, pausing to wuff madly through the grass, loping ahead again. The moon was up and bright, silvering the grass, and he recalled the line from Rumi, *The moon rises, dropping her clothes along the street.* The sound of the purr vanished in the swish of his boots, and now the rush of the river, another kind of purr, rose ahead. He passed the van, found the path, and started into the trees, from time to time flicking his flashlight into the gloom. He found the gravel bar and waved his arm in an arc, so that Goose, after a moment's hesitation, got the idea—no stick, just a romp—and splashed across the gravel into the water.

Bluey leaned against a tree, shaggy with debris combed from floods, and watched the river's rush and glitter. The low round moon shone, the stars glimmered, his dog somewhere frolicked. The assurance of nature. He had trained himself to a kind of spiritual stoicism, a life without guessing, content to need and wait. But now, not for the first time but more keenly, he felt the weakness in that attitude, the explorer who discovers the world-explaining silence, then abides, content with patience, aloof from expectation. Complacency hid there, and pride. Now a dream-foreshadowed tiger and his bewitching purr, the crew's intoxication, a home-striking talk with Ellen Auster, Dawson's mad intelligence and idea for community. That was how the world did change, by an up-welling which flowed from heart to heart. Something was approaching and should be greeted, and stoicism was a poor host.

Calculations passed through his mind. The plan was for the ecopark to become profitable in seven years. With the tiger, that might be reduced to five. Or less. If so, he could fund the dome. A fantastic idea. But it surged. He could build it at the edge of Memphis on the highway to the park, create an economy of scale. A mad idea. But let it connect, if it could. Let it build, if it could.

He stood and whistled for Goose, listened, whistled again, then heard a racket of splashing from his left as Goose raced up.

"Sit. Sit, old Goose." Goose sat, lifted his muzzle, and Bluey straddled him, stroked the dog's muzzle and eyes, slow, then slower, releasing his heart-rain.

He made a tweeting whistle, freeing Goose, and started for the path. Goose raced ahead and was soon lost in the gloom of trees. He walked without using the flashlight, trusting the moon and memory through the pools of darkness. He emerged from the forest, passed the van, started for the illumined circle of cages two hundred yards away. He stopped. He closed his eyes. Yes, he felt some inner shifting. On the surface was enthusiasm, the exploration of a new project, the comradeship of his bright-minded nephew, but something beneath supported and called, some assurance. He turned. He looked past the van into the trees. The first line of a poem came, *A forest starts behind your house.*

•

After the three of them decided to sleep under the tiger, Dawson returned to his van for his blanket and laptop so he could continue browsing the *Discourses*, which he had found on the site the fifty dollar guy had mentioned. They settled, Roger in the center, bookless, lying eyes-closed on his back, El in a blanket cave with a flashlight and her two books.

Dawson opened his computer, surfed to the book site, and saw that *The Wayfarers* was also included. He whispered across Roger's bulk, "El, *The Wayfarers* is on this site too. And a lot of other books."

She whispered back, "Search it for the word tiger. After this, Roger, we promise to be quiet."

Roger said, "Nice."

"You're nice, Roger." She shoulder-bumped him through the blankets. She added, "Annie and I are going to give Dori a thorough going over tomorrow, by the way. In case she's after your money."

Roger was silent.

El said, "We'll be nice, don't worry." Another moment's silence. "Are you worried?"

She heard Roger draw a long breath, let it out. He said, "Yes. Except I can't get it going very well with this purr. Tomorrow though, I'll probably be shrunk up like a raisin."

"Is that how you get when you worry?"

"I do, as I recall."

"Well, I'm sure she's a very nice person."

Roger said, "She seems to be."

El said, "Is that what you're worried about?"

"No. It's because I want something and may not get it."

"Roger, you sound so wise. So there's hope for everyone. Was that mean? I meant it to be funny."

"It was really funny."

She bumped him.

Dawson said, "Look on page 218. There's a passage about a guy called Munshi who walked around with two tigers. And also on page 73. There's a whole section about a guy they called the tiger mast."

•

Annie woke. Had there been a sound? She twisted to glance the clock on the headboard shelf. Three in the morning. As she left the bathroom, she saw that El's bed was empty again, the blanket gone and this time the pillow too. They would be sleeping under the tiger. Annie was not about to sleep on the grass unless they carried her mattress out there. She opened the RV door and listened. She heard the purr, clear and emphatic in the silence. She went into her bedroom and put on her robe. She was drawn to make a tour, circumambulate the tiger, wash in the purr, patrol the sleeping young ones, patrol her Dawson. When she had left them last night, he had embraced her, kissed her forehead. Her eyes had sprung with tears, which she did not hide, but also ignored. Let love be at least a little unsurprising.

She passed through the rear gap, passed the lion cage, and entered the grounds. Tomorrow these grounds would again teem with browsers. And George, the renowned surgeon, would come to give her regard and see about her for himself, poor man. She would hold his shoulders and tenderly say, George, I mean to love everyone, not anyone. He would say, well, start here.

Demijohn rose from the cedar chips and watched her, pressed his muzzle into the mesh. She could see the shadowed tiger, haunch-sitting, and under the cage the shapes of blankets. She wanted to cross to the cage and circle it, and the three blanketed figures, and bind them in a spell of protection, but first she must deal with that lion nose, which projected through the wire an inch. She put her hands on either side, brought them slowly together, touched the moist nose with her fingertips, bent closer, slowly, then closer still and kissed the nose, gently and fully. She felt a flick of warm tongue beneath her chin. She straightened, wiped her chin and mouth on her robe. Demijohn withdrew his muzzle, settled again on the cedar, watched her mildly. She wanted to summon him to the wire again, to press her lips again into his muzzle. She touched her heart, kissed her hand, blew the kiss. Demijohn received the kiss impassively, held her in his mild gaze.

The tiger watched her approach. The tops of two heads were visible under the blankets and one big-jawed face, Roger's, open-mouthed and vanished in sleep. El had told her as she gathered her blankets from the RV of Roger's thought experiment about the little boy and love and hate and his hard-minded father, and also of the online girl that would arrive tomorrow, which Annie a little deplored, since this girl might be an odd person to come so many miles on a whim, but also maybe a brave person with an attractive heart. El and she would inspect her and decide. They would invite her to tiger tea. Roger had said she had a hotel booked, so at least it was not just a long-distance hookup.

She walked carefully, lifting and placing her slippers so that the sounds of her passage were submerged in the purr. In the glare of the halogen, eyes glistened from the circle of cages. She was watched but welcome, like crossing a room in her home. The tiger stood as she approached, and as she rounded the end of the cage came forward and pressed his nose into the bars as Demijohn had done, but with the snout protruding a full four inches since the bars on his Indian-built cage were wider. She came forward, resisting the impulse to glance about for Bluey, and without hesitation grasped the snout on both sides and kissed the moist nose. She reached through the bars then and stoked under the chin, then reached farther and stroked the vibrating larynx, then realized with a shock that both her arms were in fantastical danger—she could lose her arms!—and continued to stroke. The tiger lay belly down and arched his neck and again her hands found the vibrating throat and stroked. Then she laid her hands on top of the massive head and thumb-stroked the eyes as she had seen Bluey do with dogs. The tiger accepted these attentions with benignity. She felt an ache throb, deep down, like a song needing release, like a dance undanced, and she would sing, and would dance, and would love, and that was the ache, simply put, to love, to get the world inside with welcome, and that was finally how to live, to be a heart-hawk above the muddy world and swoop down and love, then up and swoop again and love, then swoop again and love. But not be foolish and put bare hands and arms inside the cage of a destroying tiger! Wisps of thought—her hands ripped away. But if the tiger only looked like a tiger but was something else, and you recognized that, then be bold with fear. She moved her hands to the tiger's mouth, which opened. She grasped the canines. Her palms filled with the warm spikes of ivory, and she thought, to see beneath the tiger face is the truth. Something is under the world.

She laid her palms along the snout, stroked backwards, gently over the eyes, the forehead, gently over the ears. She was bright awake now, and thought of dancing, but touching the tiger was her dance. She was drained. She removed her hands. The tiger rose, turned away. She thought, there are no goodbyes. It's like a fluid, and we are in the fluid, in the belly of God—El said that—and we're dissolving and love is the fluid.

She had come to circumambulate the tiger and the sleeping young ones and now began that. As she rounded the end of the tiger cage, she saw a dark bullet emerge from the folds of blankets and trundle stiff-legged across the grass and through the stockade gap. It was Patti who she had chained and who was now loose and free, and Annie, the dare-devil who had seized a tiger's canines, felt the rough clutch of fear. She followed. Patti had vanished. She went to the rear of the RV and found the chain straightened on the grass and ending in a circle of collar. She went into the RV, found her flashlight, then went back outside. She entered the fairgrounds and spend ten minutes slowly circling the poultry building, probing shadows with the light beam, softly calling, "Patti! Patti!" At the end of the poultry building, where it flanked the midway, a security guard, a young black woman, approached. She was unconcerned but curious to find a robed woman wandering the midway. Annie explained. She said, "If you see her, could you please come rap on my door? I'm in the RV just on the other side of the zoo."

The young woman said she would. Annie returned to the RV, on the way turning off the halogen above the tiger cage—let the young ones sleep in darkness. After a duration of restlessness, she fell into a light sleep. No rap came.

•

JJ had holed up in a Holiday Inn off the interstate. He would make the three mile jump back to the fairgrounds in the morning, get there early, try to get Bluey alone and make his presentation, which had been forming up in his mind. The presentation was—The Birth of an Ecopark, a documentary that starts with the animals in the closing-down college and follows them all the way to Tennessee and their new digs, how it happens, blow by blow, hopes and fears, load the animals, drive them along, feed them, hopes and fears, etc. Which meant confessing to the hat cam, which was out there anyway, since three days ago he had posted his footage of Carlos, called *Mad Latino*, and it already had over nine million hits, internet sensation, so Carlos would be getting his check, which JJ would round up to ten grand, *Collegio por los chicos, dude*. But why were you videoing us with the secret hat cam? asks Bluey. Well, Bluey, here's the deal on that. I heard about the ecopark and wanted to get started on the project but wanted everything super candid. No trace of self-consciousness, Bluey, because if you set that tone early, you can mesmerize the audience, and later on in the film if you get some self-consciousness, which I deeply deplore, it's less obtrusive. Basic documentary one oh one. Also, it's a no slouch hat cam. 1080 HD, perfect audio, and all my equipment is top-notch. Yes, I made that video of Carlos, and I did provoke him, and I apologize, but I got carried away by humor, but that's between me and Carlos, who didn't hit it off, and he will get ten grand, by the way. It was not odd, but just a particular trait of mine to find certain things hilarious. And he will get ten grand.

He had been pacing and rehearsing his delivery in the bathroom. Now he stopped in front of the mirror and gestured clearly to himself with an extended index finger—don't dwell on Carlos. Or mention it even for now. Stay with the documentary riff. Then when the Carlos video comes up, somebody sees it, reports it to Bluey, already be into the documentary and chuckle, say, yeah, that was a little thing I did, Bluey, which might indicate a certain type of cold heartless ruthless streak in me, but it's no wonder I have that with all the torment and murder in my life. Now let's get back to work on this documentary. He sneered amusement in the mirror. What a cut-up.

He had laid his equipment out on the second bed, had battery chargers plugged into every socket. In the bed's center was his Hi-Tense drone, a four blade top-of-the-line $25,000 military beauty that he bought at the international drone convention in Las Vegas. Beside it was the foam board drone he built himself in the basement from plans and parts ordered on the internet. Putting it together, he had begun to understand design, the balance of quality and cost and function, and saw a direction there for himself, a new business, build better drones, create drone kits, have a booth in the drone show, get reviews, get a buzz. Ideas flooded. He watched videos, read books on aerodynamics and 3-D printing. He contacted flight board design companies, talked to their engineering people about what was coming, saw that if he had a company himself, was a manufacturer, they would listen to him and design for him. He talked to HD camera engineers. He talked to motor engineers. His new house could have a development lab. He could have a worthwhile project. He spoke to his hedge fund dad, who said investors were possible if they smelled money. He could have a company and a first-rate life.

But could you grow happiness over emptiness? Was the big question. If you left the basement where you were lopped off and entered a new life followed by the sweats and trembles of your lopped off self, with crazy madness poking in whenever it could, and frying pan daddy poking in, and inside a giant ball of hollow, could you leave that and be new? Could you be new on top of that? In the computer store, he had seen the fifty faces of El, and that was new. That was sea breeze in the face. That was sunlight. Wild insanity to think he could win her, and breathe sea breeze at her side, and feel the sunlight cool and fresh by her side, with her hand moving into his hand and her thumb gentle on the back of his hand.

He had come fast six hundred miles without thinking. Now he must think. And don't be crazy and do a crazy thing like kidnapping and a remote cabin. Be near her. Have her somewhere fifty feet away doing something and radiating beneficial feelings, which he had bathed in for a week via his hat cam video of her, edited down in beautiful sections with *Little Jenny Dow* behind, 210 seconds of sympathy, ending in *I do love animals, I do, I do, I do,* excellent and kind. He watched it several times each day, never while working, but as a break, seated in a folding chair, straight up facing the monitor, 210 seconds of Frisell's exultation and El meekly speaking, better than weed, better than anything. Tomorrow bring all the juiced-up packed-up equipment in the SUV, run the deep-breathing exercises the VA shrink advised, run the video to get centered, then approach Bluey in a calm confident enthusiastic-for-animals way and make your pitch, last pitch, everything riding on a single pitch.

He woke wide awake. He checked the motel clock. Four thirty-five. Had there been a sound? He had been dreaming a panicky dream, water breaking through the berms, hurry hurry. Then someone locked in a closet, scratching frantic, and a flood coming with snakes in the water. Then he heard the scratching again, and that was it, what had woken him. He got up and crossed to the door, looked through the spyhole. Nothing. Through the door, he said, "Can I help you?" Nothing. He crossed to his pants, rummaged out his five shot, crossed back, turned on the hallway light, and, squinting in the brightness, opened the door with his left hand, right hand pointing the pistol. A motion down low, and it was the robot dog lifting his black white muzzle, *Let me in.* He swept the chain and opened the door. The dog marched in, crossed to the sofa, hopped up, dropped prone, watched him.

This was eerie and impossible, but it was actual, whatever it was. Ideas about how the dog had found him flashed and fell away—scent, a fast runner, luck. Some psychic sense. Which meant a mystery, vast and deep. Whatever it was, here he was. Or she, because as the dog strutted past JJ saw he didn't have dog balls, or else they were cut off.

He sat on his bed. He confronted the dog's empty regard. He said, "Why have you come?" The dog might send telepathy, might bark some message in barky dogtalk. The dog settled his head on his paws. His eyes flicked quick around the room, then closed.

JJ turned off the light, and got back into bed. He laid the pistol on the second pillow beside him. He felt the comfort of the dog's presence, the comfort of destiny. He fell fast into the comfort of sleep.

•

After Bluey said goodnight to Annie, leaving the three young ones on the blanket with their tea, he returned to his cab. He could feel the soft snout of a poem nuzzling within and wanted a pen in his hand and his eyes closed. In the cab, he cleared away the laptop and its insistent inbox, and on white paper with a pen, he wrote the line that had come earlier, *A forest starts behind your house.* The rest came gradually and fine, in twenty minutes, likes steps going down, and at the bottom a whole round poem. He read it over many times, added words and lines and commas, struck lines and altered them and added them again, less a word here and a new word there. When he woke at four and came outside to stand in the cool grass and heard the purr gone, he reviewed the poem from memory and made a final revision, working in two more *eventuallys.* Back in the cab, he opened his laptop and wrote the poem into the computer by memory, titled it, *The Creek*. In the morning he would tell the animals.

•

El woke in a blanket cave and felt the dark cool morning outside and the halogen off. She was wide awake without the gloom of sleep. Her hand was near her face, and she fingered the blanket past her eyes, and there was the morning, the first bit of day emerging the world, and there was Roger's sleeping face four feet away, open-mouthed.

Behind her, she heard murmurs and rolled over. It was Bluey making rounds, a soft bulk in the dark bulk of dawn. He was giving treats. Now his voice raised slightly in pitch and clarified. He began to recite.

"A forest starts behind your house.
Eventually you'll want to wander there.
Go when you must,
In the daylight or the night.
There time is unimportant,
And the only light is shadow.
The eyes of beasts will follow you from thickets,
But so what?
You have as much right there as they do.
Dappled clearings, misty starlight,
This and that.
Notice what you can.
The forest is immense.
No one can notice much.
Eventually you'll find a creek,
And deeper wonder starts.
See the way the water moves.
Everyone goes upstream,

And so will you.
Eventually the earth inclines,
And you're deeply breathing.
The water's clear and cold
And mumbling something true.
Notice what you can.
No one can notice much.
Eventually wild thirst begins,
And you'll get so tired of dryness,
You'll tear out all your chest bones
To let the water in.
If you can,
Kindly let me know what happens next."

El sat up in her blanket now, and on her shoulders felt a brush of morning chill. Beside her, Roger was awake and stretched his arms above his head, making an eight foot plank of person. El rolled to her knees by his side, seized his cheeks with flat palms, pat-pat-patted them, kissed his forehead.

He said, "Hey."

She closed his eyes with thumbstrokes.

He said, "Good morning."

She said, "Good morning."

Across Roger's bulk, she saw Dawson's blanket shift. She heard his voice, "Good morning."

Roger and El said good morning.

El said, "Did you guys hear that poem?"

Roger said, "What poem?"

Dawson said, "Yes."

El said, "Bluey said a poem to the beasts."

They heard Bluey's voice at their feet. He was squatting. He said, "Good morning."

They said good morning.

El said, "That was a nice poem."

Dawson said, "You wrote it?"

Bluey said, "I walked Goose last night, and when I passed your van the first line came. The moon wrote it." He had seen them under the tiger cage, the shadowed mounds of blankets, but had spoken the poem regardless. He said, "El, wake my sister if she's not up. Three hours til showtime, folks."

•

Roger, in his tennis shoes and shorts, slung a hundred pound bag across his shoulders. This morning he wanted weight. In his cab, dressing, he had stared at his laptop and gotten a case of trembles. Probably she had written, maybe canceled the whole trip, or else was on the way to the airport with her little green suitcase, which probably she would be, trembling and thinking, like he was thinking, what am I doing?

The night before in the blanket he talked about his father and uncovered some part of his underneath self, like lifting a log in the woods and everything is moist and moving, and suddenly you're more realistic, but there's no time to think because here comes a stranger, flying from Oklahoma on a hunch, and you're clammy-handed and limp. He started across the field toward the path along the river. He would run a jolting root-jumping run. She was coming. He must run and run. As he ran, tears began to fall, and he let them streak his face.

•

After the poem, Dawson went quickly back to his van. Before sleeping, before the battery on his laptop failed, he had spent over three hours absorbed in the books, reading random passages. The practical guidance in the *Discourses* was elegant and clear, the cosmology of *God Speaks* was difficult but compelling, and in *The Wayfarers*, the eccentricities of the masts and their ecstatic relationship with Meher Baba seemed authentic. Perhaps he had found a map to the truest world. Then he closed his eyes and felt the absurdity of that claim. Then he begin to read again.

In the *Discourses*, he read that creation was teleological, that the soul gathered experiences according to its needs, that nothing was chance, and the end was union with God. If so, he was meant to be reading these books under this tiger whose purr was melting him, as it had melted Roger. But do not be duped, bright boy. Do not need belief.

But what if that were all the truth, that once you were in the universe you couldn't get out, except by the door to God, who you couldn't know because the last rule shrugs? But you could feel him drawing you with need, with quiet persistent invisible magnetism. You were God in disguise, and he was reuniting with himself eternally, and that was the whole deal, summed up. Then be clear. Be honest. Wait. And need.

As he began to brush his teeth above his little sink, his eyes wet, and then abruptly from his belly and beneath his sternum, a spasm of sobs erupted, and he began to weep.

•

Annie said, "Well, at least she didn't attack the chickens, as far as I know, anyway. I went out to the poultry building last night and this morning too. I saw Garrell, who was hanging around, seeing if the mystery beast had come back."

She had cooked the bacon and was scrambling eggs. Bluey sat with coffee at the settee. El had just entered the shower, and they could hear the faint rush of water. Annie scraped the eggs into a glass bowl, then sat across from Bluey with her coffee. His hands were cradling his coffee mug, and she laid both her hands across his, enclosing them and the mug. She would trap them until she finished.

She said, "It may be time to send me packing." She released his hands, a small nobility. Let him be free. She said, "Bluey, I have no idea how this happened. You said, well, don't touch the tiger. Definitely. And then, I did."

"I saw you."

"No, Bluey. Not then. Last night. I woke up and went to check on the kids. Bhajan was still purring, and, I don't know, I just wanted to check them. There they were, under the tiger, and I went to the tiger. Well, first Demijohn stuck his nose out for me to kiss, and I kissed him. Then I went to the tiger, and he stuck his whole muzzle out, and I kissed him too, and then, Bluey, I put my hands just automatically inside the bars and gave him a pet, all along his throat. I felt the purr vibrating. And then—" Bluey's face had sterned. She pressed on. "And then you won't believe it—" She found his hands again, not to restrain but to merge. "Here's what I did, without thinking. I stroked his face, all across his eyes, like you do. Then he opened his mouth. And I held his canines in my hands. They were so big. They were warm."

"They're full of blood."

"Really? Oh."

They sat for a moment.

Annie said, "I don't think that beast is a tiger, Bluey."

Bluey was silent. The thought settled between them unopposed.

Annie said, "Well, I guess you're past the scolding part. I even thought, oh no, he could eat my arms off. But I didn't stop." Annie rose, covered the eggs with foil. She began to butter bread for oven toast. She said, "By the way, is George coming just for me, do you think?"

"He was glad to learn you would be here."

"I'm not dreading it. I just don't want to hurt anyone. Bluey, have you any idea what's happening?"

Bluey said, "No."

"Well, love is the answer. If you had told me that a week ago I would have been bored. You told me that in Australia, and I was bored. When I was young I thought, I must take a giant breath. I must fill up with life. But it's the opposite. It's not inhaling, it's exhaling. When you sigh, you let it out, and something comes in because there's room."

"When you sigh, you first take a deep breath."

"Very true! If it were up to me, Bluey, I would let that tiger out. I'm just that wild today. Don't give me the combination."

The shower door had opened, and El stepped out in jeans and a pink T-shirt, towel-scrubbing her head. She said, "Oh, god, she wants to let Bhajan out." She threw her towel across her bed and went to the coffee pot.

Annie said, "Shall I tell her? Yes, tell El everything."

El returned to the settee with a coffee mug and sat beside Bluey. She said with indifferent reproof, "You should be spanked, at least. I heard you talking through the shower wall. And guess what, Dawson found *The Wayfarers* on his computer and found a passage about a mast that was seen at night from time to time accompanied by two tigers. The bus drivers would see him on the road. And also there was one mast they called the tiger mast, because he was so ferocious. He was on the sixth plane, which is almost God. And he wore metal bangles all over and on his neck. There's a photograph of him that we could show Haley. If we care anymore."

Bluey said, "We don't need the recipe to enjoy the food."

Annie cocked the window curtain aside with a finger. She said, "Here come the boys." El and Bluey looked through the side window and saw Dawson, in jeans and T-shirt, and Roger, in shorts, balancing on his head a bulky grain sack, walking together across the sparkling field.

•

On the run he had been thinking about his football ambition and brain trauma, then of gladiators, and he thought of himself as a gladiator, and whether he had been a gladiator in a past life, and there he was under the Coliseum in a dungeon sort of place with the other guys, armored up, waiting to go out and fight hand to hand, just the normal thing they did, because of society, which was automatically cruel, waiting for their fun. But what if he got out there and stuck his sword in the sand and shouted, *I'm done with gladiating. I'm going to be a farmer. So long.* Massive boos, and the coach makes a face. But in the boos and the coach's disgust he hears the *yes* he needs, since it isn't their life, and they're pushing on a ghost, since he isn't in that gladiator body now, he's in a farmer body, walking out to sweet fields of wheat. He had stopped crying fifteen minutes earlier over his Dori trembles and now the tears started again, thinking of the brave gladiator booed out to a better life. He came out of the woods, and there was the van with Dawson in his chair in the open doorway. He thought to clear the tears but realized no need since he was dripping sweat. Dawson had the van door open and was hunched over something, his laptop maybe, but no, just hunched over thinking. He saw Dawson's head come slowly up and saw the tears on his face before Dawson shoulder wiped them on his T-shirt sleeves. Roger swung his grain bag down, and stood heaving for breath and giving off an I-didn't-see-anything expression. Then he said anyway, "I been crying too."

Dawson burst out an odd happy laugh and said, "Why?"

Roger tilted his head with sad fun. He said, "Gladiators, man. Can you imagine?"

Dawson laughed again. He stood and seized Roger's thick body, wetting himself with sweat. He made a trembling sigh. He said, "Oh, Jesus. Oh, man."

They went up to breakfast.

21

The robot dog slurped from the toilet before they left the hotel room, then defecated beside the SUV, then snarfed her way—definitely a her—through two sausage biscuits and now sat upright and sentinel still in the passenger seat. He had called her *Patti* a few times, which didn't seem to catch, so stopped calling her anything and just said, up, or eat, or sit, which she did in her lordly robot way, treating him like a talking rock she permitted to ride along. As he dressed that morning—white T-shirt, green dress shirt, new jeans, new tennis shoes, all mall-bought on the way—a plan had firmed up, neat as tiles in his head. First fifteen minutes in Kinko's, then park in the public lot, take the dog to the rear where their trucks were parked, present the dog, present the documentary idea, offer his skillful service. Then he passed a hardware store and stopped for some rope for a leash so he wouldn't have to waste a cable from his gear box. As he paid the slow-as-hell clerk, he could feel his heart start and his hands go clammy. When he returned to the SUV, the robot dog didn't even turn her head.

He sat for a moment, craving to get out the laptop and hook up the El video with *Jenny Dow* and cool down in the hardware store parking lot, but it was already past nine, opening time, and he should have been there at eight. Christ, what was he thinking? At nine they'll be busy, Christ, and now with the rope stop he won't be there until nine thirty, or ten thirty if there's traffic And they'll be busy with crowds. But he had the dog, his ice-breaker, and the dog would lead to handshakes and amazement, and he would naturally be part of the family as a dog rescuer, which was destiny.

He gave his five bucks to the fairground parking lot guy, then followed the flaggers and nosed in. He waited until the flaggers had moved on and the other parkers had dispersed, then told the robot dog to stay, and got out. On the grass, between cars, he taped together his Kinko's contraption, a four-sided foot tall perimeter of cardboard printed with *LJBN TV NEWS.* He set the handmade helicopter on top of the SUV—he wouldn't risk exposing the expensive military model—then set the cardboard square over it. He stepped back. The copter was hidden. A flagger fast-walked by, saw the sign, flicked a smile, normal deal. He put the controller and laptop in his backpack, used his Gerber to cut the rope and tied a section to the robot dog's collar, then went around and got the dog down. He started flowing with the walkers toward the entrance, the dog nicely alongside, then peeled off, broadcasting confidence, and headed toward the edge of the lot. He passed a flagger who noticed him but gave a shit, then was in the people-empty edge of the lot, then was through a low wood slat fence, the robot dog splaying under a rail and waiting for him to find the rope. Then he and the dog were in a grassy field, and the zoo stockade was three hundred yards away.

•

After the cleaning and feeding, Roger and Dawson showered, then began spiking the crowd fence. Bluey made a treat round, offering Auden and Yeats, which the beasts raptly received. Ballyhoo, the lethargic Binturong, even lipped in his biscuit upside down and tail-suspended from the zoo link. Three news vans parked near the RV, and crews began setting satellites. Garrell arrived in his referee's shirt and this time brought his two teen-aged sons, also in black and white and with whistles. He also brought an ink pad and a large letter "z" stamp, which Annie gratefully accepted. Annie and El walked the line, already stretching to the midway, made change, chatted, and stamped the backs of hands. Since Garrell brought reinforcements, Bluey sent Dawson to the van to work on graphics.

The two crows arrived, circled twice, and settled on the tiger cage. Their arrival drew cheers from the line of people and was captured on video by all three news crews. Just before nine, El, nicely piratey in Annie's burnoose, lifted Sybil onto her towel-padded shoulder and took her place in the tiger perimeter. Bhajan rose, paced with her as she inspected the fence, then haunch sat facing the gate. At nine the crowd surged in, cameras and smart phones aloft. Some began to circle, some chatted with Bluey and Roger in the outer perimeter. More than half gathered at the tiger cage, where Sybil cautioned them to stay *back, you devils, back*. A moment later, both crows fluttered through the bars of Bhajan's cage, provoking an outcry. One bird hopped to the water bowl and began beaking water over its feathers. The other followed. A moment later, Sybil flapped from El's shoulder to the bars of the cage, clambered inside, then hop-flapped atop Bhajan's rolling shoulders. The news crews filmed. The crowd around the tiger densed. At nine ten Bhajan chuffed, and the show began.

•

When the stockade was a fifty yards away, he stopped, and the robot dog stopped beside his ankles and stood, pointed home. JJ was nerve sweating and worried about his armpits and forehead. They had washcloths in the motel room, and he should have thought ahead, but too late now. He pulled up his T-shirt and used the tail to wipe down, then crammed it back into his jeans, then undid his jeans and smoothed everything military neat, then buttoned up. He needed a good long breathe. He needed the video. He slung off his backpack, pulled out his noise-canceling headphones, opened the laptop, and in a moment had the video going, a last bliss before the Bluey meet to cool himself. He would have sat in the grass except for grass stains, so stood, holding the laptop, listening to *Jenny Dow* and watching a hard-to-see sun-washed El speak until a kind cloud crossed the sun, and El emerged bright and clear, and he felt himself cool and strengthen.

"Hey, man."

The voice was behind him, jumping him. He closed the laptop immediately but not panicky fast, giving off vibes of a professional videographer out and about. He turned. It was a long-haired skinny kid in a blue T-shirt with a rock band on the front.

The kid said, "Wow, you found Patti. Where was she?"

It was a shock question, out of the blue. He should know the answer, definitely. That should have been practiced. He flash thought, cross draw the Gerber, slash the kid's throat, throw him in the river.

He said, "I was here yesterday, and the dog must have followed me. Is this your dog?"

"No, it's my mom's. He followed you? You must be in one of the trailers. You work at the fair?"

The kid was a fast jabber. He said, "No man. The dog came to my hotel room. He scratched on my door in the night."

"No kidding? How far is your hotel?"

"On the freeway. About three miles."

"No kidding?" The kid was perked. "That's amazing. Let me ask you—did you see her following you? Did you pet her? Or did she just follow you, and you have no idea about it?"

"I have no idea about it." Menace had leaked, and he saw the kid flinch, still open but draining. JJ gave off a slant smile, made a head shake. He said, "It's weird man, but there it is."

The kid said, "You want me to take her? We have a spot where we tie her up. She got out of her collar last night. It's good you recognized her."

"Yeah, sure, take her."

Dawson took the rope. He said, "Hey, did you want a reward or something? There could be one, I guess. I have to ask Bluey."

"Tell Bluey JJ is here from the college. I came to see him."

"You know Bluey?"

"Yes, I do. I was a keeper at the college for a while. But my real thing is video. I want to make a documentary about this traveling zoo. You're in the zoo?"

"Yeah. Bluey's my uncle. I wonder if Patti recognized you. I bet she did, and I bet—"

"No, that's not it. Because I never saw that dog until yesterday."

"Oh. Well, that's right. Because she came with my mom, and we left that day. So it's a mystery." The kid smiled and diddled fingers. He said, "Have you already started your documentary? Back at the college? Is that it?" The kid gestured to the backpack where the laptop had gone.

A small pause while JJ calculated. Had the kid seen the video? Had he seen El, whom he would know? The screen had been sun-washed, but then a cloud. He gambled. "No, I was just listening to music. *Little Jenny Dow*. Ever heard it?"

"You're shitting me. You're absolutely shitting me! That was *Little Jenny Dow*? Was it by Bill Frisell?"

"Yeah, man."

"Wow! That is my favorite tune. I play that for people, and they say, yeah, nice tune, and I want to shout, fucking great tune! You like it?"

"My favorite tune, man."

"No shit! That's amazing."

JJ nodded. He should speak something comradely, but he was bushwhacked, the kid beaming into his face about his sacred El sessions, like a hallucination. He was getting slushy. He pronounced, "Yes. It is."

The kid said, "Well, this is just one more fact in a bunch of amazing facts. And you brought Patti back. And she came to your room? I'm wildly amazed. I'm Dawson, by the way."

The kid kept shooting. He could flashback skid any minute, start face jitters and bullet pings.

The skinny kid was holding his hand out. JJ took it. He said, "I'm JJ. Maybe you could let Bluey know I'm here."

From the zoo, they heard a chorus of referee whistles. JJ followed Dawson and Patti to the rear gap and into the inner perimeter. The crowd was draining back through the entrance. Bluey stood ten feet away behind the lion cage in conversation with two elderly men and a younger woman. One of the men wore a University of Oregon baseball cap. The news people eavesdropped, mikes extended. The three appeared to be serious-minded. The young woman identified herself as a mycologist and asked about food storage. Certain fungus, she said, produced psychedelic effects. There had been animal cases. One of the men asked if there had been extensive training? The other wondered if they might continue to observe? Bluey replied, no fungus, no training, and certainly, then detached himself. And that's a wrap, folks, here at the exotic animal caravan in Eugene, Oregon.

Bluey was approaching them now. JJ felt him loom like a cliff. He said, "Hey, man. Remember me?"

Bluey offered his hand, and they shook. Bluey said, "I do." Then to Dawson. "Where did you find her?"

Dawson said, with a nod to JJ, "He found her. She came to his hotel room."

Bluey looked at JJ, who felt his calm like a blow. His heart throbbed. This was the interview, all of a sudden, a fundamental moment, and he must rise and take hold and not fail, since fifty feet away through a gap in the cage perimeter he could see El, scarf-wrapped, wearing in a blue shirt with pink at the neck, charmingly schmoozing and waving as the crowd left. He said, "I was here yesterday. She must have followed me."

"Did you befriend her?"

Did he befriend her? Was it an accusation? Was it a trick? He said, "No. Not really. Dogs like me. She got out of her collar, I guess."

Bluey said, "Where did you see her?"

The question sailed over his wall like a grenade and fused fast. If she was chained, he would have had to go where she was chained, which was where? She had been free though, when he creeped the zoo. Through the cages, he saw El stride across the grounds and start a conversation with a guy in a referee shirt. She stood upright and straight-spined, and her hands flipped out and back as she talked. He must seize the grenade and toss it back. He must risk. He said, "I was waiting in line, and she came by, and I petted her."

Dawson said, "What's weird is that his motel is by the interstate. She came to his room at night and scratched." Dawson looked at JJ, and what before, between two young men, seemed amazing and cool, now, before Bluey's gravity, seemed impossible. Their minds loomed at him. The dog was not a ticket into the family. The dog could not be explained. He said, "They say dogs have a sixth sense, right?" They didn't respond. El finished her conversation with the referee and went to speak with a dark-haired woman at the gate. She moved a finger across the woman's brow, neating her hair. He said, "Well, I don't get it either." He was being inspected and suspected. Their minds were like a wind blowing his raft away from land into a dark sea. He said, "I didn't steal your dog, if that's what you're thinking."

The skinny kid's mouth surprise-opened.

Bluey said, "Of course not."

The world tipped. The professional videographer documentary presentation had come loose. He said, "Okay. Whatever. I bet you wonder what brings me."

Bluey said, "What does bring you?"

"Well, I want to make a documentary about your zoo, about all the things you do. From the very first back at the college, all the way to Tennessee. That's what I do. I'm a videographer. With every type of cool gadget. That's what I wanted to show you. You got a minute? We have to go out in the field to get reception. You can see your zoo from the air."

Dawson said, "You got a video drone?"

"Yeah, man. I do. I made it myself. That's another thing I might do, is make drones. We have to go out in the field. I got it on top of my car."

Dawson said, "Is that yours?" And pointed up.

They looked. A four-blade copter glided slowly overhead fifty feet above them.

JJ said, "No, man. C'mon. I'll show you. I got it set up." But now it was lame. And his drone was homemade. He had said that. And stupidly said about the company he planned. And he had a twenty-five thousand dollar military drone which would be stupid to mention now. He reddened. They were seeing that. Fury built. He tried to mind-jacket calm. It wouldn't come. He said, "C'mon. What say?" He heard his voice clipped and hard, the fighter voice, last stop before release. Across Dawson's shoulder, he saw El approaching, twenty feet, then ten. He saw her recognize him. He focused on the pink circle around her neck. He said, "Hi. Remember me?"

"Hi, JJ. Nice to see you. What brings you to these parts?"

Dawson said, "He found Patti."

El tilted her head and smiled a frown.

Dawson said, "She came to his hotel room last night. He was here yesterday. She must have followed him. We were trying to figure that out."

Bluey said, "You want me to come and see your drone which I would be happy to do some time, but not now. We have another batch of people just coming in." He made a brief palm-offer toward the gate which the dark-haired woman had opened. A crowd swarmed. Bluey said, "Maybe you could bring your drone here later some time."

Bluey had not mentioned the documentary, and JJ saw he was being kindly handled, like a child, which he was, to these people with their famous zoo and crowds and separate world from his, which was a frantic world with homemade drones and amateur ambitions. He felt himself smirk, breaking disguise. Then he was backing away. He said "Okay. No problem. See you." Then turned and walked and felt their minds on his back until he was through the stockade gap and out into the field, then began to trot, then run, at first only fast, and a moment later in a top speed sprint, three hundred yards to the parking lot fence, where he fell onto his knees, gasping, then dropped onto the grass on his back and closed his eyes and let his body heave. Then he rolled onto his stomach and put his face into the grass and began to weep.

•

Annie worked the line, taking cash and stamping hands, and she felt something flowing from her and felt those who hands she lifted and stamped with the blue *Z* must feel it too. She jibber-jabbered—*How old is your baby? Thank you, kind sir. Three rings? You're a three ring circus, sweetie.* She was light and warm. She was warm light glancing, and the people shined in her queenly wake.

From the zoo grounds, the chorus began, the fourth one of the morning, and gathered and rose, and conversation stilled in the pleasure of wonder. Heads lifted, faces concentrated. Then it faded, punctuated with a single hooting note from Taj, the guenon. The whistles blew. Roger opened the gate. The crowd undazed a little and began to mill out and back to the fairway.

As the fifth group entered the grounds, and Annie closed the gate behind them, she noticed the tall angular man thirty people back in the line. He wore a bundle-lashed frame backpack and an olive floppy hat and was staring at her. George, the doctor. She lifted her chin and perked a smile of recognition. He smiled back. She took five dollars from a short round teenaged boy, lifted his soft hand, and pressed the back with the stamp. His hand was dead in hers, like meat. The flow had stopped. She was bewildered and grieved, and then she was angry, first at George, an intruder who brought need, then at herself, so porous a vessel.

She took money, made change, stamped hands. She offered face smiles and felt herself redden. They would see that she had lost connection, that she was suddenly bereft. But the spasm of humiliation was oddly satisfying. She felt a faint tick of release and let the pain abide. She must leave the throne, but she would not leave the kingdom. She would not be queen, but could be a princess, shining but learning, and this was insight and joyful. She was stamping the callused hand of a young woman as that impression came, and she laughed a merry laugh. The young woman raised her eyebrows, but without suspicion.

Annie slid the stamp between her thumb and palm, then folded the young woman's hand between hers. She said, "These hands do work."

The woman smiled and said, "They do."

She could have inquired, and might have, but a tall man held out five dollars and his hand for the stamp, and many more waited, and George was fifteen people away now, and she could feel his eyes. She took the money, stamped the hand, another soul admitted. Admit them all. Let them pass through the gate in their time. Then George was three away, then two, then next, and she took his five dollars and his hand and stamped it. She said, "Should I charge you?"

He said, "I don't know. Yes. I must be charged." He smiled. Their eyes glanced together.

She felt a softness in him and felt a sudden softness toward him. He has been watching me in my princess mode and has softened to me. His hands were surgeon's hands, nicely sized and long-fingered. She reached past his hand to touch his forearm with her fingertips. She said,

"I'll see you later." And it was an invitation, and from her heart, and let it be, and see what came.

•

Dawson had followed JJ out of the stockade and saw him first fast walk, then run, then sprint. He ached after him, the stranger who loved *Little Jenny Dow*, who now ran and ran. Far away he saw the tiny figure collapse into the green of the field and vanish. He folded his arms, palms clasping upper arms, and embraced himself. He sent the embrace across the field.

He walked back to his van. A memory emerged—the Philadelphia cab driver who told him about his son's trouble with drugs. The cab driver had taken him from the airport out to Valley Forge, the house of his birth father, whom he hadn't seen for seven years, a trip dutifully arranged by his mother. He was fifteen then, and his father, who owned a dinner theater, made him welcome but had toward his son a dutiful formality, like a concierge. He stayed the week, kindly endured by his stepmother, an actor and manager of the theater, and must return to his mother, another actor, entangling herself with a new man, and thought at the end, be home nowhere, and live that way. He had the cab driver's card and called him. On the ride back, the driver, a neat thin black man with a tight carpet of gray hair, drifted again onto his son, who would be in prison for many years. At some point, he remarked, "You can't buy feeling." Through the years, those words had become precious and rung in Dawson's mind, and rung again now as he saw the distant figure of JJ rise from the grass, cross a fence, and disappear into the mass of vehicles.

That was the precious important trouble with life, that you can't buy feeling, and until you had feeling, you were home nowhere, and when you had it, you were home everywhere, and so the life project he had imagined, the dome, was good and true, because it would be a place for feeling, like a home.

He was nearing the van and river and stopped to listen and close his eyes for a moment. Instantly in his mind an image emerged, like a tree from murk, and it was a tree, and beneath it roots tangled like branches, and the roots and branches reached and twined and made a circling mass, and then a wheel, and the wheel filled with colorful intricacy, and it was a mandala and shined and vanished. It was a vision, escaping for an instant from the self thicket, flashing up and gone.

He opened his eyes. He looked toward the parking lot. There were people moving among the cars but no one recognizable as the *Little Jenny Dow* guy. He could run there, he could make a search. But he was green and incomplete. He had no power to save anyone. So save everyone. Create the dome.

•

There were three moms and a jumble of kids at the fence in front of the peacock, and Roger stopped and said to the kids, "You guys want to see something cool?" The oldest boy, around ten, said, "Yes," and the others agreed by quieting. Bluey had showed him the move that morning, and he had done it for three crowds already, but this would be the first time for mostly kids. He said, "Okay. Check this." He turned to face the cage. Spectra came forward a step, giving himself room. Roger glanced behind at the kids, made a good-chum matter-of-fact get-this head nod and spread his arms. Spectra fanned his tail, and the tail effervesced in sunlit blues and greens. A chorus of *ohs* and *ahs*. Roger held his pose for a few seconds, then folded his arms, and the tail collapsed.

One child said, "Do it again."

Roger turned. It was a girl, maybe six, and like her older brother, she had spoken for them all.

Roger said, "Everybody close your eyes for a minute."

The kids closed their eyes.

Roger said, "See that in your mind, that beautiful tail? It's still there. That's your beautiful memory that you have. So you don't need to see it again, I hope. Because I'm not supposed to do it too much because we don't want to tire old Spectra out." All but the little girl had reopened their eyes. Roger said, "Okay, open your eyes." The little girl opened her eyes, made a timid frown. Roger turned to Spectra and again wide spread his arms, and again the tail fanned, and the crowd murmured. He held, a moment, a longer moment, then collapsed the tail. He turned. The three mothers glowed. The little girl made a bright missing-tooth smile.

He moved on. He would be a good father. They would climb on Mt. Papa in the morning. He would give them two shots of peacock every day, because of love and because he would not stop noticing them.

He scanned over the crowd again and again did not see her. She was five eight and long-haired and would be alone and noticeable. He felt keenly his double life, one life the friendly crowd-talker with the zoo shirt, the other the wooer who had invited a strange girl and was afraid. He had deepened. He had some kind of protective thickness around him now, which was relaxation and confidence but also sadness that if this girl did appear in the crowd, and he could not warm, and if she felt his helpless reserve, that they would be confused and dangle like puppets, and the best would be to be realistic with their disappointment. That would be sad, but also all right. The truth was all right. He scanned the crowd.

And there she was. She had seen him and was coming, in jeans and an orange top and pony tail. She was nice-looking. She was smirking just the right kind of smirk, which said, oh well, here we are. And he felt himself flow out.

•

El saw the pony-tailed girl in orange stop in front of Roger, saw them shake hands, saw Roger laugh at something the girl said. It was lonely seeing them, but a little good too, her inner soil moistened. She was inside the tiger enclosure. A moment later, as the crowd gathered, as if summoned by her need, she saw a perfect guy come to the fence with his son or little brother, a tall, in-his-twenties guy in jeans and a tan T-shirt with fingercombed hair and a strong face soft toward his small companion, whose hand he held. She yearned toward him, then looked away. She could drift that way, work along the crowd chatting until she reached him, but went the other way as a test, felt desire resist and stretch and let go, and there was a mom and dad and boy, and the boy said, "Does he ever eat a bird?"

El and the family looked at the two crows, who stood together in the cage center making a formal stiff-stepping bird dance as the tiger paced. El said, "He never does. Or that parrot either. You want to hear something cool?" She crossed to the cage, and as Bhajan swept by with the shoulder-clinging Sybil, El murmured, "Back."

Sybil obediently cackled, "Back, you devils, back."

El returned to the fence, charmed a gathering section of crowd with an explanation of the proposed skit. She moved on. If she continued around, if she hastened a little, she might come to the perfect guy again before the next zoo chorus. She saw Roger moving along the crowd again, being the zoo bouncer, as Dawson put it, and saw the orange-topped blond girl, following, weaving in and out of people, chatting and making hand sweeps and head wags which were probably laughs. Roger was laughing. She felt a burst of love for him and thought of quick running over, introduce herself to Dori, so nice to meet you, heard so much, then jump the fence, give Roger a good hug, then run back. That morning she had thought several times of his testimony in the blanket, when he had pulled some heart plug and drained out truth and beauty. Her eyes shined to think of it, and they shined now as she stopped before five high school chums and answered about food, about the birds, about the ecopark.

Bhajan chuffed. The calls began, gliding louder, higher, finding their way, agreeing on the interval, then blasting their orchestra of cries. Then off. A monkey hoot. A yip from Nubia, then silence. Friends looked at each other with parted lips. They made joy laughs. El began her explanations. Training? No. The tiger signals? Yes. What's going on? We don't know. The last rule shrugs. Forget your malarkey. Love is in the air.

Garrell and sons gave them the customary three minutes to unwonder, then blasted the whistles. The crowd stirred moodily toward the exit, back to their lives. She had come to the perfect guy at last, turning his small companion from the fence, noticing El over his shoulder with a face smile, then appreciating her with a re-glance. She felt the glance and could have spoken but didn't. She turned to Bhajan, who waited for her as usual. She stroked his face. That morning, she had given up all pretense that this was a tiger. He was a being of some kind, tamer than she was. We must all be tamed, which means surrendered, which was why to say goodbye to the perfect guy whom she desired, but who was outside love. Maybe if he came back, or if he came back twenty times, and said, I have such hope for us. Life could be well-lived if you were tame. As she stroked the tiger's eyes, Sybil gripped her way forward over Bhajan's head, then pounced with gentle assurance onto El's forearm.

She brought the bird back through the bars, reset her burnoose with her other hand, and turned to meet the streaming crowd.

•

Bluey saw the many-bundled backpack advancing through the crowd and retrieved the blue uniform shirt, which he had hung on the back of the cage of the Phoenix, the Himalayan blue sheep. He held it up.

George inspected it. Over the left pocket the name *George* had been sewn in red letters. He said, "Damn, you thought ahead."

Bluey said, "I did. Now get it on because you're going to work. Did you encounter the lovely Miss Annie?"

"Yes, I did." George shrugged off his backpack and set it against the stockade. Phoenix cocked his head patiently at them. "I think I made quite an impression."

"She's halfway to an old woman."

"Oh stop. You can't correct fascination with truth." He took off his sweatshirt and buttoned the uniform shirt. "Good fit. So what do I do?"

"Stay with me and pay attention. Then I'll send you off to on your own."

"Do I get paid?"

"No."

"I've seen this on TV. It's all over the news."

"I know."

"So what's going on here?"

"No idea, George."

"Really? No idea?"

"What's happening is bigger than any idea I could get, so I don't think about it."

They entered the fenced area in front of the cages, thin George tailing blocky Bluey. After a few moments conversation with three piercing-festooned teenagers, the chuff sounded, and the chorus rose around them like a fluid.

•

The zoo was quiet. The animals slept. Since they were seven now, Annie spread picnic blankets in front of the RV. They ate broccoli casserole, glazed sweet potatoes, and biscuits. Dori and Roger cleaned up, El and Bluey began the evening rounds, Dawson went back to his van to work.

Annie and George set up his small tent near the tiger cage and deposited his gear inside. She led him to the end of the RV. Bluey had tightened Patti's collar, and she lay underneath in the shadows, the chain pooled at the bumper. Annie released her, and they started toward the river.

They hadn't seen each other since Thanksgiving the year before and now caught up—divorces, Annie's financial disaster. At the river, they settled on a log and watched Patti walk upstream across the gravel.

They listened to the river. A current rose between them plainer than words. George said, "Well." Then—"Are you available?"

She briefly touched his hand. "Thanks for asking. That's nice. I'm not, actually. I think I'm tired of all that now. I feel free. In a moment I'll start talking about things eternal. Things eternal are on the tip of everyone's tongue around here."

"I want to hear this purr."

"Yes, you must hear it. You're not crushed?"

He returned the brief touch. "Well, no. You haunted my marriage, I admit that. And we're sitting here now, together and free. That's as much as I ask. You say no? All right then. I am sweet and calm."

"Oh, good lord. Are you trying to say just the right thing?"

"I probably am."

Annie began to say, I wouldn't want you altogether sweet and calm, but stopped herself, then began to touch his hand again, and stopped herself. The rush of the river came up around them, and she felt something in her bath in the sound. She felt something washing away.

When they stood and called for Patti, she did not appear.

•

Roger said, "I went for a run here this morning."

"Seems kind of bumpy."

"It was. And I was—" He had begun to mention carrying the hundred pound grain bag, but stopped, an impulse against bragging.

She said, "What?"

"I was thinking about gladiators." That was true, but not what he had been going to say, so dishonest and regretted. She inspired him to be true. He felt another roll of affectation move through him. Affection rolls had been coming all afternoon, ever since she arrived from her thousand mile airplane ride with her doubtful smirk. She had eaten with the crew and was brave and friendly and now had come away with him on a river walk. From the screen of trees they could see two figures sitting on a log beside the rapids. He said, "There's Annie and George."

Dori said, "Why gladiators?"

The path curved away from the river. The diminished river sound amplified their privacy.

He said, "I guess because I play football. I was thinking of gladiators under the Coliseum waiting to come out and fight. I thought maybe I was a gladiator in a past life."

"You believe in past lives?"

"Well, it makes sense."

"Otherwise it's unfair."

He looked at her. "That's true."

"That's from my dad, actually. He's also a big believer in fate. He says, if you're supposed to drown, God will chase you through the desert with a bucket of water."

"He sounds like a cool guy."

"He is."

"What does he do?"

"He owns coffee shops, five of them actually."

"So that's where you work."

"I manage the roaster. We have a central roaster."

"You must be very knowledgeable when it comes to coffee."

"I am. It's pretty fun. I get to experiment. Different beans and different roasts."

"I bet you write that stuff—hints of blackberry, cantaloupe, and oleander."

"I do, except oleander's poison. How about blackberry and antelope, which is what I thought you said until I thought about it."

"You should put that on one of the bins, wait until somebody notices. I bet your dad would think that's funny."

"He would." She laughed. "I'll probably actually do that."

"Did you tell him you were coming out here?"

"God, no. I said I was going to a friend's." She looked at him. "So I lied to my cool dad."

He met her look. "For his own good though."

She said, "You know why I came?"

"Why?"

"I saw you on YouTube. You were on the news too, but it was mostly the YouTube video. You were talking with a bunch of kids and somebody posted it. It wasn't the one that went viral, with El and the parrot. But they tagged it *exotic animal caravan,* and I found it. I was looking for you. I think you were being a bear or something. The kids laughed."

They had been walking single file, Dori ahead. Now the path widened, and he came alongside. He could take her hand and strongly urged, but hesitated.

She took his hand. She said, "I thought you made a nice bear, so that's why I came."

They walked a moment. He lifted her hand and stroked her rings with his thumb. The rings were silver and wide and involved. He said, "I see you like rings."

"Yes, I do. Annie called me a three ring circus when she stamped my hand."

"You could have called me. I could have saved you five bucks."

"Well, damn." They smiled and walked. She said, "I think it's going pretty good, don't you?"

He laughed. "Yes, I do."

She said, "It could be past lives. Of course, maybe I killed you in a past life. I put oleander in your coffee."

"Or antelope."

They laughed.

She said, "So what's going on with the animals? Really no idea?"

Earlier he had told her about the tiger, that it was raised by a holy man, that it purred all night. He said, "It's the tiger." Then he stopped, turned her toward him, laid his hands on her shoulders, moved them to her upper arms, framed her with himself. He felt his gaze direct and smooth, and felt her in it, awake and interested. He embraced her. He felt her head nest under his chin. Her hair smelled clean and felt cool on his neck. He felt the pressure of her breasts. They released and started off again, side by side, their hands coming together. He said, "We're all in a really good mood around here. That's all we know, really."

"Feeling love?"

"Yes."

She said, "Okay, wait a minute."

He stopped, and she came in front, took his cheeks with both hands, and drew him down. She kissed him on the lips, lightly. She drew back and beamed a smile. She said, "Okay, that's plenty."

They began to walk.

She said, "Is it okay?"

He said, "Definitely."

She said, "So far, this is about the easiest date I've ever had."

•

Through the darkened windows of the van, Dawson had seen them go by, first Annie with George and her dog, then Roger with Dori, the girl who came from out of the blue all the way from Oklahoma, and whom they had all gotten to know a little at dinner. She seemed glad to live. Roger liked her.

He thought about going to get El, make the third couple by the river, or maybe she would drop by, poke her head in, let's take a walk, which he would like just then for a nice break. He didn't want to go alone and see the others paired.

Off and on all day as he worked, he had thought of the *Little Jenny Dow* guy. He was working on the stockade banners, two ten foot wide, seven foot high sections with crowds seen from behind, to be displayed on either side of the gate. It was Norman Rockwell styled, bright happy bony people, with kids and moms and American dads, except one of them he made the Little Jenny Dow guy, turning back to look with a happy smile, in white T-shirt and jeans. He had worked for six hours on the banner, taking a couple of hour breaks to read, first *The Conditions of Happiness* in the *Discourses*, then in *The Wayfarers* about the wild revered god-intoxicated people. It was soaking in amazing hidden information which might be facts, that the universe was divine, and that involution came after evolution, and that you could deepen and make contact with the soul, and that all the virtues, which had been corny and plastered on, were ancient and natural and true. As he read, excitement built. He repressed it, but it built.

He thought he saw why he had fainted. He had come to the edge where the last rule shrugged, but had heart-yearned past and broke a boundary, which splintered his mind. Whatever the deep soul was, which was under even the heart, you couldn't eat it with thought. Thought was subtraction. Good thought subtracted bad thought until you got to zero. You ate it by becoming small, which was the odd old secret, which was humility, which was why humanity loved honesty and self-effacement and what a saint is, small enough to be great. It made good clear sense of everything. You could live in terms of it and still be intelligent because it was not a thing to believe but something to experience, and it made his idea, the dome, a perfect idea and life purpose, to make a place where people could meet and love.

Now he wanted to walk, to get some air into his ideas, see if he was leaving out some giant ingredient, like people were selfish and power mad and could never be happy. He slid open the van door and stepped onto the grass. A cricket loudly chirped. There was the creamy moon, big over trees. He walked away from the path into the field, then began to trot, then bent over trotting, letting thistles bounce against his opened palms. He dropped into the grass and rolled, ending on his back. Stars glittered. Things would be simpler now. There was one thing, then everything else.

Across the grass, from the glow of the zoo, he heard a feather of sound. The purr had begun.

•

El spread the blankets, then returned to the RV for the teapot and tray of cups and spoons. Bhajan rose and turned to face her. His slab of belly swung like a pendant from his spine. Goose appeared, walked briefly around the blankets, and settled at the edge. Bhajan paced away and back, away and back, then dropped, facing the blankets, head aloft. He began to purr. The two crows, gripping the top rail of the cage, simultaneously rose their wings wide, then flapped them inward like fans folding, producing a neat, card-shuffle sound.

She sat on the blanket beside Goose, laid her hand on his head, worked one ear, then the other. The purr moved through her, and she felt it as pain. She felt it as restlessness and as discontent. She thought, that's my background mind. She thought, I am always in pain.

The guy she had seen at the tiger cage that afternoon, the perfect guy with his child or brother, had not come back. His child probably, which was why. She thought, under happiness and under confidence and success, which were cosmetic, and under all the giant pile of what you want and even what you did get, is pain, which called like a voice from a well. Well, that would be right. That would be the structure of the universe, if God got separated from himself, so long ago, long long ago in the gripping ancient tale of every life, which will end well, all right, so everything's fine at last, but it took its round-and-round time, and again and again you forgot how to live. So pain steered. She lay down, rolled Goose into herself so they were her belly to his back. She laddered her fingers along his arched throat again and again. She heard his satisfied hum under the purr like an overtone and hummed back to him, and it was the lonely song of friendship atop the song of pain.

JJ had come for her. She had seen that in his eyes, in his quick face-frozen stare and look-away. Or she was fearing, and JJ had come to make a film, what Dawson said. But Bluey did not believe that. She had seen Bluey's pensive scowl move over her after JJ fled. He would not say and shock her, but she felt him feel it. JJ might be dangerous. She had attracted him. But if he came back, Bluey would steer him, put his hand on the wheel of JJ's mind and glide him away. If he had come for her. And he had. That knowledge, and the sudden sharp background discontent unexpectedly upwelling, were weights, and the purr was in her face like a blast.

She gave Goose a farewell scrub and rose and went to the tiger. She put her hands through the bars to touch him, but he lifted his head and held it aloft and away to the side, and while her hands were extended, held it, held it, and when her hands withdrew, revolved around again.

She gripped the cool bars. She had been refused. She was behind the bars, not outside them.

She closed her eyes, and in a moment felt a grip on her right shoulder, then on her left, and heard the flutter of wings. She opened her eyes and saw peripherally the black flanks of the crows on her shoulders. One hopped-flapped through the bars, then the other, onto the cage floor, unremarkable doings in the new shiny world.

Behind her Bluey said, "I put the teabags in."

She turned. They smiled to each other. She felt his seasoning and endurance. He was long in harness. She said, "Mine with a teaspoon of honey."

And, as he prepared her tea, he began to tell her, because no one had yet told her, about Dawson's idea for a dome, a place for gathering and friendship, and it seemed to her good and inevitable, and what the world must do.

22

If he had an automatic, he could pull the trigger two or three times probably before he even felt it, shoot himself in the heart, definitely get it done. But a revolver was iffy. You might not have the strength for another pull, and a head shot could make you a vegetable, especially with a little thirty-two. But what if you dived off a building, and you do a head shot on the way down, a good idea actually. His hotel only had two stories though. So drive to town, except that was a lot of effort. It was hard to get that ambitious. Also, it was hard to move. He was encased in something like grease. He had taken a shower, which felt weird, the grease sliding around as he moved, letting him through, but if he stopped moving—he held the wash cloth in front of his face, testing—the grease held his arm and held his fingers on the wash cloth. This was an improper insane sensation. Also, what if the grease hardened, and he got trapped, and they found him in the shower with a wash cloth? They would dress him and bend him into a chair and that would be that. Put him in a hospital with feeding tubes and that would be that. So he better make the drive, find a building while he still could.

He was sitting on the edge of the bed, and it might be hard even to stand up. He stood up partway and stopped, halfway bent forward. The grease held him. He took a bent-over step, and the grease let him through, but he could feel its reluctance, and now he could see it a little, a sort of glinty blue goo swirling. He could give up any second, and the grease would hold him, and that would be that. A crappy life. He started to tuck the five shot into his pants, then saw he was naked. Ask the clerk, where's the roof, man? Sir, you are naked and covered in grease.

He laid the pistol on the dresser, opened the drawer. Socks slid easily onto his feet. He slid his feet into his loafers, lifted his jeans, smirked, then bent, cranked off the loafers. He stepped into jeans, not bothering with underwear, drew on a T-shirt. He slid the pistol into his front pocket. What else? Keys. As he stooped to lift a discarded pair of jeans from the floor, the scratching came. He let the grease hold him and listened. Long silence. He could feel the grease begin to gel. Even bent over, he was warm and comfortable. What if he didn't move from now on, and a million years from now they find him like a bug in blue grease. The silence was smooth and safe and went on and on. The scratching came again. Could he move was the question or had the grease caked? He unbent a little. The grease objected but permitted. He took a step, unbending more, then stopping still halfway bent, since the spyhole was lower than his eyes and why waste effort? At the door, he peered through the spyhole. Nothing. Scratch scratch. Had to be the robot dog which had come to be with him in his hour of need.

He straightened, rippling out blue waves, and opened the door. The dog trotted inside, robot-walked to the bed, sprung up, spun once, and dropped. The dog observed him. The dog's expression was contemptuous.

The dog said, *You greasy loser.*

The dog said, *Take and do.*

The dog said, *El is three miles away and can melt grease down to the last molecule of grease, and you can be new and what would it cost her, a minute, a second, an hour or two, and everything would melt and new life could come.*

He swung his right arm, out across his vision. He swung his left arm. The grease was faint and soupy. Just the thought of El, and the grease was soupy. The dog watched and said, *Watch out for Bluey. And the skinny kid. Sneak and see. Get a plan. Find out where she sleeps.*

When he opened the door, the dog trotted ahead, down the concrete stairway to the parking lot. On the stairs he saw he had forgotten to put on shoes, but went on because he didn't want to lose contact with the dog, who said, hurry, hurry, and anyway, a sneak in socks was good. The dog was waiting by the SUV.

•

She liked to touch him when they talked, a poke or tap or little finger beat on his knee. Roger wanted to roll her up on top of him and stroke her hair and hold her head against his chest, but resisted. He listened as she told about her family, her mother who managed a roller skating rink, her philosophical coffee dad, and her brother, in college now in zoology, and a high school safety but too slow for college football. He was a year younger, and she and her cheerleader buddies made up cheers to embarrass him.

And what about your family, Roger, let's hear all about your hard ass father and picky mother and lonely fled sister. And he did tell her and even found a way to make it funny, like an obstacle course with giant pillow hammers, and told her about football and the pros and his current working out with determined ambition. And she made a small smile and said, what about CTE, which their family had read up on after her brother got dinged and asked who won the game four times on the way home.

They were lying on the blanket, Roger on his back, elbow propped, and Dori knee hugging beside him. Bhajan sprawled on his belly, head high, and the purr flowed into their faces. They could feel themselves recognizing each other, and the CTE question came from them together, up from between them, and the answer also, which was no more football, amazing and clear. Roger felt it arrive and settle. He looked at the tiger. The tiger looked away. Roger closed his eyes. He thought, give up football. He felt something shift, something rise, something fall away.

He opened his eyes. He said, "Well, I guess I'll give up football."

She said, "Really?"

"Yeah. I been meaning to. All this time."

She turned onto her knees, faced him. She made a pout face, then a merry beam. She said, "Well, I guess I have no right to be happy, but that just makes me so happy."

Roger looked at the tiger, who glanced briefly toward him, then away. He said, "I bet we get married."

She laughed. She kissed his brow. She said, "Oh God, we probably will."

•

From the other end of the blanket, where she sat between George and Bluey, Annie saw the kiss and felt a pluck of stinginess that this young vixen was making away with one of the tribe's males. Which was the structure of her mind, that among the males she counted coup, and which was an ordinary emotion, ordinarily unnoticed, but noticed now like grime. Then raise it higher, this spot of grime, let it be a clear known flag and flap and tatter in the wind of the purr. Which she did, a small banner of possessiveness in her mind, that another female was active and alive, and hold it forth and let the banner tatter away to a flagless stick and the stick a sweet relief. What a good image, that desire is a banner-proud army marching out of you, until love blows you clear and clean, and you're an army of sticks, which is understanding. Then come out and out, little proud army of me, and blow away in this clean wind. Somewhere there's an end, but who cares for that? We have learned the dance of the bannerless sticks.

She badly wanted to dance, jump up, forget every person and herself and dance or maybe just stand and wave her arms or just stand still and let the dance be how completely you stilled, which would be a glorious dance.

Joy laughter bubbled, and she turned to George to share it. He turned his head toward her, then his eyes, which were fastened on the tiger and seemed to reluctantly release. She laughed the joy across, saw he was absorbed, and with both hands returned his head to the tiger. But he turned to her again.

She said, "I wasn't going to say anything really. I had this strong impulse to dance. El and I danced the other night. Do you like to dance?"

He said, "Well, there are times when I do. Like right now. I'm very interested in dancing."

She laughed. She stood, pulled him up with two hands. She said, "Come, sir. Let us satisfy ourselves."

She led him onto the crowd-trodden grass, took her place in his arms, ballroom style. He began a stately marching dance with tidy dips and stops and swinging turns. He delighted her with skill. She began to trust. He is a skillful man, she thought, good in a surgeon. The purr has made him graceful. To love is rich. She glided in the nest of his arms. She closed her eyes, which had wet. He would see the tears, which was all right, because they were the heart lake filling and lapping over which was common with human beings, which they were, on earth, dancing.

•

While Bluey worked, a thought-line revolved, the divinity of the universe, the old central premise, which was deep sense, but only sense, so never satisfying, and the history of ideas was the entanglement of useless corollaries. Corollaries, berries, histories, cherries, fairies. A poem of quatrains and rhymes and packed-in thought. He took the time to browse to his idea folder and wrote "corollaries, cherries, histories, high thought quatrains," saved it with the same title, and closed the file. It would be a worked-at poem though, likely without flavor, and probably go unwritten. Anyway, he had no time for poetry.

He had taken tea, searched without success for Patti with Annie, exchanged glances with Bhajan, then returned to his cab and computer. He had easily a thousand emails, half from overseas, some short but many lengthy, a tide of offers, theories, job inquiries, warnings about Satan, and sprinkled through messages from friends and colleagues. He searched for and found Haley's note, that his boss, Fuad, was returning to the states and asked for a meeting. He responded, any time, my great pleasure, searched and found the messages of friends and colleagues and responded. Tomorrow he would set Dawson the task of scanning and flagging, then write boiler plate responses that could answer in batches. Dawson would need help though and there was no one. Probably there was a service somewhere on the net you could hire to answer emails. Dawson could find it.

Behind the immediacy of the emails, the larger decision—whether to cut short the tour and proceed directly to the ecopark, or continue, which meant buying another RV, calling former students, hiring crew. At their next stop, a state fair in Nevada, they would need replacements for Garrell and his sons.

The gate was over thirty thousand today. He feared for the beasts. Though their behavior was compelled by the benign tiger, still it was compelled. He wanted to rest them and observe, which would mean a wrench in the schedule. Or they could be in Tennessee in two long days. He had instructed his site manager to stop work on the buildings and devote all manpower to completing the fencing.

The beasts seemed fine though. On his rounds, they had been animated. They had been creative. Quanna stood in the center of her enclosure with her arms akimbo, tossing her head, mouth open, clearly signaling, *throw, throw*, and when he one by one underhanded the treats through the wire, mouth-caught them all with nimble dipping steps. When all five treats were caught, she clapped, cocked her head, and watched him patiently away. The guanacos, Pumper and Nickel, stood together to make an X of their necks, first Pumper on top, then Nickel, then Pumper, then Nickel, a dexterous jabbing and fiddling. Wildly abnormal. A signal of presence. Tooey, the honey badger somersaulted. Thane the mandrill, extended his arms backward beneath his legs, then twisted them forward to lace his fingers and lock his legs. Paris, the Siberian lynx balanced a full minute on his hind legs with hardly a waver. Cloe the okapi struck her right hoof four times against the metal floor, then four times, then four times. We are here, they said. Notice.

Sybil was beak stroking one of her wings as he approached. As he held the biscuit through the bars, she came upright and spoke clearly a single word, *Bluey,* then beaked the biscuit through the wire and claw clamped it onto her perch. The mind enlarges, he thought, unmoored somehow from the brain, as when a man enlarges within he is unmoored from body, as after death consciousness is unmoored. If he said, *Sybil, tell me everything,* would she respond? But that would be insistence and somehow contrary. He poked a second biscuit through the wire. It made a muffled thump on the cedar chips. Sybil, as he walked away, made a simple loud parrot screech.

That evening, knowing he had work, he had pulled his truck closer to the stockade, so that with his cab window open he was bathed in purr. From time to time he closed his eyes to let bliss work. His thoughts drifted for explanation. What unknown potency of sound could move from the material through the subtle and mental to reach the soul? Well, of course. That was *not* the path. It was not from the world to the soul, but the other way, from the soul to the world. The purr was the manifestation, coming not *from* the tiger's throat, but *through* it, which was the structure of the universe after all, that the soul emitted the cosmos. Odd not to see that, to think first of hyoid bones, but also normal, the evidence dependent track of the science mind.

It had been three days, and all of them altered, Dawson perhaps the most. Or emerged, a better word. In days to come such terms will be commonplaces, if Meher Baba is right, and an awakening coming. He mind-said the name, *Meher Baba*. He would neither refuse nor accept. Let it come if it could.

•

Dawson sat on the grass with his laptop on crossed legs between Charlie, the Somali wild ass, and the guanacos. He had nicked the tip of his right index finger that morning as he sliced apples, and now as he typed, he had to use his middle finger, holding his band-aided index finger aloft, which made typing deliberate, which was good, since he was thinking deliberately.

He was thinking about the dome and what was good and bad in it, and typing the points out in two columns, good first, which turned out to be a short column with so far a single point. It was good because it would collect people and give them a place to play and be happy together. That was it. Like a church without ideas. A place where people could express their deep need to be friendly. That was it.

There were way more points in the bad column. They were smaller and not deeper, but more. For instance, this guy's drunk. For instance, this blowhard thinks he knows everything. For instance, he's hitting on me.

But that was the beautiful substance of the idea, that you came to the dome to be together, which was the main impulse and would correct the inevitable impulses of selfishness. Or not, since everyone was willful and had opinions to defend. How about there could be—and he wrote this in the good idea column—a big pottery bowl at the entrance where everybody had to leave two pennies as they entered. Leave your two cents at the door. Come into the dome and recognize your neighbors and play with them. Leave your opinions at the door and come on, buddy, square off with me over checkers, or learn to cook, or talk about a book.

You had to establish the attitude, which he wrote in the good ideas column, *establish the attitude,* all important, since it would be like a force field as new people came in, woolly with mistrust, and they would feel the force field soothe and settle them, and they would discover, hey, I always wanted to build a kite and have friendly relations with other people. The whole city could become a dome, and the country, and the world, all under the same sky, which, by the way, is a dome.

Then he wrote *giantly naive* in the bad points column and let it accuse him. And he imagined the venture capitalist's office and describing the dome and seeing the guy shift and smile and cut the meeting short. Dawson had run the numbers. It was not a money maker, at least at first. You had go to a foundation or the government, but politicians bickered, so a foundation. You would have to get it all in your arms and carry it into a foundation and spread it out and start the force field there, with whoever was behind the desk, and get them inside the force field, and keep spreading it until there it was, a dome where people came to enjoy each other. And if a biker gang roared up, meet them at the gate, show them the two cents bowl, hand out deodorant, and come on, guys, let's work on bikes, or play dodge ball if you're feeling jumpy. And if there is any particular hard-headed biker guy immune to the force field of kindness, he must be banned. Sorry, come back when you're ready to leave your asshole self in the two cents bowl.

He could see El sitting alone in the blanket center with Roger and Dori on one side and Annie and George on the other. The Exotic Animal Caravan was already a dome. The purr was a dome and a force field. His mother, who said she didn't want another boyfriend, was getting one. And Roger and Dori. He had the strong urge to jump on Roger and wrestle him down, which Roger would permit and enjoy, but they were having a conversation, Dori looking straight at him while Roger talked, then swinging her head in dips of understanding, the purr immensely in their faces.

Dawson felt something in him settle, some inner rain collecting, like Bluey's poem, *finds the lowest place and stills.* Everything makes sense at the lowest place, where every two cents comes to rest.

He set his laptop on the grass and rose, drawn by El's aloneness. The tiger was haunch-sitting, facing away from the blanket, and as Dawson approached, he rose, paced once around his cage and haunch sat facing him.

El said, "Did you see that?"

Dawson said, "What?"

"Oh, just he reads minds. He felt you coming. What are you working on?"

Dawson sat, embraced his knees. He said, "I have this wild idea."

"The dome?"

He looked at her. "Right."

"Bluey told me. I think it's a great idea."

"Really?"

"I do, really."

He turned to her, scrambling his legs across each other. He hunched forward. He said, "I'm trying to convince myself it's a dumb idea, and so far I can't. I'm really calm for some reason. You know, I haven't touched Bhajan yet."

Dawson got to his feet, crossed to the cage, and put his arms through the bars five feet from Bhajan, so that the tiger could come to him, or not. Annie turned from George and frowned. Roger and Dori watched. Bhajan lifted his hind quarters, strolled along the cage front, nosed Dawson's hands, then passed by, letting Dawson trail fingers along his flank, then turned and resumed his seat. A silent sigh passed through them all. Dawson crossed back to El, sat again. He leaned forward, spoke softly. "The best thing is, Roger and Dori. They are getting along great. I'm gonna wrestle him down." Dawson sprang to his feet and tackled Roger from behind, driving him to the side and down onto the blanket.

Roger said, "Help, help!"

•

The thought came, the robot dog is transfusing me, like on the chopper when they put a gallon of blood through Miguel Aqua, and Miguel was cheery all the way in and lived, the blood keeping him flush and up, and he didn't know his feet were gone until two days later. The dog is pumping in dog blood vigor. He could no longer see the greasy blue glints. He could think now and see the future, the next hour of it at least, or more, if his ideas came true.

First thing, make a sneak. She would be in the RV or a truck. Make a sneak, and take a peek. He was made of courage. Courage was running in his blood now, from the mysterious agency of the robot dog who had found him again and rescued him from becoming a statue.

He passed the gas station where he had reconnoitered the fairgrounds. It was dark, one light bulb beaming above the door, a red Slurpee sign lit in the window. He was driving fast, and when he turned the SUV onto the parking lot road, he and the robot dog tilted together against the turn, then came upright, in harmony, which was their silent relationship. At the parking lot entrance, he spun the wheel and drove through the entry chain which clanged the fenders and pinged as it flew apart. The lot was empty, no guard cars even for the walking guards. He doused the lights. He had driven though the chain, and now doused the lights and felt the form of his underneath plan, which he hadn't said in his mind yet. Cross the parking lot and park by the fence and have the SUV close in case. No decisions had been made though. Something was building though. You had to have courage, and first thing, have the SUV ready. Just the first link to accomplish in a link of things, but nothing was decided. How things got planned as you vagued through life, which everyone did. How you think of a Slurpee on a hot day. Then you're in the convenience store, and there's the Slurpee machine. Then an hour later there's a red stain on your T-shirt and an empty Slurpee cup, so you got a Slurpee and can hardly remember it. Which was the truth of life, how you got steered, then went to sleep and woke and got steered, then died, and that was life. Except if he did not shirk or look away, but instead, with dog blood pounding, forthrightly followed your deep needs.

He parked the SUV by the fence in case of a fast getaway.

•

Bluey woke from a strong dream. There was a party at his house with students and friends. Rosa was there, visiting from the land of the dead. For some reason, she wasn't permitted to speak but stayed close as he played darts with a student, who was Dawson and also El. Then he had to go to the front door to let someone in. It was raining a torrent of fierce rain. The porch was large and wooden, a farmhouse porch. On the porch was JJ in a white T-shirt, clinging and translucent with rain-water. He shivered and paced. Bluey said, "Come in," but JJ could only pace, turning back and forth on the porch like a carnival target.

Goose had woken him. He stood on his hind legs, forepaws on the sheet, and whimpered into his ear. Bluey swung his legs out of bed and sat for a moment, letting the dream set. He knew it was deep-rooted, but its sense did not emerge. He set it in memory for later when he was awake and clear.

Goose flicked his head and again whimpered. Bluey gave the dog a single ear scrub, then bent through the curtain, stretched, and cranked open the cab door. Goose scrambled past him and dropped onto the grass, then turned, looked up, and again whimpered. Then he spun in a circle and yipped.

Bluey said, "Pee, Goose. Pee pee."

He closed the cab door. There was another yip, then silence. He backed through the curtain and got into bed. If Goose demanded entry again, he would yip him awake. But he might sleep with the kids under the tiger. Which might have been why he whimpered, to be near Bhajan.

Something tugged at his mind. But he needed sleep. Just before his consciousness dropped away, he heard a single distant yip.

•

El heard the close huff of an animal, felt a moist nose against her own, and came awake. She lifted the blanket with a forearm to find Goose's head wavering in the gloom. The purr was loud above. She closed her eyes, dropped a hand across Goose's muzzle. She tried to relax toward sleep. Goose snouted the hand aside and made a short whimper. She pulled the blanket between them, rolled away. She heard the whimper again, then felt his snout against her back. Good lord. Whatever it was, in a moment he would wake the others. Besides, she could pee. She tossed the blanket aside, crawled into the circle of halogen, and stood in her hippo pajamas. Bhajan's large head was two feet away, erect and purring. Their watchman, as they slept. Goose pranced in place. She gestured open-hands, what? Goose came to a four-footed alert, blond and straight backed. She was struck with his beauty, with his essence of noble dogness. She knelt, slid hands along his cheeks and eyes, which closed and opened. He made a moaning whimper. She whispered, "What?" She scrubbed his ears, stood, made a noiseless one hand clap for him to follow. She walked past George's tent, saw the mound of a single sleeping bag, which meant he was alone. She went through the stockade gap. Goose followed. When she turned toward the RV, he made another whimper, this one emphatic. She one hand clapped again and continued walking. As she opened the RV door, she held up a palm and whispered, "Stay, Goose. I'll be right back" As she closed the RV door, she heard another whimper, then the scutter of feet.

•

JJ saw the blond dog coming in a fast trot, high-headed in the moonlight and guard dog stiff. He skinned off his T-shirt and wound it around his left forearm. He slid out his Gerber and knelt in the grass. That the dog would stream out of the fortress to attack seemed proper. But if he would kill a dog, then he was in the plan, not outside it, and he saw now, as he approached the trailers, he had partway been outside it, until the blond dog came streaming, and the knife came up hard and brutal and not dreamy. He touched the tip to the earth, then stabbed the blade hilt deep. Earth blood soaked up through his arms. Where was the robot dog? The blond dog came on, fifty yards away now. JJ looked behind him, and there, flattened against the grass, nose at his socked feet, the robot dog was hiding, or lurking, since the dog had properties.

Twenty-five yards and no hesitation. A fine straight ahead assault, splendid but unwise. JJ pulled the knife from the earth, stood on his knees, presented his shirted forearm, poised the knife low for a heart strike. He was in the plan now. He had come halfway, and the plan had rushed out to meet him.

Ten yards and the blond dog accelerated, then launched, fanged-mouthed and silent. Three feet from the wrapped forearm and cocked knife, a bundle struck, knocking the blond dog sideways and onto the grass. There was a snarl-less melee of dog feet, a sharp yip, a low grunt, then silence. The robot dog held the throat for another five seconds, then released, trotted to JJ, and stood, pointed toward the zoo. JJ fished up his keys and LED penlight and examined the body. The throat was crumpled and bloody, the eyes empty. Sad but good. Otherwise, he should knife the dog in the heart in case, and the dog was beautiful and courageous.

•

Before entering the bathroom, El eased open Annie's door, and there was Annie on her side in her bed, not in George's tent. Still, the movie had begun. They meet. Vitality is present. George was Bluey's old friend, a sober, friendly man. El wished it. She enclosed them in wide wings and urged. As she closed the door, through the partly open blinds, she saw a pin of light flash on and off. A firefly. Or something.

She finished in the bathroom, drank from her palm at the sink, then stepped out of the RV, pressing the door silently closed. She said, "Psst, psst. Goose."

Patti stepped out from the rear of the RV, followed by JJ, who said, "Can you believe it? This dog came to my room again."

23

JJ heard the RV door open and popped back into the shadow, then saw El descend the steps in pink pajamas, turn, and gently press the door closed. She made a shush sound and said, *Goose*. Then the robot dog stepped into the light, and that was his cue and sounding trumpet to enter fate. He stepped out, revealed in the halogen from the tiger cage. He spoke something about the robot dog. El looked across, fear-frozen. He made a hands tossing, shrugging gesture as he walked toward her, crafting innocence. Still, she stepped back. He stopped, pointed a finger. The point became a slow finger wag. He said, "The worst thing would be to wake everyone up. That would be the worst." It hurt him to menace, but he must. Then he shined innocence again. He said, "I came here to see if I could keep this dog. And you know what happened? Step around here. You can see in the moonlight." He turned and gestured her to follow. He veiled himself in indifference. He could not flinch. He must be a ruthless spellcaster. She followed. Her eyes were on him, but her head began to turn toward the stockade. She might bolt. He stopped. She stopped, but a step later, and the distance between them closed.

He said, "Will you take it easy, so I can just get this done?" He gestured, and she followed. Now they were past the RV, with only three hundred yard of grass between them and the parking lot and SUV. He pointed. He said, "Can you see that white spot?"

She nodded.

"Guess what that is? Come on, I'll show you."

El did not move. She said, "What is it?"

"Come on." When she did not move, he added low-voiced, "I mean it." He gestured. She followed. Her obedience was crucial, but his cruelty was agony. He had followed fate, and it split him, loving need and brutal need, and the halves were excruciating, but welded by fate, whose agent was the robot dog, pacing ahead now, leading them. They reached the dead dog.

El dropped to her knees. She said, "Oh, Goose." She lifted the dog's head. She said, "Oh, baby."

JJ said, "That dog attacked me. I didn't kill it. This other dog killed it. Come on. It's dead."

"We have to get Bluey."

"No, I can't have any Bluey. He's just what I don't want. You come with me. Don't worry. This is my last night. Now come on."

El looked at him. He could feel her evaluating chances.

He said, "I run like a deer. No harm will come to you. Even if you run, I won't hurt you. But I will catch you."

El said, "Where are we going?"

"I just want to talk to you. I've got something to show you on my computer. I made a video of you which I've been watching. Probably let's go back to my hotel room. You'll be safe. I don't want sex, so don't think that. I even hate saying that. Come on." He gestured, took a step. She took a step with him. He took another. She took another. Then they were walking toward the SUV.

El said, "You made a video?"

"Yes. Do you know the tune, *Little Jenny Dow*?"

"I've heard of it."

"I put the video to that. I watch it every day. You have no idea of the affect you have on me. I have lived a short and brutal life, you could say. But it seemed long. Here's my plan. Come to the hotel room, and we'll talk just a while. Then you can go. I had this idea of taking you to Canada, but that would mean kill everybody that came by. I won't kill anymore, don't worry."

"You killed in Iraq?"

"Yes, I did. You start to think, well, there is no death, or else that's all there is. Either all this killing will balance out because there is no death really, or else death is the natural correct state, and life popped up by accident millions of years ago, and now death has to kill it all down. That was my conclusion, that last one. Then you came. I just want to have a short talk. You may think I'm crazy and, don't worry, I admit it. My mind moves away from me sometimes. My life is about over, which is fine. You know what, I could give you a check for a million dollars. Would that be good? I could give you the whole thing. I could write a will, which I will do tonight. I know you will spend the money wisely. It's around twenty million. I'll get the clerk to sign it. You're safe."

They walked for a moment in silence.

El said, "I'm so scared. But I feel sorry for you."

"That makes sense."

Ahead of them, Patti pranced sideways, looking back, then resumed her trot.

JJ said, "See that? That dog wants me to kill you. She is willing it with all her little might. I could shoot this dog, but it might dodge the bullets. It probably could. Besides, it's my ally. One thing that makes death so great is that then it's all over, or else it's not, and you find out the truth. Why doesn't everybody kill themselves is a pretty good question."

El said, "You won't find it out in death. You can only do that in life."

"That's a perfect thing to say. That doesn't make it trite, I don't mean that. But it's the perfect thing if you like life. You say, stay with us, stay here. But some are not happy in life. I haven't met anyone that's happy. Maybe you are. You have some power. See the robot dog?" Patti had pranced sideways again, again looked back. "I'm making her nervous. She's my ally, but she's crazier than me, I bet. Watch this." JJ pulled his five shot from his pants pocket, cocked it, aimed it at the dog, who looked briefly back, then continued its methodical trot. JJ uncocked the revolver, slid it into his pocket. "She knows I won't shoot. I'll tell you one thing, this is tremendously exciting, me being here with you and this crazy dog. It's the most significant thing that ever happened to me. I'm glad about that anyway. Just an hour or two, El. I'm very relaxed. That's the first time I ever said your name to you. El is an ancient name for God. I looked it up. It's probably the most beautiful name. You can't say it without feeling it in your chest, did you know that, which I bet is why they named God that? I know it's like I stole the cross out of a church or something. Don't worry, I'm giving it back." Again Patti made a sideways stuttering step. "I got the robot dog on a string. Every time I say something that means I'm not going to kill you she gets jumpy. I'm not going to kill her! No reaction now. That's a smart dog. We're connected, and we can't fool each other."

They had come to the wooden fence. Patti slunk under the bottom rail. El and JJ straddled across the top. She followed him to the SUV's passenger door. He opened it.

He said, "Please get in, El." He heard a stifled sob, saw her shudder. She got into the passenger seat, looked straight ahead. He closed the door. He said, "That was brave. Probably you'll be stronger after this."

A car turned into the parking lot. Its headlights came directly toward them. JJ crossed to the driver's side, started the SUV, pulled away at normal speed. The car turned and parked, dousing its headlights as they passed. El turned her face into the lights, mouthing the word *help* just before the lights extinguished.

•

Roger lifted his head. The purr continued above him. But another sound had woken him.

"Sorry," said a voice beside his ear. "I was trying to be quiet."

"Dori?"

"Yes. I couldn't sleep, so I went to Walmart and got a sleeping bag. I thought I'd sleep under the tiger with you guys after all. I left room for El if she comes back."

"El?"

"Yeah. She was leaving as I came in. She was in an SUV with somebody."

"Oh, Jesus," said Roger and threw off his blanket.

•

JJ was sitting on the bed. He scraped fingernails across his temples, held his head. "Whoa," he said. "I just had a flash. My brother is fucking me. And my uncle is sucking me. That might be a memory. Oh man. I bet I could remember it all if I wanted to. Just what I wanted. All this time. But guess what, it's a trivial insight. All this time, and it's a trivial insight." El was seated on the sofa with a lamp lighting the side of her face, JJ's laptop on her knees. Patti was sprawled on the bathroom tile, watching. "Maybe it frees up your energies, but not that much. I already accepted that. I knew that's what they did. They're dead now. They killed themselves. They ruined their lives. They abused me, and it cut them off from their hearts. That's what they didn't know. That's everybody's trouble." His head sagged, then lifted. He looked at El. He said again, "That's everybody's trouble."

El said, "Yes. That we don't love."

JJ laughed. "God, you're a fountain of wisdom. I know I made you up. I know that. You say you liked the video, but I know it's crazy I made that video. But that's fine. You keep it though, if you want to. Or show it to the cops. They might want it. But I wouldn't mind if you kept it."

El closed the laptop. She said, "Oh, stop that! Just stop it. Are you going to kill yourself right in front of me? Is that it? Don't you know how awful that would be?" She burst into tears. "If you really mean it, don't do it. We have a tiger in our zoo. This tiger will make you feel much better. Completely completely better!" She stroked the tears away, jerked in breath against the next impulse of sobbing.

JJ made a low grunting sound as her pain entered him. He said, "Oh, man. How did we get here?" He let his head sag. He lifted his head. "What do you mean? Explain about the tiger."

El said, "We have a tiger that was raised by a holy man in India. He purrs all night long, which is unknown in tigers. And he—he heals us from the inside. You could have that."

There was a long silence. JJ head slowly sagged again.

El said, "It's true. You can't say anything in words about it."

JJ said, "That was good. I mean to say that about you can't say it in words. Because I was thinking, oh man, they got a cult. Have you guys got a cult?"

"No."

"Are you making this up?"

"No."

"A purring tiger with special powers. Well, that makes sense. Because here's this robot dog which is a being of some type. She's a dark being though. Earlier I was encased in grease. It's what they call catatonia, I'm fairly sure. Where you don't feel like going on. You fade into the grease. I almost did. But this dog saved me. It's coming back though, I can feel it. When I thought you were in a cult, I could feel the grease again. I know I made you up. You can't save me. It's not your fault. Here." He stood, fished his revolver from his front pocket, laid it on the laptop. "Just have it for now, while we talk. Let's talk just a short time more. I'm getting so many insights. I didn't make you up entirely. You're worth a video. You should be exalted. I think we have to exalt things because we live in the garbage. And we send people to war. Wars are completely different from everything else. I'm not going to kill myself in front you. How about this—I won't kill myself at all."

"Then let me take the gun when I leave."

He threw one hand briefly to the side, stabbed toward her with an index finger. He smiled. "Well, good point. No, you can't take the gun. I had this plan earlier. I would jump off a building and shoot myself on the way down. As insurance. Pretty soon, the nicest thing for me to do is just let you walk out the door. I'll give you some money for a cab. Oh damn, I forgot about the will. You have to take that will. Let's see." JJ rose, crossed to the desk, opened drawers. He withdrew a small scratch pad. "I'll write a note to my mother. She's the only one that would contest it. Well, my father might, so I'll write him too. This is the best I can do, El. I don't want to stay around that much longer, and beside the grease could get me before I got to a lawyer. Basically, you say you are feeling sane, and here's what you want done with your money."

"If you kill yourself you'll become a ghost. I've just been reading about that. All your karma doesn't get finished, so you have to be a ghost until it's done. That can be hundreds of years."

"That wouldn't be so bad." He began to write. *I, John Jefferson Bartle, being of sound mind—* "El, I will need your last name and address. And social security number."

"I will never take your money, JJ. I will never do it."

He looked at her for a moment. "You might change your mind though."

"I won't. Can't you see how awful that would be for me?"

JJ hung his head and sighed. He said, "Yes, I do. I see that."

"Do you think your mother and father are awful? What about them?"

JJ looked at her for a moment. "You're trying to talk me back to normal. Normal is far away. Anyway, normal is awful too. That's why those guys get guns and start killing everybody. They get broken off from normal, and there's nowhere else to go. Normal is a cheat. But I don't mind. I just don't want to sit in grease for fifty years. I'd rather be a ghost."

El covered her face, made a sobbing gasp, then looked up, bright with tears. "No no no no no. If you kill yourself it will so much break my heart. It might ruin my life. You're way way way too much of a person to do that. No, you must live, and fight out of the grease."

"Well, thank you for that, El. Hey, you know what? I'll leave the money to the zoo. I'll donate it to the zoo." He began to write. Outside the room there were engine sounds and car doors opening. El crossed the room, tried to grab the pen. He held it away, amazed.

The bay window imploded in a storm of glass. A massive tiger landed sure-footed in the room's center, tumbling the sofa, laptop and revolver onto the carpet. A bolt of brown shot from the bathroom, sprinted across the carpet, and launched itself at the tiger's throat. Bhajan's massive jaws darted forward, caught Patti's head in a vice of teeth. There was a soft *crump,* and the dog's body swung limply from the tiger's jaws.

JJ stood. He said, "That must be your tiger." The revolver had come to rest at his feet. He picked it up and put it to his temple. He saw the tiger bound forward. He fired.

24

Roger cranked open the cab door and leaned inside. He said, "Bluey, wake up. Bluey!"

Bluey's head appeared through the curtains. He said, "What is it?"

"El is gone. Dori saw her leaving the parking lot in an SUV. You were talking about that guy JJ. So would she—"

Bluey cut him off. "Is Dawson there? Ask him if he knows where JJ is staying. I'm getting dressed."

Roger turned and trotted back to the zoo grounds. He was still in his boxer shorts.

Two minutes later Bluey arrived at the tiger cage. Bhajan had stopped purring. When he saw Bluey, he bounded to the cage door and struck it with his flank. The door made a clanging boom.

Roger said, "Dawson doesn't know, Bluey. Should we call the cops?"

George said, "What's happening, Bluey? You think this guy took her?"

"He took her, yes. She wouldn't have gone with him."

Dawson fished up his phone. "I'll call 911."

They heard the booming clang again and looked at the tiger. "Wait," said Bluey. He walked to the tiger cage door. Bhajan stood, head lowered, waiting for him. As he approached, Bhajan lifted his head, lowered it, a long slow nod. Bluey lifted the lock cover.

Dori said, "What's he doing? Is he gonna—"

George said, "Bluey, what are you doing? Wait, wait." He was moving, but as he reached Bluey, the door swung open, and Bhajan bounded onto the grass. The tiger turned, a cat-fast swirl of black and orange in the halogen, and trotted to the puma's cage. He stood before the door, gazed behind him at Bluey. Bluey approached. He lifted the lock cover of Clark's cage. Beside him, the tiger's head reached his shoulder.

George said, "Maybe we should get into the tiger cage."

Dawson said, "We don't need to."

Clark's door swung open, and the puma paced out, swinging his head from side to side. Bhajan trotted to the hyena cage. As Bluey followed, he called to Dawson, "Dawson. Get the van. Run now."

Dawson sprinted.

Nubia stood at the door of her cage waiting. The massive hyena head nosed forward toward the lock as Bluey entered the code. The door opened, and she leapt onto the grass. As she fell in beside Clark, the puma bumped her with his shoulder, a greeting.

Bluey followed Bhajan to the lion cage. As they approached, Demijohn roared, and as the door swung opened roared again. He bounded onto the grass, turned sharply, fast trotted to Clark and Nubia. Bhajan wheeled away and sprinted toward the stockade gap. Demijohn, Clark, and Nubia followed.

Annie, tying her robe, emerged bare-footed from the RV as Bluey and the others came through the stockade. The van's headlights jounced across the field. They bundled inside the van and followed the running animals, who were strung out now, Bhajan in the lead. The van's headlights illuminated something blond in the green grass.

Dawson slowed. Goose's body, bloody-necked and open-eyed, flared in the headlights.

Bluey said, "Drive."

The animals reached the fence and leapt. As the van approached, Bluey said, "Go through. Break it." Dawson did. Boards exploded. One headlight shattered, but one remained and followed the racing beasts.

After a mile they passed a sheriff's cruiser coasting to a stop at an intersection. It pulled in behind them, light flashing and siren starting. It passed them, illuminating the beasts with its headlights, then killed its siren. In another mile, a second cruiser entered the chase and tailed behind the van, lights flashing, siren silent. The animals passed under the freeway, turned right onto an access road, and into the Holiday Inn parking lot. Three of them, the puma, the lion, and the hyena, turned to face the sheriff cruiser that slid to a stop at the parking lot entrance. Bhajan dove through a bay window. A pistol shot sounded. The sheriff's deputy remained in his cruiser, spoke frantically into his radio. The van passed him, stopped in front of the animals. They scrambled out. Dawson climbed through the broken window and opened the door. When they entered, they found El kneeling on the carpet holding a washcloth to JJ's head.

She said, "Get an ambulance."

Bluey walked to the two cruisers, now parked beside each other.

"There's a man shot," he said. "Call an ambulance."

He walked back to the hotel room, ushering Clark, Nubia, and Demijohn before him. When the paramedics arrived, the two deputies entered the hotel room first, guns drawn.

Bluey said, "The animals are secured in the bathroom. They are completely safe. You won't need guns."

25

Dawson's assistant entered the bathroom as Dawson was zipping his fly. His assistant propped a buttock on the sink counter, found that position static, walked along the front of the stalls, gave each door a light fist bang, watched them swing. Dawson came to the sinks, began to wash his hands.

His assistant said, "Here's a tip. Wash your dick now and then, and you won't have to wash your hands."

Dawson smiled.

His assistant propped a buttock on the counter again. He said, "Okay, greater than love is obedience. First, it's hard to imagine anything greater than love. But okay. But he hasn't given *me* any orders! Me personally. So what is obedience to me! What do I obey! I mean if you just say, no greed, lust, or anger, that's morality, which fucked up the world with self-righteousness, right? So how does this work? I can't hold it. I don't see it in a smooth way, and that's my danger."

Dawson dried his hands, began to adjust his tie in the mirror.

His assistant came off the counter, turned Dawson toward him. He said, "I'll do that. I'm the valet." He snugged the knot, stroked the tie neat.

Dawson said, "How do I look?"

His assistant observed him critically. He removed a thread from the shoulder of Dawson' suit. "You're good. I have tidied you."

Dawson said, "You did it with love?"

His assistant looked at him. His mouth opened. His good eye shined. He said, "Ah, man. It's love first, then we have to live, so then it's obedience. That's exactly what it is. It could just be love if you never did anything. But as soon as you come in contact with other people, then it's obedience! Love in action is obedience. I'm gonna write that on my forehead."

Dawson said, "Write it on your heart, sprout."

His assistant laughed. "One day I won't be squirming around so much. Right now I'm exhibiting obedience because I want to embrace you, but I don't because of wrinkles. Are you ready?"

"I guess."

"Let me adjust your bandolier." The assistant adjusted Dawson's imaginary bandolier of ideas, the jokey rift they started after Dawson stopped using notes. They had been on a speaking tour for three weeks, and in that time Dawson had learned to speak extemporaneously, letting one thought pull the next until the bandolier of bullet points was through his mind. This was their last stop before returning to the Exotic Animal Ecopark. The grand opening was Saturday. On Friday they would sleep in their cabins in the ecopark settlement.

They left the bathroom, walked down the hallway, and entered the gym. It was a middle school auditorium, and the podium was set up under the basketball goal. It was a few minutes after seven in the evening, and the bleachers were full of people from the surrounding communities, and the other end of the auditorium was dense with people standing. Dawson and his assistant sat in folding chairs behind the podium while Alice Henderson, the young school principal and coordinator of the meeting, made the introduction.

Dawson took the podium. He let the applause settle, thanked them for coming, thanked Alice, mentioned handouts would be available on tables at the exits.

He said, "Half of you, maybe most of you, are here because the Exotic Animal Caravan. Some of you may have even read the books—boy, they get those out fast—and all of you I expect have seen the videos, particularly the squad car video of those four big beasts racing through the night. So the ecopark is famous, which is great, because that's what an ecopark needs to be. The grand opening is this Saturday, and we definitely hope you'll come. The original animals will all be there, of course, plus a lot more which have been coming in from all over. And of course Bhajan will be there.

"Now I always get questions about Bhajan so I'll take a moment to address that. Bhajan is a large Bengal tiger, raised in captivity in India by a mast—also called a god-intoxicated soul. All this is in the books, and all three of them are accurate as far as they go. And at one time Bhajan purred, which is abnormal in tigers, and that purr lifted our spirits, which is how we think of it. And that's it. The rest is mystery. It happened, and it was invisible. Probably the lifting of spirits is always invisible. Which brings me to my subject tonight, which is the dome."

He told them then that in a year's time a community center would be finished, that it was free and fully funded, that it was fifteen minutes or less away from five hundred thousand people. He described its structure—a hundred and ten yards in diameter, and with seven foot high movable walls inside, so that everyone could feel there was one space for all. Fifty different groups could meet and each have fifteen hundred square feet.

He said, "Bluey Macintosh and I were talking about the dome and how it could work and the problems you could have because the world isn't perfect and people aren't either, and he laughed and said he and his wife Rosa figured out one day how to make a perfect world. He said it was simple. They would just people it with Blueys and Rosas, because they loved each other. And then you could have any kind of government, and it wouldn't matter, because everybody would be dear, and nobody would be poor and nobody would hoard, and there would be no pollution or war and people would probably have to work three or four hours a day, and then what? Paint pictures, play games, look around, see if everyone was all right. Tell stories to children. All Blueys and Rosas. And of course you guys could make a perfect world too, if you could people it with yourself and your loved ones. You might get exasperated now and then, but you would never punish anyone with lifelong poverty or ignorance. And you would never take so much that others had too little or had to live in a chemical stew, because you wouldn't think you *ought* to love and cherish people, you actually *would*.

"I like that thought experiment because it points up the central problem with living together in groups. We are thick-skinned and self-centered and don't see ourselves or our loved ones in others. And that simple truth, that we don't see ourselves in others, is pretty much the root problem, and all other problems are just results. If we can't see ourselves in others, it's hard to live together, no matter how you organize it. If we do, it's no problem at all. In a government of saints, you don't need rules. In a government of cobras, even the innocent must be imprisoned.

"A spiritual master once commented that people shout when they are angry because they are far apart and can't hear each other. When they calm down and come closer, they talk normally, and when they are closer still they begin to whisper, and when they are really in tune and love each other, they don't need words at all and are silent. That's a beautiful progression, isn't it? And I think everyone gets that it's deeply true. As we come closer in love and begin to recognize each other, it's like emerging from a fog. Oh, it's you. Good thing I didn't pull the trigger. Good thing I didn't build a fence.

"This leads to another point which I like. I can't prove it, but it's a great hypothesis, because if it's true, it solves everything, which definitely makes it worth considering. The hypothesis is that we are all one. And that there is a soul, and we are it. I don't mind using the word *God* here, but some people do, and anyway it's got a lot of fingerprints on it. So let's leave God out on the porch for a moment. If he really is infinite consciousness, he'll find something to do."

Laughter rolled through the crowd. He let it fade.

"But just imagine, what if existence is really that, a divine manifestation? And the purpose of life is to *get* that, and recognize that other people, even if they're Republicans or Democrats or Muslims, are the same soul. Pretty good hypothesis. It makes complete sense of the deep natural values of every culture. It's why everyone likes humility better than vanity. Humility recognizes other people. Vanity doesn't. We like thoughts and feelings that remind us that we are the same.

"Before I get to the dome, here's another thing Bluey said. I love Bluey Macintosh, and if the world were made just of Blueys and Dawsons I think we would all get along great. Though sadly there would be no children."

He let the laughter fade.

"Here's what Bluey said—if people are honest and patient they are compelled by the nature of existence itself to agree about everything. I love that thought. Some people instantly get that. Some people say, hey, wait a minute. But eventually everybody gets it. Honest people must agree. We're used to fighting for our opinions because we think if we give them up, we'll lose all the truth we have. But if the truth really is that we are all one, then it's something you can't fight for. You have to love for it. You might say, yeah, damnit, religions always get that backwards. But it's us. We're the religions.

"Which reminds me that I've left God on the porch. But after all that's where we mostly like him, so the neighbors can see him. If you really want to invite him in, go to the back door. He likes the kitchen best, where you do your living and feeling. Whether or not we see God on your porch, we can always tell if he's in your kitchen.

"So what is the dome? I guess it's a place to test out that hypothesis, that we are all one. And what do people do when they recognize each other? Basically they don't talk so much about what life's all about anymore. Or spend time making sure other people agree with them. They have felt love, and they know other people will figure it out when they start to love too. So they play. They make things together. They teach each other. They talk and tell stories. The dome is a place for that. I know that among the crowd tonight are representatives from clubs and organizations in several counties and most welcome to you all. I have the list—the southern cooking club, storytellers, scrapbookers. I see magicians are here, book clubs, backgammon players, eurogames. Count me in on eurogames. I'm a big fan.

"And by the way, to sort of tune everybody up when they come in, we are going to put a big bowl at the entrance and everybody has to put in two cents. That's the entry fee. Everybody has to leave their two cents at the door. Just a fun reminder to unpack a little when you enter, and also, hey, that two cents could add up."

Laughter rose and faded.

"I'm young. I know it, and I feel it. I am not disappointed yet. If the dome is a failure and nobody comes or everybody bickers, I *will* be disappointed, but I don't think that disappointment will last or go very deep. It won't disturb my hypothesis, that we are all one, because that hypothesis is not based on the outside world, but on the inside one. Anyway, I think that hypothesis is taking root, and not just in me. We are all one. When people hear that it usually feels happy and truthful and starts a little current inside them. A happy current, and I think that little happy current is the main evidence we have for divinity. At least it's the right place to begin. You don't need to believe in God in order to feel him. We got that backwards too. There's a scent in the air these days, and you smell it when young people say, it's all good, don't be a hater, and you feel it in the fact that through the internet everybody is able to see everybody else for the first time in the history of the earth. First time. We're all sort of used to the internet, or we might think it's for business or being social, but I suspect it's more amazing that anyone can imagine. It's like the world is suddenly full of mirrors, and everybody can notice everybody. Which makes some people crazy, and they get in the news, and you sometimes think it's too much too fast, and we're going to explode. But most of us aren't in the news. Almost all of us aren't in the news, or on TV or the radio blasting away at our enemies or planting bombs. I'm in the generation called the millennials. And I definitely didn't come to be a hater. I definitely didn't come to defend a point of view. I think that's what we're starting to get, maybe millennials especially. We grew up with the internet, and it's a banquet of points of views, and you get to taste them all, and you start to develop a pretty generous palette. It's in your blood. I can't prove any of this, but I sense it, and maybe you do too because here you are. We're all sort of like dogs that way. We rely on scent, and the scent in the air today is, don't be a hater, it's all good, we are one. Another name for that is love.

"We're not saints, but we're not cobras either. We're somewhere is the middle, and the dome is a place where we can come together, come out of the fog and recognize each other, and figure out how to live. That's my pitch, folks. Thank you for having me, and now I'll be happy to take questions. My assistant will hand around the microphone."

The applause was instant and thunderous.

JJ came to the podium with the radio mike. He embraced Dawson fervently.

Dawson said, "Maybe start the mike on the left there."

JJ said, "Fucking A, Mister Man." He crossed to the bleachers and handed the mike up to a young woman who had raised her hand.

•

As JJ's finger had tightened on the trigger, Bhajan's paw reached his chest. The bullet passed through the zygomatic arch, destroying the right eye and exiting the base of his nose. He woke in the hospital embedded in grease. From time to time the right side of his face flashed pain, but the pain was outside the grease and unimportant. His face on that side was snugged with bandages. When he opened his left eye he could see the grease. It sepiaed the world in soothing blue. Nurses came, fiddled and twiddled, went away. Doctors came, men and women, spoke among themselves, sometimes to him, but their words could not penetrate. They passed blue hands across his vision. They talked and moved and went away. Time passed, then stopped passing and stayed. He was in time. Time was blue and solid, and he went away.

Then he heard a voice, and time started again like a far off hum, like faded footsteps fading back. He went away again but not as far, and the voice returned, reading something now, and on and on, and the voice held up the photo of a mustachioed Italian baker, bluefaced and smiling, and on and on, and it was El's voice, and her face was there, waving in the blue, and she said *JJ, JJ, JJ.* Then they were dressing him, and he was in a wheelchair wheeling, and they drove him, and there was blue evening and blue grass and then a blue tiger, and the hum of time came up and clear, and it was the tiger purring beside him and on and on, and the Italian baker smiled, and one morning he woke and said, "I'm alive, right?"

•

A local dairy farmer offered his pasture, and they set the zoo there while the county, state, and federal investigators made inquiries. Wild animals had roamed the streets, the public had been endangered, penalties were required. The county sheriff visited the farm, spoke to Bluey. He observed the animals. He stayed for dinner. He listened to the purr until three in the morning. The next day he released the squad car video of the chase. It went wildly viral. In the end, the federal people left things to the state, the state left it to the county, and circuit court fined the zoo a hundred dollars.

JJ was discharged from the hospital in a week and a half, and at El's request, they brought him to Bhajan. George, who had extended his vacation, tended his wound. Dori returned to Oklahoma City but was back in a week. This time she stayed at the zoo, sleeping under the tiger with the others.

The animals had been released from their cages and wandered freely now in the woods and along the stream and pond. Visitors and news vans began to line the road. Eventually the stockade was erected across the pasture as a privacy screen. Fuad and Haley arrived and spent hours in conversation with Bluey. The tour was canceled, disappointing the internet. Plans were made to drive directly to the ecopark.

In the daytime, JJ wandered the forest. Bluey found him there and sat with him beside the pond and told him he was with them now and that this was his place until he wanted something else. JJ listened to the purr each night, all night awake, sitting on a blanket away from the others. He ate a single meal each day, prepared by Annie and brought by El.

JJ felt himself climbing down a ladder, coming back and down, back from madness and down into the basement of childhood and the madness there, then up again, and he was on the earth for the first time and rooting, and the weeping began, surprising him on walks or listening to the purr, sometimes waking the others. El restrained their sympathy, advising isolation. One day Dawson followed him into the woods and sat beside him and explained the universe, which he could do now in an amazed funny cooling way. The Italian baker was Meher Baba. Life is simple and interesting and worth it. He had an idea for a dome too.

26

El, the park curator, had a staff of ten, two for the office, eight for the grounds. It was October. Schools were in session, and the next day, the grand opening, the parking lots would be filled with dozens of school buses, tour buses, and cars. Bluey had hired a public relations firm in Chicago, who advised them that the ecopark would be overwhelmed for several months at least. El had made a hundred to-do lists and methodically done them, but was fretful. Probably they were ready, but also probably not. She gathered the staff, who had been working for two weeks without a day off, thanked them, gave them a pep talk, and dismissed them for the day. Sleep well. Arrive early. Try to be patient with me. Oh well. She laughed and embraced them all.

She went back to her cabin, then down to the stream behind it where Roger had made a patio for her. She removed her sandals, sat on the flat stones, and put her feet on the gravel into the pleasant shock of the moving cold. Her dog, Little Man, a rat terrier, sat beside her, waited to see if there would be anything more, a stick, an excursion into the woods? He was a rescue dog and entirely dog as far as she knew, since he had heard Bhajan's purr only once. Bhajan no longer purred, except when JJ was present. Dawson and JJ would be back tonight, so everyone was fairly excited. They would all gather at the caravan enclosure, the separate ten acres where the caravan animals had their homes. They would bring their sleeping bags. They would turn off the webcams.

Charlie, George's son, would be there too. He was the staff vet now and ran the ecopark hospital. Yesterday she brought him a wallaby with a broken foot. She could have sent a staff member but took the animal herself. He understood that. He sedated the wallaby and made his inspection. Then he kissed her, very lightly. The kiss said, here's something to think about, and she had, all day under the busyness. He had a steady friendly mind. He was Bluey's nephew, sort of. He had arrived three months ago and had heard the purr several times. Annie, who was married to George now, said, "Well, what about Charlie?" And when El blushed, Annie said, "Good lord. We fell into a karmic stew."

She heard a noise and looked up, and it was Dori, wading in tennis shoes, her belly swelling out her green stretch shorts. She and Roger had a cabin a hundred yards up the creek. He was the park horticulturist, and she was his assistant. She had become an expert backhoe operator. She also worked with George and Annie designing the coffee shop for the education center and gift shop.

Dori sat beside El on the flat stones. She said, "Shouldn't you be running around like a headless chicken?"

El smiled. She said, "Should I get us some iced tea?"

"I'd just have to pee. I pee every ten minutes about."

"Roger said you canceled the ultrasound."

"We did. I finally figured out why. We wanted it to be completely new. A birth, you know? And if you already know, then it's sort of a process or something. I know people do it. Anyway, we canceled it and felt sort of relieved, so I guess it's good. Want to feel a kick? Because, man, you can today." She guided El's hand onto her belly. "You felt that, right?"

El laughed. "That's a twitchy baby."

Dori laughed, then smiled. "It's happening to me. Man, oh man."

"You're blooming."

"Roger says I'm fruiting. Bluey said we'll build a little school. Probably just in time for your child. With Charlie."

"Oh, for god's sake."

"No secrets around here."

El said, "Especially with Annie."

"Very true. If you think it, she says it."

They laughed, dangled their feet for a moment. Dori said, "My mom and dad are coming out in a month and staying the whole time. And guess what, I turned my dad onto the *Discourses*, and he started calling me with questions, so I gave him Bluey's number, and now he bugs Bluey. I asked him first. They're buddies, now. I want them to come quick so they can hear Bhajan before he quits all the way. I want JJ to be done, but not just yet, thank you, JJ. He and Dawson came for dinner, and he talked about his life. He made us all cry and was embarrassed. He said he talks to his mother again. So good there."

"Good there."

"Who knows, he may be a movie star one day."

That summer during camp, beside teaching taekwondo, JJ had taken the role of the one-eyed pirate in Dawson's script. Then he and Dawson and fifteen of the caravan animals, including all nine carnivores, had concocted a comedic skit they called Animal Town, which involved innocent animals, village oppression, and mistaken identities, and which ended in a ferocious melee with several animals and a heroic JJ hurtling through the air. It had been videoed, and several movie studios had contacted the ecopark to inquire about using the caravan animals in film. Two had sent producers to the park and were currently developing scripts. Bluey had let JJ take the lead in the discussions since both studios liked his ease with the animals and his screen presence, including eyepatch and bullet scar, and proposed to include him in the scenarios.

Dori said, "Are you lonely, El?"

"Some."

"Well, Charlie kissed you, which all the world knows."

"About time."

They laughed.

Dori said, "When I was a little girl I used to think, my husband is out there right now, doing something. Roger said God picked me up with tweezers."

El said, "It's all tweezers when you think about it."

"Sometimes we worry we don't fight enough. He's a bit of a slob, but I'm a lazy bitcher. We're waiting for things to get harder."

"Do they have to?"

"Probably not. Anyway, it won't be boring. When Fuad's money came in, Roger's five year plan became a ten year plan."

They were both silent for a moment, pleased with each other's company, the cool water, and everything.

Dori said, "It's like you have a dream that you're living a wonderful life. Then you wake up, and oops, you actually are."

•

When the education center was finished, Bluey wanted an adjoining restaurant, and Annie had agreed to manage it. And became obsessed. For six months while the building went up, she searched books and the internet and juggled restaurant criteria—taste, expense, healthiness, presentation, profit, personnel, cleanliness, complexity of preparation. For a month, George advised and guided, then was outdistanced and simply encouraged. Now his time was split between his son's veterinary clinic and the education center. Plus he missed surgery and drove to Memphis twice a week for fourteen hour stints in an operating room.

Annie heard the thump and opened the door. It was Louie, the UPS guy, who had left a box that had better be the menus, since they were opening tomorrow. She waved to Louie, already down the walk, then took the box to the prep table and opened it. Fifty excellent menus, each a single sheet, gleaming in plastic and designed by Dawson with soft slants of color and freckles of food graphics in lovely friendly minimalism. She had finalized the bill of fare only a week ago, and he had squeezed the project in, working late in hotel rooms on his speaking tour, then sending it to the printer. The last and absolutely final entry had been a three cheese grill cheese sandwich, two Roger-grown fermented cucumber spears, and a chipotle cilantro coleslaw, faintly honeyed. Nine bucks. Such a deal.

George entered the kitchen from the rear door, still in his vet scrubs, twin smears of blood across the belly of the blue smock. He said, "Where is everybody?"

"El and I sent everybody home. I think Roger and Carlos did too." She regarded her husband mildly, giving him leave, as she sometimes thought of it, to emit himself. He emitted humor and sobriety and industry and kindness and, when she was not distracted, woke her love, as he did now. She said, "You've been operating with Charlie. You can't walk around like that tomorrow."

He kissed her directly and briefly. He turned a menu in his big hands. He said, "Gosh, they're art."

"They are."

His hands found her elbows. He stood her up from her stool, laid her head on his chest, embraced her. He said, "Don't fret. The blood is dry."

She said, "Whose blood?"

"That the blood of Charlie, not my Charlie, but our Somali ass, who had a bump on his belly."

"Is he good?"

"The tumor was benign." Charlie was the mayor of Animal Town in Dawson and JJ's skit. George said, "He's good to go for the skit." He stood her back. "Let's drink a beer by the creek, shall we?"

They got beers from the fridge and walked to the wooden footbridge which arched over the creek into the settlement. They sat beneath it on a bench where Roger had built another patio. Annie looked past her husband into the busy water, held him in patient peripheral regard, aware of the comfort of silence. Her off and on jealousy, which before had perplexed her, she better understood. She had no jealousy with old lovers because she didn't love them, and with George no jealousy because she did.

George said, "Bhajan will purr tonight. JJ is back."

"Yes."

"Here's my utopia thought for the day. Everybody must have a stranger room. Which is a guest room, but everyone calls it their stranger room because it's for strangers. You say, look, I just got into town, can I use your stranger room? But oh no, they say, sorry, there's already a stranger in there. But check with my neighbor, Jane. And Jane says, sorry, big game tonight, all the stranger rooms in town are taken. So then what? You go to the square and shout, hey, what about me! Plus, there's a blizzard. So here's the question—will love find a way?"

"And a tidal wave is coming."

"Yes, a tidal wave, for god's sake. I'm filling my heart with love, and first no stranger room and now a goddamn tidal wave!"

They laughed. They could make the points explicit, but they had made them before, and the shorthand was pleasant, and the sound of the water was pleasant.

Annie said, "I thought tomorrow after the park closes we could go out to the dome."

"And watch bulldozers?"

"I know. I want to take pictures though."

"You want to be a mom."

"I do. Dawson said he would give us a tour. He's meeting the geothermal energy people on site."

George took her hand. He said, "Everything is love and restlessness. That should be a book. Actually, it's every book. That's profound."

Annie said, "You are quite profound."

•

The time between five and seven was precious to Bluey. The animals had been fed. His head keeper, Carlos, who had come from California with his snow-hating wife, had dismissed his crew, and Roger had dismissed the grounds crew and landscapers. Half of both crews lived in the dormitory, but that was set on the park's perimeter, and the park was quiet and wild. He drove his golf cart through Roger's recently planted bamboo forest—next year the pandas would arrive—past the dromedaries and Arabian horses—gifts from Fuad—and parked at the gate of the exotic animal caravan. Inside the specially fenced ten acres the original cages had been arranged in a central clearing. The doors had been removed, and each night the beasts returned to their old homes to sleep. Around the perimeter of the ten acres, level with the twelve foot fencing, ran a raised wooden walk with viewing platforms every fifty yards. Trails could be seen crossing and vanishing under the golden cloud of the hardwoods. The internet was busy with rumors that here lions lived with lambs, and the public relations firm advised that this part of the park would of course be the greatest draw. Each platform had drinking fountains and vending machines, and two, on opposite sides, had tiny, Annie-managed cafes and ice cream freezers.

Bluey tapped in the combination and entered. The ten acres had been Roger's first project. A creek wandered along the edge, hesitated in a pond, then fell away in a rocky fall and vanished into a screened culvert under the fence. Beside the creek, they had cleared a meadow, which Roger edged with blue-flowered pickerelweed and orange-flowered trumpet creeper for the hummingbirds. The trees, a native mix of pine and hardwood, were hung with vines and studded beneath with beautyberry, fringetree, and dozens more native species, some goodlooking, some tasty, some both. A sinuous perimeter path of fine-textured hardwood bark intersected other paths which disappeared into the forest. It was an Eden. Spectators would witness carnivores coexisting with their prey. There would be questions. There would be speculation. There would be insistence. But from Bluey and his keepers there would be only a smile and a shrug.

Clark the puma emerged from a thicket. A well-chewed branch of spicebush dropped from his jaws. He grazed his flank along Bluey's knee. Bluey seized the scruff of his neck, gave it a friendly shake, traced two fingertips hard along the spine as it slipped past. Taj chi-chied from a pine tree, and Bluey looked up in time to catch the pine cone that was sailing toward his head. Bluey pointed a finger at the monkey, made a low grunt of disapproval, but tossed the cone back. Taj caught it nimbly with a single hand, then let it fall to the forest floor, accepting his reprimand.

Bluey made a loud two-fingered whistle, announcing his presence, then headed into the forest toward the creek and meadow. Cloe the okapi, trotted down an intersecting path and swung in beside him. Shindig the spider monkey, clung to Cloe's neck, and his buddy Chortle, the raccoon, clung to him. As Bluey walked, he stroked muzzles, ears, eyes, and spines. He passed behind the circle of caravan cages and, fifty yards farther on, entered the meadow at the head of a troop of more than half of the caravan animals. Others splashed across the creek or arrived from alternate paths until the entire caravan, save Charlie and Bart, was assembled. They milled, awaiting his division into the day's teams.

Roger, following Bluey's instruction, had planted two semicircles of haspberry bushes at each end of the meadow. These were the prisons in their daily game of jail tag, Bluey's prescription for exercise. He served as director and referee—tag disputes were common—and was empowered, by imperial fiat, to free any prisoner when the game needed balance or drama, which authority he exercised with careless implacable injustice.

He divided the teams, calling names and waving animals into sides, balancing each contestant against another similar in skill—Tooey the honey badger against Thane the mandrill, Alfie the wild dog against Paris the Siberian lynx, Demijohn the lion against Bhajan, Pumper and Nickel, not always, but today on opposite sides.

Bluey knew Charlie was in the infirmary and now noticed Bart's absence. He said, "Where's Bart?"

Sybil, who had perched on the shoulder of Phoenix, the Himalayan blue sheep, said, "Sick."

Bluey said, "How?"

Sybil said, "Foot."

"Where?"

"Zoo."

Bluey held his hands wide, meaning, listen all. He spoke slowly. "Okay. I go to Bart. You all play. I will come back. One two three!" He swung his hands down. The meadow exploded with leaping, snarling, baaing, chittering, and howling.

Bluey walked fast back to the zoo compound and found Bart the ostrich nested in his cage on a pad of straw. As Bluey approached, Bart presented his foot. The great toenail on his single-pronged foot had been broken away, exposing a crust of red flesh. Bluey ran his hands gently along the muscular neck, then down-patted consultation and authority. He said, "We will fix. All well."

He fished up his cell phone.

Charlie answered, "Yeah, Bluey."

"Bart tore off a toenail. Salve and a wrap at least. He's in his cage. Can you come early?"

"On my way."

They hung up. Bluey said, "Charlie doctor comes. Stay here quiet."

Bart swung his head faintly.

Bluey said, "I go to the game. They kill each other."

Again the head swung. Bluey traced the fingertips of both hands along the neck. He offered his cheek, which Bart lightly pecked. As he returned toward the meadow, he took a side path into the cemetery field where he made a slow circuit of the flower grown-graves of Goose and Patti. Then instead of returning directly to the meadow, he took the short path to the creek and began to pick his way along the stones. He reached the big stone with the flat footrest rock beneath it and sat, his boots a few inches from the tumbling water.

The cacophony from the meadow was insistent, and without his witness, their play would eventually lose flavor. But he took a selfish minute to savor the voice of the water. He felt his mind urge to think, as always in quiet moments, but he tucked the urge into its accustomed fold of patience. Thinking could not conclude. Thinking saw and stopped.

He had read all of the *Discourses* now and *God Speaks* twice, and had nearly finished the twenty volumes of *Lord Meher*, Meher Baba's biography. He had a picture in his mind of what Baba called impressions, or sanskaras, how they built a body of mind and desire and wound and evolved through all being and species to human beings, then finally involved and thinned until divine love was felt and the universe made sense, then vanished altogether in realization. Somehow. Then a mast and a tiger, a purr, and the rapid sanskaric thinning of a gathered pool of souls. And Patti, whose soul, he guessed, had claimed a burden, perhaps the sanskaras of her brother animals, and given her life, more Jesus than Judas.

And so the ecopark, made sound with Fuad's money, would thrive and proclaim its theme of unity with nature, and Dawson's dome, made possible with JJ's money, would be built and proclaim its theme of human unity, and the caravan animals, who were no longer wholly animal, would inspire and amaze for years to come. Visitors would arrive from around the world. Researchers already clamored for position. The summer camp program for kids would expand. A college of animal care would be established next year. He and his old boss, Rudy Wheeler, still in California and teaching at a small college, were designing buildings and planning curricula. Three independent websites were devoted to the ecopark and caravan animals, and their webmasters had visited the park several times. The ecopark coordinated ticket sales with them, and already tickets were available by reservation only.

From the webmasters, and from the movie studio people, and from the community of zoo professionals, Bluey hid nothing—except that Sybil could speak and that the others could understand. That disclosure would further amaze but also disturb. Government could take notice, and the animal's freedom could be endangered. Sybil had been cautioned, and he, El, and Carlos were the only keepers currently permitted inside the enclosure. Science might lose an opportunity, but the relation of consciousness to matter, the primordial mystery, was best—and most stably—penetrated by the accumulation of scientific data.

"I thought you'd be here." Roger's voice came from the right. He stopped on the bank ten feet from Bluey.

Bluey said, "Sit. I suppose you sprayed?"

"Oh, yeah." The cool weather had stopped the chiggers, but ticks were still possible. Roger nested on the bank, letting his boot tops cover with water. He said, "I should velcro a cushion on that rock. I see you here sometimes."

"It's a good spot."

The creek filled the silence. Roger said, "I bet you get poems here. Dori and I are reading poems to each other. There is something silent in a poem that points."

"Well, Christ, that's true."

"I just said a beautiful thing."

"You did."

"Also, we're reading the *Discourses*. Now we're reading the *Nature of the Ego and Its Termination*. It has about the inferiority and superiority complexes, and, man, do I have those. So now I'm thinking all about my parents, and Dori's thinking about high school, and we're just thinking about everything. She put a picture of Baba in every room. I said, Dori, this is about inner experience. She says, Baba pictures are the small end of a telescope. You look through and see the universe."

"You are unworthy of her."

"True. Damn, I already forgot what I said about poems. What did I say?"

"There's a silence that points."

"Ah. By the way, when's the last time you told us a poem? As JJ might say, you are one selfish fucker."

"Maybe tonight. I just finished it."

The noise of animal melee from the meadow suddenly ceased, which meant one of the teams had prevailed, and Bluey was needed. Bluey stood, shouted, "BLUEY COMES!" Then to Roger—"We better get started."

Roger said, "I'll make the fire. So what's the title of tonight's poem?"

"*A Letter to Myself.*"

"I like it already."

They parted, Roger to the caravan perimeter and fire pit, Bluey back to the meadow, where he found the animals had begun the game they called tumble jumble. Bluey had cautioned them about the game but had not entirely forbidden it. It consisted of two lines of animals with one animal after another rushing between them. The goal was to push or trip the running animal off its feet, whereupon the others would make a jumble, or pile of animals on top of him. Even the small animals participated, hence Bluey's caution. As he approached, Shindig the spider monkey made the run, and was being nudged and bumped, with more drama than sincerity. He chittered merrily and was through. Bump the sun bear was next, and he was fair game. Nubia butted him into Demijohn, who rolled him over, and the jumble was on. Animals collided and bounced like balls. By instinctual code, the larger animals found the bottom, then the middle sized, and last the birds, Spectra and Sybil and the two crows, Harry and Mabel, prancing and hopping about the moving mass beneath them. The game was fairly dangerous and had already resulted in split lips and cuts, but so far no broken bones. It was essentially a rugby scrum, and though Bluey made his disapproval known, he let the game abide somewhere between forbidden and tolerated. All of them, the carnivores particularly, needed the release.

Now he shouted, "STOP! STOP!"

The mound of animals ceased convulsing and began to unpeel. Bluey said, "Who is hurt?"

The animals milled and emitted happy chagrin. None came forward.

Bluey said, "Oz, come." The meerkat bounded and leapt, and Bluey caught him against his chest. Bluey tapped the fur above the meerkat's left eye, then showed Oz a bloody finger. There was a sickle shaped split in the fur. Bluey said, "You are hurt. Charlie Doctor is coming." He tossed Oz who landed on the grass, scampered, then sat up at attention and waited. Bluey swept his gaze, grave-facing them all, but only briefly. Then, with a glance at Bhajan, he said, "Tonight JJ comes. Come on. We make the fire."

The animals gave voice and started, some running, toward the zoo compound. Bluey caught Bhajan's eye, who slowed and curved to his side. Sybil flapped dutifully onto Bhajan's shoulder. But she was seldom needed anymore.

Over the months that followed the shooting, the questions to Bhajan, most from El and Dawson, had been met with silence and finally fallen away. Who was the mast who raised you? Had he met Meher Baba? Are you stationed on the planes? Why Patti? Eventually Bhajan's silence instructed them. They came to see that in the world that had opened to them, the inner world, every essential question is asked by its answer. The rest is information.

Still, whether purring or not, the tiger's presence was a balm and gave off some inner perfume. Bluey let his hand fall onto the massive neck, stroked, then stroked between the eyes. It was perhaps too familiar, but what was he to do? The being walking besides him looked like a tiger. On impulse, he nudged his hip into Bhajan's shoulder, an act of play and mischief. Bhajan swung his head, caught Bluey's eye, and roared mightily. Bluey laughed. He felt a powerful impulse of love. Tonight he would say a poem, out loud, to human beings. Tomorrow the park would open, and something new would begin, a new work moving under the slow diligence of destiny to some unknown end, no different now than before, or at any time, except more joy, and love. He would say a poem.

27

Letter to Myself

Eventually, you'll get a taste for God.
Maybe you'll get everything you want someday,
And you'll say, why, it's just the same as if I didn't get it.
Maybe you'll get old and tired of being stubborn.
You'll say, all right, then, what?
Maybe what I'm saying now will turn a key in your heart.
But I know better than that.
The longing you are longing for
Must come most naturally, like hunger and courage,
And simple as sight,
The way shyness from a young girl falls
When love makes up her mind.
That's true, but also this,
That God is standing across a green field,
Shouting and waving his arms,
While you're munching like an ox with your head down.
Well.
Everything is simple
Because everything is true.
Every lie knows the truth it hides.
Therefore, eat.
Make a trail of dung.
Love has made God patient.
Time is his caress.
Still, take this good advice—
Make your trail straight.
Don't make it complicated.
And if you see something bright
Waving its arms from across a field,
Stop chewing for a minute.
Try to notice it.

About the author

I live on three and a half acres near Durham, North Carolina, with a wife, Cynthia, and a dog, Blue, both excellent companions. The idea for *Bhajan* came thirty-five years ago. I didn't write it that year, or the next, and so on. I tried now and then, but not hard. I needed to ripen, and knew it, and eventually did. I began to write three years ago in a cabin built especially to write this book. I plan to write more there.

In a sense, *Bhajan* is a letter to the twenty year old kid I was when I first noticed the inner world and became a seeker. Now, after a dozen or so trips to India to visit the tomb of Meher Baba and be in company with his *mandali*, the companions who lived with him, I am less a seeker than a pursuer.

What else? I grew up in Arizona, then in the Alaskan wilderness. I live beside a creek. I have beloved children and grandchildren. I enjoy thinking. I am also a potter and make millefiori porcelain jewelry. Visit www.bluebusstudiostore.com to see it.

What else? A whole vast life, like yours.

Tim Garvin

Questions for discussion

1) In Writing 101, writing students are reminded that characters must change. How do the characters in the story change? Who changes the most?
2) On page 214, Bluey tells El that "honesty is a kind of surrender, and, if you have patience, it leads past opinion to wonder." Is this a new way to think about honesty? Or an ancient one?
3) If the tiger is a trope, or literary device, what does he stand for?
4) Dawson is inspired by the dream of a community dome where everyone can leave their two cents worth of opinion at the door (page 354) and enjoy each other's company. Would anyone go? Would you?
5) Just before Dawson faints, he experiences a frenetic thought train (page 275) that ends with *the last rule must shrug* "…*so* thought has to shrug too. Thought poops out. That's appealing to me. Very appealing." Why is that so appealing to him?
6) On page 308, Roger makes his blanket burrito speech about the eighteen year old black youth, who he imagines moving backwards in time until he is three, and much loved, then growing forward until he is eighteen again, and is feared and hated. He concludes that God cannot hate because he never looks away. What do you think?
7) On page 39, El tells Bluey that she came to the Exotic Animal College after she heard him tell a couple of guys at a party that if conservatives and liberals made a list of virtues the lists would

be identical except perhaps for their order. Would your list be the same as your liberal or conservative friends?

8) Do you share Bluey's dedication to preserving the animals of the earth? Has *Bhajan* made their plight clearer for you?
9) On page 114, JJ says, "Everybody on earth was hollowed out like zombies, or else why poverty, why war, why my stuff instead of our stuff?" Is this part of a delusion, or is he in some way correct?
10) Was JJ's redemption a surprise? Was it somehow foreshadowed?
11) On page 254, as Dawson drives to Eugene, he encounters a line of cars and squints, "…making the cars into a column of weary refugees. They were fleeing a disaster in the city. Was it war? They fled emptiness. They rushed to the fair's tinsel wonderland to spectate and forget." Is this too harsh? Or is he right?
12) In Annie's tirade against God on page 191, she says, "Vagueness is atheism's best argument." What do you think?
13) On page 247, after imaging the irked white southerner with "his wild trapped pride" entering the black church, Annie falls to her knees in the RV. What was her emotional state at that moment? Was it an aberration? Or deeply normal?
14) On the next to last page, this statement appears: "They came to see that in the world that had opened to them, the inner world, every essential question is asked by its answer. The rest is information." What sort of question is asked by its answer?
15) In the ending poem, *Letter to Myself*, Bluey writes: "Everything is simple because everything is true. Every lie knows the truth it hides." This is Tim Garvin speaking now—and commenting that, for myself, those lines shine with beauty, and express the truth that once you are in the universe you cannot get out except by the door to love. And everyone will.

Made in the USA
Charleston, SC
16 May 2015